The Green Man Revisited

CLASSIC ENGLISH SHORT STORIES

D0805042

The Green Man Revisited

━━

CLASSIC ENGLISH SHORT STORIES

SELECTED BY
ROGER SHARROCK

Oxford   New York
OXFORD UNIVERSITY PRESS
1988

Oxford University Press, Walton Street, Oxford OX2 6DP
Oxford New York Toronto
Delhi Bombay Calcutta Madras Karachi
Petaling Jaya Singapore Hong Kong Tokyo
Nairobi Dar es Salaam Cape Town
Melbourne Auckland

and associated companies in
Beirut Berlin Ibadan Nicosia

Oxford is a trade mark of Oxford University Press

First published as English Short Stories of Today, Fourth Series 1976
First issued, with the title The Green Man Revisited, as an
Oxford University Press paperback 1988

British Library Cataloguing in Publication Data

[English short stories of today. 4th Series]
The green man revisited : classic English
short stories.
I. Sharrock, Roger
823'.01'08 [FS]
ISBN 0-19-282190-3

Library of Congress Cataloging in Publication Data
English short stories of today. Fourth series.
The Green man revisited : classical English short stories/
selected by Roger Sharrock. p. cm.
Originally published: Englished short stories of today. Fourth
series. London : Oxford University Press for the English
Association, 1976.
Bibliography: p.
1. Short stories, English. 2. English fiction—20th century.
I. Sharrock, Roger. II. Title.
PR1309.S5E544 1988 823'.01'08—dc 19
ISBN 0-19-282190-3 (pbk.)

Printed in Great Britain by
The Guernsey Press Co. Ltd.
Guernsey, Channel Islands

PREFACE

THESE stories are by writers from almost every major national group which provides a public for literature in the English language—British, American, West Indian, West African, Indian, South African, Australian, and New Zealand. They serve to demonstrate, not only that English is a world language as never before, but also that it is beginning to produce a world literature. Beneath the differences of background which we encounter in reading Dan Jacobson on an Afrikaans township, R. K. Narayan on a southern Indian villager, and Susan Hill and Elizabeth Taylor on the lives lived in English south-coast hotels and boarding houses, we begin to detect the presence of the same themes: in a complex world, failures of understanding between cultures, between generations and individuals, and the strenuous, usually unrewarded, effort at communication across these barriers. But this demonstration of internationally shared complexity and confusion is incidental; the stories have been chosen for their intrinsic excellence and for the variety of approaches to the short-story form which they present. Most of them are work of the last fifteen years or so.

What is a short story? The excellence of English is to be rich and suggestive rather than precise and it is perhaps unfortunate that we have this ambiguous expression 'short story' instead of a single word like the French *conte* or the German *Erzählung*. Short stories may vary in length from a few hundred words as in the tiny reminiscence of Frank Sargeson's 'A Hen and Some Eggs' to a narrative of several thousand words like George Mackay Brown's 'Tithonus' in which years pass and people have children, age and die. 'Short' must not make us think that a short story is a kind of stunted or compressed novel. Readers of English need to be reminded of this fact because the short story is not really a native growth. The inspiration came from abroad, from France and Russia and America. English and Irish writers went to school to Guy de Maupassant, to Chekhov, to Henry James, and later to Ernest

Hemingway. But before the last decade of the nineteenth century English short fiction did indeed trail behind the novel and embodied something of the heaviness and excessive detail of Victorian furniture and suety Victorian meals. The revolution came when it was seen that the short story must aim at a goal wholly different from that of the novel. It must attempt to capture the essence of an experience or a relationship, or the atmosphere of a place or time; to do this it must practise the greatest economy of form, dispensing with full characterization, with the luxury of minor characters, with any but the simplest of plots. It may sometimes have no plot at all to speak of. Unlike most novels, it may never move to the climax of a completed action. Things may appear to be left in the air, the situation remaining much as before, but if a feeling has been communicated and our sensibility, however imperceptibly, changed by it, then the story has been successful. Every phrase, if not every word, counts: often (but not always) the short story may approximate more than other forms of fiction to the lyric poem (Coleridge's 'the best words in the best order'). Another parallel might be with that faithful, even scientifically, optically faithful, recording of a scene attempted by the great impressionist painters; and it is worth noting that the rise of the short story in France coincided with the rise of the impressionist movement.

Forms are real and powerful in literature. We could not read without an awareness of them, however unconscious may be our acknowledgement that the lines our eyes are passing over belong to a detective story or a work of science fiction which can trace its ancestry to *Gulliver's Travels*. But there are no pure Platonic literary forms, only numbers of works which fall into patterns; and the patterns recur. I have in the previous paragraph tried to define the short story as it developed within the last hundred years as a distinctive form of writing. But I would not wish to put in too exclusive a claim for what may be called the 'art' short story. I would not want to ring it round, and, having rightly dismissed Dickens, Thackeray, and Wilkie Collins from the premises, insist that all further comers after Poe, Chekhov, and Joyce should take their dirty extravert boots off and aspire to cultivate a single delicate chord. The spatial metaphor of a chosen territory betrays; it is better to think of the short story formally as a clearing in a forest with many tracks entering it and other tracks being blazed out of it. Like other literature it is progressive, a way of doing something by taking over where others have left off and continuing in a new direction. One of the tracks is a kind of story which must go back to the Stone Age and for which we have a good single word in English, the tale. Unlike some art short stories, the tale has a beginning, a middle, and an end. It may be the sort of anecdote from real life which unliterary people tell to each other because it is funny, tragic, or shocking, and has that particular satisfying shape that makes it—like a story. When the imaginary person (who is really Forster himself) in E. M. Forster's *Aspects of the Novel* (1927) says sadly: 'Yes, oh yes, the novel must tell a story', he is revealing that Forster and Bloomsbury did not relish a tale for its own sake (which is why in Forster plot and incident creak so terribly under the passionate symbolism and muted sympathies). But in earlier civilizations the demand for a tale was satisfied by works as diverse as the Icelandic sagas, the *Arabian Nights*, and the *Decameron*. The parables of the New Testament are tales, each containing a complete action, and the packed moral suggestiveness of their extraordinary simplicity and brevity makes many modern impressionistic short stories seem long-winded and pretentious. The form is still flourishing in the twentieth century alongside our more characteristically contemporary interest in the introspective and the unfinished. It is exhibited in Chinua Achebe's 'Uncle Ben's Choice', a ghost story and the first story in this collection. Kingsley Amis's ghost story which comes next is an interesting contrast: not having traditional folklore to rely on as Achebe has, he is concerned with the problem of how to achieve the convincing thrill of the ghost story within a sophisticated contemporary setting. Another accomplished tale, quite different again, is Elizabeth Taylor's 'A Dedicated Man', but here the interest of pure story is enriched by psychological penetration into peculiarities of human motive.

The peculiar, the eccentric, the lonely, the downright mad: these, with children and old people, make up a great part of the population of the modern short story. I do not consider that this bias constitutes an indictment of the writers on the grounds of narrowness of sympathy or neglect of the facts of modern social life. If a similar bias were to be discovered in the contemporary novel, as I suspect it might, then the indictment might be lodged. For the novel has as its business to deal with social man as well as the individual; it must really give some account of those who marry and work and vote and of their social relations and milieux. If these are neglected, then something is wrong. But the spare form of the short story cannot concern itself with the vast complexity of the modern social world; it is a form for the pre-social and the post-social, the child and the old man, before the intense circle of experience widens and after it narrows again, or for the lonely and alienated. Having learned this when I began to read for this selection, I feared at first that I should not find enough amusing and delightful stories, but as I went on I realized that I need not have worried. Stories like Olivia Manning's 'A Spot of Leave' and John Updike's 'Should Wizard Hit Mommy?' show in their very different circumstances and characters that even the failure of people to communicate across their personal barriers (cultural differences, the gap of child and parent) can be a subject of high comedy.

Up to about forty years ago there were a number of widely-circulating magazines like the old *London* and *Strand* in which writers of all kinds, unless they were aggressively experimental, could find a market for stories. In a changing historical atmosphere, with a widening fissure between serious and popular readership, short stories of note continued to appear in *New Writing*, *Penguin New Writing*, and *Horizon*. But since the last war the number of outlets has decreased. Mr. Alan Ross's *London Magazine* has kept the flag flying in a difficult period and introduced many new writers, some of them represented in these pages. The radio has brought a new public and encouraged a new form of story, casual and colloquial, without the artistic self-consciousness of many post-Hemingway collo-

quial stories written for the page. In this volume 'The Green
Man Revisited' is an example of the radio story. The economics
of the contemporary short story may be hard, but looking over
this collection I hope readers will agree with me, bearing in
mind the age range of the writers, that the form is not in a
period of decline but of exciting development. I only wish the
exigencies of space had allowed me to include more experimental
work, the anti-stories and surrealist fantasies of the last few
years, but I hope there may be room for those in a later series.
And perhaps the smoke has not sufficiently cleared from the
impact of Jorge Luis Borges.

There are a number of good books on the short story. One by
an Irishman, Frank O'Connor, *The Lonely Voice. A Study of the
Short Story* (Macmillan, 1963) is brilliant and wayward; another
by H. E. Bates is a superb short survey by a craftsman in the
form of the whole modern tradition of the story from Gogol and
Poe onwards, but unfortunately it has not been revised to cover
the post-war period (*The Modern Short Story: a Critical Survey*,
Nelson, 1941). Brief but suggestive remarks by another distinguished practitioner may be found in the preface to Graham
Greene's *Collected Stories* (Bodley Head and William Heinemann,
1972). Two more substantial studies deserve notice: T. O.
Beachcroft, *The Modest Art: a Survey of the Short Story in English*
(Oxford University Press, 1968) devotes some space to ancient
prototypes of the short story and recurring themes before dealing
fully with the masters of the form from the nineteenth century
onwards. Walter Allen, *The Short Story in English* (Clarendon
Press, Oxford, 1981) starts out from Scott and Poe and with
discussion of origins and affinities, and then reviews the achieve-
ment of individual writers down to the present day with the
judgement and perceptiveness to be expected of one who is both
critic and short-story writer. Those readers who, like myself,
regret the absence from the following pages for reasons of space
of any story by a Welsh writer may consult *Twenty-Five Welsh
Short Stories*, ed. Gwyn Jones and I. F. Elis and the introduction
to that volume.

ROGER SHARROCK

CONTENTS

CONTENTS

CHINUA ACHEBE

Uncle Ben's Choice

IN THE year nineteen hundred and nineteen I was a young clerk in the Niger Company at Umuru. To be a clerk in those days is like to be a minister today. My salary was two pounds ten. You may laugh but two pounds ten in those days is like fifty pounds today. You could buy a big goat with four shillings. I could remember the most senior African in the company was one Saro man on ten-thirteen-four. He was like Governor-General in our eyes.

Like all progressive young men I joined the African Club. We played tennis and billiards. Every year we played a tournament with the European Club. But I was less concerned with that. What I liked was the Saturday night dances. Women were surplus. Not all the waw-waw women you see in townships today but beautiful things like this.

I had a Raleigh bicycle, brand new, and everybody called me Jolly Ben. I was selling like hot bread. But there is one thing about me—we can laugh and joke and drink and do otherwise but I must always keep my sense with me. My father told me that a true son of our land must know how to sleep and keep one eye open. I never forget it. So I played and laughed with everyone and they shouted 'Jolly Ben! Jolly Ben!' but I knew what I was doing. The women of Umuru are very sharp; before you count A they count B. So I had to be very careful. I never showed any of them the road to my house and I never ate the food they cooked for fear of love medicines. I had seen many young men kill themselves with women in those days, so I remembered my father's word: Never let a handshake pass the elbow.

I can say that the only exception was one tall, yellow, salt-water girl like this called Margaret. One Sunday morning I was playing my gramophone, a brand-new HMV Senior. (I never believe in second-hand things. If I have no money for a new one I just keep myself quiet; that is my motto.) I was playing this record and standing at the window with my chewing-stick in my mouth. People were passing in their fine-fine dresses to one church nearby. This Margaret was going with them when she saw me. As luck would have it I did not see her in time to hide. So that very day—she did not wait till tomorrow or next tomorrow—but as soon as church closed she returned back. According to her she wanted to convert me to Roman Catholic. Wonders will never end! Margaret Jumbo! Beautiful thing like this. But it is not Margaret I want to tell you about now. I want to tell you how I stopped all that foolishness.

It was one New Year's Eve like this. You know how New Year can pass Christmas for jollity, for we end-of-month people. By Christmas Day the month has reached twenty-hungry but on New Year your pocket is heavy. So that day I went to the Club.

When I see you young men of nowadays say you drink, I just laugh. You don't know what drink is. You drink one bottle of beer or one shot of whisky and you begin to holler like craze-man. That night I was taking it easy on White Horse. *All that are desirous to pass from Edinburgh to London or any other place on their road, let them repair to the White Horse cellar.* . . . God Almighty!

One thing with me is I never mix my drinks. The day I want to drink whisky I know that that is whisky-day; if I want to drink beer tomorrow then I know it is beer-day; I don't touch any other thing. That night I was on White Horse. I had one roasted chicken and a tin of Guinea Gold. Yes, I used to smoke in those days. I only stopped when one German doctor told me my heart was as black as a cooking-pot. Those German doctors were spirits. You know they used to give injections in the head or belly or anywhere. You just point where the thing is paining you and they give it to you right there—they don't waste time.

What was I saying? . . . Yes, I drank a bottle of White Horse and put one roasted chicken on top of it . . . Drunk? It is not in my dictionary. I have never been drunk in my life. My father used to say that the cure for drink is to say no. When I want to drink I drink, when I want to stop I stop. So about three o'clock that night I said to myself, you have had enough. So I jumped on my new Raleigh bicycle and went home quietly to sleep.

At that time our senior clerk was jailed for stealing bales of calico and I was acting in that capacity. So I lived in a small company house. You know where G. B. Olivant is today? . . . Yes, overlooking the River Niger. That is where my house was. I had two rooms on one side of it and the store-keeper had two rooms on the other side. But as luck would have it this man was on leave, so his side was vacant.

I opened the front door and went inside. Then I locked it again. I left my bicycle in the first room and went into the bed-room. I was too tired to begin to look for my lamp. So I pulled my dress and packed them on the back of the chair, and fell like a log into my big iron bed. And to God who made me, there was a woman in my bed. My mind told me at once it was Margaret. So I began to laugh and touch her here and there. She was hundred per cent naked. I continued laughing and asked her when did she come. She did not say anything and I suspected she was annoyed because she asked me to take her to the Club that day and I said no. I said to her: if you come there we will meet, I don't take anybody to the Club as such. So I suspected that is what is making her vex.

I told her not to vex but still she did not say anything. I asked her if she was asleep—just for asking sake. She said nothing. Although I told you that I did not like women to come to my house, but for every rule there must be an exception. So if I say that I was very angry to find Margaret that night I will be telling a white lie. I was still laughing when I noticed that her breasts were straight like the breasts of a girl of sixteen—or seventeen, at most. I thought that perhaps it was because of the way she was lying on her back. But when I touched the hair and it was soft like the hair of a European my laughter was quenched by force. I touched the hair on her head and it was the same. I jumped out of the bed and shouted: 'Who are you?' My head swelled up like a barrel and I was shaking. The woman sat up and stretched her hands to call me back; as she did so her fingers touched me. I jumped back at the same time and shouted again to her to call her name. Then I said to myself: How can you be afraid of a woman? Whether a white woman or a black woman, it is the same ten and ten pence. So I said: 'All right, I will soon open your mouth,' at the same time I began to look for matches on the table. The woman suspected what I was looking for. She said, 'Biko akpakwana ọku.'

I said: 'So you are not a white woman. Who are you? I will strike the matches now if you don't tell me.' I shook the matches to show her that I meant business. My boldness had come back and I was trying to remember the voice because it was very familiar.

'Come back to the bed and I will tell you,' was what I heard next. Whoever told me it was a familiar voice told me a lie. It was sweet like sugar but not familiar at all. So I struck the matches.

'I beg you,' was the last thing she said.

If I tell you what I did next or how I managed to come out of that room it is pure guess-work. The next thing I remember is that I was running like a craze-man to Matthew's house. Then I was banging on his door with my both hands.

'Who is that?' he said from inside.

'Open,' I shouted. 'In the name of God above, open.'

I called my name but my voice was not like my voice. The door opened very small and I saw my kinsman holding a matchet in his right hand.

I fell down on the floor, and he said, 'God will not agree.'

It was God Himself who directed me to Matthew Obi's house that night because I did not see where I was going. I could not say whether I was still in this world or whether I was dead. Matthew poured cold water on me and after some time I was able to tell him what happened. I think I told it upside down otherwise he would not keep asking me what was she like, what was she like.

'I told you before I did not see her,' I said.

'I see, but you heard her voice?'

'I heard her voice quite all right. And I touched her and she touched me.'

'I don't know whether you did well or not to scare her away,' was what Matthew said.

I don't know how to explain it but those words from Matthew opened my eyes. I knew at once that I had been visited by Mami Wota, the Lady of the River Niger.

Matthew said again: 'It depends what you want in life. If it is wealth you want then you made a great mistake today, but if you are a true son of your father then take my hand.'

We shook hands and he said: 'Our fathers never told us that a man should prefer wealth instead of wives and children.'

Today whenever my wives make me vex I tell them: 'I don't blame you. If I had been wise I would have taken Mami Wota.' They laugh and ask me why did I not take her. The youngest one says: 'Don't worry, Papa, she will come again; she will come to morrow.' And they laugh again.

But we all know it is a joke. For where is the man who will choose wealth instead of children? Except a crazy white man like Dr. J. M. Stuart-Young. Oh, I didn't tell you. The same night that I drove Mami Wota out she went to Dr. J. M. Stuart-Young, a white merchant and became his lover. You have heard of him? . . . Oh yes, he became the richest man in the whole country. But she did not allow him to marry. When he died, what happened? All his wealth went to outsiders. Is that good wealth? I ask you. God forbid.

KINGSLEY AMIS
The Green Man Revisited

I WANT to tell you about a very odd experience I had a few months ago—not so as to entertain you, but because I think it raises some very basic questions about, you know, what life is all about and to what extent we run our own lives. Rather worrying questions. Anyway, what happened was this . . .

My wife and I had been staying the weekend with her uncle and aunt in Westmorland, near a place called Milnethorpe. Both of us—Jane and I, that is—had things to do in London on the Monday morning, and it's a long drive from there down to Barnet, where we live, even though a good half of it is on the M6. So I said: 'Look, don't let's break our necks trying to get home in the light' (this was in August). 'Let's take it easy and stop somewhere for dinner and reckon to get home about half-past ten or eleven.' Jane said okay.

So we left Milnethorpe in the middle of the afternoon, took things fairly easily, and landed up about half-past seven or a quarter to eight at the place we'd picked out of one of the food guides before we started. I won't tell you the name of the place, because the people who run it wouldn't thank me if I did. Please don't go looking for it. I'd advise you not to.

Anyway, we parked the car in the yard and went inside. It was a nice-looking sort of place: pretty old, built a good time ago, I mean, done up in a sensible sort of way, no muzak and no bloody silly blacked-out lighting, but no olde-worlde nonsense either. I got us both a drink in the bar and went off to see about a table for dinner. I soon found the right chap, and he said: 'Table for two in half an hour—certainly, sir. Are you in the bar? I'll get someone to bring you the menu in a few minutes.' Pleasant sort of chap, a bit young for the job.

I was just going off when a sort of paunchy business-type came in and said something like 'Mr. Allington not in tonight?'

and the young fellow said: 'No, sir, he's taken the evening off.'
'All right, never mind.'

Well, I'll tell you why in a minute, but I turned back to the
young fellow and said, 'Excuse me, but is your name Palmer?'
and he said: 'Yes, sir.' I said, 'Not David Palmer by any
chance?' and he said: 'No, sir. Actually, the name's George.'
I said, or rather burbled: 'A friend of mine was telling me
about this place, said he'd stayed here, liked it very much,
mentioned you—anyway, I got half the name right, and Mr.
Allington is the proprietor, isn't he?' 'That's correct, sir.'

I went straight back to the bar, went up to the barman and
said: 'Fred?' He said: 'Yes, sir.' I said, 'Fred Soames?' and he
said: 'Fred Browning, sir.' I just said, 'Wrong Fred'—not very
polite, but it was all I could think of. I went over to where my
wife was sitting and I'd hardly sat down before she asked:
'What's the matter?'

What was the matter calls for a bit of explanation. In 1969
I published a novel called *The Green Man*, which was not only
the title of the book but also the name of a sort of classy pub,
or inn, where most of the action took place—very much the
kind of establishment we were in that evening. Now the landlord of The Green Man was called Allington, and his deputy
was called David Palmer, and the barman was called Fred
Soames. Allington is a very uncommon name—I wanted that
for reasons nothing to do with this story. The other two aren't,
but to have got Palmer and Fred right, so to speak, as well as
Allington was a thumping great coincidence—staggering, in
fact. But I wasn't just staggered, I was very alarmed. Because
The Green Man wasn't only the name of the pub in my book:
it was also the name of a frightening creature, a sort of solid
ghost, conjured up out of tree branches and leaves and so on,
that very nearly kills Allington and his young daughter. I
didn't want to find I was right about that too.

Jane was very sensible, as always. She said stranger coincidences had happened and still been just coincidences, and
mightn't I have come across an innkeeper called Allington
somewhere, half-forgotten about it and brought it up out of my
unconscious mind when I was looking for a name for an

innkeeper to put in the book, and now the real Allington had moved from wherever I'd seen him before to this place. And Palmer and Fred really are very common names. And I'd got the name of the pub wrong. (I'm still not telling you what it's called, but one of the things it isn't called is The Green Man.) And my pub was in Hertfordshire and this place was . . . off the M6. All very reasonable and reassuring.

Only I wasn't very reassured. I mean, I obviously couldn't just leave it there. The thing to do was get hold of this chap Palmer and see if there was, well, any more to come. Which was going to be tricky if I wasn't going to look nosey or mad or something else that would shut him up. Neither of us ate much at dinner, though there was nothing wrong with the food. We didn't say much, either. I drank a fair amount.

Then, half-way through, Palmer turned up to do his everything-all-right routine, as I'd hoped he would, and as he would have done in my book. I said yes, it was fine, thanks, and then I said we'd be very pleased if he'd join us for a brandy afterwards if he'd got time, and he said he'd be delighted. Jolly good, but I was still stuck with this problem of how to dress the thing up.

Jane had said earlier on, why didn't I just tell the truth, and I'd said that since Palmer hadn't reacted at all when I gave him my name when I was booking the table, he'd only have my word for the whole story and might think I was off my rocker. She'd said that of course she'd back me up, and I'd said he'd just think he'd got two loonies on his hands instead of one. Anyway, now she said: '*Some* people who've read *The Green Man* must have mentioned it—fancy that, Mr. Palmer, you and Mr. Allington and Fred are all in a book by somebody called Kingsley Amis.' Obvious enough when you think of it, but like a lot of obvious things, you have got to think of it.

Well, that was the line I took when Palmer rolled up for his brandy: I'm me and I wrote this book and so on. Oh really? he said, more or less. I thought we were buggered, but then he said, 'Oh yes, now you mention it, I do remember some chap saying something like that, but it must have been two or three years ago'—as if that stopped it counting for much. 'I'm not much of a reader, you see,' he said.

'What about Mr. Allington,' I said, 'doesn't he read?' 'Not what you'd call a reader,' he said. Well, that was one down to me, or one up, depending on how you look at it, because *my* Allington was a tremendous reader—French poetry and all that. Still, the approach had worked after a fashion, and Palmer very decently put up with being cross-questioned on how far this place corresponded with my place in the book. Was Mrs. Allington blonde? There wasn't a Mrs. Allington any more: she'd died of leukemia quite a long time ago. Had he got his widowed father living here? (Allington's father, that is.) No, Mr. Allington senior, and his wife, lived in Eastbourne. Was the house, the pub, haunted at all? Not as far as Palmer knew, and he'd been there three years. In fact, the place was only about two hundred years old, which completely clobbered a good half of my novel, where the ghosts had been hard at it more than a hundred years earlier still.

Nearly all of it was like that. Of course, there were some questions I couldn't ask, for one reason or another. For instance, was Allington a boozer, like my Allington, and, even more so, had this Allington had a visit from God? In the book, God turns up in the form of a young man to give Allington some tips on how to deal with the ghosts, who he, God, thinks are a menace to him. No point in going any further into that part.

I said nearly all the answers Palmer gave me were straight negatives. One wasn't, or rather there were two points where I scored, so to speak. One was that Allington had a fifteen-year-old daughter called Marilyn living in the house. My Allington's daughter was thirteen, and called Amy, but I'd come somewhere near the mark—too near for comfort. The other thing was a bit harder to tie down. When I'm writing a novel, I very rarely have any sort of mental picture of any of the characters, what they actually look like. I think a lot of novelists would say the same. But, I don't know why, I'd had a very clear image of what my chap David Palmer looked like, and now I'd had a really good look at George Palmer, this one here, he was nearly the same as I'd imagined: not so tall, different nose, but still nearly the same. I didn't care for that.

Palmer, George Palmer, said he had things to see to and took off. I told Jane about the resemblance. She said I could easily have imagined that, and I said I supposed I might. 'Anyway,' she said, 'what do you think of it all?' I said it could still all be coincidence. 'What could it be if it isn't coincidence?' she asked. I'd been wondering about that while we were talking to Palmer. Not an easy one. Feeling a complete bloody fool, I said I thought we could have strayed into some kind of parallel world that slightly resembles the world I had made up —like in a Science Fiction story. She didn't laugh or back away. She looked round and spotted a newspaper someone had left on one of the chairs. It was that day's *Sunday Telegraph*. She said: 'If where we are is a world that's parallel to the real world, it's bound to be different from the real world in all sorts of ways. Now you read most of the *Telegraph* this morning, the real *Telegraph*. Look at this one and see if it's any different.' Well, I did, and it wasn't: same front page, same article on the trade unions by Perry, that's Peregrine Worsthorne, same readers' letters, same crossword down to the last clue. Well, that was a relief.

But I didn't stay relieved, because there was another coincidence shaping up. It was a hot night in August when all this happened, and Allington was out for the evening. It was on a hot night in August, after Allington had come back from an evening out, that the monster, the Green Man, finally takes shape and comes pounding up the road to tear young Amy Allington to pieces. That bit begins on page 225 in my book, if you're interested.

The other nasty little consideration was this. Unlike some novelists I could name, I invent all my characters, except for a few minor ones here and there. What I mean is, I don't go in for just renaming people I know and bunging them into a book. But, of course, you can't help putting *something* of yourself into all your characters, even if it's a surly bus-conductor who only comes in for half a page. Obviously, this comes up most of all with your heroes. None of my heroes, not even old Lucky Jim, are me, but they can't help having pretty fair chunks of me in them, some more than others. And Allington in that book was one of the some. I'm more like him than I'm like most of the others: in particular, I'm more like my Maurice Allington in my book than the real Allington, who, by the way, turned out to be called John, seemed (from what I'd heard) to be like my Maurice Allington. Sorry to be long-winded, but I want to get that quite clear.

So, if, by some fantastic chance, the Green Man, the monster, was going to turn up here, he, or it, seemed more likely to turn up tonight than most nights. Furthermore, I seemed better cast for the part of the young girl's father, who manages in the book to save her from the monster, than this young girl's father did.

I tried to explain all this to Jane. Evidently I got it across all right, because she said straight away: 'We'd better stay here tonight, then.' 'If we can,' I said, meaning if there was a room. Well, there was, and at the front of the house too—which was important, because in the book that's the side the monster appears on.

While one of the blokes was taking our stuff out of the car and upstairs, I said to Jane: 'I'm not going to be like a bloody fool in a ghost story who insists on seeing things through alone, not if I can help it—I'm going to give Bob Conquest a ring. Bob's an old chum of mine, and about the only one I felt I could ask to come belting up all this way (he lives in Battersea) for such a ridiculous reason. It was just after ten by this time, and the Green Man wasn't scheduled to put in an appearance till after 1 a.m., so Bob could make it all right, if he started straight away. Fine, except his phone didn't answer: I tried twice.

Jane said: 'Get hold of Monkey. I'll speak to him.' Monkey, otherwise known as Colin, is her brother: he lives with us in Barnet. Our number answered all right, but I got my son Philip, who was staying the weekend there. He said Monkey was out at a party, he didn't know where. So all I could do was the necessary but not at all helpful job of saying we wouldn't be home till the next morning. So that was that. I mean, I just couldn't start getting hold of George Palmer and asking him to sit up with us into the small hours in case a ghost came along. Could any of you? I should have said that Philip hasn't got a car.

We stayed in the bar until it closed. I said to Jane at one point: 'You don't think I'm mad, do you? Or silly or anything?' She said: 'On the contrary, I think you're being extremely practical and sensible.' Well, thank God for that. Jane believes in ghosts, you see. My own position on that is exactly that of the man who said: 'I don't believe in ghosts, but I'm afraid of them.'

Which brings me to one of the oddest things about this whole business. I'm a nervous type by nature: I never go in an aeroplane; I won't drive a car (Jane does the driving); I don't even much care for being alone in the house. But, ever since we'd decided to stay the night at this place, all the uneasiness and, let's face it, the considerable fear I'd started to feel as soon as these coincidences started coming up, it all just fell away. I felt quite confident, I felt I knew I'd be able to do whatever might be required of me.

There was one other thing to get settled. I said to Jane—we were in the bedroom by this time: 'If he turns up, what am I going to use against him?' You see, in the book, Maurice Allington has dug up a sort of magic object that sort of controls the Green Man. I hadn't. Jane saw what I was driving at. She said she'd thought of that, and took off and gave me the plain gold cross she wears round her neck, not for religious reasons: it was her grandmother's. That'll fix him, I thought, and, as before, I felt quite confident about it.

After that, we more or less sat and waited. At one point a car drove up and stopped in the car park. A man got out and went in the front door. It must have been Allington. I couldn't see much about him except that he had the wrong colour hair, but when I looked at my watch it was eight minutes to midnight, the exact time when the Allington in the book got back after his evening out the night he coped with the creature. One more bit of . . . call it confirmation.

I opened our bedroom door and listened. Soon I heard footsteps coming upstairs and going off towards the back of the house, then a door shutting, and then straight away the house seemed totally still. It can't have been much later that I said to Jane: 'Look, there's no point in me hanging round up here. He might be early, you never know. It's a warm night, I might as well go down there now.' She said: 'Are you sure you don't want me to come with you?'

'Absolutely sure,' I said, 'I'll be fine. But I do want you to watch from the window here.'

'Okay,' she said. She wished me luck and we clung to each other for a bit, and then off I went.

I was glad I'd left plenty of time, because getting out of the place turned out to be far from straightforward. Everything seemed to be locked and the key taken away. Eventually I found a scullery door with the key still in the lock. Outside it was quite bright, with a full moon, or not far off, and a couple of fairly powerful lights at the corners of the house. It was a pretty lonely spot, with only two or three other houses in sight. I remember a car went by soon after I got out there, but it was the only one. There wasn't a breath of wind. I saw Jane at our window and waved, and she waved back.

The question was, where to wait. If what was going to happen—assuming something was—went like the book, then the young girl, the daughter, was going to come out of the house because she'd thought she'd heard her father calling her (another bit of magic), and then this Green Man creature was going to come running at her from one direction or the other. I couldn't decide which was the more likely direction.

A bit of luck: near the front door there was one of those heavy wooden benches. I sat down on that and started keeping watch, first one way, then the other, half a minute at a time. Normally, ten minutes of this would have driven me off my head with boredom, but that night somehow it was all right. After some quite long time, I turned my head from right to left on schedule and there was a girl, standing a few yards away: she must have come round that side of the house. She was wearing light-green pyjamas—wrong colour again. I was going to speak to her, but there was something about the way she was standing . . .

She wasn't looking at me: in fact, I soon saw she wasn't looking at anything much. I waved my hand in front of her eyes, the way they do in films when they think someone's been hypnotized or something. I felt a perfect idiot, but her eyes didn't move. Sleepwalking, presumably: not in the book. Do people walk in their sleep? Apparently not: they only pretend to, according to what a psychiatrist chum told me afterwards, but I hadn't heard that then. All I knew, or thought I knew, was this thing everybody's heard somewhere about it being dangerous to wake a sleepwalker. So I just stayed close to the girl and went on keeping watch. A bit more time went by, and then, sure enough, I heard, faintly but clearly, the sound I'd written about: the rustling, creaking sound of the movement of something made of tree branches, twigs and clusters of leaves. And there it was, about a hundred yards away, not really much like a man, coming up at a clumsy, jolting sort of jog-trot on the grass verge, and accelerating.

I knew what I had to do. I started walking to meet it, with the cross ready in my hand. (The girl hadn't moved at all.) When the thing was about twenty yards away I saw its face, which had fungus on it, and I heard another sound I'd written about coming from what I suppose you'd have to call its mouth, like the howling of wind through trees. I stopped and steadied myself and threw the cross at it, and it vanished— immediately. That wasn't like the book, but I didn't stop to think about it. I didn't stop to look for the cross, either. When I turned back, the girl had gone. So much the better. I rushed back into the inn and up to the bedroom and knocked on the door—I'd told Jane to lock it after me.

There was a delay before she came and opened it. I could see she looked confused or something, but I didn't bother with that, because I could feel all the calm and confidence I'd had earlier, it was all just draining away from me. I sat her down on the bed and sat down myself on a chair and just rattled off what had happened as fast as I could. I must have forgotten she'd been meant to be watching.

By the time I'd finished I was shaking. So was Jane. She said: 'What made you change your mind?'

'Change my mind—what about?'

'Going out there,' she said: 'getting up again and going out.'

'But,' I said, 'I've been out there all the time.'

'Oh no you haven't,' she said. 'You came back up here after about twenty minutes, and you told me the whole thing was silly and you were going to bed, which we both did.' She seemed quite positive.

I was absolutely shattered. 'But it all really happened,' I said. 'Just the way I told you.'

'It couldn't have,' she said. 'You must have dreamed it. You certainly didn't throw the cross at anything because it's here, you gave it back to me when you came back the first time.'

And there it was, on the chain round her neck.

I broke down then. I'm not quite clear what I said or did. Jane got some sleeping-pills down me and I went off in the end. I remember thinking rather wildly that somebody or other with a funny sense of humour had got me into exactly the same predicament, the same mess, as the hero of my book had been in: seeing something that must have been supernatural and just not being believed. Because I knew I'd seen the whole thing: I knew it then and I still know it.

I woke up late, feeling terrible. Jane was sitting reading by the bed. She said: 'I've seen young Miss Allington. Your description of her fits and, she said, she used to walk in her sleep.' I asked her how she'd found out, and she said she just had: she's good at that kind of thing. Anyway, I felt better straight away. I said it looked as if we'd neither of us been dreaming, even if what I'd seen couldn't be reconciled with what she'd seen, and she agreed. After that we rather dropped the subject in a funny sort of way. We decided not to look for the cross I'd thrown at the Green Man. I said we wouldn't be able to find it. I didn't ask Jane whether she was thinking what I was thinking: that looking would be a waste of time because she was wearing it at that very moment.

We packed up, made a couple of phone-calls rearranging our appointments, paid the bill, and drove off. We still didn't talk about the main issue. But then, as we were coming off the Mill Hill roundabout—that's only about ten minutes from home—Jane said: 'What do you think happened to sort of make it all happen?' I said: 'I think someone was needed there to destroy that monster. Which means I was guided there at that time, or perhaps the time could be adjusted. I must have been, well, sent all that stuff about the Green Man and about Allington and the others.'

'To make sure you recognized the place when you got there and knew what to do,' she said. 'Who did all the guiding and the sending and so on?'

'The same chap who appeared in my book to tell Allington what he wanted done.'

'Why couldn't he have fixed the monster himself?'

'There are limitations to his power.'

'There can't be many,' she said, 'if he can make the same object be in two places at the same time.'

Yes, you see, she'd thought of that too. It's supposed to be a physical impossibility, isn't it? Anyway, I said, probably the way he'd chosen had been more fun. 'More fun,' Jane repeated. She looked very thoughtful.

As you'll have seen, there was one loose end, of a sort. Who or what was it that had taken on my shape to enter that bedroom, talk to Jane with my voice, and share her bed for at any rate a few minutes? She and I didn't discuss it for several days. Then one morning she asked me the question more or less as I've just put it.

'Interesting point,' I said. 'I don't know.'

'It's more interesting than you think,' she said. 'Because when . . . whoever it was got into bed with me, he didn't just go to sleep.'

I suppose I just looked at her.

'That's right,' she said. 'I thought I'd better go and see John before I told you.' (That's John Allison, our GP.)

'It was negative, then,' I said.

'Yes,' Jane said.

Well, that's it. A relief, of course. But in one way, rather disappointing.

GEORGE MACKAY BROWN

Tithonus

FRAGMENTS FROM THE DIARY OF A LAIRD

THEY are all, especially the women, excited in Torsay today. There is a new child in the village, a little girl. The birth has happened in a house where—so Traill the postman assured me—no one for the past ten years has expected it. The door of Maurice Garth the fisherman and his wife Armingert had seemed to be marked with the sign of barrenness. They were married twenty-one years ago, when Maurice was thirty and Armingert nineteen. One might have expected a large family, five or six at least, from such a healthy devoted pair. (They had both come from tumultuous households to the cold empty cottage at the end of the village.) But the years passed and no young voice broke the quiet dialogue of Maurice and Armingert. To all the islanders it seemed a pity: nothing but beautiful children could have come from their loins.

I was hauling my dinghy up the loch shore this afternoon— it was too bright a day, the trout saw through every gesture and feint—when I saw the woman on the road above. It seemed to me then that she had been waiting to speak to me for some time. I knew who she must be as soon as she opened her mouth. The butterings of her tongue, and the sudden knife flashes, had been described to me often enough. She was Maggie Swintoun. I had been well warned about her by the factor and the minister and the postman. Her idle and wayward tongue, they told me, had done harm to the reputation of more than one person in Torsay; so I'm sure that when I turned my loch-dazzled face to her it did not wear a welcoming expression.

'O sir, you'll never guess,' she said, in the rapt secret voice of all news bearers. 'A bairn was born in the village this morning, and at the Garth cottage of all places—a girl. I think it's right that you should know. Dr. Wayne from Hamnavoe took it into the world. I was there helping. I could hardly believe it when they sent for me.'

The face was withdrawn from the loch side. A rare morning was in front of her, telling the news in shop, smithy, manse, and at the doors of all the crofts round about.

I mounted my horse that, patient beast, had been cropping the thin loch-side grass all morning and cantered back to The Hall over the stony dusty road.

Now I knew why a light had been burning at two o'clock in the cottage at the end of the village. I had got up at that time to let Tobias the cat in.

This is the first child to be born in the island since I came to be laird here. I feel that in some way she belongs to me. I stood at the high window of The Hall looking down at the Garth cottage till the light began to fade.

The generations have been renewed. The island is greatly enriched since yesterday.

I suppose that emotionally I am a kind of neutral person, in the sense that I attract neither very much love nor very much dislike. It is eight years since I arrived from London to live in the island that my grand-uncle, the laird of Torsay, a man I had never seen in my life, left to me. On the slope behind the village with its pier and shop and church is The Hall—the laird's residence—that was built in the late seventeenth century, a large elegant house with eighteen rooms, and a garden, and a stable. I am on speaking terms with everyone in the village and with most of the farmers and crofters in the hinterland. Certain people—William Copinsay the shopkeeper, Maggie Swintoun, Grossiter from the farm of Wear—I pass with as curt a nod as I can manage. If I do have a friend, I suppose he must be James MacIntosh who came to be the schoolmaster in the village two summers ago. We play chess in the school-house every Friday night, summer and winter. Occasionally, when he is out walking with his dog, he calls at my place and we drink whatever is in the whisky decanter. (But I insist that his dog, a furtive collie called Joe who occasionally

bares his teeth at passers-by, is not let further than the kitchen—
Tobias must not be annoyed.) MacIntosh comes from Perth.
He is a pleasant enough man. I think his chief interest is politics,
but I do nothing to encourage him when he starts about the
Irish question, or the Liberal schism, or the suffragettes, or
what the Japanese can be expected to do in such and such an
eventuality. I am sure, if I let him go on, that some fine evening he will declare himself to be a socialist. I set the decanter
squarely between us whenever I hear the first opinionated mur-
murings; in those malty depths, and there alone, will any
argument be.

I think MacIntosh is quite happy living in this island. He is
too lazy and too good-natured to be hustled about in a big city
school. It is almost certain that he has no real vocation for his
job. He has gone to the university, and taken an arts degree, and
then enrolled in teaching for want of anything better. But perhaps I do him wrong; perhaps he is dedicated after all to make
'clever de'ils' of the Torsay children. At any rate, the parents
and the minister—our education committee representative—
seem to have no objection to him. My reason for thinking that
he is without taste or talent for the classroom is that he never
mentions his work to me; but there again it could simply be,
as with politics, that he receives no encouragement.

There is a curious shifting relationship between us, sometimes cordial, sometimes veiled and hostile. He becomes aware
from time to time of the social gulf between us, and it is on these
occasions that he says and does things to humble me—I must
learn that we are living now in the age of equality. But under
it all he is such a good-natured chap; after ten minutes or so of
unbated tongues we are at peace again over chess-board or
decanter.

Last night MacIntosh said, between two bouts of chess in the
school-house, 'It's a very strange thing, I did not think I could
ever be so intrigued by a child. Most of them are formed of the
common clay after all. O, you know what I mean—from time
to time a beautiful child, or a clever child, comes to the school,
and you teach him or her for a year or two, then away they go
to the big school in the town, or back to work on the farm, and

you never think more about them. But this pupil is just that wee bit different.'

'What on earth are you talking about?' I said.

'The Garth girl who lives at the end of the village—Thora— you know, her father has the fishing boat *Rain Goose*.'

'Is that her name, Thora?' I said. (For I had seen the quiet face among a drift of school-children in the playground, at four o'clock, going home then alone to Maurice and Armingert's door. I had seen bright hair at the end of the small stone pier, waiting for a boat to come in from the west. I had seen the solemn clasped hands, bearing the small bible, outside the kirk door on a Sunday morning. But beyond that the girl and I had never exchanged a single word. As I say, I did not even know her name till last night.)

'She is a very strange girl, that one,' said MacIntosh. 'There is a *something* about her. Would you please not drop your ash on the mat? (There's an ash tray.) I'm not like some folk. I can't afford to buy a new mat every month. Mrs. Baillie asked me to mention it to you.'

My pipe and his dog cancel each other out. Mrs. Baillie is his housekeeper.

'To me she looks an ordinary enough child,' I said. 'In what way is she different?'

MacIntosh could not say how this girl was different. She was made of the common clay—'like all of us, like all of us,' he hastened to assure me, thereby putting all the islanders, including the laird and Halcro the beachcomber, on the same footing. Still, there was something special about the girl, he insisted, goodness knows what. . . .

MacIntosh won the third hard-fought game. He exulted. Victory always makes him reckless and generous. 'Smoke, man, smoke in here any time you like. To hell with Mrs. Baillie. Get your pipe out. I'll sweep any ash up myself.'

I met Thora Garth on the brae outside the kirk as I was going home from the school-house. She put on me a brief pellucid unsmiling look as we passed. She was carrying a pail of milk from the farm of Gardyke.

Fifteen years ago, in my grand-uncle's day, the island women stopped and curtsied whenever the laird went past. A century ago a single glance from the great man of The Hall turned them to stone in their fields.

All that is changed.

Traill the postman had put a letter through my window while I was at the school-house. The familiar official writing was on the envelope. I lit the lamp. I was secure in my island for another six months. The usual hundred pounds was enclosed, in a mixture of tens and fives and singles. There was no message; there was usually no need for the Edinburgh lawyer to have anything special to say. He had simply to disburse in two instalments the two hundred pounds a year that my grand-uncle left me, so that I can live out my life as a gentleman in the great Hall of Torsay.

Thora Garth returned this morning from the senior school in Hamnavoe, at the end of her first session there. I happened to be down at the pier when the weekly mail steamer drew alongside. Several islanders were there, as always on that important occasion. The rope came snaking ashore. A seaman shouted banter to the fishermen and Robbie Tenston the farmer of Dale (who had just come out of the hotel bar). The minister turned away, pretending not to have heard the swear-words. I found Maurice Garth standing beside me. 'What's wrong with the creels today?' I said to him. . . . 'I'm expecting Thora,' Maurice said in that mild shy murmur that many of the islanders have. 'She should be on the boat. It's the summer holidays—she'll be home for seven weeks.'

Sure enough, there was the tilted serious freckled face above the rail. She acknowledged her father with a slight sideways movement of her hand. At that moment I was distracted by an argument that had broken out on the pier. Robbie Tenston of Dale was claiming possession of a large square plywood box that had just been swung ashore from the *Pomona*.

'Nonsense,' cried William Copinsay the general merchant. 'Don't be foolish. It's loaves. It's the bread I always get from the baker in the town on a Friday.'

And indeed—though I hated to agree with Copinsay—there

was no doubt that the box contained bread; the incense of new baking drifted across the pier.

'Don't you call me a fool,' said Robbie Tenston in his dark dangerous drinking voice. 'This is a box of plants, if you want to know. It's for my wife's greenhouse. The market gardener wrote to say that it was coming on the boat today. That's why I'm here, man. Let go of it now.'

Copinsay and Robbie Tenston had each laid hands on the rope that was round the box. A circle of onlookers gathered raggedly about them.

The trouble was, the label had somehow got scraped off in transit. (But Robbie must have been stupid to have missed that delicious smell of new rolls and loaves. Besides, roots and greenery would never have weighed so much.)

They wrestled for the box, both of them red in the face. It had all the makings of a disgraceful scene. Four of the crew had stopped working. They watched from the derrick, delighted. The skipper leaned out of his cabin, grinning eagerly. They could have told who owned the box by rights, but they wanted the entertainment to go on for some time yet.

Mr. Evelyn the minister attempted to settle the affair. 'Now now,' he said, 'now now—it is simply a matter of undoing the rope—please, Mr. Copinsay—Robert, I beg you—and looking inside.'

They paid no attention to him. The farmer dragged the box from the weaker hands of the merchant. Copinsay's face was twisted with rage and spite. 'You old miserly bastard!' shouted Robbie.

The skipper leaned further out of his cabin. He put his pipe carefully on the ledge and clapped his hands. Maggie Swintoun and a few other women came down the pier from their houses, attracted by the hullabaloo.

At that point Copinsay flung himself on Robbie Tenston and began to scratch at his face like a woman. He screamed a few falsetto incoherences.

The dispute had reached a dangerous stage. (I felt that, as the chief man in the island, I should be doing something about it, but I am morbidly afraid of making a fool of myself in front of these people.) Robbie could have taken the merchant in his great earth-red hands and broken him. He could have picked him up and flung him into the sea. He tried first of all to shake himself free from the hysterical clutchings of William Copinsay. He struck Copinsay an awkward blow on the shoulder. They whirled each other round like mad dancers between the horse-box and the gangway. Then—still grappling—they achieved some kind of a stillness; through it they glared at each other.

God knows what might have happened then.

It was Thora Garth who restored peace to the island. It was extraordinary, the way the focus shifted from the two buffoons to the girl. But suddenly everyone on the pier, including the skipper and the fighters and myself, was looking at her alone. She had left the steamer and was standing on the pier beside the disputed box. She had one hand on it, laid flat. With the other she pointed to William Copinsay.

'The box belongs to him,' she said quietly. 'Robbie, the box belongs to Mr. Copinsay.'

That was the end of the fracas. Robbie Tenston seemed to accept her verdict at once. He pushed Mr. Copinsay away. He muttered a grudging 'Well, don't let him or anybody ever call me a fool again.' He walked up the pier, his face encrimsoned, past Maggie Swintoun and the other women who were flocking to the scene, too late, with their false chorus of commiseration and accusation. 'That Robbie Tenston should be reported to the police,' said Maggie Swintoun flatly. 'It's that pub to blame. It should be closed down. Drink is the cause of all the trouble in Torsay. Them in authority should be doing something about it.' . . . She kept looking at me out of the corner of her eye.

Mr. Copinsay sat on his box of bread and began to weep silently.

I could not bear any more of it.

The seamen had returned to their work, swinging ashore mail-bags, crates of beer, saddlery, a bicycle, newspapers. Steve Mack the skipper was lighting his pipe and looking inland to the island hills as if nothing untoward had happened.

I left the women cluck-clucking with sympathy around

Copinsay Agonistes. I took my box of books that was sent each month from the library in the town—there was never likely to be any fighting about that piece of cargo—and walked up the pier.

From the gate of The Hall I looked back at the village. Thora Garth was greeting her mother in the open door of their cottage. Maurice carried his daughter's case. The woman and the girl—the one was as tall as the other now—leaned towards each other and kissed briefly. The dog barked and danced around them.

On the top of the island, where the road cuts into the shoulder of the hill, a small dark figure throbbed for a minute against the sky. It was Robbie Tenston bearing his resentment and shame home to Dale.

This evening I called in at the hotel bar for a glass of beer—a thing I rarely do; but it has been, for Orkney, a warm day, and also I must confess I am missing James MacIntosh already—he went home to Perth for the summer vacation two days ago. Seven weeks without chess and argument is a long time.

Maurice Garth was sitting in the window seat drinking stout. I took my glass of beer across to his table.

'Well,' I said, 'and how is Thora liking the big school in Hamnavoe?'

'She isn't clever,' he said, smiling. 'I doubt she won't go very far as a scholar. But what is there for a lass to do in Torsay nowadays? Everybody's leaving the island. I suppose in the end she might get some kind of a job in the town.'

'It was remarkable,' I said, 'the way Thora put a stop to that fight on the pier this morning.'

'Oh, I don't know,' said Maurice. 'That pair of idiots! Any fool could have seen that it was a bread box. I hope we'll hear no more about it. I hope there isn't going to be any trouble about it with the police.'

'They might have done each other an injury,' I said. 'It was your Thora who brought them to their senses. I never saw anything quite so astonishing.'

'No, no,' said Maurice, raising his hand. 'Don't say that. Thora's just an ordinary lass. There's nothing so very strange about it. Thora just pointed out what was what to that pair of fools. Say no more about it.'

Maurice Garth is a placid man. Such vehemence is strange, coming from him. But perhaps it was that he had drunk too many glasses of stout.

There has been a fine morsel of scandal in the village this morning. The Swintoun woman has been going about the doors at all hours, her cheeks aflame with excitement. It seems that the younger son of Wear, the main farm in the island, has been jilted. Everything has been set fair for a wedding for three months past. Consignments of new furniture, carpets, curtains, crockery have been arriving in the steamer from Hamnavoe; to be fetched later the same afternoon by a farm servant in a cart. They do things in style at Wear. The first friends have gone with their gifts, even. I myself wandered about the empty caverns of this house all one morning last week, considering whether this oil painting or that antique vase might be acceptable. The truth is, I can hardly afford any more to give them a present of money. In the end I thought they might be happy with an old silk sampler framed in mahogany that one of my grand-aunts made in the middle of Queen Victoria's reign. It is a beautiful piece of work. At Wear they would expect something new and glittery from the laird. I hoped, however, that the bride might be pleased with my present.

The Rev. Mr. Evelyn was going to have made the first proclamation from the pulpit next Sunday morning. (I never attend the church services here myself, being nominally an Episcopalian, like most of the other Orkney lairds.)

Well, the island won't have to worry any more about this particular ceremony, for—so Traill the postman told me over the garden wall this morning—the prospective bride has gone to live in a wooden shack at the other end of the island—a hut left over from the Kaiser's war—with Shaun Midhouse, a deck hand on the *Pomona*, a man of no particular comeliness or gifts —in fact, a rather unprepossessing character—certainly not what the women of Torsay would call 'a good catch', by any means.

I am sorry for Jack Grossiter of Wear. He seems a decent enough young chap, not at all like some others in the household. His father of all men I dislike in Torsay. He is arrogant and overbearing towards those whom he considers his inferiors; but you never saw such cap-raisings and foot-scrapings as when he chances to meet the minister or the schoolmaster or myself on the road. He is also the wealthiest man in the island, yet the good tilth that he works belongs to me, and I am forbidden by law to charge more than a derisory rent for it. I try not to let this curious situation influence me, but of course it does nothing to sweeten my regard for the man. In addition to everything else he is an upstart and an ignoramus. How delighted he was when his only daughter Sophie married that custom house officer two years ago—that was a feather in his cap, for according to the curious snobbery of folk like Grossiter a man who has a pen-and-paper job is a superior animal altogether to a crofter who labours all his life among earth and blood and dung. The eldest son Andrew will follow him in Wear, no doubt, for since that piece of socialism was enacted in parliament in 1882 even death does not break the secure chain of a family's tenure. . . . For Andrew, in his turn, a good match was likewise negotiated, no less than Mr. Copinsay the merchant's daughter. Wear will be none the poorer for that alliance. Only Jack Grossiter remained unmarried. Whom he took to wife was of comparatively small importance—a hill croft would be found for him when the time came. I could imagine well enough the brutish reasonings of the man of Wear, once his second son began to be shaken with the ruddiness and restlessness of virility. There was now, for instance, that bonny respectable well-handed lass in the village—Thora Garth—what objection could there be to her? She would make a good wife to any man, though of course her father was only a fisherman and not over-burdened with wealth. One afternoon—I can picture it all—the man of Wear would have said a few words to Maurice Garth in the pub, and bought him a dram. One evening soon after that Jack Grossiter and Thora would have been left alone together in the sea-bright room above the shore; a first few cold words passed between them. It gradually became known in the village that they were engaged. I have seen them, once or twice this summer, walking along the shore together into the sunset.

Now, suddenly, this has shaken the island.

The first unusual thing to happen was that Thora went missing, one morning last week. She simply walked out of the house with never a word to her parents. There had been no quarrel, so Armingert assured the neighbours. For the first hour or two she didn't worry about Thora; she might have walked up to Wear, or called on Minnie Farquharson who was working on the bridal dress. But she did not come home for her dinner, and that was unusual, that was a bit worrying. Armingert called at this door and that in the afternoon. No-one had seen Thora since morning. Eventually it was Benny Smith the ferryman who let out the truth, casually, to Maurice Garth, at the end of the pier, when he got back from Hamnavoe in the early evening. He had taken Thora across in his boat the *Lintie* about ten o'clock that morning. She hadn't said a word to him all the way across. It wasn't any concern of his, and anyway she wasn't the kind of young woman who likes her affairs to be known.

Well, that was a bit of a relief to Maurice and Armingert. They reasoned that Thora must suddenly have thought of some necessary wedding purchase; she would be staying over-night with one of her Hamnavoe friends (one of the girls she had been to school with); she would be back on the *Pomona* the next morning.

And in fact she did come back on Friday on board the *Pomona*. She walked at once from the boat to her parents' door. Who was trailing two paces behind her but Shaun Midhouse, one of the crew of the *Pomona*? Thora opened the cottage door and went inside (Shaun lingered at the gate). She told her mother—Maurice was at the lobsters—that she could not marry Jack Grossiter of Wear after all, because she had discovered that she liked somebody else much better. There was a long silence in the kitchen. Then her mother asked who this other man was. Thora pointed through the window. The deck-hand was shuffling about on the road outside with that hangdog look that he has when he isn't working or drinking. 'That's my man,'

Thora said—'I'm going to live with him.' Armingert said that she would give much pain and grief to those near to her if she did what she said she was going to do. Thora said she realized that. 'I'm sorry,' she said. Then she left the cottage and walked up the brae to the farm of Wear. Shaun went a few paces with her through the village, but left her outside the hotel and went back on board the *Pomona*; the boat was due to sail again in ten minutes.

Thora wouldn't go into the farmhouse. She said what she had to say standing in the door, and it only lasted a minute. Then she turned and walked slowly across the yard to the road. The old man went a few steps after her, shouting and shaking his fists. His elder son Andrew called him back, coldly—his father mustn't make a fool of himself before the whole district. Let the slut go. His father must remember that he was the most important farmer in Torsay.

Jack had already taken his white face from the door—it hasn't been seen anywhere in the island since. I am deeply sorry for him.

I ought to go along and see these people. God knows what I can say to them. I am hopeless in such situations. I was not created to be a bringer of salves and oils.

I saw the minister coming out of the farmhouse two days ago. . . .

The eastern part of the island is very desolate, scarred with peat-bogs and Pictish burial places. During the war the army built an artillery battery on the links there. (They commandeered the site—my subsequent granting of permission was an empty token.) All that is left of the camp now, among concrete foundations, is a single wooden hut that had been the officers' mess. No-one has lived there since 1919—inside it must be all dampness and mildew. Tom Christianson the shepherd saw, two days after the breaking of the engagement, smoke coming from the chimney of the hut. He kept an eye on the place; later that afternoon a van drove up; Shaun Midhouse carried from van to hut a mattress, a sack of coal, a box of groceries. He reported the facts to me. That night, late, I walked between the hills and saw a single lamp burning in the window.

Thora Garth and Shaun Midhouse have been living there for a full week now—as Mr. Copinsay the merchant says, 'in sin'; managing to look, as he says it, both pained and pleased.

Two nights ago Armingert and Maurice came to see me.

'Shaun Midhouse is such a poor weed of a creature,' said Armingert in my cold library. 'What ever could any girl see in the likes of *that*?'

Maurice shook his head. They are, both these dear folk, very troubled.

'Jack Grossiter is ill,' said Armingert. 'I never saw a boy so upset. I am very very sorry for him.'

'I will go and see him tomorrow,' I said.

'What trouble she has caused,' said Armingert. 'I did not think such a thing was possible. If she had suddenly attacked us with a knife it would have been easier to bear. She is a bad cruel deceptive girl.'

'She is our daughter,' said Maurice gently.

'We have no business to inflict our troubles on you,' said Armingert. 'What we have come about is this, all the same. We understand that you own that war-time site. They are sitting unbidden in your property, Thora and that creature. That is what it amounts to. You could evict them.'

I shook my head.

'You could have the law on them,' she insisted. 'You could force them out. She would have to come home then, if you did that. That would bring her to her senses.'

'I'm sorry,' I said. 'There is something at work here that none of us understands, some kind of an elemental force. It is terrible and it is delicate at the same time. It must work itself out in Thora and Shaun Midhouse. I am not wise enough to interfere.'

There was silence in the library for a long time after that.

Armingert looked hurt and lost. No doubt but she is offended with me.

'He is right,' said Maurice at last. 'She is our daughter. We must just try to be patient.'

Then they both got to their feet. They looked tired and sad. They who had been childless for so long in their youth are now childless again; and they are growing old; and an area of their

life where there was nothingness twenty years ago is now all
vivid pain.

I knew it would happen some day: that old school-house dog
has savaged one of the islanders, and a child at that. I was in the
garden, filling a bowl with gooseberries, when I heard the terrible outcry from the village, a mingling of snarls and screams.
'Joe, you brute!' came James MacIntosh's voice (it was a still
summer evening; every sound carried for miles)—'Bad dog!
Get into the house this minute!' . . . And then in a soothing
voice, 'Let's see your leg then. It's only a graze, Mansie. You
got a fright, that's all. . . . That bad Joe. . . . Shush now, no
need to kick up such a row. You'll deafen the whole village.'
. . . This Mansie, whoever he was, refused to be comforted.
The lamentation came nearer. I heard the school-house door
being banged shut (my garden wall is too high to see the village): James MacIntosh had gone indoors, possibly to chastise
his cur. Presently a boy, sobbing and snivelling in spasms,
appeared on the road. He leaned against a pillar to get his
breath. 'Hello,' I said, 'would you like some gooseberries?'

Greed and self-pity contended in Mansie's face. He unlatched the gate and came in, limping. There was a livid
crescent mark below his knee. He picked a fat gooseberry from
my bowl. He looked at it wonderingly. His lips were still
shivering with shock.

'That damn fool of a dog,' I said. 'Did he seize you then?
You'd better come into the kitchen. I'll put some disinfectant
on it. I have bandages.'

The cupped palm of his hand brimmed with gooseberries.
He bit into several, one after the other, with a half-reluctant
lingering relish. Then he crammed six or seven into his mouth
till his cheek bulged. His brown eyes dissolved in rapture; he
closed them; there was a runnel of juice from one corner of his
mouth to his chin.

The day was ending in a riot of colour westward. Crimson
and saffron and jet the sea blazed, like stained glass.

'The disinfectant,' I said. 'It's in the kitchen.'

He balanced the last of the gooseberries on the tip of his

tongue, rolled it round inside his mouth, and bit on it. 'It's nothing,' he said. 'I was in the village visiting my grand-da. It was me to blame really. I kicked Joe's bone at the school gate. I must be getting home now. Thora'll be wondering about me.' . . .

So, he was one of the Midhouse boys. He looked like neither of his parents. He had the shy swift gentle eyes of Maurice his grandfather. He relished gooseberries the way that old Maurice sipped his stout in the hotel bar.

'And anyway,' he said, 'I wouldn't come into your house to save my life.'

'What's wrong with my house?' I said.

'It's the laird's house,' he said. 'It's The Hall. I'm against all that kind of thing. I'm a communist.' (He was maybe ten years old.)

'There isn't anything very grand about this great ruckle of stones,' I said. 'It's falling to pieces. You should see the inside of it. Just look at this wilderness of a garden. I'll tell you the truth, Mansie—I'm nearly as poor as Ezra the tinker. So come in till I fix your leg.'

He shook his head. 'It's the principle of it,' said Mansie. 'You oppressed my ancestors. You taxed them to death. You drove them to Canada and New Zealand. You made them work in your fields for nothing. They built this house for you, yes, and their hands were red carrying up stones from the shore. I wouldn't go through your door for a pension. What does one man want with a big house like this anyway? Thora and me and my brothers live in two small rooms up at Solsetter.'

'I'm sorry, Mansie,' I said. 'I promise I won't ever be wicked like that again. But I am worried about that bite on your leg.'

'It's the same with the kirk,' said Mansie. 'Do you think I could have just one more gooseberry? I would never enter that kirk door. All that talk about sin and hell and angels. Do you know what I think about the bible? It's one long fairy-tale from beginning to end. I'm an atheist, too. You can tell the minister what I said if you like. I don't care. I don't care for any of you.'

The rich evening light smote the west gable of The Hall. The great house took, briefly, a splendour. The wall flushed and darkened. Then with all its withered stonework and ramshackle rooms it began to enter the night.

The gooseberry bush twanged. The young anarchist was plucking another fruit.

'I don't believe in anything,' he said. 'Nothing at all. You are born. You live for a while. Then you die. My grandma died last year. Do you know what she is now? Dust in the kirkyard. They could have put her in a ditch, it would have been all the same. When you're dead you're dead.'

'You'd better be getting home then, comrade, before it's dark,' I said.

'Do you know this,' he said, 'I have no father. At least, I do have a father but he doesn't live with us any more. He went away one day, suddenly. Oh, a while ago now, last winter. Jock Ritch saw him once in Falmouth. He was on a trawler. We don't know where he is. I'm glad he's gone. I didn't like him. And I'll tell you another thing.'

'Tomorrow,' I said. 'You must go home now. You must get that bite seen to. If you don't, some day there'll be an old man hobbling round this village with a wooden leg. And it'll be you, if you don't show that wound to your mother right away.'

'Rob and Willie and me,' he said, 'we're bastards. I bet I've shocked you. I bet you think I said a bad word. You see, Thora was never married. Thora, she's my mother. I suppose you would say "illegitimate" but it's just the same thing. The gooseberries were good. They're not your gooseberries though. They belong to the whole island by rights. I was only taking my share.'

The darkness had come down so suddenly that I could not say when the boy left my door. I was aware only that one smell had been subtracted from the enchanting cluster of smells that gather about an island on a late summer evening. A shadow was gone from the garden. I turned and went inside, carrying the bowl of gooseberries. (There would be one pot of jam less next winter.) I traversed, going to the kitchen, a corridor with an ancient ineradicable sweetness of rot in it.

I have been ill, it seems. I still feel like a ghost in a prison of bone. I have been very ill, James MacIntosh says. 'I thought you were for the kirkyard,' he told me last night. 'That's the truth. I thought an ancient proud island family was guttering out at last.' . . . He said after a time, 'There's something tough about you, man. I think you'll see the boots off us all.' He put the kettle on my fire to make a pot of tea. 'I don't suppose now,' he said, 'that you'll be up to a game of chess just yet. Quite so.' He is a sweet considerate man. 'I'll fill your hot-water bottle before I go,' he said, 'it's very cold up in that bedroom.'

The whole house is like a winter labyrinth in the heart of this summer-time island. It is all this dampness and rot, I'm sure, that made me so ill last month. The Hall is withering slowly about me. I cannot afford now to re-slate the roof. There is warping and woodworm and patches of damp everywhere. The three long corridors empty their overplus of draught into every mildewed bedroom. Even last October, when the men from the fishing boat broke the billiard-room window, going between the hotel and the barn dance at Dale, I had to go without tobacco for a fortnight or so until the joiner was paid. Not much can be done these days on two hundred pounds a year.

'James,' I said, 'I'm going to shift out of that bedroom. Another winter there and I'd be a gonner. I wonder if I could get a small bed fitted into some corner of the kitchen—over there, for example, out of the draught. I don't mind eating and sleeping in the same room.'

This morning (Saturday) MacIntosh came up from the school house with a small iron folding bed. 'It's been in the out-house since I came to Torsay,' he said. 'The last teacher must have had it for one of his kids. It's a bit rusty, man, but it's sound, perfectly sound. Look for yourself. If you'll just shift that heap of books out of the corner I'll get it fixed up in no time.'
. . .

We drank some tea while blankets and pillows were airing at the kitchen fire. I tried to smoke my pipe but the thing tasted foul—the room plunged; there was a blackness before my eyes; I began to sweat. 'You're not entirely well yet by any means,' said the schoolmaster. 'Put that pipe away. It'll be a week or two before you can get over the door, far less down to the hotel for a pint. I'm telling you, you've been very ill. You don't seem to realize how desperate it was with you. But for one thing only you'd be in the family vault.'

People who have been in the darkness for a while long to know how it was with them when they were no longer there to observe and evaluate. They resent their absence from the dear ecstatic flesh; they suspect too that they may have been caught out by their attendants in some weakness or shame that they themselves make light of, or even indulge, in the ordinary round. At the same time there is a kind of vanity in sickness. It sets a person apart from the folk who only eat and sleep and sorrow and work. Those dullards become the servants of the hero who has ventured into the shadowy border-land next to the kingdom of death—the sickness bestows a special quality on him, a seal of gentility almost. There are people who wear their scars and pock-marks like decorations. The biography of such a one is a pattern of small sicknesses, until at last the kingdom he has fought against and been fascinated with for so long besets him with irresistible steel and fire. There is one last trumpet call under a dark tower. . . .

This afternoon, by means of subtle insistent questions, I got from James MacIntosh the story of my trouble. He would much rather have been sitting with me in amiable silence over a chess-board. I knew of course the beginning of the story; how I had had to drag myself about the house for some days at the end of May with a gray quake on me. To get potatoes from the garden—a simple job like that—was a burdensome penance. The road to the village and the tobacco jar on Mr. Copinsay's shelf was a wearisome 'via crucis', but at last I could not even get that far. My pipe lay cold on the window-sill for two days. Sometime during the third day the sun became a blackness.

'Pneumonia,' said James MacIntosh. 'That's what it was. Dr. Wayne stood in the school-house door and barked at me. *The laird up yonder, your friend, he has double pneumonia. By rights he should be in the hospital in Kirkwall. That's out of the question, he's too ill. He'll have to bide where he is* . . . *Now then* (says he) *there's not a hell of a lot I can do for him. That's the truth. It's a dicey thing, pneumonia. It comes to a crisis. The sick man reaches a crossroads, if you understand what I mean. He lingers there for an hour or two. Then he simply goes one way or the other. There's no telling. What is essential though* (says the old quack) *is good nursing. There must be somebody with him night and day—two, if possible, one to relieve the other. Now then, you must know some woman or other in the island who has experience of this kind of thing. Get her.* . . . And out of the house he stumps with his black bag, down the road, back to the ferry-boat at the pier.

'So there you lay, in that great carved mahogany bed upstairs, sweating and raving. Old Wayne had laid the responsibility fairly and squarely on me. I had to get a nurse. But what nurse? And where? The only person who does any kind of nursing in the island is that Maggie Swintoun—at least, she brings most of the island bairns into the world, and it's her they generally send for when anybody dies. But nursing—I never actually heard of her attending sick folk. And besides, I knew you disliked the woman. If you were to open your eyes and see that face at the foot of the bed it would most likely, I thought, be the end of you. But that didn't prevent Mistress Swintoun from offering her services that same day. There she stood, keening and whispering at the foot of the stair—she had had the impudence to come in without knocking. *I hear the laird isn't well, the poor man* (says she). *Well now, if there's anything I can do. I don't mind sitting up all night.* . . . And the eyes of her going here and there over the portraits in the staircase and over all the silver plate in the hall-stand. *Thank you all the same,* said I, *but other arrangements have been made.* . . . Off she went then, like a cat leaving a fish on a doorstep. I was worried all the same, I can tell you. I went down to the village to have a consultation with Minnie Farquharson the seamstress. She knows everybody in Torsay, what they can do and what they can't do. She demurred. In the old days there would have been no difficulty: the island was teeming with kindly capable women who would have been ideal for the job. But things are different now, Minnie pointed out. Torsay is half empty. Most of the houses are in ruin. The young women are away in the towns, working in shops and offices. All that's left in the way of women-folk are school bairns and "puir auld bodies". She honestly couldn't think of a single suitable person. "*Now* (says she) *I doubt you'll have to put an advertisement in "The Orcadian*".

'I knew, as I walked back up the brae, that by the time the advertisement—"Wanted, experienced private nurse to attend gentleman"—had appeared, and been answered, and the nurse interviewed and approved and brought over to Torsay, there would have been no patient for her to attend to. The marble jaws would have swallowed you up. . . .

'When I turned in at the gate of The Hall, I saw washed sheets and pillow-cases hanging in the garden, between the potato patch and the gooseberry bushes, where no washing has ever flapped in the wind for ten years and more. (You hang your shirts and socks, I know, in front of the stove.) I went into the house. The fire was lit in the kitchen. The windows along the corridor were open, and there was a clean sweet air everywhere instead of those gray draughts. I'm not a superstitious man, but I swear my hand was shaking when I opened the door of your bedroom. And there she was, bent over you and putting cold linen to the beaded agony on your face.'

'Who?' I said.

'And there she stayed for ten days, feeding you, washing you, comforting you, keeping the glim of life in you night and day. Nobody ever relieved her. God knows when she slept. She was never, as far as I could make out, a minute away from your room. But of course she must have been, to cook, wash, prepare the medicines, things like that. She had even set jars of flowers in odd niches and corners. The house began to smell fragrant.'

I said, 'Yes, but who?'

'She told me, standing there in your bedroom that first day, that I didn't need to worry any longer. She thought she could manage. What could I do anyway, she said, with the school bairns to teach from ten in the morning till four in the afternoon? And she smiled at me, as though there was some kind of conspiracy between us. And she nodded, half in dismissal and half in affirmation. I went down that road to the schoolhouse with a burden lifted from me, I can tell you. *Well, if he doesn't get better*, I thought, *it won't be for want of a good nurse.*'

'You haven't told me her name,' I said.

'On the Thursday old Wayne came out of The Hall shaking his head. I saw him from the school window. He was still shaking his head when he stepped on board the *Lintie* at the pier. That was the day of the crisis. I ran up to your house as soon as the school was let out at half past three (for I couldn't bear to wait till four o'clock). The flame was gulping in the lamp all right. Your pulse had no cohesion or rhythm. There were great gaps in your breathing. I stood there, expecting darkness and silence pretty soon. What is it above all that a woman gives to a man? God knows. Some strong pure dark essence of the earth that seems not to be a part of the sun-loving clay of men at all. The woman was never away from your bedside that night. I slept, on and off, between two chairs in the kitchen. At sunrise next morning you spoke for the first time for, I think, twelve days. You asked for—of all things—a cup of tea. But the nurse, she was no longer there.'

'For God's sake,' I said, 'tell me who she is.'

'You'll have to be doing with my crude services,' said James MacIntosh, 'till you're able to do for yourself. You should be out and about in a week, if this good weather holds. I thought I told you who she was.'

'You didn't,' I said.

'Well now,' he said, 'I thought I did. It was Thora Garth, of course.'

This morning I had a visit from a young man I have never seen before. It turns out that he is a missionary, a kind of lay Presbyterian preacher. There has been no minister in Torsay since the Rev. Mr. Evelyn retired three years ago; the spiritual needs of the few people remaining have been attended to, now and then, by ministers from other islands.

This missionary is an earnest young bachelor. He has a sense of vocation but no humour. Someone in the village must have told him about me. 'Mister, you'd better call on the old man up at The Hall. You'll likely be able to understand the posh way he speaks. He only manages down to the village once a week nowadays for his tobacco and his margarine and his loaf. He has nothing to live on but an annuity—nowadays, with the price of things, it would hardly keep a cat. The likes of him is too grand of course to apply for Social Security. God knows what way he manages to live at all. He's never been a church man, but I'm sure he'd be pleased to see an educated person like you.' . . . I can just imagine Andrew Grossiter, or one of the elders, saying that to the newcomer some Sunday morning after the service, pointing up the brae to the big house with the fallen slates and the broken sundial.

So, here he was, this young preacher, come to visit me out of Christian duty. He put on me a bright kind smile from time to time.

'I like it here, in Torsay,' he said. 'Indeed I do. It's a great change from the city. I expect it'll take me a wee while to get used to country ways. I come from Glasgow myself. For example, I'm as certain as can be that someone has died in the village this morning. I saw a man carrying trestles into one of the houses. There was a coffin in the back of his van. By rights I should have been told about it at once. It's my duty to visit the bereaved relatives. I'll be wanted of course for the funeral. Ah well, I'll make enquiries this afternoon sometime.'

He eyed with a kind of innocent distaste the sole habitable room left in my house, the kitchen. If I had known he was coming I might have tidied the place up a bit. But for the sake of truth it's best when visitors come unexpectedly on the loaf and cracked mug on the table, the unmade bed, the webbed windows, and all the mingled smells of aged bachelordom.

'Death is a common thing in Torsay nowadays,' I said. 'Nearly everybody left in the village is old. There's hardly a young person in the whole island except yourself.'

'I hope you don't mind my visiting you,' said the missionary. 'I understand you're an episcopalian. These days we must try to be as ecumenical as we can. Now sir, please don't be offended at what I'm going to say. It could be that, what with old age and the fact that you're not so able as you used to be, you find yourself with less money than you could be doing with—for example, to buy a bag of coal or a bit of butcher-meat.'

'I manage quite well,' I said. 'I have an annuity from my grand-uncle. I own this house. I don't eat a great deal.'

'Quite so,' he said. 'But the cost of everything keeps going up. Your income hardly covers the little luxuries that make life a bit more bearable. Now, I've been looking through the local church accounts and I've discovered that there are one or two small bequests that I have the disposal of. I don't see why you shouldn't be a beneficiary. They're for every poor person in the island, whatever church he belongs to, or indeed if he belongs to no church at all.'

'I don't need a thing,' I said.

'Well,' he said, 'if ever you feel like speaking to me about it. The money is there. It's for everybody in Torsay who needs it.'

'Torsay will soon require nothing,' I said.

'I must go down to the village now and see about this death,' he said. 'I noticed three young men in dark suits coming off the *Pomona* this morning. They must be relatives of some kind. . . . I'll find my own way out. Don't bother. This is a fascinating old house right enough. These stones, if only they could speak. God bless you, now.'

He left me then, that earnest innocent young man. I was glad in a way to see the back of him—though I liked him well enough—for I was longing for a pipeful of tobacco, and I'm as certain as can be that he is one of those evangelicals who disapprove of smoking and drinking.

So, there is another death in the island. Month by month Torsay is re-entering the eternal loneliness and silence. The old ones die. The young ones go away to farm in other places, or to car factories in Coventry or Bathgate. The fertile end of the island is littered with roofless windowless crofts. Sometimes, on a fine afternoon, I take my stick and walk for an hour about my domain. Last week I passed Dale, which Robbie Tenston used to farm. (He has been in Australia for fifteen years.) I pushed open the warped door of the dwelling-house. A great gray ewe lurched past me out of the darkness and nearly knocked me over. Birds whirred up through the bare rafters. There were bits of furniture here and there—a table, a couple of chairs, a wooden shut-bed. A framed photograph of the Channel Fleet still hung at the damp wall. There were empty bottles and jam

jars all over the floor among sheep-turds and bird-splashes. . . .
Most of the farm houses in Torsay are like that now.

It is an island dedicated to extinction. I can never imagine
young people coming back to these uncultivated fields and
eyeless ruins. Soon now, I know, the place will be finally abandoned to gulls and crows and rabbits. When first I came to
Torsay fifty years ago, summoned from London by my grand-
uncle's executor, I could still read the heraldry and the Latin
motto over the great Hall door. There is a vague shape on the
sandstone lintel now; otherwise it is indecipherable. All that
style and history and romance have melted back into the
stone.

Life in a flourishing island is a kind of fruitful interweaving
music of birth and marriage and death: a trio. The old pass
mildly into the darkness to make way for their bright grandchildren. There is only one dancer in the island now and he
carries the hour-glass and the spade and the scythe.

How many have died in the past few years? I cannot remember all the names. The severest loss, as far as I am concerned,
is James MacIntosh. The school above the village closed ten
years ago, when the dominie retired. There were not enough
pupils to justify a new teacher. He did not want to leave Torsay
—his whole life was entirely rooted here. He loved the trout
fishing, and our chess and few drams twice a week; he liked to
follow the careers of his former pupils in every part of the
world—he had given so much of his life to them. What did he
know of his few remaining relatives in Perthshire? 'Here I am
and here I'll bide,' he said to me the day the school closed. I
offered him a croft a mile away—Unibreck—that had just been
vacated: the young crofter had got a job in an Edinburgh
brewery. James MacIntosh lived there for two winters, reading
his 'Forward' and working out chess moves from the manual he
kept beside his bed. . . . One morning Maggie Swintoun put
her head in at my kitchen door when I was setting the fire. 'O
sir,' she wailed, 'a terrible thing has happened!' Every broken
window, every winter cough, every sparrow-fall was stuff of
tragedy to Maggie Swintoun. I didn't bother even to look
round at the woman—I went on laying a careful stratum of

sticks on the crumpled paper. 'Up at Unibreck,' she cried, 'your friend, poor Mr. MacIntosh the teacher. I expected it. He hasn't been looking well this past month and more.' . . . She must have been put out by the coal-blackened face I turned on her, for she went away without rounding off her knell. I gathered later that the postman, going with a couple of letters to the cottage, had found James MacIntosh cold and silent in his armchair. . . . I know he would have liked to be buried in Torsay. Those same relatives that he had had no communication with for a quarter of a century ordered his body to be taken down to Dundee. There he was burned in a crematorium and his dust thrown among alien winds.

Maggie Swintoun herself is a silence about the doors of the village. Her ghost is there, a shivering silence, between the sea and the hill. In no long time now that frail remembered keen will be lost in the greater silence of Torsay.

The shutters have been up for two years in the general store. William Copinsay was summoned by a stroke one winter evening from his money bags. They left him in the kirkyard, with pennies for eyes, to grope his way towards that unbearable treasure that is laid up (some say) for all who have performed decent acts of charity in their lives; the acts themselves, subtleties and shadows and gleams in time being (they say again) but fore-reflections of that hoarded perdurable reality. (I do not believe this myself. I believe in the 'twelve winds' of Housman that assemble the stuff of life for a year or two and then disperse it again.) Anyway, William Copinsay is dead.

Grossiter died at the auction mart in Hamnavoe, among the beasts and the whisky-smelling farmers, one Wednesday afternoon last spring.

Of course I know who has died in Torsay today. I knew hours before that young missionary opened his mouth. I had seen the lamp burning in a window at the end of the village at two o'clock in the morning.

It is not the old man who has died, either. His death could not have given me this unutterable grief that I felt then, and still feel. The heart of the island has stopped beating. I am the laird of a place that has no substance or meaning any more.

I will go down to the cottage sometime today. I will knock at the door. I will ask for permission to look into that still face.

The only child I have had has been taken from me; the only woman I could ever have loved; the only dust that I wished my own dust to be mingled with.

But in the fifty years that Thora Garth and I have lived in this island together we have never exchanged one word.

MORLEY CALLAGHAN

The Runaway

IN THE lumber-yard by the lake there was an old brick building two storeys high and all around the foundations were
heaped great piles of soft sawdust, softer than the thick moss in
the woods. There were many of these golden mounds of dust
covering that part of the yard right down to the blue lake. That
afternoon all the fellows followed Michael up the ladder to the
roof of the old building and they sat with their legs hanging
over the edge looking out at the whitecaps on the water.
Michael was younger than some of them but he was much bigger, his legs were long, his huge hands dangled awkwardly at
his sides and his thick black hair curled up all over his head.
'I'll stump you all to jump down,' he said suddenly, and without thinking about it, he shoved himself off the roof and fell on
the sawdust where he lay rolling around and laughing.

'You're all stumped,' he shouted, 'You're all yellow,' he said,
coaxing them to follow him. Still laughing, he watched them
looking down from the roof, white-faced and hesitant, and
then one by one they jumped and got up grinning with relief.

In the hot afternoon sunlight they all lay on the sawdust pile
telling jokes till at last one of the fellows said, 'Come on up on
the old roof again and jump down.' There wasn't much enthusiasm among them, but they all went up to the roof again and
began to jump off in a determined, desperate way till only
Michael was left and the others were all down below grinning
up at him and calling, 'Come on, Mike. What's the matter
with you?' Michael longed to jump down there and be with
them, but he remained on the edge of the roof, wetting his lips,
with a silly grin on his face, wondering why it had not seemed
such a long drop the first time. For a while they thought he was
only kidding them, then they saw him clenching his fists. He
was trying to count to ten and then jump, and when that
failed, he tried to take a long breath and close his eyes.

In a while the fellows began to jeer at him; they were tired of waiting and it was getting on to dinner-time. 'Come on, you're yellow, do you think we're going to sit here all night?' they began to shout, and when he did not move they began to get up and walk away, still jeering. 'Who did this in the first place? What's the matter with you guys?' he shouted.

But for a long time he remained on the edge of the roof, staring unhappily and steadily at the ground. He remained all alone for nearly an hour while the sun like a great orange ball getting bigger and bigger rolled slowly over the gray line beyond the lake. His clothes were wet from nervous sweating. At last he closed his eyes, slipped off the roof, fell heavily on the pile of sawdust and lay there a long time. There were no sounds in the yard, the workmen had gone home. As he lay there he wondered why he had been unable to move; and then he got up slowly and walked home feeling deeply ashamed and wanting to avoid everybody.

He was so late for dinner that his stepmother said to him sarcastically, 'You're big enough by this time surely to be able to get home in time for dinner. But if you won't come home, you'd better try staying in tonight.' She was a well-built woman with a fair, soft skin and a little touch of gray in her hair and an eternally patient smile on her face. She was speaking now with a restrained, passionless severity, but Michael, with his dark face gloomy and sullen, hardly heard her; he was still seeing the row of grinning faces down below on the sawdust pile and hearing them jeer at him.

As he ate his cold dinner he was rolling his brown eyes fiercely and sometimes shaking his big black head. His father, who was sitting in the armchair by the window, a huge man with his hair nearly all gone so that his smooth wide forehead rose in a beautiful shining dome, kept looking at him steadily. When Michael had finished eating and had gone out to the veranda, his father followed, sat down beside him, lit his pipe and said gently, 'What's bothering you, son?'

'Nothing, Dad. There's nothing bothering me,' Michael said, but he kept on staring out at the gray dust drifting off the road.

His father kept coaxing and whispering in a voice that was

amazingly soft for such a big man. As he talked, his long fingers
played with the heavy gold watch fob on his vest. He was talking about nothing in particular and yet by the tone of his voice
he was expressing a marvellous deep friendliness that somehow
seemed to become a part of the twilight and then of the darkness. And Michael began to like the sound of his father's voice,
and soon he blurted out, 'I guess by this time all the guys
around here are saying I'm yellow. I'd like to be a thousand
miles away.' He told how he could not force himself to jump off
the roof the second time. But his father lay back in the armchair laughing in that hearty, rolling, easy way that Michael
loved to hear; years ago when Michael had been younger and
he was walking along the paths in the evening, he used to try
and laugh like his father only his voice was not deep enough
and he would grin sheepishly and look up at the trees overhanging the paths as if someone hiding up there had heard
him. 'You'll be all right with the bunch, son,' his father was
saying. 'I'm betting you'll lick any boy in town that says you're
yellow.'

But there was the sound of the screen door opening, and
Michael's stepmother said in her mild, firm way, 'If I've
rebuked the boy, Henry, as I think he ought to be rebuked, I
don't know why you should be humouring him.'

'You surely don't object to me talking to Michael.'

'I simply want you to be reasonable, Henry.'

In his grave, unhurried way Mr. Lount got up and followed
his wife into the house and soon Michael could hear them
arguing; he could hear his father's firm, patient voice floating
clearly out to the street; then his stepmother's voice, mild at
first, rising, becoming hysterical till at last she cried out wildly,
'You're setting the boy against me. You don't want him to
think of me as his mother. The two of you are against me. I
know your nature.'

As he looked up and down the street fearfully, Michael began
to make prayers that no one would pass by who would think,
'Mr. and Mrs. Lount are quarrelling again.' Alert, he listened
for faint sounds on the cinder path, but he heard only the frogs
croaking under the bridge opposite Stevenson's place and the

far-away cry of a freight train passing behind the hills. 'Why did Dad have to get married? It used to be swell on the farm,' he thought, remembering how he and his father had gone fishing down at the glen. And then while he listened to the sound of her voice, he kept thinking that his stepmother was a fine woman, only she always made him uneasy because she wanted him to like her, and then when she found out that he couldn't think of her as his mother, she had grown resentful. 'I like her and I like my father. I don't know why they quarrel. They're really such fine people. Maybe it's because Dad shouldn't have sold the farm and moved here. There's nothing for him to do.' Unable to get interested in the town life, his father loafed all day down at the hotel or in Bailey's flour-and-feed store but he was such a fine-looking, dignified, reticent man that the loafers would not accept him as a crony. Inside the house now, Mrs. Lount was crying quietly and saying, 'Henry, we'll kill each other. We seem to bring out all the very worst qualities in each other. I do all I can and yet you both make me feel like an intruder.'

'It's just your imagination, Martha. Now stop worrying.'

'I'm an unhappy woman. But I try to be patient. I try so hard, don't I, Henry?'

'You're very patient, dear, but you shouldn't be so suspicious of everyone and everybody, don't you see?' Mr. Lount was saying in the soothing voice of a man trying to pacify an angry and hysterical wife.

Then Michael heard footsteps on the cinder path, and then he saw two long shadows flung across the road: two women were approaching, and one was a tall, slender girl. When Michael saw this girl, Helen Murray, he tried to duck behind the veranda post, for he had always wanted her for his girl. He had gone to school with her. At night-time he used to lie awake planning remarkable feats that would so impress her she would never want to be far away from him. Now the girl's mother was calling, 'Hello there, Michael,' in a very jolly voice.

'Hello, Mrs. Murray,' he said glumly, for he was sure his father's or his mother's voice would rise again.

'Come on and walk home with us, Michael,' Helen called.

Her voice sounded so soft and her face in the dusk light seemed so round, white and mysteriously far away that Michael began to ache with eagerness. Yet he said hurriedly, 'I can't. I can't tonight,' speaking almost rudely as if he believed they only wanted to tease him.

As they went on along the path and he watched them, he was really longing for that one bright moment when Helen would pass under the high corner light, though he was thinking with bitterness that he could already hear them talking, hear Mrs. Murray saying, 'He's a peculiar boy, but it's not to be wondered at since his father and mother don't get along at all,' and the words were floating up to the verandas of all the houses: inside one of the houses someone had stopped playing a piano, maybe to hear one of the fellows who had been in the lumberyard that afternoon laughing and telling that young Lount was scared to jump off the roof.

Still watching the corner, Michael suddenly felt that the twisting and pulling in the life in the house was twisting and choking him. 'I'll get out of here. I'll go away,' and he began to think of going to the city. He began to long for freedom in strange places where everything was new and fresh and mysterious. His heart began to beat heavily at the thought of this freedom. In the city he had an uncle Joe who sailed the lakeboats in the summer months and in the winter went all over the south from one race-track to another following the horses. 'I ought to go down to the city tonight and get a job,' he thought: but he did not move; he was still waiting for Helen Murray to pass under the light.

For most of the next day, too, Michael kept to himself. He was up-town once on a message, and he felt like running on the way home. With long sweeping strides he ran steadily on the paths past the shipyard, the church, the railway tracks, his face serious with determination.

But in the late afternoon when he was sitting on the veranda reading, Sammy Schwartz and Ike Hershfield came around to see him. 'Hello Mike, what's new with you?' they said, sitting on the steps very seriously.

'Hello, Sammy, hello, Ike. What's new with you?'

They began to talk to Michael about the coloured family that had moved into the old roughcast shack down by the tracks. 'The big coon kid thinks he's tough,' Sammy said. 'He offered to beat up any of us so we said he wouldn't have a snowball's chance with you.'

'What did the nigger say?'

'He said he'd pop you one right on the nose if you came over his way.'

'Come on, guys. Let's go over there,' Michael said. 'I'll tear his guts out for you.'

They went out to the street, fell in step very solemnly, and walked over to the field by the tracks without saying a word. When they were about fifty paces away from the shack, Sammy said, 'Wait here. I'll go get the coon,' and he ran on to the unpainted door of the whitewashed house calling, 'Oh, Art, oh, Art, come on out.' A big coloured boy with closely cropped hair came out and put his hand up, shading his eyes from the sun. Then he went back into the house and came out again with a big straw hat on his head. He was in his bare feet. The way he came walking across the field with Sammy was always easy to remember because he hung back a little, talking rapidly, shrugging his shoulders and rolling the whites of his eyes. When he came close to Michael he grinned nervously, flashing his teeth, and said, 'What's the matter with you white boys? I don't want to do no fighting.' He looked scared.

'Come on. Get ready. I'm going to do a nice job on you,' Michael said.

The coloured boy took off his big straw hat and with great care laid it on the ground while all the time he was looking mournfully across the field and at his house, hoping maybe that somebody would come out. Then they started to fight, and Michael knocked him down four times, but he, himself, got a black eye and a cut lip. The coloured boy had been so brave and he seemed so alone, licked and lying on the ground, that they sat down around him, praising him, making friends with him and gradually finding out that he was a good ball player, a left-handed pitcher who specialized in a curve ball, and they agreed they could use him, maybe, on the town team.

Lying there in the field, flat on his back, Michael liked it so much that he almost did not want to go away. Art, the coloured boy, was telling how he had always wanted to be a jockey but had got too big; he had a brother who could make the weight. So Michael began to boast about his Uncle Joe who went around to all the tracks in the winter making and losing money at places like Saratoga, Blue Bonnets and Tia Juana. It was a fine, friendly, eager discussion about far-away places.

It was nearly dinner-time when Michael got home; he went in the house sucking his cut lip and hoping his mother would not notice his black eye. But he heard no movement in the house. In the kitchen he saw his stepmother kneeling down in the middle of the floor with her hands clasped and her lips moving.

'What's the matter, Mother?' he asked.

'I'm praying,' she said.

'What for?'

'For your father. Get down and pray with me.'

'I don't want to pray, Mother.'

'You've got to,' she said.

'My lip's all cut. It's bleeding. I can't do it,' he said.

Late afternoon sunshine coming through the kitchen window shone on his stepmother's graying hair, on her soft smooth skin and on the gentle, patient expression that was on her face. At that moment Michael thought that she was desperately uneasy and terribly alone, and he felt sorry for her even while he was rushing out of the back door.

He saw his father walking toward the woodshed, walking slow and upright with his hands held straight at his side and with the same afternoon sunlight shining so brightly on the high dome of his forehead. He went right into the woodshed without looking back. Michael sat down on the steps and waited. He was afraid to follow. Maybe it was because of the way his father was walking with his head held up and his hands straight at his sides. Michael began to make a small desperate prayer that his father should suddenly appear at the woodshed door.

Time dragged slowly. A few doors away Mrs. McCutcheon

was feeding her hens who were clucking as she called them. 'I can't sit here till it gets dark,' Michael was thinking, but he was afraid to go into the woodshed and afraid to think of what he feared.

So he waited till he could not keep a picture of the interior of the shed out of his thoughts, a picture that included his father walking in with his hands as though strapped at his sides and his head stiff, like a man they were going to hang.

'What's he doing in there, what's he doing?' Michael said out loud, and he jumped up and rushed to the shed and flung the door wide.

His father was sitting on a pile of wood with his head on his hands and a kind of beaten look on his face. Still scared, Michael called out, 'Dad, Dad,' and then he felt such relief he sank down on the pile of wood beside his father and looked up at him.

'What's the matter with you, son?'

'Nothing. I guess I just wondered where you were.'

'What are you upset about?'

'I've been running. I feel all right.'

So they sat there quietly till it seemed time to go into the house. No one said anything. No one noticed Michael's black eye or his cut lip.

Even after they had eaten Michael could not get rid of the fear within him, a fear of something impending. In a way he felt that he ought to do something at once, but he seemed unable to move; it was like sitting on the edge of the roof yesterday, afraid to make the jump. So he went back of the house and sat on the stoop and for a long time looked at the shed till he grew even more uneasy. He heard the angry drilling of a woodpecker and the quiet rippling of the little water flowing under the street bridge and flowing on down over the rocks into the glen. Heavy clouds were sweeping up from the horizon.

He knew now that he wanted to run away, that he could not stay there any longer, only he couldn't make up his mind to go. Within him was that same breathless feeling he had had when he sat on the roof staring down, trying to move. Now he walked around to the front of the house and kept going along the path as far as Helen Murray's house. After going around to the back door, he stood for a long time staring at the lighted window, hoping to see Helen's shadow or her body moving against the light. He was breathing deeply and smelling the rich heavy odours from the flower garden. With his head thrust forward he whistled softly.

'Is that you, Michael?' Helen called from the door.

'Come on out, Helen.'

'What do you want?'

'Come on for a walk, will you?'

For a moment she hesitated at the door, then she came toward him, floating in her white organdie party dress over the grass toward him. She was saying, 'I'm dressed to go out. I can't go with you. I'm going down to the dance hall.'

'Who with?'

'Charlie Delaney.'

'Oh, all right,' he said. 'I just thought you might be doing nothing.' As he walked away he called back to her, 'So long, Helen.'

It was then, on the way back to the house, that he felt he had to go away at once. 'I've got to go. I'll die here. I'll write to Dad from the city.'

No one paid any attention to him when he returned to the house. His father and stepmother were sitting quietly in the living-room reading the paper. In his own room he took a little wooden box from the bottom drawer of his dresser and emptied it of twenty dollars and seventy cents, all that he had saved. He listened solemnly for sounds in the house, then he stuffed a clean shirt into his pocket, a comb, and a toothbrush.

Outside he hurried along with his great swinging strides, going past the corner house, on past the long fence and the bridge and the church, and the shipyard, and past the last of the town lights to the highway. He was walking stubbornly with his face looking solemn and dogged. Then he saw the moonlight shining on the hay stacked in the fields, and when he smelled the oats and the richer smell of sweet clover he suddenly felt alive and free. Headlights from cars kept sweeping by and already he was imagining he could see the haze of bright light hanging over the city. His heart began to thump with eagerness. He put out his hand for a lift, feeling full of hope. He looked across the fields at the dark humps, cows standing motionless in the night. Soon someone would stop and pick him up. They would take him among a million new faces, rumbling sounds, and strange smells. He got more excited. His Uncle Joe might get him a job on the boats for the rest of the summer; maybe, too, he might be able to move around with him in the winter. Over and over he kept thinking of places with beautiful names, places like Tia Juana, Woodbine, Saratoga and Blue Bonnets.

ELSPETH DAVIE

Concerto

A BOUT halfway through the concerto some of those sitting in the organ gallery, facing the rest of the audience and overlooking the orchestra, become aware of a disturbance in the body of the hall. The seats in this gallery face the conductor who for the last minutes has been leaning out over the rostrum whacking down a thicket of cellos with one hand and with the other cunningly lifting the uncertain horns higher and still higher up into a perilous place above the other instruments. Behind him the whole auditorium opens out, shell-shaped, its steep and shallow shelves, boxes, and ledges neatly packed with people. The sloping ground floor and overhanging gallery have few empty seats and the place has a smooth appearance—a sober mosaic of browns and greys flicked here and there with scarlet.

At last the horns make it. But there is a quavering on the long-drawn-out top note which brings a momentary grimace to the conductor's mouth as though he had bitten through something sour. The horn-players lower their instruments and stare in front of them with expressionless faces. At any other time some eyes in this audience might have studied the faces closely to discover which man had produced the wavering note —whether there was a corresponding wavering in the eyes of one of them or a slight wryness about the lips. But not tonight. Tonight all eyes have been directed to another spot.

The disturbance comes from the middle stalls. Down there a man has got to his feet and is leaning over the row in front. He appears to be conducting on his own account. He too entreats, he exhorts. He too encourages something to rise. Now a small group of people are up on their feet, and just as the horns extricate themselves, this man who is conducting operations down in the stalls manages to persuade the group to lift something up out of the darkness between the narrow seats. It is a tricky business, but at last a man is pulled clear and comes into view in a horizontal position, his long legs and his shoulders supported by several persons who have started to shuffle sideways with their burden along the row. Everyone now seems anxious to support this thin figure. Each leg is held by at least three people and the arms are carried on either side by two men and two women. Someone cups his head. Another handles the feet. Even those who are too far away to be actually supporting any part of his body feel it their duty to stretch out a finger simply to touch him, as a sacred object might be touched in a procession. He moves, propelled by these reverent touches, bouncing a little in the anxious arms. It is almost as though he were bouncing in time to a great pounding of drums. For since the horn-players lowered their instruments the music has grown violent in tempo and volume.

But suddenly without warning the violent music stops. There is a second of stunning silence. Then the solo violinist who has stood patiently for some time letting the waves of sound crash over his bowed head, begins a series of scales which climb very quietly, one after the other, up onto a note so high that the silence can also be heard like a slight hiss directly above his head. This silence and the icy note of the single violin come as a shock to those whose eyes are riveted on the scene going on down below. For it is no longer merely a mimed scene floating in the middle distance. The silence has shifted it nearer as though a protective membrane which sealed it off had been abruptly ripped. Now there are sounds coming up—ordinary sounds which in the circumstances sound horrible. There is a dull bumping and dragging of feet, a rustling and breathing, low voices arguing. Obviously the thing is beginning to get the upper hand. It is attracting more and more interest. Heads are turning and the people in the organ gallery can see the round, blank, listening faces on either side change suddenly to keen, watchful profiles. There are even heads peering from the plush-covered front rows of the dress circle—the silver heads and craning necks of elderly ladies, long-trained never to peer or crane.

But there is one head which, shockingly, has not turned at all

after the first quick glance behind. It is the man who is seated
at the end of the row immediately in front of that from which
the invalid has been lifted. Everyone else in his row is up ready
to help. The man must have skin of leather and iron nerves.
Eyes which might have scrutinized the horn-players now study
his face to see whether he is going to relent, to find out if there
is about him the slightest flicker of an uneasy conscience. But
no. What kind of man is this? Is he the sort of man who might
see his own mother carried past on a stretcher without shifting
his legs out of the way? He does not turn his head even when
the horizontal figure is moving directly behind his seat. At that
moment, however, the man and woman who are holding an
arm, suddenly let it go—the better to support the fainting
man's back while manoeuvring the awkward turn into the
middle aisle of the hall. The arm swings down heavily and
deals the man still seated in front a clout over the ear. It is an
admonitory blow, as though from his deepest unconscious or
perhaps from death itself, the invalid is aware there is still
someone around who is not giving him the same tender attention all the others have shown.

There is now a fervent longing for the music to gather its
forces again and crush the disturbance before it gets out of
hand. But there is no hint of this happening. The violinist is
still playing his icy scales, accompanied as though from remo-
test space by the strings and woodwinds. A man of fifty, he is
tall and exceedingly thin with a bony hatchet face and fairish-
grey hair brushed back from his brow. This brow gives the
impression of being unnaturally exposed, as though his skull,
and particularly the bone of his temples, had resisted a continual pressure of music which would have caused most other
skulls to cave in. His eyes are deepset and give him a sightless
look while he is playing. Strangely enough he is not unlike the
man who is being carried out up the aisle. One is narrow and
vertical with huge hands like an elongated Gothic cathedral
figure—grotesque or splendid, depending on how the light
might fall from a stained glass window. The other is stiff, horizontal and grey like the stretched-out figure on a tomb. The
prostrate man has his own look of dedication, though in his

case it is not to music, for by his collapse he has destroyed any
possibility of listening.

These two figures, the vertical and the horizontal, in their
terrifying absorption, their absolute disregard for everything
else, seem somehow related. Both have their supporters, though
now it seems that the horizontal has the greater following. The
devoted, inner circle round him have made sure of that. Great,
ever-widening rings of curiosity ripple out towards him, inter-
linking with the rings still concentrating on the violinist and
causing even there a shimmer of awareness. The conductor of
the devotees in the stalls is now walking backwards up the aisle
on his tiptoes, well in front of the others. With his right hand he
beckons reassuringly to the group coming up after him and
with his powerful left he attempts to quell any sign of interference from those sitting on either side of the aisle. But those
nearest the door, paralysed till now, suddenly spring to their
feet and fight for first place to heave their weight against it.
The doors crash outward and the heaped figures pitch through.

This crash has coincided to a split second with the quietest
bars of the concerto—that point where not only the soloist but
all other players have lowered their instruments—all, that is to
say, except the flute. This flute has started up as though playing
solely for the benefit of the group just outside the door, visible
in the brilliant light of the vestibule. As though involved in a
ritual dance they crouch, rise, bend, and kneel beneath the
hands of their leader who is now signalling to invisible figures
further out. Someone carrying a jug and tumbler appears and
kneels, and a chinking of glass comes from the centre of the
group. It is a light sound but clear as a bell, and it combines
with the flute in a duet which can be heard to the furthest
corners of the hall.

At this point several people turn their eyes, in desperation,
and stare at the unmoving man sitting now quite isolated at the
end of his row. No one could say why it is imperative to turn to
him. Isn't he a brute, after all—a stubborn, fat man with a
crimson face, conspicuous only in being a figure of monumental
unhelpfulness? Yet something about the man suggests that, like
some squat, purple-cheeked Atlas, he is supporting the whole

weight of the hall on his shoulders. The short, bulging neck holds up the overhanging gallery. The legs are planted like pillars to the floor, and over his paunch the fingers come together in a massive lock. His bottom is sunk into the plush of his seat like a bulbous root into the deep earth. Nothing can budge him now. He is dedicated to absolute immobility, and the whole house knows it.

This man has never taken his eyes off the violinist. He stares ahead, unblinking—his blue, slightly protuberant eyes fixed. It is as though on him rather than on the conductor has now fallen the responsibility of holding audience and orchestra together—of pushing back the white heads in the dress circle, checking the obstreperous group outside the door, and by a superhuman effort of will turning the curious eye of the audience back into a listening ear. The soloist lifts his violin and for the first time throws a piercing glance down into the body of the hall. He exchanges one look with the immobile man sitting there. There is no recognizable emotion in this look, nothing that would ordinarily be called human warmth. Yet the man below glows and shines for an instant as though caught in a flare of brilliant light. The violinist raises his bow and begins to play.

In the meantime one of the group outside in the vestibule has at last remembered about the open doors. He pulls them to violently and the drama outside is shut away, at any rate from the ears—for figures can still be seen moving about behind the obscure glass. All the same there is a feeling of uneasiness—a feeling that the fellow lying behind that door will not allow himself to be shut away and forgotten after swaying the entire audience. This unease is justified. Scarcely have those around the door drawn their first breath of relief before it swings open again and the leader of the group strides in. His air is even more commanding than before. Now he looks like an ambassador from an important state. He walks along the empty row looking for something, before starting to tip up the seats and feel about on the floor. By this time the music has again gathered volume and nobody can hear the sound of the seats, though he is as skilful and rhythmical in the way he raps them back as the man behind the kettledrums. And now he is finished with that row and goes into the one in front where the stout man is sitting. He works his way along the seats, tipping, patting, and groping till he reaches him. Now he is actually feeling around the other's feet. But the man—this rapt buddha of non-helpfulness—shifts neither his legs nor his eyes. He allows the other to squeeze past him, to glare at him, and even to push his foot aside.

At first there is mounting curiosity as to what the searcher will come up with. Yet the seated man has managed to concentrate most of this curiosity upon himself and then, by not moving a hair or allowing his attention to swerve for an instant, has redirected it up towards the orchestra. This is something which almost amounts to an athletic feat. The sheer effort of lifting the crowd on his eyeballs alone is appalling.

The swing doors again open and a woman appears and moves diffidently, apologetically, down the gangway, all the time looking towards the searcher and waiting for a sign. But the man is now working along a row further back and keeps shaking his head. Suddenly he disappears. He has pounced on something down there. It is a long handbag in imitation plum-coloured leather with a zip pocket at the back—useful but not elegant. An advertisement would describe it as a bag which could go anywhere. And it has been kicked around a lot. Already it has travelled back a couple of rows and sideways ten feet or so. The man and woman join up enthusiastically and are soon on their way out again, the woman peering meantime into the bag to assure herself that, in spite of the hideous confusion of the last ten minutes, everything is intact inside, right down to the fragile mirror in the lid of her compact.

Now some of those in the audience had imagined it might be a pair of spectacles the man was hunting for—spectacles belonging to the fainting man who, added to the horrors of coming to in a strange place, would find himself unable to focus on the strange faces looming over him. A few have never been able to shake off a suspicion that all this time these spectacles have been lying, ground to powder, under the stubborn heels of the man sitting at the end of the row. At sight of the handbag, however, some tie linking them to the group outside the door snaps for ever. As the man and woman finally push their way out there is a glimpse of a deserted vestibule. The group, as though sensing a defeat, have disappeared.

The music is sweeping to its climax. One by one each section of the orchestra is gathered up and whirled higher and higher in a struggle to reach the four, slow, separate chords which end the concerto. On this level plateau they at last emerge into safety, and the end is in sight. The fourth and final chord crashes down, submerging all doubts, and a great burst of clapping and stamping follows it. For a while the stout man refuses to join in the applause. One might even imagine he was receiving some of it for himself, along with the soloist, the conductor, and the rest of the orchestra. But now for the first time he lowers the heavy lids of his eyes towards the ground and allows himself a discreet smile. Then he lifts his hands and begins to clap. His applauding heels shuffle the floor.

SUSAN HILL

Cockles and Mussels

Both the lounge and dining-room of the Delacourt Guest House commanded a view of the sea.

'There is nothing at all gloomy *here*, nobody has to suffer some dark, poky bedroom with outlook on to a wall,' said Mrs. Muriel Hennessy, the proprietress. Though she did not count the cook, Mrs. Rourke.

There had been, until five years ago, a Mr. Hennessy, dealer in fine wines and spirits. In the early days of their marriage, they had gone around the Châteaux of France together every spring, tasting, buying. But Mr. Hennessy had begun to drink, two, and later three, bottles of sherry a day, the relationship had soured, his wife had put money aside, secretly, in a building society account.

After his death, she had waited six, decent months before leaving their bungalow in the home counties and travelling to the sea, to make her fresh start with the Delacourt Guest House.

'It has always been a little, private longing of mine,' she had told her friends, giving a small sherry party to say goodbye, 'to be of some service to others, give a few, retired people a very comfortable and happy home.' Though, in fairness she was forced to admit to prospective clients that her charges were somewhat higher for the larger, front bedrooms.

A year ago, Miss Avis Parson had come into money from a deceased aunt, and then she had been able to take one of these, to move from a pink room overlooking the garden, into a blue room, overlooking the sea.

Mrs. Hennessy was fond of saying laughingly that Miss Parson had 'served her time', she deserved to come into her inheritance. For she did not like to think of any of her residents pinching and scraping, anxious about where the next month's rent was coming from.

It was not the quietness, not the gentle slope of the Guest House garden, down towards the promenade, not the different moods of the sea, for which Miss Parson was grateful. They pleased her well enough, but nothing happened, it was all a little dull.

'I am sixty-nine,' she said, brushing her white hair, which was as long as it had ever been when she was a young girl, 'I am not like old Mr. Brotherton, who is fit only to doze and dream and remember little incidents of his naval past. I have my eyes open to modern life and what goes on about me.' For, from the side window of the blue bedroom, she could see towards the Lower Bay, and it was to the Lower Bay that the day trippers came. Mrs. Muriel Hennessy, and, indeed, all the property owners and shopkeepers and residents of the upper town, held day trippers in the lowest possible esteem. 'They are not *real* visitors,' she would say, bringing the tea trolley with their late, hot drinks around the lounge, 'they come in chara-bancs and throw away their litter, they do nothing for the image of the town.'

And, along the foreshore and up and down the narrow streets of the Lower Bay were all the most common attractions, the souvenir gift shops full of rose-painted pottery and highly varnished shells, the ice cream and fish and chip parlours with tall stools set against eau de nil marble counters, the rifle ranges and the five shilling photographers and the sellers of novelty balloons.

At the far end of the foreshore was the Fun Fair, and, opposite the Fun Fair, beside the lifeboat house, the shellfish booths, where cockles and mussels and winkles and shrimps were shovelled into little paper cones and sprinkled with malt vinegar.

'Everything is so vulgar on the Lower Bay,' said Mrs. Hennessy, 'everything is so cheap and nasty, it smells so, I wonder anyone at all can bear it.'

But, in her heart Miss Avis Parson felt that life as it should be lived was lived along the foreshore of the Lower Bay. At night, she drew the curtains of her side window and sat, watching the flickering lights of the amusement arcade and the Fun

Fair, saw the big wheel turn round in an arc of gold and mauve and the water chute cascade electric blue. If she opened her window, and the breeze was in the right direction, she could hear the shrieks and cries of girls as their skirts went above their heads on the swing-boats, the crack and pop of bullets on the rifle range. The hours between ten and midnight, when everything was abruptly doused and darkened, filled Miss Parson with excitement and little, sudden spurts of longing. I have lived too sheltered a life, she thought, I have never known enough about the truth of things, about what really goes on. For she had been companion to her father in his Rectory—Miss Parson the Parson's daughter, said the village children, though she did not mind—and later, to her unmarried brother in Wales, the years in which she had meant to do this and that had slipped too quickly by.

That summer, when she moved into her more expensive, blue front room at the Delacourt Guest House, the weather was almost always good, the days long and hot and the beaches bright and noisy with day trippers.

Mrs. Hennessy turned away importunate families, evening after evening, at the door. 'I am not a hotel for passing visitors, I am entirely devoted to the care of the elderly, of my permanent residents,' she told them, smoothing down the skirts of her pastel linen dresses, watching them go off in their laden cars, hot and tired and disappointed down the drive.

In the afternoons, tea was served on the terrace and the deckchairs were occupied by old Mr. Brotherton and Mrs. de Vere and the Misses Phoebe and Ethel Haynes, sleeping under striped umbrellas to shade them from the glare of the sun.

Miss Parson took little solitary walks up Cliff Terrace, behind the Guest House, and the desire to venture along into the streets and shops and arcades of the Lower Bay became an obsession with her. Though she would have said nothing about it, and she was not, in any case, anxious to chat a great deal with any of her fellow guests, she saw herself as both younger than they were and somehow less permanent, for was she not entirely free, might she not suddenly choose to move on? She had money, she had her health, one day she might buy a flat in some quiet place abroad, might go on a cruise or pay an extended visit to her old school friend in Edinburgh. She reviewed her situation daily. And, meanwhile, she longed to mingle with the crowds who came in charabancs and private cars, to unmask the noisy secrets of the ghost train and eat shrimps and winkles with her fingers, sitting beside the sea.

It was only her sudden discovery of the drinking habits of Mrs. Rourke which, for a short while, diverted her attention.

When the lights of the Fun Fair were switched out, Miss Parson left her chair by the window, after drawing the curtains again, and prepared herself for bed. As long as there had been something to watch and listen to, the attraction of roundabout music and the lights flickering in the sky, she was never tired, her mind was filled with pictures of the scene, couples arm-in-arm together and the mothers of grown-up families, ridiculous in cardboard hats, middle-aged romances brought to a point of decision among the dodgems. But later, in the abrupt darkness, she remembered that she was sixty-nine years old and knew nothing, was ready to climb a little stiffly into her divan bed. But before doing so, she went quietly along the corridor to the bathroom, and it was just outside the bathroom that Miss Parson first found the cook, Mrs. Rourke, her eyes curiously glazed, unable to focus on Miss Parson's face, and her hand clutching at the bare wall. Mrs. Rourke had been cook for seven months, at the Delacourt Guest House.

The following day, old Mr. Brotherton complained again, loudly, about the quality of the mashed potato. 'There are lumps,' he said querulously, paddling them about in the serving dish with a spoon, 'there are more lumps at every meal, every day there are more.'

Rita, the day-time waitress, shot him an evil look, but in the kitchen she exaggerated the nature and number of the complaints to Mrs. Hennessy.

'You needn't think the staff have never noticed,' she added, balancing four vegetable dishes along her outstretched arm, 'it isn't as if any of *us* are exactly satisfied.'

Mrs. Hennessy lifted a fork out of the remaining potatoes,

and peered into them. She could not see any lump, and had she not had trouble and worry enough over cooks, in years past? Was this not always the season for groundless complaints? The heat was proving too much for them. She decided to say nothing.

Some nights later, Miss Parson heard the uncertain footsteps of the cook fumbling along her corridor, the slight brushing of her guiding hand, along the wall. When she opened the door, a few moments later, the faint, sour smell of Mrs. Rourke's whisky hung about on the air.

In her narrow back bedroom, at the far end of the landing, Mrs. Ruby Rourke lay with her coat still on, feet propped up on her pillow, and looked down at her own ankles. A fine pair of legs, for a woman your age, she thought, the finest pair of legs for miles. And her eyes filled with sudden tears of pride, that years of standing beside sinks and ovens had not thickened the muscles or spread the veins. Only her feet were bad now, the bunions sticking out like red noses on their side, under the fine stockings.

A year ago, she had been cooking for thirty-five secretarials in a London hostel, and when they had passed her by on the stairs, going out to dinners and parties with a stream of young men, she had looked at their legs and not had any cause to envy them, had seen over-fleshed knees and thick calves, lack of any shapeliness or finesse. And they've other lessons to learn, she had thought, looking at herself in the wardrobe mirror, it takes a woman in her fifties to know how to enjoy herself. *I* wouldn't be in their shoes, wouldn't be eighteen or twenty again, thank you very much.

But in the nights she had woken and heard them clattering up the stairs, laughing inconsiderately, and had not been able to get to sleep again for hours, had been obliged to get up and search about in her wardrobe for a bottle of gin. In the mornings, the skin around her eyes looked puffed and swollen.

When she had been asked to leave the hostel, there had not been another job in London, in the end she had had to travel up here and apply to the Delacourt Guest House.

'Oh, I like old people, I like to see they get nourishing meals,' she had told Mrs. Hennessy, crossing her legs to reveal their elegant shape, under the short black skirt. 'I couldn't get along with those young girls, oh, no, couldn't take to their noisy, selfish little ways. It was something like living in a zoo, Mrs. Hennessy, and half the food picked and poked at in a *very* dissatisfied way.'

'I daresay they were dieting, Mrs. Rourke, that is what young girls all do, nowadays.' Mrs. Hennessy was looking at the careful make-up and wondering what age the woman might really be, and if there were not something a little unsuitable about vanity, in an institutional cook.

'I am fifty,' said Mrs. Rourke, who was fifty-seven, 'and I am thankful that I have never had to diet, my figure is all that it should be.'

Mrs. Hennessy had inclined her head and begun to wonder about the lack of any recent references. But in the end the problem was solved for her, by the absence of any other applicant.

On the last Friday in July the temperature reached 84 degrees and the season for day trippers was at its height.

Sitting in the garden of the Delacourt Guest House, Miss Parson felt restless, felt the summer again passing her by, and was irritated with those around her, by the talk of the Misses Haynes, who were spiritualists, and the snores of old Mr. Brotherton. I have no place here, she thought, it is a house for old and dying people and I shall begin to grow like them, the trivialities of everyday life here will assume a greater and greater importance, the times of meals will be all I have to look forward to. And it will be my own fault.

For she had been both startled and aroused by her discovery that Mrs. Rourke came home the worse for drink. *She* has some kind of experience and pleasure, Miss Parson thought, some merrymaking and delight in life, she is a woman unafraid of the world, she has the courage of her convictions and laughs in the face of propriety. For the drunkenness of the cook seemed to her entirely romantic, it had no weak or pathetic aspect.

The hard, straight sunlight lay across the Victorian house, and the terrace and garden, it was too hot, now, for any of the residents except Miss Parson herself, and old Mr. Brotherton, snoring under a panama hat. From the beaches came the high, sharp cries of children, the sea glittered in ridges for miles out.

I have no courage, I am too concerned about the opinions of others, too afraid of their displeasure. I am anxious to walk down on to the Lower Bay and see the sights, observe the people, anxious to eat cockles and mussels and go along into the Fun Fair, and is that not a very slight, harmless ambition? Yet I have sat here for week after week and only ventured out into the respectable, upper part of the town, only walked the streets and bought from the shops approved of by women like Mrs. Hennessy. It is a very poor thing, I do not deserve to have any excitement out of life, any new experiences, I am made of flimsier stuff than a cook!

In her agitation, Miss Parson got up quickly from the striped deckchair and began to walk round and round the garden, rubbing her fingers about in the palms of her hands, wanting to make a decision.

On the hot, Saturday evening, Miss Parson ate very little supper, and did not go into the lounge afterwards, to take coffee.

'I have some business in the town—a friend to see,' she said hastily, in reply to the inquisitive expression of Mrs. Hennessy, for none of the guests ever went far, in the evenings. But then, she was annoyed with herself, for she paid good money to live here, she was her own mistress, why was it at all necessary to explain her doings in that flustered way?

'On Saturday night, Miss Parson? Oh, are you quite sure that you are wise? The town is so full of rowdy strangers, I am a little concerned as to whether you will be quite safe.'

Miss Parson would have said, and that is why I am all the more eager to go, but little Mrs. Pardue, with the pink bald patch showing through her grey hair, said, 'Rowdy people do not come up to *this* end of the town, I am thankful to say,' and in the subsequent murmur of relief and agreement, Miss Parson slipped out.

She felt not merely excited but guilty. The Lower Bay was,

in a sense, quite forbidden territory, in the tacit agreement of the residents of the Delacourt, and she could only guess at what they might say of her visit, were they to find out. One or two of them did not entirely like her. 'There is just *something* about Miss Parson,' Miss Phoebe Haynes had said, 'she is not really altogether one of us.'

On leaving Cliff Terrace, Miss Parson made a detour, up to the top of the hill and around the avenue, for someone might be watching her, unseen, from a bedroom window, and then a report would be made at once to the lounge, and to Mrs. Hennessy. The ghost of Miss Parson's father warned her, as she altered course and made for the Harbour road, that she was acting a lie. The road dipped and the Guest House was out of sight. And I do not care, Miss Parson said, gripping her pouched black handbag, I have done nothing with my freedom, nothing at all, it is quite time I grasped at my opportunities and enjoyed some small, innocent adventure.

She wore well-fitting leather shoes, and a lightweight coat, in case the evening should turn chilly, for she did not intend to return early to the Delacourt Guest House.

From her back bedroom window, Mrs. Rourke saw Miss Parson set out up Cliff Terrace, and then, glancing up again from powdering carefully around her eyes, saw her turn, and go off towards the Lower Bay.

'Well!' she said to her own image in the mirror, and was taken once again by the elegance of her own figure, the shapeliness of leg and ankle. She had always insisted, at every place of employment, upon Saturday as one of her regular nights off, everything happened on a Saturday, you never knew your luck.

For a long time Miss Parson simply walked slowly along the pavements, looking at people's faces. These are the old and the modern young, mingling together, she thought, these are the day trippers, this is life. Middle-aged men in shirts, open over sun-reddened chests, wore pressed-paper hats in imitation of cowboys or undertakers or policemen, and Miss Parson stared into their eyes, anxious to learn the secrets of enjoyment. It was very crowded, very warm in among the booths and cafés, the

night air flashed with multi-coloured lights, and along the pier
they bobbed, orange and green and red, reflected in the dark
sea.

I am very happy, I am watching the world go by, discover-
ing things I never knew, Miss Parson told herself, sitting down
on a foreshore bench while she emptied sand out of her shoes,
there is nothing to be ashamed of or snobbish about it, that I
can see. Loudspeakers sent the metallic beat of popular music
out across the street.

Somewhere, far down beyond the green railings and the
piled-up deckchairs, the long, pale shelf of sand, the edge of the
sea, creaming and stirring a little in the darkness. I would like
to walk there, too, thought Miss Parson, it is many years since
I have been on a beach at night. Though as children they had
spent their holidays at Bexhill, and she had walked the dog
Beaver out, after dark, smelling the salt and the green smell of
seaweed and imagining her own future, filled with rich, name-
less excitements.

A car began to hoot on the roadway, nosing into the back of
jaywalkers. Miss Parson got up and went across to the Seagull
Milk Bar, to perch uncertainly on a high stool with tubular
steel legs and drink a cup of expensive tea. All around her,
everyone moved, laughed and chatted across the tables, over
plates of waffles and haddock, peas and chips and every movement reflected brightly in the mirrors above the counter, so
that Miss Parson, watching, felt uncertain of which was real
and which the image. Under a table, a small child in green
bathing trunks dribbled lemonade gently on to its bare legs
from the end of a straw.

'There you go, my duck,' a man said, helping her down from
the precarious stool, and she noticed the reddish hairs, matted
all the way up his arms.

But it was going through the glittering golden archway of
the Fun Fair, and standing just a little way inside, which
brought home to her where she had come, alone on a Saturday
evening, how many unwritten rules of proper conduct she had
disobeyed. For a moment, she held her breath and was doubt-
ful, would have gone quickly away, the noise and the clamour

of people and machines and lights around her was more than she felt able to take. The smell of the place came out towards her. But then, she went ahead, fumbling in her purse for money, and joined the queue leading to the switchback railway.

On the fourth, reckless plunge over the crest of the metal track and down, down, slicing into the darkness, Miss Parson opened her eyes and saw that the woman next to her was clutching on to her sleeve, eyes huge in her melon-shaped face.

'Oh!' she said, 'Oh!' and the hand gripped tighter, though no sound coming out of the woman's mouth could be heard above the noise, there was only the purse of her lips, purple-looking under the artificial lights. She is laughing, Miss Parson realized suddenly, there is nothing wrong with her whatsoever, she is simply laughing, and she felt friendly, warmed by the careless grasping of the stranger's hand, the gesture of conviviality on the switchback.

As they climbed and plunged again, Miss Parson thought of old Mr. Brotherton, and of Mrs. Hennessy, stout and managerial in a linen dress, and began to laugh, to feel superior to all of them, as one who has outwitted everyone else in the battle of life, discovered some amazing secret.

Returning to the ground again, she was obliged to lean for some moments against the ticket booth, unable quite to recover her breath. Overhead, the big wheel spun in a flashing circle, as if gathering speed to take off like a top into the sky.

The cockles were hard to eat, she was uncertain which way to prise them out of their hard, little shells, and in her mouth they tasted as they smelled, strong as brine and heavily vinegared. But there was something rich and coarse and satisfying about eating such things, and about queueing up to buy more, to hover in her choice between the brown-pink whiskered shrimps and mussels, rubber-smooth and yet curiously gritty in the mouth.

The foreshore was now more crowded than ever, the voices more raucous, shrieking and cat-calling and squabbling, now and then. Miss Parson got up from her bench when the man next to her began to slip sideways heavily and to snore like old Mr. Brotherton, huge hands upturned and loose on his trousers. But, after all, it is only another human being, she told herself, only another aspect of life, and she felt herself expanding and blossoming with new insights and knowledge, open to a stream of experience.

A trickle of juice was left in the paper cone after she had eaten the last mussel, so that, in screwing it up, she stained her coat sleeve. The smell was blotted at once into the cloth, and came up sharply into her nostrils. It would stay there, now, certain proof, in all the months to come, of her evening in the Lower Bay, her new-found courage.

A gang of men and girls came stepping out in a row, arms linked, breasting the whole width of the road, and singing, and for a second Miss Parson was caught up among them, she could see the white teeth and peacock-painted eyes of the girls, smell the men's sweat, and then they parted and went on like the tide, leaving her behind.

In the orange-painted Bingo Booth, opening out on to the street, a game finished and, looking up from her unsuccessful card, the cook, Mrs. Rourke, saw Miss Avis Parson. Earlier, she had found one or two people to talk to, someone had bought her a drink, but it had come to nothing, the bar had emptied and filled up again and she was left to apply fresh lipstick and do something herself about the empty glass.

'Well, now!' she said, therefore, touching Miss Parson lightly on the arm, for familiar company was suddenly better than none, better than the old routine of trying to strike up a new acquaintance. 'Well, here's a thing!'

Though a thought crossed her mind, to wonder if the old girl might not be a bit unwell, a bit wandering all of a sudden, standing down here and smelling of shellfish and vinegar on a July Saturday night. She had always had a peculiar fear of madness.

'It has all been a splendid treat, Mrs. Rourke, this is a whole new world to me. I have been telling myself for so long, promising myself, you know, that I would be as bold as could be and venture down among the holidaymakers, and now here I am! But I am really just a little bit tired, I do confess to you, my feet are feeling rather swollen.'

It did not surprise her, for nothing was surprising now, when Mrs. Rourke, too, took hold of her arm.

'It's the sand,' she said, confidentially, nodding into Miss Parson's face, 'the sand gets into them, plays them up. You can't tell me.'

'Yes? Well then, that is very likely the case and perhaps I have had enough for one day, perhaps I should be getting home. . . .'

Miss Parson thought that the cook might be older than she looked, though she admired her care for her own appearance, the brightness of rouge and lipstick and the height of her heels. They were walking uphill now, between the last of the gift shops, and away from the sea, and Miss Parson saw that everyone, here, was arm-in-arm with everyone else, it must be the way of things, the air was close with bonhomie.

'My treat, dear,' said Mrs. Rourke, making her way firmly between backs and elbows to the lounge bar. 'What's it to be?'

But, sitting at the little, low table and surreptitiously easing a shoe from off one of her feet, Miss Parson felt depressed, thought perhaps it is all a little aimless, all too trivial to count as life, perhaps I have been wrong to come riding on switchbacks and eating strange food and drinking sweet sherry in the Lower Bay.

Mrs. Rourke was telling her some story, her eyes protuberant in a flushed face, and Miss Parson thought of the nights when she had found her leaning unsteadily against the Guest House wall, wondered in a moment of panic where it would all end.

Mrs. Rourke had forgotten exactly who she was with, was launched, now, into the full tale of her bad treatment at the hands of her previous employers, the London secretarial school.

'Take no nonsense, good cooks are in short supply, my hubbie would have said.' She wiped lipstick carefully off her glass with the corner of a handkerchief. 'He was a chauffeur,' she told the dazed Miss Parson. 'There wasn't anything you could tell Rourke about the tricks of employers.'

'I think I really should like to be getting back now,' said Miss Avis Parson. But when she stood, the lounge tipped and spun round, there was a curious, high-pitched echo inside her head.

In the Delacourt Guest House, Mrs. Hennessy switched off the parchment-shaded lamps in the lounge, and closed the top windows, wondering if she had been wise to let Miss Parson have a key.

The whole street seemed to be singing, now, everyone came pouring out on to the pavements as the stalls and cafés began to close, and the smell of beer and human bodies mingled with the faint ozone of the sea.

'Steady she goes,' said Mrs. Rourke, stepping off the kerb and on to it again sharply. 'Take it gently.'

'Oh, the nice fresh air, the nice, *nice*, fresh air.'

Can't hold a drink, thought Mrs. Rourke with disgust, doesn't know the first thing about it. Aloud she said, 'We're two merry lonely old ladies,' as they came up the Harbour road, leaving the trippers behind them, facing the stars, 'two lonely old souls.'

There is something wrong, thought Miss Parson, something very wrong indeed, I do not wish to be here, led along the streets by a drunken cook, and called an old woman and lonely, there is nothing at all like that about me, and she can know nothing. I would prefer to forget this incident. But, climbing Cliff Terrace, her legs felt weak under her and she was obliged to hold on to Mrs. Rourke's arm again for a little support.

'It's a bit of a hole, Miss Parson, a bit of a one-eyed hole. I'm used to a good deal better than this, I deserve it, you know, this is not the sort of carry-on I'm accustomed to.'

I do not trust you, Miss Parson thought, I have learned a very great deal tonight, about the ways of the world, and I do not feel able to trust you, you will not get away with anything with me. But she could not altogether follow what the other woman was saying.

'Come along, old girl.'

But Miss Parson had stopped and bent over to examine her shoes. Behind them, the lights of the Fun Fair were gutted, the whole of the bay was given over once more to the incoming sea.

At four, Miss Parson woke in severe abdominal pain, so that, after staggering to the bathroom and back again, she collapsed at the side of her bed and was forced to crawl up, hand-over-hand, and ring the service bell.

Towards morning, the doctor was called, for the pain and sickness had worsened, she became delirious and then semi-conscious.

At breakfast in the dining-room there was an air of alarm and expectancy, questions were asked and speculations aroused, and old Mr. Brotherton refused to eat more than a triangle of toast. 'It is the cook,' he muttered, leaning forward and speaking up so that he should be heard quite clearly at all the tables, 'the food is bad, it is not surprising that Miss Parson has been taken ill. Something should be said to the cook, I have said so before, I hope you will all bear me out.'

So that, throughout the next few days, when Miss Parson's condition worsened and, in the end she was taken to the hospital, the cry grew louder of 'the cook, the cook' as a crowd might mutter, 'Guilty! Guilty! Off with her head!' And Mrs. Hennessy, who had discovered the gin and whisky bottles in Mrs. Rourke's wardrobe, felt that more than goodwill was now at stake, something public would have to be done.

'It is acute food poisoning,' she told Mrs. Rourke, sitting at the desk in her tidy office, 'the doctor is extremely worried, Miss Parson is quite dangerously sick.'

Nor was she pleased when the lies came out so glibly, the long, garbled tale about Miss Parson's eating cockles and mussels and drinking alcohol in the Lower Bay. For surely they *were* lies, she thought, when the cook had been formally dismissed, surely the aloof, prim little Miss Parson would never have been so foolish? Though Mrs. Hennessy recalled that there had so often been a strange look on her face, a furtive, secretive expression, and perhaps she had been growing a little senile, perhaps there was a hardening of the arteries and she had begun to act in that way common among the old, as though a new, alien personality had been suddenly assumed.

Well then, it will not do for her to come back *here*, for this is only a Guest House, not a nursing or a geriatric home, I am neither trained nor equipped nor willing to cater for the senile and unreliable, the responsibility would be altogether too great. She thought that there were no relatives of Miss Parson, but somewhere, an old school friend—in Edinburgh? Or perhaps, simply, the doctor could fill out a form and the whole thing be done locally, some suitable home would be quickly found.

In the event, that was not necessary, Miss Avis Parson died in her bed at the General Hospital of a heart attack, following the ravages of food poisoning. The doctor, bringing the news to Mrs. Hennessy, warned against any future use of shellfish, cockles or mussels, shrimps or crab, in the cooking at the Delacourt Guest House.

'Old people,' he said, almost apologetically, standing on the doorstep beside his car, 'nothing indigestible, nothing, really, in the seafood line, Mrs. Hennessy, take my advice upon it.'

It was only out of respect for the memory of the recently deceased Miss Parson that she did not speak of her own, long-existing ban on all crustacea from the menus of the Delacourt.

On the train, Mrs. Rourke lifted her coat up on to the rack, tidied up her face in the tiny, rectangular mirror, and then walked along to the buffet car for a drink. She had found, only the day after her dismissal from the Guest House, an appointment as cook to a boys' approved school in rural Norfolk. They had not asked for an interview or anything more than verbal references simply because they were, they said, desperate, they would take her on a month's probation.

Like one of the bloody inmates, Mrs. Rourke thought bitterly, imagining the remoteness of the countryside, the absence of any Gaiety and Life, like a bloody prisoner myself. But then she rebuked herself, for she did not like to swear, it was a sign of weakness, a loosening of her grip. Instead, she looked down into her glass for a moment, and then drank, quickly, to the memory of the seaside, and of Miss Avis Parson.

DAN JACOBSON

The Zulu and the Zeide

O L D man Grossman was worse than a nuisance. He was a
source of constant anxiety and irritation; he was a menace
to himself and to the passing motorists into whose path he would
step, to the children in the streets whose games he would break
up, sending them flying, to the householders who at night
would approach him with clubs in their hands, fearing him a
burglar; he was a butt and a jest to the African servants who
would tease him on street corners.

It was impossible to keep him in the house. He would take
any opportunity to slip out—a door left open meant that he
was on the streets, a window unlatched was a challenge to his
agility, a walk in the park was as much a game of hide-and-seek
as a walk. The old man's health was good, physically; he was
quite spry, and he could walk far, and he could jump and
duck if he had to. All his physical activity was put to only one
purpose: to running away. It was a passion for freedom that
the old man might have been said to have, could anyone have
seen what joy there could have been for him in wandering aim-
lessly about the streets, in sitting footsore on pavements, in
entering other people's homes, in stumbling behind advertisement hoardings that fenced undeveloped building plots, in toil-
ing up the stairs of fifteen-storey blocks of flats in which he had
no business, in being brought home by large young policemen
who winked at Harry Grossman, the old man's son, as they
gently hauled his father out of their flying-squad cars.

'He's always been like this,' Harry would say, when people
asked him about his father. And when they smiled and said:
'Always?' Harry would say, 'Always. I know what I'm talking
about. He's my father, and I know what he's like. He gave my
mother enough grey hairs before her time. All he knew was to
run away.'

Harry's reward would come when the visitors would say:

'Well, at least you're being as dutiful to him as anyone can be.'

It was a reward that Harry always refused. 'Dutiful? What can you do? There's nothing else you can do.' Harry Grossman knew that there was nothing else he could do. Dutifulness had been his habit of life; it had had to be, having the sort of father he had, and the strain of duty had made him abrupt and be-grudging. He even carried his thick, powerful shoulders curved inwards, to keep what he had to himself. He was a thick-set, bunch-faced man, with large bones, and short, jabbing ges-tures; he was in the prime of life, and he would point at the father from whom he had inherited his strength, and on whom the largeness of bone showed now only as so much extra lean-ness that the clothing had to cover, and say: 'You see him? Do you know what he once did? My poor mother saved enough money to send him from the old country to South Africa: she bought clothes for him, and a ticket, and she sent him to her brother, who was already here. He was going to make enough money to bring me out, and my mother and my brother, all of us. But on the boat from Bremen to London he met some other Jews who were going to South America, and they said to him: 'Why are you going to South Africa? It's a wild country, the blacks there will eat you. Come to South America and you'll make a fortune.' So in London he exchanges his ticket. And we don't hear from him for six months. Six months later he gets a friend to write to my mother asking her please to send him enough money to pay for his ticket back to the old country— he's dying in the Argentine, the Spaniards are killing him, he says, and he must come home. So my mother borrows from her brother to bring him back again. Instead of a fortune he brought her a new debt, and that was all.'

But Harry was dutiful, how dutiful his friends had reason to see again when they would urge him to try sending the old man to a home for the aged. 'No,' Harry would reply, his features moving heavily and reluctantly to a frown, a pout, as he showed how little the suggestion appealed to him. 'I don't like the idea. Maybe one day when he needs medical attention all the time I'll feel differently about it, but not now, not now. He wouldn't like it, he'd be unhappy. We'll look after him as long as we can. It's a job. It's something you've got to do.'

More eagerly Harry would go back to a recital of the old man's past. 'He couldn't even pay for his own passage out. I had to pay the loan back. We came out together—my mother wouldn't let him go by himself again, and I had to pay off her brother who advanced the money for us. I was a boy—what was I?—sixteen, seventeen, but I paid for his passage, and my own, and my mother's and then my brother's. It took me a long time, let me tell you. And then my troubles with him weren't over.' Harry even reproached his father for his myopia; he could clearly enough remember his chagrin when shortly after their arrival in South Africa, after it had become clear that Harry would be able to make his way in the world and be a support to the whole family, the old man—who at that time had not really been so old—had suddenly, almost dramatically, grown so short-sighted that he had been almost blind without the glasses which Harry had had to buy for him. And Harry could remember too how he had then made a practice of losing the glasses or breaking them with the greatest frequency, until it had been made clear to him that he was no longer expected to do any work. 'He doesn't do that any more. When he wants to run away now he sees to it that he's wearing his glasses. That's how he's always been. Sometimes he recognizes me, at other times, when he doesn't want to, he just doesn't know who I am.'

What Harry said was true. Sometimes the old man would call out to his son, when he would see him at the end of a passage, 'Who are you?' Or he would come upon Harry in a room and demand of him, 'What do you want in my house?'

'Your house?' Harry would say, when he felt like teasing the old man. 'Your house?'

'Out of my house!' the old man would shout back.

'Your house? Do you call this your house?' Harry would reply, smiling at the old man's fury.

Harry was the only one in the house who talked to the old man, and then he did not so much talk to him, as talk of him to others. Harry's wife was a dim and silent woman, crowded out by her husband and the large-boned sons like himself that she had borne him, and she would gladly have seen the old man in an old-age home. But her husband had said no, so she put up with the old man, though for herself she could see no possible better end for him than a period of residence in a home for aged Jews which she had once visited, and which had impressed her most favourably with its glass and yellow brick, the noiseless rubber tiles in its corridors, its secluded grassed grounds, and the uniforms worn by the attendants to the establishment. But she put up with the old man; she did not talk to him. The grandchildren had nothing to do with their grandfather—they were busy at school, playing rugby and cricket, they could hardly speak Yiddish, and they were embarrassed by him in front of their friends; when the grandfather did take notice of them it was only to call them Boers and *goyim* and *shkotzim* in sudden quavering rages which did not disturb them at all.

The house itself—a big single-storied place of brick, with a corrugated iron roof above and a wide stoep all around—Harry Grossman had bought years before. In the continual rebuilding the suburb was undergoing it was beginning to look old-fashioned. But it was solid and prosperous, and indoors curiously masculine in appearance, like the house of a widower. The furniture was of the heaviest African woods, dark, and built to last, the passages were lined with bare linoleum, and the few pictures on the walls, big brown and grey mezzotints in heavy frames, had not been looked at for years. The servants were both men, large ignored Zulus who did their work and kept up the brown gleam of the furniture.

It was from this house that old man Grossman tried to escape. He fled through the doors and the windows and into the wide sunlit streets of the town in Africa, where the blocks of flats were encroaching upon the single-storied houses behind their gardens. In these streets he wandered until he was found.

It was Johannes, one of the Zulu servants, who suggested a way of dealing with old man Grossman. He brought to the house one afternoon Paulus, whom he described as his 'brother'. Harry Grossman knew enough to know that 'brother' in this context could mean anything from the son of one's mother to a friend from a neighbouring *kraal*, but by the speech that Johannes made on Paulus' behalf he might indeed have been the latter's brother. Johannes had to speak for Paulus, for Paulus knew no English. Paulus was a 'raw boy', as raw as a boy could possibly come. He was a muscular, moustached, and bearded African, with pendulous ear-lobes showing the slits in which the tribal plugs had once hung; on his feet he wore sandals the soles of which were cut from old motor-car tyres, the thongs from red inner tubing. He wore neither hat nor socks, but he did have a pair of khaki shorts which were too small for him, and a shirt without any buttons; buttons would in any case have been of no use for the shirt could never have closed over his chest. He swelled magnificently out of his clothing, and above there was a head carried well back, so that his beard, which had been trained to grow in two sharp points from his chin, bristled ferociously forward under his melancholy and almost mandarin-like moustache. When he smiled, as he did once or twice during Johannes' speech, he showed his white, even teeth, but for the most part he stood looking rather shyly to the side of Harry Grossman's head, with his hands behind his back and his bare knees bent a little forward, as if to show how little he was asserting himself, no matter what his 'brother' might have been saying about him.

His expression did not change when Harry said that it seemed hopeless, that Paulus was too raw, and Johannes explained what the baas had just said. He nodded agreement when Johannes explained to him that the baas said that it was a pity that he knew no English. But whenever Harry looked at him, he smiled, not ingratiatingly, but simply smiling above his beard, as though saying: 'Try me.' Then he looked grave again as Johannes expatiated on his virtues. Johannes pleaded for his 'brother'. He said that the baas knew that he, Johannes, was a good boy. Would he, then, recommend to the baas a boy who was not a good boy too? The baas could see for himself, Johannes said, that Paulus was not one of these town boys, these street loafers: he was a good boy, come straight from the *kraal*. He was not a thief or a drinker. He was strong, he was a hard

worker, he was clean, and he could be as gentle as a woman.
If he, Johannes, were not telling the truth about all these things,
then he deserved to be chased away. If Paulus failed in any
single respect, then he, Johannes, would voluntarily leave the
service of the baas, because he had said untrue things to the
baas. But if the baas believed him, and gave Paulus his chance,
then he, Johannes, would teach Paulus all the things of the
house and the garden, so that Paulus would be useful to the
baas in ways other than the particular task for which he was
asking the baas to hire him. And, rather daringly, Johannes
said that it did not matter so much if Paulus knew no English,
because the old baas, the *oubaas*, knew no English either.

It was as something in the nature of a joke—almost a joke
against his father—that Harry Grossman gave Paulus his
chance. He was given a room in the servants' quarters in the
backyard, into which he brought a tin trunk painted red and
black, a roll of blankets, and a guitar with a picture of a cowboy
on the back. He was given a houseboy's outfit of blue denim
blouse and shorts, with red piping round the edges, into which
he fitted, with his beard and his physique, like a king in exile
in some pantomime. He was given his food three times a day,
after the white people had eaten, a bar of soap every week,
cast-off clothing at odd intervals, and the sum of one pound
five shillings per week, five shillings of which he took, the rest
being left at his request, with the baas, as savings. He had a
free afternoon once a week, and he was allowed to entertain
not more than two friends at any one time in his room. In all
the particulars that Johannes had enumerated, Johannes was
proved reliable. Paulus was not one of these town boys, these
street loafers. He did not steal or drink, he was clean and he
was honest and hard-working. And he could be as gentle as a
woman.

It took Paulus some time to settle down to his job; he had to
conquer not only his own shyness and strangeness in the new
house filled with strange people—let alone the city, which,
since taking occupation of his room, he had hardly dared to
enter—but also the hostility of old man Grossman, who took
immediate fright at Paulus and redoubled his efforts to get

away from the house upon Paulus' entry into it. As it happened, the first result of this persistence on the part of the old
man was that Paulus was able to get the measure of the job, for
he came to it with a willingness of spirit that the old man could
not vanquish, but could only teach. Paulus had been given no
instructions, he had merely been told to see that the old man
did not get himself into trouble, and after a few days of bewilderment Paulus found his way. He simply went along with the
old man.

At first he did so cautiously, following the old man at a distance, for he knew the other did not trust him. But later he was
able to follow the old man openly; still later he was able to
walk side by side with him, and the old man did not try to
escape from him. When old man Grossman went out, Paulus
went too, and there was no longer any need for the doors and
windows to be watched, or the police to be telephoned. The
young bearded Zulu and the old bearded Jew from Lithuania
walked together in the streets of the town that was strange to
them both; together they looked over the fences of the large
gardens and into the shining foyers of the blocks of flats;
together they stood on the pavements of the main arterial
roads and watched the cars and trucks rush between the tall
buildings; together they walked in the small, sandy parks, and
when the old man was tired Paulus saw to it that he sat on a
bench and rested. They could not sit on the bench together, for
only whites were allowed to sit on the benches, but Paulus
would squat on the ground at the old man's feet and wait until
he judged the old man had rested long enough, before moving
on again. Together they stared into the windows of the subur-
ban shops, and though neither of them could read the signs
outside the shops, the advertisements on billboards, the traffic
signs at the side of the road, Paulus learned to wait for the
traffic lights to change from red to green before crossing a
street, and together they stared at the Coca-Cola girls and the
advertisements for beer and the cinema posters. On a piece of
cardboard which Paulus carried in the pocket of his blouse
Harry had had one of his sons print the old man's name and
address, and whenever Paulus was uncertain of the way home,

he would approach an African or a friendly-looking white man and show him the card, and try his best to follow the instructions, or at least the gesticulations which were all of the answers of the white men that meant anything to him. But there were enough Africans to be found, usually, who were more sophisticated than himself, and though they teased him for his 'rawness' and for holding the sort of job he had, they helped him too. Neither Paulus nor old man Grossman were aware that when they crossed a street hand-in-hand, as they sometimes did when the traffic was particularly heavy, there were people who averted their eyes from the sight of this degradation, which could come upon a man when he was senile and dependent.

Paulus knew only Zulu, the old man knew only Yiddish, so there was no language in which they could talk to one another. But they talked all the same: they both commented on or complained to each other of the things they saw around them, and often they agreed with one another, smiling and nodding their heads and explaining again with their hands what each happened to be talking about. They both seemed to believe that they were talking about the same things, and often they undoubtedly were, when they lifted their heads sharply to see an aeroplane cross the blue sky between two buildings, or when they reached the top of a steep road and turned to look back the way they had come, and saw below them the clean impervious towers of the city thrust nakedly against the sky in brand-new piles of concrete and glass and facebrick. Then down they would go again, among the houses and the gardens where the beneficent climate encouraged both palms and oak trees to grow indiscriminately among each other—as they did in the garden of the house to which, in the evenings, Paulus and old man Grossman would eventually return.

In and about the house Paulus soon became as indispensable to the old man as he was on their expeditions out of it. Paulus dressed him and bathed him and trimmed his beard, and when the old man woke distressed in the middle of the night it would be for Paulus that he would call—'*Der schwarzer*,' he would shout (for he never learned Paulus' name), '*vo's der schwarzer*'—

and Paulus would change his sheets and pyjamas and put him back to bed again. 'Baas *Zeide*,' Paulus called the old man, picking up the Yiddish word for grandfather from the children of the house.

That was something that Harry Grossman told everyone of. For Harry persisted in regarding the arrangement as a kind of joke, and the more the arrangement succeeded the more determinedly did he try to turn it into a joke not only against his father but against Paulus too. It had been a joke that his father should be looked after by a raw Zulu: it was going to be a joke that the Zulu was successful at it. 'Baas *Zeide*! That's what *der schwarzer* calls him—have you ever heard the like of it? And you should see the two of them, walking about in the streets hand-in-hand like two schoolgirls. Two clever ones, *der schwarzer* and my father going for a promenade, and between them I tell you you wouldn't be able to find out what day of the week or what time of day it is.'

And when people said, 'Still that Paulus seems a very good boy,' Harry would reply:

'Why shouldn't he be? With all his knowledge, are there so many better jobs that he'd be able to find? He keeps the old man happy—very good, very nice, but don't forget that that's what he's paid to do. What does he know any better to do, a simple kaffir from the *kraal*? He knows he's got a good job, and he'd be a fool if he threw it away. Do you think,' Harry would say, and this too would insistently be part of the joke, 'if I had nothing else to do with my time I wouldn't be able to make the old man happy?' Harry would look about his sitting-room, where the floorboards bore the weight of his furniture, or when they sat on the stoep he would measure with his glance the spacious garden aloof from the street beyond the hedge. 'I've got other things to do. And I had other things to do, plenty of them, all my life, and not only for myself.' The thought of them would send him back to his joke. 'No, I think the old man has just about found his level in *der schwarzer*—and I don't think *der schwarzer* could cope with anything else.'

Harry teased the old man to his face too, about his 'black friend', and he would ask him what he would do if Paulus went away; once he jokingly threatened to send the Zulu away. But the old man didn't believe the threat, for Paulus was in his room at the time, and the old man simply left Harry and went straight to Paulus, and sat in the room with him. Harry did not follow him: he would never have gone into any of his servants' rooms, least of all that of Paulus. For though he made a joke of him to others, to Paulus himself he always spoke gruffly, unjokingly, with no patience. On that day he had merely shouted after the old man, 'Another time he won't be there.'

Yet it was strange to see how Harry Grossman would always be drawn to the room in which he knew his father and Paulus to be. Night after night he came into the old man's bedroom when Paulus was dressing or undressing the old man; almost as often Harry stood in the steamy, untidy bathroom when the old man was being bathed. At these times he hardly spoke, he offered no explanation of his presence. He stood dourly and silently in the room, in his customary powerful, begrudging stance, with one hand clasping the wrist of the other and both supporting his waist, and he watched Paulus at work. The backs of Paulus' hands were smooth and hairless, they were paler on the palms and at the finger-nails, and they worked deftly about the body of the old man, who was submissive under their ministrations. At first Paulus had sometimes smiled at Harry while he worked, with his straightforward, even smile in which there was no invitation to a complicity in patronage, but rather an encouragement to Harry to draw forward. After the first few evenings Paulus no longer smiled at his master, but he could not restrain himself, even under Harry's stare, from talking in a soft, continuous flow of Zulu, to encourage the old man and to exhort him to be helpful and to express his pleasure in how well the work was going. When Paulus at last wiped the gleaming soapsuds from his hands he would occasionally, when the old man was tired, stoop low and with a laugh pick him up and carry him easily down the passage to his bedroom. Harry would follow; he would stand in the passage and watch the burdened, bare-footed Zulu until the door of his father's room closed behind them both.

Only once did Harry wait on such an evening for Paulus to

re-appear from his father's room. Paulus had already come out, had passed him in the narrow passage, and had already subduedly said: 'Good night, baas,' before Harry called suddenly:

'Hey! Wait!'

'Baas,' Paulus said, turning his head. Then he came quickly to Harry. 'Baas,' he said again, puzzled to know why his baas, who so rarely spoke to him, should suddenly have called him like this, when his work was over.

Harry waited again before speaking, waited long enough for Paulus to say: 'Baas?' once more, to move a little closer, and to lift his head for a moment before lowering it respectfully.

'The *oubaas* was tired tonight,' Harry said. 'Where did you take him? What did you do with him?'

'Baas?'

'You heard what I said. What did you do with him that he looked so tired?'

'Baas—I—' Paulus was flustered, and his hands beat in the air, but with care, so that he would not touch his baas. 'Please baas.' He brought both hands to his mouth, closing it forcibly. He flung his hands away. 'Johannes,' he said with relief, and he had already taken the first step down the passage to call his interpreter.

'No!' Harry called. 'You mean you don't understand what I say? I know you don't,' Harry shouted, though in fact he had forgotten until Paulus had reminded him. The sight of Paulus' puzzled and guilty face before him filled him with a lust to see this man, this nurse with the face and the figure of a warrior, look more puzzled and guilty yet; and Harry knew that it could so easily be done, it could be done simply by talking to him in the language he could not understand. 'You're a fool,' Harry said. 'You're like a child. You understand nothing, and it's just as well for you that you need nothing. You'll always be where you are, running to do what the white baas tells you to do. Look how you stand! Do you think I understood English when I came here?' Then with contempt, using one of the few Zulu words he knew: '*Hamba!* Go! Do you think I want to see you?'

'*Au* baas!' Paulus exclaimed in distress. He could not remonstrate; he could only open his hands in a gesture to show that he understood neither the words Harry used, nor in what he had been remiss that Harry should have spoken in such angry tones to him. But Harry gestured him away, and had the satisfaction of seeing Paulus shuffle off like a schoolboy.

Harry was the only person who knew that he and his father had quarrelled shortly before the accident that ended the old man's life. That was one story about his father he was never to repeat.

Late in the afternoon they quarrelled, after Harry had come back from the shop in which he made his living. He came back to find his father wandering about the house, shouting for *der schwarzer*, and his wife complaining that she had already told the old man at least five times that *der schwarzer* was not in the house: it was Paulus' afternoon off.

Harry went to his father, and he too told him, '*Der schwarzer's* not here.' The old man turned away and continued going from room to room, peering in through the doors. '*Der schwarzer's* not here,' Harry repeated 'What do you want him for?'

Still the old man ignored him. He went down the passage towards the bedrooms. 'What do you want?' Harry called after him.

The old man went into every bedroom, still shouting for *der schwarzer*. Only when he was in his own bare bedroom did he look at Harry. 'Where's *der schwarzer*?'

'I've told you ten times I don't know where he is. What do you want him for?'

'I want *der schwarzer*.'

'I know you want him. But he isn't here.'

'I want *der schwarzer*.'

'Do you think I haven't heard you? He isn't here.'

'Bring him to me,' the old man said.

'I can't bring him to you. I don't know where he is.' Harry steadied himself against his own anger. He said quietly: 'Tell me what you want. I'll do it for you. I'm here, I can do what *der schwarzer* can do for you.'

'Where's *der schwarzer*?'

'I've told you he isn't here,' Harry shouted. 'Why don't you tell me what you want? What's the matter with me—can't you tell me what you want?'

'I want *der schwarzer.*'

'Please,' Harry said. He threw out his arms towards his father, but the gesture was abrupt, almost as though he were thrusting him away. 'Why can't you ask me? You can ask me —haven't I done enough for you already? Do you want to go for a walk?—I'll take you for a walk. What do you want? Do you want—do you want—?' Harry could not think what his father might want. 'I'll do it,' he said. 'You don't need *der schwarzer.*'

Then Harry saw that his father was weeping. His eyes were hidden behind the thick glasses that he had to wear: his glasses and beard made of his face a mask of age. But Harry knew when the old man was weeping—he had seen him crying too often before, when they had found him at the end of a street after he had wandered away, or even, years earlier, when he had lost another of the miserable jobs that seemed to be the only ones he could find in a country in which his son had, later, prospered.

'Father,' Harry asked, 'what have I done? Do you think I've sent *der schwarzer* away?' His father turned away, between the narrow bed and the narrow wardrobe. 'He's coming—' Harry said, but he could not look at his father's back, at his hollowed neck, on which the hairs that Paulus had clipped glistened above the pale brown discolorations of age—Harry could not look at the neck turned stiffly away from him while he had to try to promise the return of the Zulu. He dropped his hands and walked out of the room.

No one knew how the old man managed to get out of the house and through the front gate without having been seen. But he did manage it, and in the road he was struck down by a man on a bicycle. It was enough. He died a few days later in the hospital.

Harry's wife wept, even the grandsons wept; Paulus wept. Harry himself was stony, and his bunched, protuberant features were immovable; they seemed locked upon the bones of his face. A few days after the funeral he called Paulus and

Johannes into the kitchen and said to Johannes: 'Tell him he must go. His work is finished.'

Johannes translated for Paulus, and then, after Paulus had spoken, he turned to Harry. 'He says, yes baas.' Paulus kept his eyes on the ground; he did not look up even when Harry looked directly at him. Harry knew that this was not out of fear or shyness, but out of courtesy for his master's grief— which was what they could not but be talking of, when they talked of his work.

'Here's his pay.' Harry thrust a few notes towards Paulus, who took them in his cupped hands, and retreated.

Harry waited for them to go, but Paulus stayed in the room, and consulted with Johannes in a low voice. Johannes turned to his master. 'He says, baas, that the baas still has his savings.'

Harry had forgotten about Paulus' savings. He told Johannes that he had forgotten, and that he did not have enough money at the moment, but would bring the money the next day. Johannes translated and Paulus nodded gratefully. Both he and Johannes were subdued by the death there had been in the house.

Harry's dealings with Paulus were over. He took what was to have been his last look at Paulus, but this look stirred him once more against the Zulu. As harshly as he told Paulus that he had to go, so now, implacably, seeing Paulus in the mockery and simplicity of his houseboy's clothing, feeding his anger to the very end, Harry said: 'Ask him what he's been saving for. What's he going to do with the fortune he's made?'

Johannes spoke to Paulus and came back with a reply. 'He says, baas, that he is saving to bring his wife and children from Zululand to Johannesburg. He is saving, baas,' Johannes said, for Harry had not seemed to understand, 'to bring his family to this town also.'

The two Zulus were bewildered to know why it was then that Harry Grossman's clenched, fist-like features should have fallen from one another, or why he stared with such guilt and despair at Paulus, while he cried, 'What else could I have done? I did my best!' before the first tears came.

BENEDICT KIELY

God's Own Country

THE plump girl from Cork City who was the editor's secretary came into the newsroom where the four of us huddled
together, and said, so rapidly that we had to ask her to say it
all over again: Goodness gracious, Mr. Slattery, you are, you
really are, smouldering.

She was plump and very pretty and enticingly perfumed and
every one of the four of us, that is everyone of us except Jeremiah, would have been overjoyed to make advances to her
except that, being from Cork City, she talked so rapidly that
we never had time to get a word in edgeways. She said: Goodness gracious, Mr. Slattery, you are, you really are, smouldering.

Now that our attention had been drawn to it, he really was
smouldering. He sat, crouched as close as he could get to the
paltry coal fire: the old ramshackle building, all rooms of no
definable geometrical shape, would have collapsed with Meru-
lius Lacrymans, the most noxious form of dry rot, the tertiary
syphilis of ageing buildings, if central heating had ever been
installed. Jeremiah nursed the fire between his bony knees. He
toasted, or tried to toast, his chapped chilblained hands above
the pitiful glow. The management of that small weekly newspaper were too mean to spend much money on fuel; and in
that bitter spring Jeremiah was the coldest man in the city. He
tried, it seemed, to suck what little heat there was into his
bloodless body. He certainly allowed none of it to pass him by
so as to mollify the three of us who sat, while he crouched,
working doggedly with our overcoats and woollen scarves on.
The big poet who wrote the cinema reviews, and who hadn't
been inside a cinema since he left for a drink at the inter-
mission in *Gone With The Wind* and never went back, was
typing, with woollen gloves on, with one finger; and for panache
more than for actual necessity he wore a motor-cycling helmet

with fleece-lined flaps over his ears. The big poet had already told Jeremiah that Jeremiah was a raven, a scrawny starved raven, quothing and croaking nevermore, crumpled up there in his black greatcoat over a fire that wouldn't boil an egg. Jeremiah only crouched closer to the fire and, since we knew how cold he always was, we left him be and forgot all about him, and he might well have gone on fire, nobody, not even himself, noticing, if the plump pretty secretary, a golden perfumed ball hopping from the parlour into the hall, hadn't bounced, warming the world, being the true honey of delight, into the room.

It was the turned-up fold of the right leg of his shiny black trousers. He extinguished himself wearily, putting on, to protect the fingers of his right hand, a leather motoring-gauntlet. He had lost, or had never possessed, the left-hand gauntlet. He moved a little back from the fire, he even tried to sit up straight. She picked up the telephone on the table before me. Her rounded left haunch, packed tightly in a sort of golden cloth, was within eating distance, if I'd had a knife and fork. She said to the switch that she would take that call now from where she was in the newsroom. She was silent for a while. The golden haunch moved ever so slightly, rose and fell, in fact, as if it breathed. She said: Certainly, your Grace.

—No, your Grace.

—To the island, your Grace.

—A reporter, your Grace.

—Of course, your Grace.

—And photographer, your Grace.

—An American bishop, your Grace.

—How interesting, your Grace.

—Confirmation, your Grace.

—All the way from Georgia, your Grace.

—Goodness gracious, your Grace.

—Lifeboat, your Grace.

—Yes, your Grace.

—No, your Grace.

—Next Thursday, your Grace.

—I'll make a note of it, your Grace.

—And tell the editor when he comes in from the nunciature, your Grace.

The nunciature was the place where the editor, promoting the Pope's wishes by promoting the Catholic press, did most of his drinking. He had a great tongue for the Italian wine.

—Lifeboat, your Grace.

—Absolutely, your Grace.

—Goodbye, your Grace.

The big poet said: That wouldn't have been His Grace you were talking to?

—That man, she said, thinks he's three rungs of the ladder above the Pope of Rome and with right of succession to the Lord Himself.

She made for the door. The gold blinded me. She turned at the door, said to us all, or to three of us: Watch him. Don't let him make a holocaust of himself. Clean him up and feed him. He's for the Islands of the West, Hy-Breasil, the Isle of the Blest, next Thursday with the Greatest Grace of all the Graces, and a Yankee bishop who thinks it would do something for him to bestow the holy sacrament of confirmation on the young savages out there. Not that it will do much for them. It would take more than two bishops and the Holy Ghost. . . .

She was still talking as she vanished. The door crashed shut behind her and the room was dark again, and colder than ever. Jeremiah was visibly shuddering, audibly chattering, because to his bloodlessness and to the chill of the room and of the harsh day of east wind, had been added the worst cold of all: terror.

—Take him out, the big poet said, before he freezes us to death. Buy him a hot whiskey. You can buy me one when I finish my column.

As he tapped with one gloved finger and, with a free and open mind and no prejudice, critically evaluated what he had not seen, he also lifted up his voice and sang: When the roses bloom again down by yon river, and the robin redbreast sings his sweet refrain, in the days of auld lang syne, I'll be with you sweetheart mine, I'll be with you when the roses bloom again.

In Mulligan's in Poolbeg Street, established 1782, the year of the great Convention of the heroic patriotic Volunteers at Dungannon when the leaders of the nation, sort of, were inspired by the example of American Independence, I said to Jeremiah: Be a blood. Come alive. Break out. Face them. Show them. Fuck the begrudgers. Die, if die you must, on your feet and fighting.

He said: It's very well for you to talk. You can eat.

—Everybody, for God's sake, can eat.

—I can't eat. I can only nibble.

—You can drink, though. You have no trouble at all with the drink.

His first hot whiskey was gone, but hadn't done him any good that you'd notice.

—Only whiskey, he said, and sometimes on good days, stout. But even milk makes me ill, unless it's hot and with pepper sprinkled on it.

I pretended to laugh at him, to jolly him out of it, yet he really had me worried. For he was a good helpless intelligent chap, and his nerves had gone to hell in the seminary that he had had to leave, and the oddest rumours about his eating or non-eating habits were going around the town. That, for instance, he had been seen in a certain hotel, nibbling at biscuits left behind by another customer, and when the waiter, who was a friend of mine, asked him in all kindness did he need lunch, he had slunk away, the waiter said, like a shadow that had neither substance nor sunshine to account for its being there in the first place. He was no man, I had to agree, to face on an empty stomach a spring gale, or even a half or a hatful of a gale, on the wild western Atlantic coast.

—And the thought of that bishop, he said, puts the heart across me. He's a boor and a bully of the most violent description. He's a hierarchical Genghis Khan.

—Not half as bad as he's painted.

—Half's bad enough.

So I told some story, once told to me by a Belfast man, about some charitable act performed by the same bishop. It didn't sound at all convincing. Nor was Jeremiah convinced.

—If he ever was charitable, he said, be sure that it wasn't his own money he gave away.

—You won't have to see much of him, Jeremiah. Keep out of his path. Don't encounter him.

—But I'll encounter the uncandid cameraman who'll be my constant companion. With his good tweeds and his cameras that all the gold in the mint wouldn't buy. How do the mean crowd that run that paper ever manage to pay him enough to satisfy him? He invited me to his home to dinner. Once. To patronise me. To show me what he had and I hadn't. He ran out six times during dinner to ring the doorbell, and we had to stop eating and listen to the chimes. A different chime in every room. Like living in the bloody belfry. Searchlights he has on the lawn to illuminate the house on feast-days. Like they do in America, I'm told. Letting his light shine in the uncomprehending darkness. Some men in this town can't pay the electricity bill, but he suffers from a surplus. And this bishop is a friend of his. Stops with him when he comes to town. His wife's uncle is a monsignor in His Grace's diocese. Practically inlaws. They call each other by their Christian names. I was permitted and privileged to see the room the bishop sleeps in, with its own special bathroom, toilet seat reserved for the episcopal arse, a layman would have to have his arse specially anointed to sit on it. Let me tell you that it filled me with awe. When they have clerical visitors, he told me, they couldn't have them shaving in the ordinary bathroom. I hadn't the courage to ask him was there anything forbidding that in Canon Law, Pastoral Theology, or the Maynooth Statutes. God look down on me between the two of them, and an American bishop thrown in for good luck. They say that in the United States the bishops are just bigger and more brutal.

—Jeremiah, I said severely, you're lucky to be out with that cameraman. He'll teach you to be a newsman. Just study how he works. He can smell news like, like . . .

The struggle for words went on until he helped me out. He was quick-witted; and even on him the third hot whiskey was bound to have some effect: to send what blood there was in his veins toe-dancing merrily to his brain.

—Like a buzzard smells dead meat, he said.

Then the poet joined us. Having an inherited gift for cobbling he had recently cobbled for himself a pair of shoes but, since measurement was not his might, they turned out to be too big even for him, thus, for any mortal man. But he had not given up hope of encountering in a public bar some Cyclopean for whose benefit he had, in his subconscious, been working, and of finding him able and willing to purchase those shoes. He carried them, unwrapped, under his arm. They always excited comment; and many were the men who tried and failed to fill them. That night we toured the town with them, adding to our company, en route, an Irish professor from Rathfarnham, a French professor from Marseilles, a lady novelist, a uniformed American soldier with an Irish name, who came from Boston and General Patch's army which had passed by Marseilles and wrecked it in the process. Outside Saint Vincent's hospital in Saint Stephen's Green a total stranger, walking past us, collapsed. He was a very big man, with enormous feet. But when the men from Boston and Marseilles, and the poet and myself, carried him into the hospital he was dead.

All that, as you are about to observe, is another story.

We failed, as it so happened, to sell the shoes.

On that corner of the western coast of Ireland the difference between a gale and a half-gale is that in a half-gale you take a chance and go out, in a gale you stay ashore.

The night before the voyage they rested in a hotel in Galway City. The wind rattled the casements and now and again blew open the door of the bar in which Jeremiah sat alone, until well after midnight, over one miserable whiskey. Nobody bothered to talk to him, not even in Galway where the very lobsters will welcome the stranger. The bar was draughty. He wore his black greatcoat, a relic of his clerical ambitions. It enlarged his body to the point of monstrosity, and minimized his head. Dripping customers came and drank and steamed and went again. When the door blew open he could see the downpours of rain hopping like hailstones on the street. The spluttering radio talked of floods, and trees blown down, and crops destroyed, and an oil-tanker in peril off the Tuskar Rock. The cameraman had eaten a horse of a dinner, washed it down with the best wine, said his prayers, and gone to bed, to be, he said, fresh and fit for the morning. Jeremiah was hungry, but less than ever could he eat: with fear of the storm and of the western sea as yet unseen and of the bull of a bishop and, perhaps too, he thought, that visiting American would be no better. At midnight he drained his glass dry and afterwards tilted it several times to his lips, drinking, or inhaling, only wind. He would have ordered another whiskey but the bar was crowded by that time, and the barman was surrounded by his privileged friends who were drinking after hours. The wind no longer blew the door open for the door was double-bolted against the night. But the booming, buffeting, and rattling of the storm could still be heard, at times bellowing like a brazen bishop, threatening Jeremiah. The customers kept coming and crowding through a dark passage that joined the bar and the kitchen. They acted as if they had spent all day in the kitchen and had every intention of spending all night in the bar. Each one of them favoured Jeremiah with a startled look where he sat, black, deformed by that greatcoat, hunched-up in his black cold corner. Nobody joined him. He went to bed, to a narrow, hard, excessively-white bed with a ridge up the middle and a downward slope on each side. The rubber hot-water bottle had already gone cold. The rain threatened to smash the window-panes. He spread his greatcoat over his feet, wearing his socks in bed, and, cursing the day he was born, fell asleep from sheer misery.

Early next morning he had his baptism of salt water, not sea-spray but rain blown sideways and so salty that it made a crust around the lips.

—That out there, said the cameraman in the security of his car, is what they call the poteen cross.

The seats in the car were covered with a red plush, in its turn covered by a protective and easily-washable, transparent plastic that Jeremiah knew had been put there to prevent himself or his greatcoat or his greasy, shiny pants from making direct contact with the red plush.

—Did you never hear of the poteen cross?

—No, said Jeremiah.

They had stopped in a pelting village on the westward road. The doors were shut, the windows still blinded. It was no morning for early rising. The sea was audible, but not visible. The rain came bellying inshore on gusts of wind. On a gravelled space down a slope towards the sound of the sea stood a huge bare black cross: well, not completely bare for it carried, criss-crossed, the spear that pierced, that other spear that bore aloft the sponge soaked in vinegar; and it was topped by a gigantic crown of thorns. The cameraman said: When the Redemptorist Fathers preached hellfire against the men who made the poteen, they ordered the moonshiners, under pain of mortal sin, to come here and leave their stills at the foot of the cross. The last sinner to hold out against them came in the end with his still but, there before him, he saw a better model that somebody else had left, so he took it away with him. There's a London magazine wants a picture of that cross.

—It wouldn't, said Jeremiah, make much of a picture.

—With somebody beside it pointing up at it, it wouldn't be so bad. The light's not good. But I think we could manage.

—We, said Jeremiah.

—You wouldn't like me, he said, to get up on the cross? Have you brought the nails?

He posed, nevertheless, and pointed up at the cross. What else could he do? We saw the picture afterwards in that London magazine. Jeremiah looked like a sable bloated demon trying to prove to benighted sinners that Christ was gone and dead and never would rise again. But it was undeniably an effective picture. Jeremiah posed and pointed. He was salted and sodden while the cameraman, secure in yellow oilskins and sou'wester, darted out, took three shots, darted in again, doffed the oilskins, and was as dry as snuff. They drove on westwards.

—That coat of yours, said the cameraman. You should have fitted yourself out with oilskins. That coat of yours will soak up all the water from here to Long Island.

—Stinks a bit too, he said on reflection. The Beeoh is flying.

That was meant to be some sort of a joke and, for the sake

of civility, Jeremiah tried to laugh. They crossed a stone bridge over a brown-and-white, foaming, flooded river, turned left down a byroad, followed the course of the river, sometimes so close to it that the floodwater lapped the edge of the road, sometimes swinging a little away from it through a misted landscape of small fields, thatched cabins dour and withdrawn in the storm, shapeless expanses of rock and heather, until they came to where the brown-and-white water tumbled into the peace of a little land-locked harbour. The lifeboat that, by special arrangement, was to carry the party to the island was there, but no lifeboatmen, no party. A few small craft lay on a sandy slope in the shelter of a breakwater. Jeremiah and the cameraman could have been the only people alive in a swamped world. They waited: the cameraman in the car with the heat on; Jeremiah, to get away from him for a while, prowling around empty cold sheds that were, at least, dry, but that stank of dead fish and were floored with peat-mould terrazzoed, it would seem, by fragments broken from many previous generations of lobsters. Beyond the breakwater and a rocky headland the sea boomed, but the water in the sheltered harbour was smooth and black as ink. He was hungry again but knew that if he had food, any food other than dry biscuits, he wouldn't be able to eat it. All food now would smell of stale fish. He was cold, as always. When he was out of sight of the cameraman he pranced, to warm himself, on peat-mould and lobsters. He was only moderately successful. But his greatcoat, at least, steamed.

The rain eased off, the sky brightened, but the wind seemed to grow in fury, surf and spray went up straight and shining into the air beyond the breakwater, leaped it and came down with a flat slap on the sandy slope and the sleeping small craft. Then, like Apache on an Arizona skyline, the people began to appear: a group of three, suddenly, from behind a standing rock; a group of seven or eight rising sharply into sight on a hilltop on the switchback riverside road, dropping out of sight into a hollow, surfacing again, followed by other groups that appeared and disappeared in the same disconcerting manner. As the sky cleared, the uniform darkness breaking up into bullocks of black wind-goaded clouds, the landscape of rock and heather, patchwork fields divided by grey, high, drystone walls, came out into the light; and from every small farmhouse thus revealed, people came, following footpaths, crossing stiles, calling to each other across patches of light green oats and dark-green potatoes. It was a sudden miracle of growth, of human life appearing where there had been nothing but wind and rain and mist. Within three-quarters of an hour there were a hundred or more people around the harbour, lean hard-faced fishermen and small farmers, dark-haired laughing girls, old women in coloured shawls, talking Irish, talking English, posing in groups for the cameraman who in his yellow oil-skins moved among them like a gigantic canary. They waved and called to Jeremiah where he stood, withdrawn, and on the defensive, in the sheltered doorway of a fish-stinking shed.

A black Volkswagen came down the road followed by a red Volkswagen. From the black car a stout priest stepped forth, surveyed the crowd like a general estimating the strength of his mustered troops, shook hands with the cameraman as if he were meeting an old friend. From the red car a young man stepped out, then held the door for a gaunt middle-aged lady who emerged with an effort, head first: the local schoolteachers, by the cut of them. They picked out from the crowd a group of twelve to twenty, lined them up, backs to the wall, in the shelter of the breakwater. The tall lady waved her arms and the groups began to sing.

—Ecce sacerdos magnus, they sang.

A black limousine, with the traction power of two thousand Jerusalem asses on the first Holy Thursday, came, appearing and disappearing, down the switchback road. This was it, Jeremiah knew, and shuddered. On the back of an open truck behind the limousine came the lifeboatmen, all like the camera-man, in bright yellow oilskins.

—This is God's own country, said the American bishop, and ye are God's own people.

Jeremiah was still at a safe distance, yet near enough to hear

the booming clerical-American voice. The sea boomed beyond
the wall. The spray soared, then slapped down on the sand,
sparing the sheltered singers.

—Faith of our fathers, they sang, living still, in spite of
dungeon, fire, and sword.

Circling the crowd the great canary, camera now at ease,
approached Jeremiah.

—Get with it, Dracula, he said.

He didn't much bother to lower his voice.

—Come out of your corner fighting. Get in and get a story.
That Yank is news. He was run out of Rumania by the Com-
munists.

—He also comes, said Jeremiah, from Savannah, Georgia.

—So what?

—He doesn't exactly qualify as a Yankee.

—Oh Jesus, geography, said the cameraman. We'll give you
full marks for geography. They'll look lovely in the paper
where your story should be. If he came from bloody Patagonia,
he's here now. Go get him.

Then he was gone, waving his camera. The American bishop,
a tall and stately man, was advancing, blessing as he went, to
the stone steps that went down the harbour wall to the moored
lifeboat. He was in God's own country and God's own people,
well-marshalled by the stout parish priest, were all around him.
The Irish bishop, a tall and stately man, stood still, thoughtfully watching the approaching cameraman and Jeremiah
most reluctantly plodding in the rear, his progress, to his relief,
made more difficult by the mush of wet peat-mould underfoot,
growing deeper and deeper as he approached the wall where
sailing hookers were loaded with fuel for the peatless island.
Yet, slowly as he moved, he was still close enough to see clearly
what happened and to hear clearly what was said.

The bishop, tall and stately and monarch even over the
parish priest, looked with a cold eye at the advancing cameraman. There was no ring kissing. The bishop did not reach out
his hand to have his ring saluted. That was odd, to begin with.
Then he said loudly: What do you want?

—Your Grace, said the great canary.

He made a sort of a curtsey, clumsily, because he was hobbled in creaking oilskins.

—Your Grace, he said, out on the island there's a nona-genarian, the oldest inhabitant, and when we get there I'd like to get a picture of you giving him your blessing.

His Grace said nothing. His Grace turned very red in the face. In increased terror, Jeremiah remembered that inlaws could have their tiffs and that clerical inlaws were well known to be hell incarnate. His Grace right-about-wheeled, showed to the mainland and all on it a black broad back, right-quick-marched towards the lifeboat, sinking to the ankles as he thundered on in the soft wet mould, but by no means abating his speed which could have been a fair five miles an hour. His long coat-tails flapped in the wind. The wet mould fountained up like snow from a snow-plough. The sea boomed. The spray splattered. The great canary had shrunk as if plucked. Jere-miah's coat steamed worse than ever in the frenzy of his fear. If he treats his own like that, he thought, what in God's holy name will he do to me? Yet he couldn't resist saying: That man could pose like Nelson on his pillar watching his world collapse.

The canary cameraman hadn't a word to say.

Once aboard the lugger the bishops had swathed themselves in oilskins provided by the lifeboat's captain, and the camera-man mustered enough of his ancient gall to mutter to Jeremiah that that was the first time that he or anybody else had seen canary-coloured bishops.

—Snap them, said Jeremiah. You could sell it to the maga-zines in Bucharest. Episcopal American agent turns yellow.

But the cameraman was still too crestfallen, and made no move, and clearly looked relieved when the Irish bishop, tall and stately even if a little grotesque in oilskins, descended carefully into the for'ard foxhole, sat close into the corner, took out his rosary beads and began to pray silently: he knew the tricks of his western sea. Lulled by the security of the land-locked sheltered harbour, the American bishop, tall and stately even if a little grotesque in oilskins, stood like Nelson on the foredeck. He surveyed the shore of rock, small fields, drystone

walls, small thatched farmhouses, oats, potatoes, grazing black
cattle, all misting over for more rain. Then he turned his back
on the mainland and looked at the people, now marshalled all
together by the parish priest and the two teachers in the lee of
the harbour wall. The choir sang: Holy God, we praise thy
name. Lord of all, we bow before thee.

An outrider of the squall of rain that the wind was driving
inshore cornered cunningly around harbour wall and headland, and disrespectfully spattered the American bishop.
Secure in oilskins and the Grace of state he ignored it. The
cameraman dived into the stern foxhole. Jeremiah by now was
so sodden that the squall had no effect on him. An uncle of his,
a farmer in the County Longford, had worn the same heavy
woollen underwear winter and summer and argued eloquently
that what kept the heat in kept it out. That soaking salty
steaming greatcoat could, likewise, stand upright on its own
against the fury of the Bay of Biscay. It was a fortress for
Jeremiah; and with his right hand, reaching out through the
loophole of the sleeve, he touched the tough stubby oaken
mast, a talismanic touch, a prayer to the rooted essence of the
earth to protect him from the capricious fury of the sea. Then
with the bishop, a yellow figurehead, at the prow, and Jeremiah, a sable figurehead, at the stern, they moved smoothly
towards the open ocean; and, having withdrawn a little from
the land, the bishop raised his hand, as Lord Nelson would not
have done, and said: This is God's own country. Ye are God's
own people.

The choir sang: Hail Glorious Saint Patrick, dear Saint of
our isle.

From the conscripted and marshalled people came a cheer
loud enough to drown the hymn; and then the sea, with as
little regard for the cloth as had the Rumanian Reds, struck
like an angry bull and the boat, Jeremiah says, stood on its
nose, and only a miracle of the highest order kept the American
bishop out of the drink. Jeremiah could see him, down, far
down at the bottom of a dizzy slope, then up, far up, shining
like the sun between sea and sky, as the boat reared back on its
haunches and Jeremiah felt on the back of his head the blow of

a gigantic fist. It was simply salt seawater in a solid block, striking and bursting like a bomb. By the time he had wiped his eyes and the boat was again, for a few brief moments, on an even keel, there were two bishops sheltering in the for'ard fox-hole: the two most quiet and prayerful men he had ever seen.

—On the ocean that hollows the rocks where ye dwell, Jeremiah recited out as loudly as he could because no ears could hear even a bull bellowing above the roar and movement and torment of the sea.

—A shadowy land, he went on, has appeared as they tell. Men thought it a region of sunshine and rest, and they called it Hy-Breasil the Isle of the Blest.

To make matters easier, if not tolerable, he composed his mind and said to himself: Lifeboats can't sink.

On this harshly-ocean-bitten coast there was the poetic legend of the visionary who sailed west, ever west, to find the island where the souls of the blest are forever happy.

—Rash dreamer return, Jeremiah shouted, oh ye winds of the main, bear him back to his own native Ara again.

For his defiance the sea repaid him in three thundering salty buffets and a sudden angled attack that sent the boat hissing along on its side and placed Jeremiah with both arms around the mast. In the brief following lull he said more quietly, pacifying the sea, acknowledging its power: Night fell on the deep amid tempest and spray, and he died on the ocean, away far away.

He was far too frightened to be seasick, which was just as well, considering the windy vacuum he had for a stomach. The boat pranced and rolled. He held on to the mast, but now almost nonchalantly and only with one arm. The sea buffeted him into dreams of that luckless searcher for Hy-Breasil, or dreams of Brendan the Navigator, long before Columbus, sailing bravely on and on and making landfall on Miami Beach. Secure in those dreams he found to his amazement that he could contemn the snubbed cameraman and the praying bishops hiding in their foxholes. He, Jeremiah, belonged with the nonchalant lifeboatmen studying the sea as a man through the smoke of a good pipe might look at the face of a friend. One of them, indeed, was so nonchalant that he sat on the hatch-roof above the bishops, his feet on the gunwale chain so that, when the boat dipped his way, his feet a few times went well out of sight in the water. Those lifeboatmen were less men than great yellow seabirds and Jeremiah, although a land-lubber and as black as a raven, willed to be with them as far as he could, for the moment, go. He studied on the crazy pattern of tossing waters the ironic glint of sunshine on steel-blue hills racing to collide and crash and burst into blinding silver. He recalled sunshine on quiet, stable, green fields that he was half-reconciled never to see again. He was on the way to the Isle of the Blest.

Yet it was no island that first appeared to remind him, after two hours of trance, that men, other than the lifeboat's crew and cargo, did exist: no island, but the high bird-flight of a dozen black currachs, appearing and disappearing, forming into single file, six to either side of the lifeboat, forming a guard of honour as if they had been cavalry on display in a London park, to escort the sacerdotes magni safely into the island harbour. Afterwards Jeremiah was to learn that lifeboats could sink and had done so, yet he says that even had he known through the wildest heart of that voyage it would have made no difference. Stunned, but salted, by the sea he arose a new man.

The parish church was a plain granite cross high on a windy, shelterless hilltop. It grew up from the rock it was cut from. No gale nor half-gale, nor the gates of hell, could prevail against it.

To west and south-west the land sank, then swept up dizzily again to a high bare horizon and, beyond that there could be nothing but monstrous seacliffs and the ocean. To east and north-east small patchwork fields, bright green, dark green, golden, netted by greystone walls, dotted by white and golden cabins all newly limewashed and thatched for the coming of the great priests, sloped down to a sea in the lee of the island and incredibly calm. The half-gale was still strong. But the island was steady underfoot. Far away the mainland, now a bit here, now a bit there, showed itself, glistening, out of the wandering squalls.

—Rock of ages cleft for me, he hummed with a reckless merriment that would have frightened him if he had stopped to reason about it, let me hide myself in thee. He was safe in the arms of Jesus, he was deep in the heart of Texas. The granite cruciform church was his shelter from the gale, providing him, by the protection of its apse and right arm, with a sunny corner to hide in and smoke in. He was still giddy from the swing of the sea. He was also, being, alas, human and subject to frailty, tempted to rejoice at the downfall and humiliation of another. He hath put down the mighty, he began to chant but stopped to consider that as yet there was little sign of the lowly being exalted.

This corner of the cross was quiet. One narrow yellow grained door was securely shut. All the bustle, all the traffic was out around the front porch: white-jacketed white-jerseyed islanders sitting on stone walls, women in coloured shawls crowding and pushing, children hymn-singing in English, Irish, and Latin, real Tower of Babel stuff, the cameraman photographing groups of people, and photographing the bishops from a safe distance, and the church from every angle short of the one the angels saw it from. He was no longer a great clumsy canary. He was splendid in his most expensive tweeds. He was, nevertheless, a cowed and broken man.

For back at the harbour, at the moment of disembarkation, it had happened again.

The two bishops, divested of oilskins, tall and black but not stately, are clambering up a ladder on to the high slippy quay-side, and they are anything but acrobatic. Jeremiah, a few yards away, is struggling to tear from his body his sodden greatcoat, to hang it to dry under the direction of an island-man, in the lee of a boathouse where nets are laid to dry. The cameraman has jocosely snapped him. Then he directs the camera on the clambering bishops only to be vetoed by a voice, iron and Irish and clanging.

—Put away that camera, the Irish voice says, until the opportune time.

—Why Peter, says the American voice, that would make a fun picture.

—In Ireland we don't want or need fun pictures of the hierarchy. We're not clowns.

It is arguable, Jeremiah thinks. He recalls that archbishops, on their own territory and when in full regimentals, are entitled to wear red boots. But he keeps his back turned on the passing parade in sudden terror that his eyes might reveal his thoughts. He hears the cameraman say: Your Grace, there is on the island the oldest inhabitant, a nonagenarian. I'd like to . . .

But there is no response. The procession has passed on. Fickle, Jeremiah knows, is the favour of princes, particularly when, like the Grand Turk, they are related to you. But whatever or how grievous the cause of offence had been that led to these repeated snubs, Jeremiah feels for the first time, burning through empty belly and meagre body, the corps-spirit of the pressman. Who in hell, anyway, is a bishop that he won't stand and pose like any other mortal man? All men are subject to the camera. Face up to it, grin, watch the little birdie. Only murderers are allowed to creep past, faces covered. If he won't be photographed, then to hell with him. He will be scantily written about, even if he is Twenty Times His Grace. And to hell also with all American bishops and Rumanian Reds, and with all colour stories of confirmations and of simple island people who, more than likely, spend the long winter nights making love to their own domestic animals which, as far as Jeremiah is concerned, they have a perfect right to do.

So here in the corner of the granite cross he had found peace. He didn't need to see the nonsense going on out there. When the time came to type, as no doubt it would, the Holy Ghost would guide his fingertips. The moment on the quay-side mingled with the moment in the shelter of the church and he realized, for the first time since anger had possessed him, that he had left his greatcoat still drying with the nets. He had been distracted by a call to coffee and sandwiches intended to keep them from collapsing until the show was over. But to hell, too, he decided with all greatcoats; a man could stand on his own legs. He smoked, and was content, and heard far away the voices of children, angels singing. Then the narrow, yellow, grained door opened, a great venerable head, a portion of surpliced body, appeared, a voice louder than the choirs of angels said: Come here, pressman.

Jeremiah went there.

—On the alert I'm glad to see, His Grace said. Waiting to see me. What can I do for you?

Jeremiah, to begin with, bent one knee and kissed his ring. That little bit of ballet enabled him to avoid saying whether he had or had not been on the alert, waiting for an interview.

—You must be starved, His Grace said. That was a rough journey.

They were in the outer room of the sacristy. The walls were mostly presses all painted the same pale yellow, with graining, as the narrow door. In an inner room the American bishop, head bowed, was talking to two tiny nuns. From one of the presses His Grace took a bottle and a half-pint tumbler and half-filled the tumbler with Jameson neat.

—Throw that back, he ordered. 'Twill keep the wind out of your stomach.

He watched benevolently while Jeremiah gasped and drank. The whiskey struck like a hammer. How was His Grace to know that Jeremiah's stomach had in it nothing at all, but wind? Jeremiah's head spun. This, he now knew, was what people meant when they talked about the bishop's bottle. His Grace restored bottle and glass to the press.

—We mustn't, he said, shock the good sisters.

He handed Jeremiah a sheaf of typescript. He said: It's all there. Names. History. Local lore. All the blah-blah, as you fellows say. Here, have a cigar. It belongs to our American Mightyship. They never travel without them. God bless you now. Is there anything else I can do for you?

Jeremiah's head had ceased to spin. His eyes had misted for a while with the warmth of the malt on an empty stomach, but now the mist cleared and he could see, he felt, to a great distance. The malt, too, had set the island rocking but with a gentle soothing motion.

—There's a man here, he said, the oldest inhabitant, a nonagenarian. The cameraman who's with me would like a picture.

—No sooner said than done, oh gentleman of the press. That should make a most edifying picture. I'll call himself away from the nuns. We'll just have time before the ceremony.

But, for reasons never known to me or Jeremiah, he laughed all the time as he led the way around the right arm of the cross to the front of the church; and brought with him another cigar for the cameraman, and shook hands with him, and offered him his ring to be kissed.

Apart from Jeremiah and the cameraman and the island doctor it was a clerical dinner, the island parish priest as host, a dozen well-conditioned men sitting down to good food, and wines that had crossed from Spain on the trawlers without paying a penny to the revenue.

—One of the best men in the business, said His Grace, although he'd sell us all body and soul to the *News of the World*.

He was talking about the cameraman, and at table, and in his presence. But he was laughing, and inciting the gathering to laughter. Whatever cloud there had been between the relatives had blown away with the storm, or with Jeremiah's diplomacy. So Jeremiah felt like Tallyrand. He was more than a little drunk. He was confirmed and made strong by the sea and the bishop's whiskey. He was hungry as hell.

—And Spanish ale, he muttered, shall give you hope, my dark Rosaleen.

His mutter was overheard, relayed around the table, and accepted as unquestionable wit. He was triumphant. He ate. He fell to, like a savage. He drank, he said afterwards— although we suspected that he had conned the names from a wine merchant's list, red and white Poblet, and red Rioja, and red Valdapenas, and another wine that came from the plain to the west of Tarragona where the Cistercians had a monastery: the lot washed down with Fundadór brandy which the American bishop told him had been the brandy specially set aside for the Conclave of Pope John the Twenty-third.

—Thou art Peter, said Jeremiah, and upon this rock.

Once again the remark was relayed around the table. Awash

on the smuggled products of Spain, Jeremiah was in grave danger of becoming the life and soul of the party.

A boy-child had that day been born on the island. The American bishop had asked the parents could he baptize the child and name it after himself.

—Episcopus Americanus O'Flaherty, said Jeremiah.

Pope John's Fundadór circled the board. The merriment knew no bounds. His Grace told how the great traveller, O'Donovan, had dwelt among the Turkomans of ancient Merv, whom he finally grew to detest because they wouldn't let him go home, but who liked him so much they called all their male children after him: O'Donovan Beg, O'Donovan Khan, O'Donovan Bahadur, and so on.

—It was the custom in ancient Merv, said His Grace, to call the newborn babes after any distinguished visitor who happened to be in the oasis at the time.

—It was not the custom in Rumania, said Jeremiah.

Renewed merriment. When the uproar died down, the American bishop, with tears in his eyes, said: But this is God's Own Country. Ye are God's Own People.

Jeremiah got drunk, but nobody minded. Later, outside a bar close by the harbour, he was photographed feeding whiskey out of a basin to a horse. The horse was delighted. The picture appeared in a London magazine, side-by-side with a picture of the nonagenarian flanked by bishops.

—You got him to pose, said the cameraman, when he rusted on me.

He meant, not the horse, but the bishop.

—Jer, he said, you'll make a newsman yet.

So, as Jer, a new man, eater of meat and vegetables, acknowledged gentleman of the press, he came back from the Isle of the Blest, sitting on the hatch above the bishops, feet on the gunwale chain. He was not beyond hoping that the swing of the sea and the tilt of the boat might salt his feet. It didn't. The easy evening sway would have lulled a child in the cradle.

—Episcopus Americanus O'Flaherty, he said to the lifeboatman who sat beside him and who had enough Latin to clerk Mass.

—True for you, said the lifeboatman. Small good that chris-
tening will do the poor boy. As long as he lives on that island
he'll never be known as anything but An Teasbog Beag—the
Little Bishop. If he goes to the States itself, the name could
follow him there. His sons and even his daughters will be
known as the Little Bishops. Or his eldest son may be called
Mac an Easboig, the Son of the Bishop. They'll lose O'Flaherty
and be called Macanespie. That's how names were invented
since the time of King Brian Boru who bate the Danes.

Behind them the island stepped away into the mist: the
wanderer, crazed for Hy-Breasil, would never find it. The rain
would slant for ever on rocks and small fields, on ancient forts
and cliffs with seabirds crying around them, on currachs riding
the waves as the gulls do. Visitors would be enthralled by
ancient ways, and basking sharks captured. But as long as
winds rage and tides run, that male child, growing up to be a
lean tanned young man in white jacket and soft pampooties,
leaning into the wind as he walks as his forebears have always
done, courteous as a prince but also ready to fight at the drop
of a half-glass of whiskey, sailing with the trawlers as far away
as the Faroes, will continue, because of this day, to be known
as the Little Bishop.

In the foxhole underneath Jeremiah, the American bishop
was telling the Irish bishop and the cameraman that in the
neighbourhood of the Okeefenokee Swamp, out of which the
Suwannee River drags its corpse, and generally in the state of
Georgia, there were many Southern Baptists with Irish Catholic names.

The water in the land-locked harbour was deadly still, and
deep purple in the dusk. Sleepy gulls foraged on the edge of the
tide, or called from inland over the small fields. Jer's greatcoat
was still on the island, dry by now, and stiff with salt. He never
wanted to see it again.

Shadowy people gathered on the harbour wall. The choir
sang: Sweet Sacrament Divine, dear home of every heart.

—Ye are God's own people, said the American bishop. This
is God's own country.

—Fuck, said the cameraman and in a painfully audible voice.

BERNARD MALAMUD

The Silver Crown

G ANS, the father, lay dying in a hospital bed. Different
doctors said different things, held different theories.
There was talk of an exploratory operation but they thought
it might kill him. One doctor said cancer.

'Of the heart,' the old man said bitterly.

'It wouldn't be impossible.'

The young Gans, Albert, a high school biology teacher, in
the afternoons walked the streets in sorrow. What can anybody
do about cancer? His soles wore thin with walking. He was
easily irritated; angered by the war, atom bomb, pollution,
death, obviously the strain of worrying about his father's illness. To be able to do nothing for him made him frantic. He
had done nothing for him all his life.

A female colleague, an English teacher he had slept with
once, a girl who was visibly aging, advised, 'If the doctors
don't know, Albert, try a faith healer. Different people know
different things; nobody knows everything. You can't tell
about the human body.'

Albert laughed mirthlessly but listened. If specialists disagree
who do you agree with? If you've tried everything what else
can you try?

One afternoon after a long walk alone, as he was about to
descend the subway stairs somewhere in the Bronx, still burdened by his worries, uneasy that nothing had changed, he
was accosted by a fat girl with bare meaty arms who thrust a
soiled card at him that he tried to avoid. She was a stupefying
sight, retarded at the very least. Fifteen, he'd say, though she
looks thirty and probably has the mentality of age ten. Her
skin glowed, face wet, fleshy, the small mouth open and would
be forever; eyes set wide apart on the broad unfocused face,
either washed-out green or brown, or one of each—he wasn't
sure. She seemed not to mind his appraisal, gurgled faintly.

Her thick hair was braided in two ropelike strands; she wore
bulging cloth slippers, bursting at seams and soles; a faded red
skirt down to massive ankles; and a heavy brown sweater vest,
buttoned over blown breasts, though the weather was still hot
September.

The teacher's impulse was to pass by her outthrust plump
baby hand. Instead he took the card from her. Simple curiosity
—once you had learned to read you read anything? Charitable impulse?

Albert recognized Yiddish and Hebrew but read in English:
'Heal The Sick. Save The Dying. Make A Silver Crown.'

'What kind of silver crown would that be?'

She uttered impossible noises. Depressed, he looked away.
When his eyes turned to hers she ran off.

He studied the card. 'Make A Silver Crown.' It gave a
rabbi's name and address no less: Jonas Lifschitz, close by in
the neighborhood. The silver crown mystified him. He had
no idea what it had to do with saving the dying but felt he
ought to know. Although at first repelled by the thought, he
made up his mind to visit the rabbi and felt, in a way, relieved.

The teacher hastened along the street a few blocks until he
came to the address on the card, a battered synagogue in a
store, Congregation Theodor Herzl, painted in large uneven
white letters on the plate-glass window. The rabbi's name, in
smaller, gold letters, was A. Marcus. In the doorway to the
left of the store the number of the house was repeated in tin
numerals, and on a card under the vacant name plate under
the mezuzah, appeared in pencil, 'Rabbi J. Lifschitz. Retired.
Consultations. Ring The Bell.' The bell, when he decided to
chance it, did not work—seemed dead to the touch—so Albert,
his heartbeat erratic, turned the knob. The door gave easily
enough and he hesitantly walked up a dark flight of narrow
wooden stairs. Ascending, assailed by doubts, peering up
through the gloom, he thought of turning back but at the
first-floor landing compelled himself to knock loudly on the
door.

'Anybody home here?'

He rapped harder, annoyed with himself for being there,

engaging in the act of entrance—who would have predicted it an hour ago? The door opened a crack and that broad, badly formed face appeared. The retarded girl, squinting one bulbous eye, made noises like two eggs frying, and ducked back, slamming the door. The teacher, after momentary reflection, thrust it open in time to see her, bulky as she was, running swiftly along the long tight corridor, her body bumping the walls before she disappeared into a room at the rear.

Albert entered cautiously, with a sense of embarrassment, if not danger, warning himself to depart at once; yet stayed to peek curiously into a front room off the hallway, darkened by lowered green shades through which thread-like rivulets of light streamed. The shades resembled faded maps of ancient lands. An old gray-bearded man with thickened left eyelid, wearing a yarmulke, sat heavily asleep, a book in his lap, on a sagging armchair. Someone in the room gave off a stale odor, unless it was the armchair. As Albert stared, the old man awoke in a hurry. The small thick book on his lap fell with a thump to the floor, but instead of picking it up, he shoved it with a kick of his heel under the chair.

'So where were we?' he inquired pleasantly, a bit breathless.

The teacher removed his hat, remembered whose house he was in, and put it back on his head.

He introduced himself. 'I was looking for Rabbi J. Lifschitz. Your—ah—girl let me in.'

'Rabbi Lifschitz; this was my daughter Rifkele. She's not perfect, though God who made her in His image is Himself perfection. What this means I don't have to tell you.'

His heavy eyelid went down in a wink, apparently involuntarily.

'What does it mean?' Albert asked.

'In her way she is also perfect.'

'Anyway she let me in and here I am.'

'So what did you decide?'

'Concerning what if I may ask?'

'What did you decide about what we were talking about—the silver crown?'

His eyes roved as he spoke; he rubbed a nervous thumb and

forefinger. Crafty type, the teacher decided. Him I have to watch myself with.

'I came here to find out about this crown you advertised,' he said, 'but actually we haven't talked about it or anything else. When I entered here you were sound asleep.'

'At my age—' the rabbi explained with a little laugh.

'I don't mean any criticism. All I'm saying is I am a stranger to you.'

'How can we be strangers if we both believe in God.'

Albert made no argument of it.

The rabbi raised the two shades and the last of daylight fell into the spacious high-ceilinged room, crowded with at least a dozen stiff-back and folding chairs, plus a broken sofa. What kind of operation is he running here? Group consultations? He dispensed rabbinic therapy? The teacher felt renewed distaste for himself for having come. On the wall hung a single oval mirror, framed in gold-plated groupings of joined metal circles, large and small; but no pictures. Despite the empty chairs, or perhaps because of them, the room seemed barren.

The teacher observed that the rabbi's trousers were a week from ragged. He was wearing an unpressed worn black suit-coat and a yellowed white shirt without a tie. His wet grayish-blue eyes were restless. Rabbi Lifschitz was a dark-faced man with brown eye pouches and smelled of old age. This was the odor. It was hard to say whether he resembled his daughter; Rifkele resembled her species.

'So sit,' said the old rabbi with a light sigh. 'Not on the couch, sit on a chair.'

'Which in particular?'

'You have a first-class humour.' Smiling absently he pointed to two kitchen chairs and seated himself in one.

He offered a thin cigarette.

'I'm off them,' the teacher explained.

'I also.' The old man put the pack away. 'So who is sick?' he inquired.

Albert tightened at the question as he recalled the card he had taken from the girl: 'Heal The Sick, Save The Dying.'

'To come to the point, my father's in the hospital with a serious ailment. In fact he's dying.'

The rabbi, nodding gravely, dug into his pants pocket for a pair of glasses, wiped them with a large soiled handkerchief and put them on, lifting the wire earpieces over each fleshy ear.

'So we will make then a crown for him?'

'That depends. The crown is what I came here to find out about.'

'What do you wish to find out?'

'I'll be frank with you.' The teacher blew his nose and slowly wiped it. 'My cast of mind is naturally empiric and objective—you might say non-mystical. I'm suspicious of faith healing but I've come here, frankly, because I want to do anything possible to help my father recover his former health. To put it otherwise, I don't want anything to go untried.'

'You love your father?' the rabbi clucked, a glaze of sentiment veiling his eyes.

'What I feel is obvious. My real concern right now mainly is how does the crown work. Could you be explicit about the mechanism of it all? Who wears it, for instance? Does he? Do you? Or do I have to? In other words, how does it function? And if you wouldn't mind saying, what's the principle, or rationale, behind it? This is terra incognita for me, but I think I might be willing to take a chance if I could justify it to myself. Could I see a sample of the crown, for instance, if you have one on hand?'

The rabbi, with an absent-minded start, seemed to interrupt himself about to pick his nose.

'What is the crown?' he asked, at first haughtily, then again, gently. 'It's a crown, nothing else. There are crowns in Mishna, Proverbs, Kabbalah; the holy scrolls of the Torah are often protected by crowns. But this one is different, this you will understand when it does the work. It's a miracle. A sample doesn't exist. The crown has to be made individual for your father. Then his health will be restored. There are two prices——'

'Kindly explain what's supposed to cure the sickness,' Albert said. 'Does it work like sympathetic magic? I'm not nay-saying, you understand. I just happen to be interested in all kinds of phenomena. Is the crown supposed to draw off the illness like some kind of poultice, or what?'

'The crown is not a medicine, it is the health of your father. We offer the crown to God and God returns to your father his health. But first we got to make it the way it must be made—this I will do with my assistant, a retired jeweler. He has helped me to make a thousand crowns. Believe me, he knows silver—the right amount to the ounce according to the size you wish. Then I will say the blessings. Without the right blessings, exact to each word, the crown don't work. I don't have to tell you why. When the crown is finished your father will get better. This I will guarantee you. Let me read you some words from the mystic book.'

'The Kabbalah?' the teacher asked respectfully.

'Like the Kabbalah.'

The rabbi rose, went to his armchair, got slowly down on his hands and knees and withdrew the book he had shoved under the misshapen chair, a thick small volume with faded purple covers, not a word imprinted on it. The rabbi kissed the book and murmured a prayer.

'I hid it for a minute,' he explained, 'when you came in the room. It's a terrible thing nowadays, goyim come in your house in the middle of the day and take away that which belongs to you, if not your life itself.'

'I told you right away that your daughter had let me in,' Albert said in embarrassment.

'Once you mentioned I knew.'

The teacher then asked, 'Suppose I am a non-believer? Will the crown work if it's ordered by a person who has his doubts?'

'Doubts we all got. We doubt God and God doubts us. This is natural on account of the nature of existence. Of this kind doubts I am not afraid so long as you love your father.'

'You're putting it as sort of a paradox.'

'So what's so bad about a paradox?'

'My father wasn't the easiest man in the world to get along with, and neither am I for that matter, but he has been generous to me and I'd like to repay him in some way.'

'God respects a grateful son. If you love your father this will go in the crown and help him to recover his health. Do you understand Hebrew?'

'Unfortunately not.'

The rabbi flipped a few pages of his thick tome, peered at one closely and read aloud in Hebrew which he then translated into English. ' "The crown is the fruit of God's grace. His grace is love of creation." These words I will read seven times over the silver crown. This is the most important blessing.'

'Fine. But what about those two prices you mentioned a minute ago?'

'This depends how quick you wish the cure.'

'I want the cure to be immediate, otherwise there's no sense to the whole deal,' Albert said, controlling anger. 'If you're questioning my sincerity, I've already told you I'm considering this recourse even though it goes against the grain of some of my strongest convictions. I've gone out of my way to make my pros and cons absolutely clear.'

'Who says no?'

The teacher became aware of Rifkele standing at the door, eating a slice of bread with lumps of butter on it. She beheld him in mild stupefaction, as though seeing him for the first time.

'Shpeter, Rifkele,' the rabbi said patiently.

The girl shoved the bread into her mouth and ran ponderously down the passageway.

'Anyway, what about those two prices?' Albert asked, annoyed by the interruption. Every time Rifkele appeared his doubts of the enterprise rose before him like warriors with spears.

'We got two kinds crowns,' said the rabbi. 'One is for 401 and the other is 986.'

'Dollars, you mean, for God's sake?—that's fantastic.'

'The crown is pure silver. The client pays in silver dollars. So the silver dollars we melt—more for the large-size crown, less for the medium.'

'What about the small?'

'There is no small. What good is a small crown?'

'I wouldn't know, but the assumption seems to be the bigger

the better. Tell me, please, what can a 986 crown do that a 401 can't? Does the patient get better faster with the larger one? It hastens the reaction?'

The rabbi, five fingers hidden in his limp beard, assented.

'Are there any other costs?'

'Costs?'

'Over and above the quoted prices?'

'The price is the price, there is no extra. The price is for the silver and for the work and for the blessings.'

'Now would you kindly tell me, assuming I decide to get involved in this, where am I supposed to lay my hands on 401 silver dollars? Or if I should opt for the 986 job, where can I get a .pile of cartwheels of that amount? I don't suppose that any bank in the whole Bronx would keep that many silver dollars on hand nowadays. The Bronx is no longer the Wild West, Rabbi Lifschitz. But what's more to the point, isn't it true the mint isn't making silver dollars all silver any more?'

'So if they are not making we will get wholesale. If you will leave with me the cash I will order the silver from a wholesaler, and we will save you the trouble to go to the bank. It will be the same amount of silver, only in small bars, I will weigh them on a scale in front of your eyes.'

'One other question. Would you take my personal check in payment? I could give it to you right away once I've made my final decision.'

'I wish I could, Mr. Gans,' said the rabbi, his veined hand still nervously exploring his beard, 'but it's better cash when the patient is so sick, so I can start to work right away. A check sometimes comes back, or gets lost in the bank, and this interferes with the crown.'

Albert did not ask how, suspecting that a bounced check, or a lost one, wasn't the problem. No doubt some customers for crowns had stopped their checks on afterthought.

As the teacher reflected concerning his next move—should he, shouldn't he?—weighing a rational thought against a sentimental, the old rabbi sat in his chair, reading quickly in his small mystic book, his lips hastening along silently.

Albert at last got up.

'I'll decide the question once and for all tonight. If I go ahead and commit myself on the crown I'll bring you the cash after work tomorrow.'

'Go in good health,' said the rabbi. Removing his glasses he wiped both eyes with his handkerchief.

Wet or dry? thought the teacher.

As he let himself out of the downstairs door, more inclined than not toward trying the crown, he felt relieved, almost euphoric.

But by the next morning, after a difficult night, Albert's mood had about-faced. He fought gloom, irritation, felt flashes of hot and cold anger. It's throwing money away, pure and simple. I'm dealing with a clever confidence man, that's plain to me, but for some reason I am not resisting strongly. Maybe my subconscious is telling me to go along with a blowing wind and have the crown made. After that we'll see what happens— whether it rains, snows, or spring comes. Not much will happen, I suppose, but whatever does, my conscience will be in the clear.

But when he visited Rabbi Lifschitz that afternoon in the same roomful of empty chairs, though the teacher carried the required cash in his wallet, he was still uncomfortable about parting with it.

'Where do the crowns go after they are used and the patient recovers his health?' he cleverly asked the rabbi.

'I'm glad you asked me this question,' said the rabbi alertly, his thick lid drooping. 'They are melted and the silver we give to the poor. A mitzvah for one makes a mitzvah for another.'

'To the poor you say?'

'There are plenty poor people, Mr. Gans. Sometimes they need a crown for a sick wife or a sick child. Where will they get the silver?'

'I see what you mean—recycled, sort of, but can't a crown be re-used as it is? I mean do you permit a period of time to go by before you melt them down? Suppose a dying man who recovers gets seriously ill again at a future date?'

'For a new sickness you will need a new crown. Tomorrow the world is not the same as today, though God listens with the same ear.'

'Look, Rabbi Lifschitz,' Albert said impatiently, 'I'll tell you frankly that I am inching toward ordering the crown, but it would make my decision a whole lot easier all around if you would let me have a quick look at one of them—it wouldn't have to be for more than five seconds—at a crown-in-progress for some other client.'

'What will you see in five seconds?'

'Enough—whether the object is believable, worth the fuss and not inconsequential investment.'

'Mr. Gans,' replied the rabbi, 'this is not a showcase business. You are not buying from me a new Chevrolet automobile. Your father lays now dying in the hospital. Do you love him? Do you wish me to make a crown that will cure him?'

The teacher's anger flared. 'Don't be stupid, rabbi, I've answered that. Please don't sidetrack the real issue. You're working on my guilt so I'll suspend my perfectly reasonable doubts of the whole freaking business. I won't fall for that.'

They glared at each other. The rabbi's beard quivered. Albert ground his teeth.

Rifkele, in a nearby room, moaned.

The rabbi, breathing emotionally, after a moment relented.

'I will show you the crown,' he sighed.

'Accept my apologies for losing my temper.'

The rabbi accepted. 'Now tell me please what kind of sickness your father has got.'

'Ah,' said Albert, 'nobody is certain for sure. One day he got into bed, turned to the wall and said, "I'm sick." They suspected leukemia at first but the lab tests didn't confirm it.'

'You talked to the doctors?'

'In droves. Till I was blue in the face. A bunch of ignoramuses,' said the teacher hoarsely. 'Anyway, nobody knows exactly what he has wrong with him. The theories include rare blood diseases, also a possible carcinoma of certain endocrine glands. You name it, I've heard it, with complications suggested, like Parkinson's or Addison's disease, multiple sclerosis, or something similar, alone or in combination with other sicknesses. It's a mysterious case, all in all.'

'This means you will need a special crown,' said the rabbi.

The teacher bridled. 'What do you mean special? What will it cost?'

'The cost will be the same,' the rabbi answered dryly, 'but the design and the kind of blessings will be different. When you are dealing with such a mystery you got to make another one but it must be bigger.'

'How would that work?'

'Like two winds that they meet in the sky. A white and a blue. The blue says, "Not only I am blue but inside I am also purple and orange." So the white goes away.'

'If you can work it up for the same price, that's up to you.'

Rabbi Lifschitz then drew down the two green window shades and shut the door, darkening the room.

'Sit,' he said in the heavy dark, 'I will show you the crown.'

'I'm sitting.'

'So sit where you are, but turn your head to the wall where is the mirror.'

'But why so dark?'

'You will see light.'

He heard the rabbi strike a match and it flared momentarily, casting shadows of candles and chairs amid the empty chairs in the room.

'Look now in the mirror.'

'I'm looking.'

'What do you see?'

'Nothing.'

'Look with your eyes.'

A silver candelabrum, first with three, then five, then seven burning bony candlesticks appeared like ghostly hands with flaming fingertips in the oval mirror. The heat of it hit Albert in the face and for a moment he was stunned.

But recalling the games of his childhood, he thought, who's kidding who? It's one of those illusion things I remember from when I was a kid. In that case I'm getting the hell out of here. I can stand maybe mystery but not magic tricks or dealing with a rabbinical magician.

The candelabrum had vanished, although not its light, and

he now saw the rabbi's somber face in the glass, his gaze addressing him. Albert glanced quickly around to see if anyone was standing at his shoulder, but nobody was. Where the rabbi was hiding at the moment the teacher did not know; but in the lit glass appeared his old man's lined and shrunken face, his sad eyes, compelling, inquisitive, weary, perhaps even frightened, as though they had seen more than they had cared to but were still looking.

What's this, slides or home movies? Albert sought some source of projection but saw no ray of light from wall or ceiling, nor object or image that might be reflected by the mirror.

The rabbi's eyes glowed like sun-filled clouds. A moon rose in the blue sky. The teacher dared not move, afraid to discover he was unable to. He then beheld a shining crown on the rabbi's head.

It had appeared at first like a braided mother-of-pearl turban, then had luminously become—like an intricate star in the night sky—a silver crown, constructed of bars, triangles, half-moons, and crescents, spires, turrets, trees, points of spears; as though a wild storm had swept them up from the earth and flung them together in its vortex, twisted into a single glowing interlocked sculpture, a forest of disparate objects.

The sight in the ghostly mirror, a crown of rare beauty— very impressive, Albert thought—lasted no longer than five short seconds, then the reflecting glass by degrees turned dark and empty.

The shades were up. The single bulb in a frosted lily fixture on the ceiling shone harshly in the room. It was night.

The old rabbi sat, exhausted, on the broken sofa.

'So you saw it?'

'I saw something.'

'You believe what you saw—the crown?'

'I believe I saw. Anyway, I'll take it.'

The rabbi gazed at him blankly.

'I mean I agree to have the crown made,' Albert said, having to clear his throat.

'Which size?'

'Which size was the one I saw?'

'Both sizes. This is the same design for both sizes, but there is more silver and also more blessings for the $986 size.'

'But didn't you say that the design for my father's crown, because of the special nature of his illness, would have a different style, plus some special blessings?'

The rabbi nodded. 'This comes also in two sizes—the $401 and $986.'

The teacher hesitated a split second. 'Make it the big one,' he said decisively.

He had his wallet in his hand and counted out fifteen new bills—nine one hundreds, four twenties, a five and a single—adding to $986.

Putting on his glasses, the rabbi hastily counted the money, snapping with thumb and forefinger each crisp bill as though to be sure none had stuck together. He folded the stiff paper and thrust the wad into his pants pocket.

'Could I have a receipt?'

'I would like to give you a receipt,' said Rabbi Lifschitz earnestly, 'but for the crowns there are no receipts. Some things are not a business.'

'If money is exchanged, why not?'

'God will not allow. My father did not give receipts and also my grandfather.'

'How can I prove I paid you if something goes wrong?'

'You have my word, nothing will go wrong.'

'Yes, but suppose something unforeseen did,' Albert insisted, 'would you return the cash?'

'Here is your cash,' said the rabbi, handing the teacher the packet of folded bills.

'Never mind,' said Albert hastily. 'Could you tell me when the crown will be ready?'

'Tomorrow night before Shabbos, the latest.'

'So soon?'

'Your father is dying.'

'That's right, but the crown looks like a pretty intricate piece of work to put together out of all those odd pieces.'

'We will hurry.'

'I wouldn't want you to rush the job in any way that would

—let's say—prejudice the potency of the crown, or for that matter, in any way impair the quality of it as I saw it in the mirror—or however I saw it.'

Down came the rabbi's eyelid, quickly raised without a sign of self-consciousness.

'Mr. Gans, all my crowns are first-class jobs. About this you got nothing to worry about.'

They then shook hands. Albert, still assailed by doubts, stepped into the corridor. He felt he did not, in essence, trust the rabbi; and suspected that Rabbi Lifschitz knew it and did not, in essence, trust him.

Rifkele, panting like a cow for a bull, let him out the front door, perfectly.

In the subway, Albert figured he would call it an investment in experience and see what came of it. Education costs money but how else can you get it? He pictured the crown as he had seen it established on the rabbi's head, and then seemed to remember that as he had stared at the man's shifty face in the mirror the thickened lid of his right eye had slowly dropped into a full wink. Did he recall this in truth, or was he seeing in his mind's eye and transposing into the past something that had happened just before he left the house? What does he mean by his wink?—not only is he a fake but he kids you? Uneasy once more, the teacher clearly remembered, when he was staring into the rabbi's fish eyes in the glass, after which they had lit in visionary light, that he had fought a hunger to sleep; and the next thing there's the sight of the old boy, as though on the television screen, wearing this high-hat magic crown.

Albert, rising, cried, 'Hypnosis! The bastard magician hypnotized me! He never did produce a silver crown, it's out of my imagination—I've been suckered!'

He was outraged by the knavery, hypocrisy, fat nerve of Rabbi Jonas Lifschitz. The concept of a curative crown, if he had ever for a moment believed in it, crumbled in his brain and all he could think of were 986 blackbirds flying in the sky. As three curious passengers watched, Albert bolted out of the car at the next stop, rushed up the stairs, hurried across the street, then cooled his impatient heels for twenty-two minutes till the next train clattered into the station, and he rode back to the stop near the rabbi's house. Though he banged with both fists on the door, kicked at it, 'rang' the useless bell until his thumb was blistered, the boxlike wooden house, including dilapidated synagogue store, was dark, monumentally starkly still, like a gigantic, slightly tilted tombstone in a vast graveyard; and in the end unable to arouse a soul, the teacher, long past midnight, had to head home.

He awoke next morning cursing the rabbi and his own stupidity for having got involved with a faith healer. This is what happens when a man—even for a minute—surrenders his true beliefs. There are less punishing ways to help the dying. Albert considered calling the cops but had no receipt and did not want to appear that much a fool. He was tempted, for the first time in six years of teaching, to phone in sick; then take a cab to the rabbi's house and demand the return of his cash. The thought agitated him. On the other hand, suppose Rabbi Lifschitz was seriously at work assembling the crown with his helper; on which, let's say, after he had bought the silver and paid the retired jeweler for his work, he made, let's say, a hundred bucks clear profit—not so very much; and there really *was* a silver crown, and the rabbi sincerely and religiously believed it would reverse the course of his father's illness? Although nervously disturbed by his suspicions, Albert felt he had better not get the police into the act too soon because the crown wasn't promised—didn't the old gent say—until before the Sabbath, which gave him till sunset tonight.

If he produces the thing by then, I have no case against him even if it's a piece of junk. So I better wait. But what a dope I was to order the $986 job instead of the $401. On that decision alone I lost $585.

After a distracted day's work Albert taxied to the rabbi's house and tried to rouse him, even hallooing at the blank windows facing the street; but either nobody was home or they were both hiding, the rabbi under the broken sofa, Rifkele trying to shove her bulk under a bathtub. Albert decided to wait them out. Soon the old boy would have to leave the house to step into the shul on Friday night. He would speak to him, warn him to come clean. But the sun set; dusk settled on the earth; and though the autumn stars and a sliver of moon gleamed in the sky, the house was dark, shades drawn; and no Rabbi Lifschitz emerged. Lights had gone on in the little shul, candles were lit. It occurred to Albert, with chagrin, that the rabbi might be already worshipping; he might all this time have been in the synagogue.

The teacher entered the long, brightly lit store. On yellow folding chairs scattered around the room sat a dozen men holding worn prayer books, praying. The Rabbi A. Marcus, a middle-aged man with a high voice and a short reddish beard, was dovening at the Ark, his back to the congregation.

As Albert entered and embarrassedly searched from face to face, the congregants stared at him. The old rabbi was not among them. Disappointed, the teacher withdrew.

A man sitting by the door touched his sleeve.

'Stay awhile and read with us.'

'Excuse me, I'd like to but I'm looking for a friend.'

'Look,' said the man, 'maybe you'll find him.'

Albert waited across the street under a chestnut tree losing its leaves. He waited patiently—till tomorrow if he had to.

Shortly after nine the lights went out in the synagogue and the last of the worshippers left for home. The red-bearded rabbi then emerged with his key in his hand to lock the store door.

'Excuse me, rabbi,' said Albert, approaching. 'Are you acquainted with Rabbi Jonas Lifschitz, who lives upstairs with his daughter Rifkele—if she is his daughter?'

'He used to come here,' said the rabbi with a small smile, 'but since he retired he prefers a big synagogue on Mosholu Parkway, a palace.'

'Will he be home soon, do you think?'

'Maybe in an hour. It's Shabbat, he must walk.'

'Do you—ah—happen to know anything about his work on silver crowns?'

'What kind of silver crowns?'

'To assist the sick, the dying?'

'No,' said the rabbi, locking the shul door, pocketing the key, and hurrying away.

The teacher, eating his heart, waited under the chestnut tree till past midnight, all the while urging himself to give up and go home but unable to unstick the glue of his frustration and rage. Then shortly before 1 a.m. he saw some shadows moving and two people drifting up the shadow-encrusted street. One was the old rabbi, in a new caftan and snappy black Homburg, walking tiredly. Rifkele, in sexy yellow mini, exposing to above the big-bone knees her legs like poles, walked lightly behind him, stopping to strike her ears with her hands. A long white shawl, pulled short on the right shoulder, hung down to her left shoe.

'On my income their glad rags.'

Rifkele chanted a long 'boooo' and slapped both ears with her pudgy hands to keep from hearing it.

They toiled up the ill-lit narrow staircase, the teacher trailing them.

'I came to see my crown,' he told the pale, astonished rabbi, in the front room.

'The crown,' the rabbi said haughtily, 'is already finished. Go home and wait, your father will soon get better.'

'I called the hospital before leaving my apartment, there's been no improvement.'

'How can you expect so soon improvement if the doctors themselves don't know what is the sickness? You must give the crown a little more time. God Himself has trouble to understand human sickness.'

'I came to see the thing I paid for.'

'I showed you already, you saw before you ordered.'

'That was an image of a facsimile, maybe, or something of the sort. I insist on seeing the real thing, for which I paid close to one thousand smackers.'

'Listen, Mr. Gans,' said the rabbi patiently, 'there are some things we are allowed to see which He lets us see them. Sometimes I wish He didn't let us. There are other things we are not allowed to see—Moses knew this—and one is God's face, and another is the real crown that He makes and blesses it. A miracle is a miracle, this is God's business.'

'Don't you see it?'

'Not with my eyes.'

'I don't believe a word of it, you faker, two-bit magician.'

'The crown is a real crown. If you think there is magic, it is on account those people that they insist to see it—we try to give them an idea. For those who believe, there is no magic.'

'Rifkele,' the rabbi said hurriedly, 'bring to Papa my book of letters.'

She left the room, after a while, a little in fright, her eyes evasive; and returned in ten minutes, after flushing the toilet, in a shapeless long flannel nightgown, carrying a large yellowed notebook whose loose pages were thickly interleaved with old correspondence.

'Testimonials,' said the rabbi.

Turning several loose pages, with trembling hand he extracted a letter and read it aloud, his voice husky with emotion.

' "Dear Rabbi Lifschitz: Since the miraculous recovery of my mother, Mrs. Max Cohen, from her recent illness, my impulse is to cover your bare feet with kisses. Your crown worked wonders and I am recommending it to all my friends. Yours truly and sincerely, (Mrs.) Esther Polatnik." '

'This is a college teacher.'

He read another. ' "Dear Rabbi Lifschitz, Your $986 crown totally and completely cured my father of cancer of the pancreas, with serious complications of the lungs, after nothing else had worked. Never before have I believed in miraculous occurrences, but from now on I will have less doubts. My thanks to you and God. Most sincerely, Daniel Schwartz." '

'A lawyer,' said the rabbi.

He offered the book to Albert. 'Look yourself, Mr. Gans, hundreds of letters.'

Albert wouldn't touch it.

'There's only one thing I want to look at, Rabbi Lifschitz, and it's not a book of useless testimonials. I want to see my father's silver crown.'

'This is impossible. I already explained to you why I can't do this. God's word is God's law.'

'So if it's the law you're citing, either I see the crown in the next five minutes, or the first thing tomorrow morning I'm reporting you and your activities to the Bronx County District Attorney.'

'Booo-ooo,' sang Rifkele, banging her ears.

'Shut up!' Albert said.

'Have respect,' cried the rabbi. 'Grubber yung!'

'I will swear out a complaint and the D.A. will shut you down, the whole freaking plant, if you don't at once return the $986 you swindled me out of.'

The rabbi wavered in his tracks. 'Is this the way to talk to a rabbi of God?'

'A thief is a thief.'

Rifkele blubbered, squealed.

'Sha,' the rabbi thickly whispered to Albert, clasping and unclasping his gray hands. 'You'll frighten the neighbors. Listen to me, Mr. Gans, you saw with your eyes what it looks like the real crown. I give you my word that nobody of my whole clientele ever saw this before. I showed you for your father's sake so you would tell me to make the crown which will save him. Don't spoil now the miracle.'

'Miracle,' Albert bellowed, 'it's a freaking fake magic, with an idiot girl for a come-on and hypnotic mirrors. I was mesmerized, suckered by you.'

'Be kind,' begged the rabbi, tottering as he wandered amid empty chairs. 'Be merciful to an old man. Think of my poor child. Think of your father who loves you.'

'He hates me, the son-of-a-bitch, I hope he croaks.'

In an explosion of silence the girl slobbered in fright.

'Aha,' cried the wild-eyed rabbi, pointing a finger at God in heaven.

'Murderer,' he cried, aghast.

Moaning, father and daughter rushed into each other's arms, as Albert, wearing a massive, spike-laden headache, rushed down the booming stairs.

An hour later the elder Gans shut his eyes and expired.

OLIVIA MANNING

A Spot of Leave

A T FIVE O'CLOCK, when the afternoon was deepening into
violet-scented, spring twilight, Phillips and Aphrodite met
for tea at Larides'. This was the hour when the Alexandrine
Greeks drank coffee. Sometimes men dropping into the café
from offices and women pausing in their shopping, would
stand at the counter and eat with a silver, two-pronged fork,
a couple of cakes. The counter displayed immense chocolate
boxes tied with ribbons. The cakes were rich and elaborate:
sponge-cake, macaroon or feather-fine pastry laden with cream,
strawberries, chocolate, icing, nuts, preserved fruits, rich jams,
or chestnut paste. They were displayed behind glass.

'And the ladies,' thought Phillips in his captain's uniform,
his young face decorated with a cavalry moustche he would
have shrunk from wearing when a civilian clerk, 'the ladies
are like the cakes.'

They came and went in the shop, charming in their flowered
silks, their furs, their confectionery hats, their sheer silk stockings from the United States and their delicate shoes. Each
whose husband was of the necessary income-level wore like a
trophy on her ring finger a diamond of at least two carats. All
were completed with flowers and perfumes, as though a
fashionable wedding might be sprung on them at any moment.
Phillips, staring at them with his slightly bulging, stone-blue
eyes, nodded agreement with himself: 'Just like the cakes—
and I wouldn't mind a bite.'

'It is shocking, don't you think, such a display?' said
Aphrodite.

'Shocking?' Phillips turned to her and laughed. 'Far from
it.'

'But in Palestine you lack sugar.'

'Well, the civilians are a bit short.'

'Here they have too much, yet they refuse to export. In this window last week there was a wedding cake—eight cakes on top of one another, white with sugar. And in Palestine children are ill for need of it.'

'Too bad,' agreed Phillips, looking back into the shop's bustle and fluffing up his moustache with his hand as dark eyes glanced towards him. He had admired Aphrodite's English every time he had been at a loss for something to say, but his ear was more intrigued by the chirruping, inaccurate French of the ladies who moved among the bows on the chocolate-boxes like flowers among butterflies. The men were as elegant. Phillips noticed one—small, elderly, plump, exquisite in silver-grey with pointed shoes—who followed a shopgirl and supervised her packing of a satin-covered box. He moved like a bright insect through the garden of sweets and women, pausing his long, quivering, forefinger over the trays of fondants, darting it like a sting when he made his choice, then rejecting and choosing again, making, un-making and re-making his mind with agitation.

'Wonder who the old boy's buying those for!' said Phillips.

'For himself.'

'Surely not.'

'Yes.' Aphrodite gave a decided shake of her head. 'He is a relative of mine. He is very rich. He always buys himself a box when he makes money on the Bourse. Every day he makes more money except when it looks as though the war might end soon, then the Bourse is frightened.'

'Really!' After some reflection Phillips said: 'You have a lot of relatives.'

'Everyone has a lot of relatives,' said Aphrodite.

Beyond the giant window-bottles filled with crystallized fruits, violets and angelica, went a stream of people: smart Greeks, rich Egyptians, some wearing the fez, servants in galabiahs, French sailors with red pom-poms on their hats and every sort of English and Allied serviceman.

Some French officers, from the pale-grey battleships that had lain motionless in Alexandria harbour since the fall of France, sat at the near-by table. They drank coffee like the Greeks. They, thought Aphrodite, had become at home here because they had adapted themselves at once. The English tried to make a place adapt itself to them. Phillips, for instance, had settled into his basket-chair and without consulting her had at once ordered tea. He had got it just as he had wanted it—hot and strong with milk and sugar. Larides' had learnt to serve it that way the day the first Englishman explained his needs. The Wrens, A.T.S., and nurses, when they arrived, had proved more exacting, for they required the old tea to be emptied out of the pots and fresh tea put in for each customer —but, they, too, got what they wanted. They sat round the tables with the confident look of the girls she had seen in tea-shops when she went to stay with her husband's family at Littlehampton.

'You like the tea here?' she asked Phillips.

'Just the job,' he answered. 'Laid on as mother made it.'

'Your nurses,' said Aphrodite, watching the table opposite, 'they do not approve of us, do they? They have seen men dying and they think here are all these people who only make money out of the war.'

'They're jealous,' declared Phillips. 'They know you've got nice silk stockings and they've only got cotton ones. You have got nice silk stockings, haven't you?' he gazed humorously under the table. 'That's what we like to see when we get a spot of leave.'

'Don't women wear silk stockings in Jerusalem?'

'Well, yes, they do if they can get them—but I used to be up in the blue, you know. I can remember what a treat it was to see you girls nicely dressed. And it's still a treat. I'm glad your husband doesn't take too dim a shufti of me trotting you round a bit.'

'Why should he?' asked Aphrodite. 'He's an Englishman.'

'Even an Englishman can be jealous.'

'We are modern,' said Aphrodite, as though the suggestion of jealousy were an insult. She thought back to a few years before when, unmarried, she had the reputation of being the most 'modern' girl in Alexandria. Indeed, so 'modern' had her behaviour been that it had led to endless rows at home and her mother had said: 'You will never get a husband now.

There is not a Greek of good family who would have you.'
'Then I'll marry an Englishman,' she said, and she did.

'My parents did not like me to marry James. He was only a
clerk in the English bank—but I loved him. I love Englishmen.
They are so intelligent, such breadth of mind, so "modern"—
the Greeks are like Orientals. In England women are free.'

'Well, I suppose they are,' Phillips agreed without enthusiasm. 'But nice girls aren't too free.'

'My parents wanted me to marry a rich cotton-merchant.
An old man who was always drunk. A Copt, too! Think of it.
"You can reform him," my mother said, but I said: "Why
should I? If he wants to be drunk all the time, it is of no
interest to me." Then James was sent to work in Cairo and
they were glad. I said nothing. I pretended I had forgotten
him. Then one day I started to cry with a toothache. "What I
suffer," I said. "Oh, what I suffer!" They were alarmed and
said I must go to our dentist in Cairo. So I went and he made
an X-ray of my teeth and one had twisted roots. "Look,
mother," I said, "look at my insides—how terrible!" So they
agreed I should go to stay with my aunt in Cairo and have my
teeth mended. When I was two days in Cairo I got married to
James.'

'Good Lord!' commented Phillips. 'What did the pater say?'

'You mean my father? He said much, but in the end it is all
right. He is a banker. He used influence and James was
brought back here to a position.'

'O.K. for James, eh?'

'We are very happy.'

'Oh, are you!' Phillips showed a twinge of annoyance that
made Aphrodite smile.

She was reminded of the days before her happy marriage
when she had roused endless twinges of jealousy in the young
men of Alexandria. Now, after two years of contentment with
James, she felt afresh the glow of the chase. In a moment the
situation, which she had scarcely grasped before, fell into
position and she saw herself in control. Looking upon Phillips
as her natural victim, Aphrodite's eyes and colour grew
brighter and her whole manner eased into an indolent charm.

'Tell me about your home in England,' she said, as she pushed back her teacup and lit a cigarette.

'Oh!' Phillips was disconcerted for a moment, but he was not unprepared. Ever since he had got through the O.C.T.U. and his office experience had led him to a job in Pal Base, he had been readjusting his background.

Aphrodite, watching him as she listened to him, saw him quite newly as rather handsome in his youthful, blue-eyed fairness. His moustache hid his worse feature, his small, prim mouth. She began to build up from what was attractive in him, the elements of romance. She knew exactly how it should continue from here and she would let it continue. She listened with all the necessary smiling interest, the glow, the flattering absorption in him that was to be his undoing. When Phillips, looking up into her fixed dark glance, blushed slightly, she thought: 'He is sweet, and only a boy.'

'What is your mother like?' she asked, keeping him talking.

'Rather handsome, the mater. Dresses awfully well, but a bit severe with the poor old pater. Plays golf, too.' He added this last touch, which he had not thought of before, and the picture came into focus.

'Have you a photograph of her?' asked Aphrodite.

'Yes—at least, I mean, no. Not with me,' Phillips blushed again.

After a smiling pause Aphrodite said: 'Tonight my husband is going out for a business meeting. Come in and have a drink and keep me company.'

' 'Fraid I can't. I've got a date with another fellow on leave from my office.'

She looked surprised rather than hurt, but smiled: 'I hope you're not going to Maisie's House.'

He gave her a startled stare. There was a long silence before he suggested they should meet next day for tea.

'Of course,' said Aphrodite. 'And would you like to walk with me along the Corniche?'

'I don't mind,' Phillips's manner was neither eager nor indifferent. Aphrodite could interpret his manner as she wished.

When he had seen her to a taxi, he called one for himself and started back to his hotel by the sea. Settled into his corner, watching out at the brilliance of the street in that moment before darkness and the blackout fell, he contemplated his life now lived in expensive hotels, expensive restaurants, taking tea with the daughters of wealthy bankers, jumping into taxis . . . and he murmured to himself in the almost forgotten argot of the desert: 'Bit of all right, eh, chum?'

Aphrodite's flat in the Sharia Cherif Pasha was as English as its basic Frenchness permitted. Her father had also presented her with a small house at Stanley Bay, where she and James spent the summer. She had, she realized, all she could wish. James had the characteristics she most admired in the English. He was better-looking than Phillips, he was considerate yet met her on an equal footing and showed no resentment of her intelligence. She could not had she wished have found cause for discontent, yet now she felt she was missing an excitement she must find again.

When James came home to supper, she said: 'You know Phillips, the young officer?'

'What about him?'

'You wouldn't mind, would you, if I went to bed with him?'

James did not glance up from his soup as he said: 'I'm tired and I've got to go out to that damned meeting.'

'You wouldn't mind, would you?'

'Mind what?' asked James irritably.

'What I asked—if I slept with Phillips?'

'I don't know,' James kept his glance on his plate. 'I haven't thought about it.'

'But we thought about it a long time ago. We agreed we'd be modern.'

'Then why ask me? You know you can do what you like.'

Aphrodite sighed. She wanted to get these formalities over. Almost she wished now the whole business were over and Phillips safely back in Jerusalem. Yet she was determined to go through with it and in her determination she felt a little drunk, a little lifted above the realities of her everyday life. 'I don't want to deceive you,' she said. 'I want you to be happy about it.'

'All right,' said James. 'I'm happy. Now shut up.'

When he went out, Aphrodite moved restlessly about the flat. She remained in a state of restless inactivity next day until it was time to meet Phillips. James did not speak at breakfast or at luncheon. Phillips, she knew, had only three days more leave and the knowledge filled her with a sense of urgency so that she ached with nervous strain. She ordered the house from habit and she was conscious of James with a worried impatience that was painful to her. What she felt for him was, she knew, intact, but it must remain at a standstill while she lived through this interlude that would prove to her that she was missing nothing.

After luncheon she left the house before James. 'I may not be back for dinner,' she said. He did not reply.

She met Phillips in a café near the old harbour. It was a brilliant spring day and the sea had in it the first green and purple that would deepen with summer. On the other side of the circular harbour was the castle. It stood, on the site of the ancient Pharos, cleanly edged against the sea's colour as though blown bone-white by the wind. The water within the harbour arms sprang up and down.

As they followed the Corniche road with the wind in their faces, Phillips said: 'I've been thinking of having a couple of days in Cairo.'

'You mean, after your leave?'

'No, I'd have to go tomorrow.'

'Alone?' asked Aphrodite.

'Well, the chap from my office is going. I thought of going with him.'

Aphrodite, silent, stared ahead.

'But I don't think I'll go. I like it here.'

'Ah!' Aphrodite smiled. 'Perhaps you do not want to leave me?'

Phillips cleared his throat as though he were doing a comic turn and gave her a coy glance: 'That's about it,' he said.

Conversation became easier after that. On one side of them the concrete houses and blocks of flats stretched far out of sight into the desert. On the other side splashed the mildly choppy sea, its border of rock yellow and porous like rotting cheese.

'It reminds me of Worthing,' said Phillips. 'The only thing is we don't have date palms.'

'I know. I've been to Littlehampton.'

'Good Lord, have you?' and they talked about England and English seaside towns. Aphrodite was gaily critical, while Phillips was nostalgically respectful. They passed Stanley Bay with its closed bathing huts and air of popular entertainment shut up for the winter. The houses still stretched on. In the distance, too far away to be reached, appeared among palms a white-domed palace, the only Oriental thing in sight. They came at last to a thin shelf of rock through which the ancients had cut holes. On a gusty day like this the sea came spouting through them.

'There!' said Aphrodite. 'Isn't that interesting? In the old days people used to fix musical instruments in the holes so the sea could play tunes.'

'Why on earth did they do that?'

'For amusement.'

'Rum idea.'

'But isn't it interesting? I brought you to see it.'

'Did you? Hell of a length this Corniche—as you call it. Better go back now,' and he swung round without waiting for her agreement. Now the wind was behind them, blowing their hair forward. Right at the other end of the great curve of the shore, the main part of the town, growing steely blue as the light failed, was neatly built-up on a bulge of land. A few barrage-balloons were beginning to rise like silver kidneys on threads above the harbour. The wind was growing cold.

'How about a taxi?' said Phillips at Stanley Bay. When they found one and settled inside it, Aphrodite placed herself comfortably against his shoulder. Some minutes passed before he thought to slip an arm round her.

'Now to brew up,' he said with satisfaction.

'What does that mean?'

'Tea, of course. Where shall we go?'

'The same place,' Aphrodite whispered warmly. 'The same table.'

'O.K.,' said Phillips, and: 'We're in luck,' as they entered Larides' and saw their table was free.

When the tea was poured out, when they were pressing their forks through the luscious softness of coffee-cream cakes, Aphrodite felt the moment had come to clarify and speed up the situation. Phillips might have an Englishman's shyness, but he had only three days' more leave.

'I spoke to my husband about you,' she said.

'What did you tell him? Something nice?'

'Of course. I told him I wanted to sleep with you.'

Phillips raised his eyes and fixed them on her. Even then he had little expression, but he blushed more darkly than he had done for years. 'Good Lord!' he dropped his glance. 'What made you tell him that?'

'Because I didn't want to deceive him. He must know.'

Phillips put a lump of cake into his mouth before he mumbled: 'But there isn't anything for him to know.'

Aphrodite heard because she had been listening: 'You mean you don't want to?'

Phillips swallowed down the last of his cake and pulled himself together. His manner became rather aggressive: 'You ought to know better,' he said. 'A married lady! And you said you were happy.'

'What difference does that make?'

He refused to reply. She drank some tea. There was another pause before she said with a nervous giggle: 'Why don't you want to?'

'Hell, let's drop the subject.' Phillips frowned in indignation and his voice had lost much of its gentility. A hard and edgy silence settled on them. Aphrodite tried once or twice to break it with an anecdote about this person or that passing through the café, but Phillips was unresponsive. When they parted his manner was still cold. He did not suggest their meeting again.

James, supposing Aphrodite would be out, came home late that evening. He found her sitting alone in darkness. As he switched on the light, he said: 'Home early. Did the beautiful romance fall through?'

She did not answer. She was lying back against her chair and sobbing. He stared at her for some moments, then went to her and slid his arm round her. 'What's the matter?' he asked.

She pressed her face against his middle: 'He didn't want me. Now I know I'm getting old.'

'Nonsense,' he said. 'It just showed what a fool he was.'

'No. I know. I know I'm getting old.'

GORDON MEYER

The Circle

T HE four of them were sitting on the terrace after dinner, and Brynhild (Mrs. Elizalde's father had been a devotional Wagner-goer) had just said: 'This weather: it's not right; it ought to be cold now.' It was May, winter.

A straight line produced through the Elizaldes' terrace, their golf-green lawns undulating punctiliously through the pines, to cross the coastal drive, the duned shore, the Plata's indistinguishable rendezvous with the ocean, would first touch land 3,500 miles south, on the polar continent. The Elizaldes, retired, part-wintering on the fashionable peninsula, enjoyed it all at room temperature, from behind plate-glass; noiselessly except for the rustle of a page.

The couple sat at points distant from each other on the circle of six white wrought-iron cushioned garden chairs described to Brynhild's specifications; two other positions were occupied by their guests: Mr. Broadhurst, 'the chargé' as Brynhild called him; and, diametrically opposite her, beautiful Zulema Camargo, daughter of the Commander of the Armed Forces.

Brynhild's friend, Mirabel Watts, just returned to the republic from her yearly three months at home (England), had not arrived. Leonard Elizalde had gone off to his room again; he was supposed to be getting engaged to Zulema during her stay with his parents. If so, his mother thought, he was certainly leaving it to the last night.

Brynhild in any Latin American gathering, which this was not, was outstanding. She wore blue, as now, to quote the colour of her eyes. Even though her hair, too, was turning that colour, the men's gaze would focus on her to the damage of the younger women's morale. But she had, they told each other, geography on her side, being, on their continent, exotic; and forgave her with difficulty.

Zulema saw her beauty as not earthy; picturesque, safely

non-voluptuous, suggesting Botticelli, except it was colder. Beauty that could be loved, she thought, only visibly. She asked herself how (knowing the men of her continent) Doctor Elizalde had let this turn into marriage.

As for herself, Zulema Camargo sat there in a striking silk yellow and black dress, in a cold fury: it was books again.

Was there anything duller than a well-informed English-woman? Especially when corroded by anxiety to be right. The señora de Elizalde had to make the official pronunciamento on such catechisms as the distances between various points on the earth, historical dates, what people said, and, above all, names of books and authors. She moved in fact in a realm of books.

She also excelled at crosswords and other intellectual games; and as she received regularly the best London Sunday newspapers, visitors to 'Windward' were soon shown up by those donnish little proofs of one's ignorance.

The house was so atmospheric with academic competition, Zulema suspected character to be judged according to general knowledge; and in a fortnight had learned the folly of confident utterance such as everybody in her world made.

But it wasn't only knowledge, general or particular: everything had to be right. If not, no place for it in Mrs. Elizalde's world. No right to be there, in fact. Even the weather, as she had just demonstrated.

Of course, it followed that Brynhild must herself always be right; otherwise there might be no place for her in her own world. Impossible situation.

'Creative writing' Brynhild was saying, '*can* be taught,' and all Zulema Camargo's muscles stiffened. 'You remember that man Dominguez, Richard, who worked at your Ministry back in 1950?'

Ricardo Elizalde, Richard to his English wife except in formal matrimonial acrimony, folded his large hands; the gesture a carefully placed stress on his composure. 'Dominguez came to the Ministry of Foreign Affairs in 1952.'

'No. In 1950.'

The Doctor, in a tone now of total mildness, said:

'I remember: it was in 1952.' And Brynhild reached her
flash-point of rightness.

'Absolute nonsense! It was in 1950, the year you had the
new wing added to the Ministry.'

Softly, slowly the Doctor replied: 'But my dear, I had to
authorize his pension . . .'

It was almost the identical tone, and was amputated.

'We-ell my dear, all I can sa-ay (immensely long-drawn out)
is that someone at your Ministry was having a little fun and
games at the government's expense!'

Mrs. Elizalde looked round either side of her cigarette
slanted in its black holder, and it seemed to Zulema that
nothing could now follow this except the scraping of chairs.

'Roma locuta est, causa finita est!' said a voice a little too
quickly, and there was the chargé looking up into the air. He
had his watertight compartments: business, jolly, didactic,
contrived tomfoolery; the last two had interflooded. His real
credentials at Mrs. Elizalde's social occasions were preciseness
and a psychasthenia for quotations.

Mrs. Elizalde, eyelids fluttering, also looked nowhere in
particular, as though in silent unison with the chargé. The
case was indeed finished: the Doctor did not appeal.

But that categoricalness, really it lay less in what Brynhild
said, which was often just silly, than in that slow scything
English drawl. Maybe she was right just now, maybe not—
what did it matter?—but she wasn't always: last night at
dinner she (Zulema) hadn't finished saying Sicily was the
largest island in the . . . when the scythe had cut in: Oh but
su-rely . . . !

'Well this Dominguez fellow decided to learn to write . . .'

When the mosquito door to the terrace squeaked, a girl in
grey uniform called her mistress to the telephone, Zulema felt
it was a hot day on which she had just entered an air-
conditioned room.

Easy conversation broke out. Laughter escaped, although
subdued. Possibly it would increase. The chargé began.

Beira, Port Said, Katmandu were the settings of the first

three anecdotes. Cyprus, Jordania and Indonesia did not delay in adding themselves. And the Duke used to ring him up from the port: Broadhurst, I'm coming up for one of those curries. Hot as hell I want it!

An example of what stealth could achieve in a few minutes.

Nevertheless, the Doctor settled back more comfortably, lit a cigar, remarking on the efficacy of his country's cigars (he knew they were not good) against mosquitos. It drew down Indonesia on him. Straight up in his chair the chargé sat, as though in a ceremonial howdah; his eyes were cold blue, the skin raw-beef Saxon red.

The Doctor didn't know where mosquitos were worse than on a certain river running through one of his estancias. 'It's like the Jordan, just like the Jordan' came the sharp ruling; and there the Doctor's river ended. In Zulema the little interest remaining vanished altogether the next time the mosquito door squeaked.

Leonard, a boy with a reed-like physique, greeted the chargé, took the empty chair on his mother's right. Zulema watched him pour himself over it. He ended up with his left arm hanging down over the side, as if shot; his right foot, booted in suede, lay over his left knee, and, owing to the body's now collapsed position, came to rest on a level with his narrow dark head. His right hand gripped his knee tightly. She understood: he was now positioned for attack or defence, and he reminded her of a crane on the dockside, the jib in the lowered position. He was as complicated as he now looked; he had just been educated in England. She supposed he would acknowledge her in his own fashion. His ears were beautiful enough to bite.

At dinner they had privately aggravated each other—about poetry. She would pick up a book of poems: Ah! Esta me *fascina*! Me en*cant*a! After reading the first verse, she would give it to him: Read that! Before he could finish three lines she would have torn it from him. On to something else.

She knew he was irritated by all this, by her 'lack of reason' as he put it, her thoughtless wordstreams, her questions which were not questions, 'because they are not properly formed, Zulema'. She knew she didn't always know what it was she wanted to know, that in two minutes she might have forgotten what it was she had asked; she knew she threw out her nets of words to catch something on which she might be able to depend. She was looking for some kind of a lead. Other people had got somewhere, she could see that, and she wanted to be there too, and all at once. But she felt instinctively that Leonardo had reached the stage only in words.

Nevertheless, she often felt with him a sense of inferiority. There were times when she didn't know what to say, and walked as if on stepping-stones. She didn't want him to feel like he did to her, and to counterbalance it, would, in argument, assume disdain. She didn't feel it, but sketched it in on her face; it was something else she was acquiring from him.

But she would learn. She would learn to joke about him, in company too. That would break up his secret and tacit assault on her, such as he was carrying out now.

And she knew that already she had touched his secret interior. How would he be now? That was the current question. She was always having to guess how he was going to react. But alone, how different he was. . . .

Another grey-uniformed servant appeared, approached him. Zulema watched him regard the girl with deliberate and prolonged criticalness: if he could embarrass her, she couldn't embarrass him.

After a moment, her gaze faltered, she offered tribute in the form of a feeble smile, as though he had at last done to her what she may have often hoped he would.

'Usual,' he said, and turned swiftly across Zulema's line of vision to the chargé d'affaires. 'I was just finishing reading *Pygmalion* again.'

'Ah! *Pygmalion*' said the chargé, and nothing more; he looked at the Doctor, who was regarding his son. No support for *Pygmalion* there.

'Have you read *Pygmalion*, Zulema?'

Accepting his way of saying hallo, she said, 'Yes, when I was thirteen.'

'Oh and what possessed you to do so so early?' Leonard said, and waited, illuminated now.

'Because I just loved it.'

She thought: He wonders how I could say I loved it before reading it. She saw how she was beginning to think.

'You say that with the sort of enthusiasm you might have for a meringue!'

Meant as a graceful winning shot. There was also between them the stress of deeper things unsaid; she was accustomed to them being uttered at a much earlier stage. She said sharply, 'And why not?', and there was silence.

Their tension had become public, prevented conversation gathering way. The Doctor meanwhile had withdrawn into himself, to resume for a few moments more the year-by-year plotting of the interval widening between himself and his son, the alliance tightening with the mother.

As ambassador, he had lived in London, been well received by its society, feeling more at home than is usually possible for a charming foreigner to feel: after all, in England he had met Brynhild. (In point of fact, at the Anglo-Brazilian Society's Ball at the Park Lane Hotel.) And he had moved among the English long enough to know when an ambiente is more than a hundred per cent. English.

So he told himself he was not against the English educational system, only the result of it in his son, who, in spite of their enmity, did not know how to say hallo to him.

The chargé d'affaires had sensed this atmosphere; thoughtfully he devised a remark about the recent political disturbances. He addressed the Doctor and Leonard: riots couldn't interest young and pretty Latin Americans.

But Zulema said at once:

'Those are the sort of men I'd have no trouble in killing.' Sharply the chargé turned. Leonard with a smile disapproved:

'You yourself, Zulema?'

'Yes, of course. Why not?'

'But how,' he patronized, 'would you do it?' He was deliberately almost laughing.

Zulema shrugged her bare shoulders. 'Shoot them!'

The chargé wanted her to have another chance. 'Really shoot them? Come now!'

Shrewd negotiator, with the necessary lack of penetration to the human heart, he was also interested professionally; he had a report to complete.

'Yes' said Zulema.

The Doctor had not taken his eyes off her, not because he was the only one present who understood her.

Leonard remained smiling. The chargé for the moment said nothing; he was imagining it. Then:

'But tell me where?' he brightened. 'Or in the heart, or in the head? Tell me where you'd shoot them dead?'

Zulema didn't know why even with this he was pleased; she regarded him as one would a point of aim:

'In the head.'

'Make an *awful* mess!' Leonard was looking up into a ceibo tree.

'I wouldn't have to clean it.' She dismissed her questioners.

She'd do it, my god, the chargé noted. Her father, a man totally uninterested in books, had described how he would deal with agitators, slackers and revolutionaries. Of course: out here it was Haves and Have-nots in a big way. Not like those at home, but those who had never counted how much they had against those able to exist without hope. Movement from one to the other rare, or impossible. It reminded him of reading De Tocqueville. And how each side helped its members! The Have families coming to the rescue of each other, as if slight impoverishment were shipwreck. For this girl, the 'others' were animals and so to be treated: curt commands, no answering back, instant obedience, blows if necessary. She wasn't morbid, much less cruel, oh no: warm, gay, vital. . . . True product of her system, though. Yes, it was very interesting.

Zulema had read him correctly.

What could he understand with his statistics? He had no means of knowing that the majority of the people were useful for nothing, but lived by fishing, trapping, idling—as the Indians had done. Only, these had the lotería. They were also the sort that had broken into one of her family's houses, robbed, drank and ate, leaving the whisky bottles filled with their

urine, the beds with their excreta. They had a sense of humour.
And it was her instinct to shoot them: as one would a dog with
rabies.

The mosquito door creaked again. 'To *return* . . . to the
matter of creative writing . . . !' A stranger would recognize
the loud order for attention. 'Ah Lennie darling, so you decided
to come down and grace us with your presence. And Zulema
waiting there for you, in that lovely dress. Isn't she a picture?'
Brynhild's eyes, now a pair of compasses, retraced her circle.
'Now let's have Leonard's views, shall we? But first, a kiss for
your mamá.'

Sitting down opposite her, Brynhild with vigorous thumps
of a cigarette on a silver case, re-emphasized her chairmanship.
A procedure that had to be learned: when she had lit the
cigarette, the conference would resume.

But no, this time it appeared there were private agenda to be
cleared up first. The heads of mother and son inclined towards
each other in a renewal of ties, a bringing of each other up to
date with inventories of parochial doings. Gossip. The door
behind which they had retired said in bold letters: Mother and
Son in conference. Zulema stared unbelievingly.

The chargé was temporarily cut off. To reach the Doctor, he
would have to talk across Mrs. Elizalde, which would not do
really. In any case Doctor Elizalde's attention was going
another way.

Zulema had turned deliberately to the disposal of husband
and father:

'Shall we go and have an ice-cream afterwards?' and Mrs.
Elizalde stopped talking.

So sharply had her head turned, it appeared she had been
struck in the neck.

Zulema found herself looking at two cold pale blue diamond-
hard lozenges; the glacial hatred ran a diameter across the
circle for no more than a second, by watch-timing. She returned
her gaze to the Doctor; she would go on.

He was shifting a little in his chair. For some moments there was silent incoherence; the six of them composed a perfect model of centrifugence.

Zulema had kept her eyes on the Doctor.

'Well, yes . . . we could . . . I suppose (he consulted his wife) you wouldn't care——?'

She also had her eyes on him. '*Certainly* not! Darling must you really go to those dreadful places?'

The doctor was now very conscious of Zulema's unwavering gaze. He looked at his wife, however, and no one could have interpreted the faint smile. With a patient equivocal submission he said:

'Well . . . I suppose that if I want an ice-cream, then I *must* go to one of those places!' He put his large head on one side. 'You don't mind, do you?'

Mrs. Elizalde looked away from him at once. She looked at something evidently familiar to her, although no one else had ever seen it. She looked to her left, and down at something as if it were lying in a corner, as it might have been a dog; and spoke to that something.

'Not at all, but if you want an ice-cream *so* badly, we can send out for one.'

First the Doctor hesitated, then rallied.

'Well, I don't know. . . . Personally I do think it would be rather ni-ice to have one, don't you think?'

Zulema caught her breath. He had drawn out the words in a slightly drawling, strained fashion: a miniature replica of his wife's manner. She was sure it wasn't intentional: no one could have ever said the Doctor was capable of gaucherie. Perhaps it was an example of how two people living together a long, long time assimilated something of each other; the way dogs and their masters were said to do.

'Well I really don't know . . .' said Mrs. Elizalde.

Her lips tightened, puckered, she looked again at the thing in the corner.

Then looked round, fastening attention. 'We were talking about creative writing . . . I say it can be taught, and should be.'

It was to be expected that her recovery should be the

quickest, after the collapse of the ice-cream project. No one else was ready except perhaps the chargé, and he, Zulema had seen, liked to speak last.

The Doctor was making that sequence of little vocal sounds, prelude to one of the pondered replies he would never discharge.

'But how?' The crease in the lower part of Leonard's handsome face told Zulema he was convicting someone in advance. The either-or was his technique. Whatever the other person said placed them in one of these two categories. In either case his answer lay in ambush, and the original point discarded in favour of the demonstration that the other person had been trapped in the Leonard dichotomy.

He had told her it was logic ('not the way the people here use the word lógico'); and she supposed it all must have something to do with his English university education. Of course, a black and white world would do away with colours.

'But how?' he was saying; and then in his elegant stutter: 'I mean, I mean. . . .'

'Robert Louis Stevenson . . .' said his mother, and the Doctor sank a little deeper into his chair.

Dreadful. Things that *others* had said, expended things from expended situations. Dead unfertile world. From such people she could learn nothing unavailable in a public library. Perfect examples of 'the donkey that swallowed the books' (did that phrase exist in English?). The world in which with Leonardo she would have to live.

In her striking yellow and black dress she sat back in her white iron seat, her jewellery flashed from her ears, neck and wrists, and no one, not even Leonardo, looked at her; they were examining the question of creative writing.

It was not quite true; the Doctor was not examining the question of creative writing.

'Our daughter Holly,' said the loud voice, 'is studying creative writing. I don't mean (she added quickly) that that is her main subject: she's actually at La Seetay Oonivairsitay in Paris.'

This was for the chargé; he said:

'Really!'

'She speaks six languages. Including Russian.'

'Russian!' Now he did sit up.

'And all fluently. As a matter of fact (Brynhild fluttered her eyelids rapidly as though having a brief vision of angels), it got so expensive, that we had to stop the Russian, and then, do you know, the school wrote and told us that she was so good, they would give her the Russian lessons for nothing. Wasn't that wonderful?'

There was a ragged chorus of assent.

'Besides her B.A., she's now taken her Doctorate of Law. She paints. She plays the piano beautifully. And, well, really (her eyelids fluttered again), I don't know what she doesn't do.'

I could tell you Zulema thought.

'At the moment she's in New York on a visit; then she goes to Mexico, Peru, Colombia and Brazil on a scholarship. Everything paid.' Her mouth shut, the eyebrows lifted.

'And after that?' said the chargé, calculating the whisky left in his glass.

'After that, she returns to La Seetay Oonivairsitay. Now I wonder what's happened to Mirabel.' Brynhild's gaze went down the undulating lawns to the coastal boulevard, as though Mirabel might drop out of one of the tall palm trees.

'Is that Mirabel the wife of Robert Pratt, the oil man?' asked the chargé.

'You know her then?'

'I met them in Venezuela; you know how all the English people know each other.'

'Do I not! You know (she collected attention in a raking circular gaze), Mirabel's daughter is only 19, and she is such a beautiful daughter, really such a beautiful girl.' She looked at Zulema for just a moment. 'Mirabel took her to London to meet some nice young English boys, and what does the poor child do but throw herself into the arms of the first Latin American she meets there. She's going to marry an Argentine!'

She paused; everyone, recognizing the curtain-drop, remained silent.

'Of course, Mirabel's simply *distraught*! Can you *imagine* what it is for her! And this poor fellow, to make matters a thousand times worse, is just in England on an engineering scholarship.'

God, God, God, said Zulema under her breath savagely.

At that moment the two dogs began barking furiously; a female figure, deposited by a friend's car, was ascending the brilliantly lit lawns. Her clothes, to Zulema, identified the nationality long before the individual features became distinguishable.

It seemed certain that Brynhild was back in England, sighting a fox break from a distant covert; the warm night thrilled to the long 'Hall-o-o!'

Brynhild patted the vacant chair beside her, Mirabel seated herself with breathless dutifulness in it, the duologue commenced immediately.

The amazing, the infuriating thing was that again no one else thought of assembling their own conversation; they listened, watched, waited to be spoken to.

With her own people, she was used to brilliant, fast, superficial, instinctual and, above all, gay discussion, in which a great deal of laughter was to be heard; and after which nobody would have thought of remembering what had been said.

She looked at Doctor Elizalde, suddenly felt inconsolably sorry for him.

Yesterday, when accident had left the two of them alone at the table of a little eating place at which they had stopped on a drive through the surrounding country, he had said to her: You know, I never knew that something like this could be so enjoyable.

His wife never seemed to understand the need for an art of superficiality—why presumably she would never invite the daughter of an ex-colleague of the Doctor's known for her brilliant aimless talk. With Brynhild conversation had to be aimed. The world was ordered; one could see it in nature. She was one of those positivists who believe that when conversation stops it is because there is nothing to say.

How did Ricardo endure it all? Sitting there night after

night, his mouth shut, in a membership of English guests. Didn't he ever feel the urge to resign?

Possibly. He'd given her that book by an English writer who had visited the Far East: 'I think he's a little neurotic, but it's extremely funny; let me have it back when you've finished.' Every page had a comment making the English look ridiculous; and the action of lending the book to her was the Doctor's tacit comment: everything he could not say. Perhaps such little subterfuges helped him last out the unpeopled winters on this pine-strewn peninsular Utopia.

She asked him.

He replied. At first, for Brynhild, it was like a wireless station faintly heard behind the one she wanted.

'Oh,' he said easily, 'but I don't really miss people. I just shut myself up with my books. I have my intellectual communion with myself. I reason with myself, I even . . .' he laughed a little. 'I even contradict myself!'

He thought about this for a moment, seemed to find it intriguing.

'And how do you spend your day, when the two of you are alone?'

'I get up at half-past seven, have a little breakfast in my room, then go back to bed and play patience for an hour. Then I bath and dress, by which time it's about ten-thirty. At ten-thirty I take the two spaniels for a walk, and one of them, Flotsam, always gets lost. So I return to the house, get out the station-waggon, and look for her. By the time I get back, it's lunch-time, and my wife and I meet for the first time. After lunch I take a siesta for an hour or so; then I write letters for about two hours, after which I change and join my wife for a whisky, or two, and at seven we will dine. After dinner, we play patience together, and at eleven we are in bed.' He smiled. 'You must try it sometime!'

Did he know then? She shuddered, not only at the routine, but at the expropriation of him.

The astonishing thing was how Brynhild had brought off the abduction in his own country; operating, as it were, behind the enemy lines. Her children (she always thought of them as

Brynhild's) turned out to be agents she'd passed through the lines, for indoctrination in her own people's beliefs and subsequent recall to the campaign ground.

The Ricardo softened up by a hundred subtle blows delivered before his departure from England, was the finished product in front of her; so finished, he would never again be one hundred per cent his own nationality even with his compatriots. They would always say, 'He's more English than one of us', or 'He's been Englished'. Here, in his own country, he dressed in soft elegant English tweeds, a cape, suede shoes, carried gloves; even said 'My dear'. He would never retreat from this now. He'd been taken over—taken prisoner, one might say? Why not say it? The English had more than the two main methods of conquest.

He sat before her, fixed in the amber of the English situation.

The chargé was again isolated; it was possible he was growing a little sulky about it. It is true Leonard sat next to him, but his fingernails rhythmically clicking on his glass; something that looked like discontent did not invite conversation. There were four frequency bands, two double, two single sets.

'It interested me what you were saying last night about feelings,' said Zulema to the Doctor and Mrs. Elizalde began to suffer from background interference. 'I used to give into mine, but now I keep them inside me, and this upsets me mentally and physically.' She ended quite loudly.

Doctor Elizalde saw a control only half achieved; he recognized a message being relayed through him for his son. Leonard seemed not to have heard.

The Doctor began to explain his own philosophy. 'I have learned another way of dealing with the matter. In the moment I was about to explode——'

'So you did explode!'

Mirabel was looking at Brynhild who seemed to have forgotten what she was saying.

'Oh yes.' The Doctor said it quite gravely. 'And in that moment I would stop and try to find a reason for the other person's——'

'Didn't you order whisky, Zulema?' said a hard voice.

Zulema looked at her gin and tonic. 'Yes, but this is all right.' She returned to the Doctor, having missed something; he was now saying:

'Eventually I was even able to prevent——'

'No, no, no! If you ordered whisky, you must have it. That is (Brynhild tempered it a little), the girl must bring you what you ordered; then you can change it if you wish.'

'. . . prevent these things occurring.' Maybe he was talking experimentally, she thought.

'You did *order* whisky, didn't you?' said the voice, louder still.

You have a way of omitting my name just when it should be used, Zulema said to her mentally. 'Yes,' she said again, and shrugged in a way that seemed to infuriate the older woman; 'but I don't care, it's not important.'

Brynhild was trembling when she rose and unnecessarily shouted 'Miriam!'

She went to the terrace door, pushed the bell for long seconds; Zulema said:

'When were you able to make this change in you?'

The Doctor made a nervous movement, he unclasped his hands. 'Oh . . . about three, perhaps four years a——' and his wife swung round.

'Ricardo! Didn't you order soda? You did order soda, I distinctly heard you.'

Hearing himself called by the Spanish form, the Doctor sat back apologetically, adjusting the crease in his trousers; then, courageously jerking his head up, said in his stilted, never quite correct and charming English:

'Yes, I did pass that order, but it doesn't matter now!'

He looked away from his wife, to Zulema, smiled; uncertainly she thought.

Brynhild, standing by the door, had succeeded in holding the attention of everyone. There came a scuffling movement from the other side of the door.

'What *is* happening? Why did you bring no soda for the Doctor? And the señorita Camargo ordered whisky, not gin and tonic! One doesn't drink gin and tonic *after* dinner.'

The girl mumbled her way towards escape, Brynhild's inquisition pursuing her all the way to the frontier of all those rooms a guest would never see. Zulema, understanding, found it unbearable.

'But it doesn't matter, Brynhild.'

Brynhild turned to her, in loud triumph cried, 'That is just where you are *wrong*! It *does* matter. All these things matter.'

If you had at this moment, Zulema thought, four men round you and no women, it would certainly not matter.

The chargé was smiling the affair off to himself, curate-fashion. Leonard was prick-earedly studying the ice in his glass as his mother sat down again.

She was quivering. Suddenly Zulema knew what to do; she leaned forward, looked with a fixed sweetness at the woman nearly three times her age.

'You're furious! Aren't you?'

A ritual had been interrupted.

The intruder was laughing; she was laughing in such a way that the older woman could not believe anything but that the girl was on her side; which Zulema understood was what one aimed for in order to get the best out of a child.

Brynhild's face had begun to flush with anger; all at once it changed as if against her will. It broke up, remained an instant in a vacuum, then took on new lineaments; Brynhild smiled. Sun after storm.

'Yes!' She burst out laughing. 'At least I *was*!' she corrected herself.

Everything ran down gently, stopped with the quiet perfection ending the slow movement of a Beethoven quartet. Pressures came off; in various mouths the taste of whisky or brandy returned.

Propitious moment, thought someone, for departure. The chargé got up, saying he thought he really ought to be going; a decree was issued that the Doctor should drive him to his hotel, Mirabel to her home. The Doctor, who had his mind on something else, got up awkwardly. This was because he had got up ambiguously: for the chargé and Mirabel, as he meant

Brynhild to interpret it; for Zulema, as he wanted Zulema to understand it. For himself, he didn't know what he would end by doing, until his wife said, 'You stay and talk to me, Zulema dear,' and he recognized an order.

At this, Leonard put his hands in his jacket pockets, seemed to fail to find something, and disappeared. Brynhild, still in her chair, lit another cigarette.

Zulema saw the light go on in Leonard's room. Presently through the window came the portentous opening of the Linz symphony. That was another thing: his tastes. Standard, unadventurous. Dutiful reflection of the programmes she saw advertised in Brynhild's Sunday papers.

'He's a funny boy, Lennie; even as a child he was never demonstrative. Especially in public.'

Brynhild was disposed to talk. Zulema did not want to talk, certainly not with Brynhild; she wanted to think.

Who did these English think they were, with their eternal talk of good manners? Their idea of good manners was that no one should be late for a meal, not even for a cocktail party; that there should be just two drinks before dinner, the second being known as 'the other half'; that one never ate one's bread before the food was served, nor addressed the servants direct, nor got up from the table before the hostess, not for any emergency; that there should be no second helpings; that the conversation should be about books; and lastly, that young people should be ignored.

Even that wasn't all: they let their private tensions entwine and trice up their guests, so that one sat there all the time at full stretch.

As for that corrosive anxiety to be always right, she now suspected Brynhild desired it only in terms of other people being wrong. If everybody were to agree with her at the outset, what would she do for self-expression?

The two weeks at 'Windward' had been a school term; and Leonardo was a product of that school. Tomorrow she was going home.

'You really are *very* beautiful, my dear, you know. . . .'

Brynhild was looking straight at her.

Zulema started. It was a trick, a trap even. The last thing Brynhild should have ever said to her. She was going to collect satisfaction for the ice-cream suggestion. She looked at Brynhild cautiously. The older woman remained, cigarette-holder poised, as if above a final judgement. So coldly: as though I were a picture in a gallery.

No, but it wasn't quite like that. In Brynhild's look floated something indefinable. She realized that Brynhild was perfectly sincere—they were alone for one thing. Brynhild, for some reason was nicer with her when they were alone together. And Leonardo was the same.

But she didn't trust Brynhild after that look over the ice-cream business, which of course had been cuttingly defeated; so she resisted the temptation to let the focus remain on her beauty.

'Will you go to the estancia before it gets too cold?' she asked, and for some moments, did not realize what was happening: Brynhild was relating everything so casually, as if discussing household shopping.

'My dear, I would always go, whenever Richard went. But since four years ago I have never been, and never will again. At that time we had received a letter from a girl friend of Holly's, in London, saying she was coming out, and would love to look us up. I wasn't well at the time, so I put her off. The next thing was a letter from Cartagena; she was apparently on a cruise, headed this way, obviously expecting to see us. She asked me to reply to the ship in Río.

'Well, I didn't.' Brynhild briefly re-examined herself on this. 'We'd had a terrific season here at the Punta, for one thing, and I just wanted to be alone with Richard. But about a week or two later we got a telephone call from Montevideo, and of course I had to tell her to come on. She did—with all her luggage.'

Brynhild leaned forward, carefully tapped ash into a tray; she had to describe the girl. 'She was what you'd call a stunner. That is to say, what we would call her. And of course, the inevitable happened.'

Zulema found herself being regarded a little closer. 'I think you must have noticed Ricardo's a susceptible man.'

Zulema said nothing; she had noticed that Brynhild had called him Ricardo.

'He also began spending money as I had never known him spend it. Every other day he would buy her something; when I remonstrated with him, he got very angry with me and said that for him she was like a daughter. The argument we had about *that* didn't improve matters.

'I knew she had only a thirty-day visa, so after about three weeks, I told her I could help her with the exit formalities. To my astonishment, she told me Ricardo was having her visa extended; which as ex-Foreign Minister he could do without any trouble.

'She then began saying how much she'd like to visit Santa Margarita, our largest estancia. But by now it wasn't only that I was feeling ill, so I put my foot firmly down and said, No, I was sorry but it would have to be another time.

'Two days later she had the impertinence to ask Ricardo at lunch; and in front of me he said, "Yes".'

It was the first time she had heard Brynhild not speaking for effect.

'You must understand that by now I was neither eating nor sleeping properly. I felt an outsider in my own home. When they kissed each other goodnight, I had to look the other way. And to make it a thousand times worse, when the girl wasn't present, Ricardo was always talking about her.

'So when he agreed to take her, something seemed to snap inside me; the fight went out of me.'

'You mean you didn't go?' This part Zulema couldn't understand.

'No. They went alone, and they stayed three weeks, during which I had the doctor sometimes twice a day. By that time, friends were asking me openly when the girl was going, and Mirabel, whom you met tonight advised me to tell Ricardo when he came back that if the girl wasn't out in a week, I would leave.

'My dear, when they finally came back and I saw their

faces, I realized I wasn't prepared to take the risk. . . . They came back as if it were all the most natural thing in the world.' Brynhild's lips drooped. 'I suppose it was. I decided to talk to her alone, and even then I knew it was a gamble. However, it came off; it was a short conversation, if that's what you call it. She went.'

Brynhild drew a breath, as if resenting the memory. Suddenly she cried:

'It lasted five whole months. *In my whole life I have never suffered so much torture.*'

Her pause, after this, created a dead silence heavy with what she could not add.

What had been dredged up subsided again inside her. 'We're together again of course, in a way of speaking, but we both know something has gone, and that we're together perhaps because there is no other distraction for him in the house. . . .

'The curious thing is that Richard is now nicer to me than at any other time in our marriage. And I am horrid to him. And even jealous!' At last she smiled.

Zulema, very still in her chair, stared at the transmuted Brynhild; it wasn't then in answer to her question that Brynhild had told her.

'I suppose she was something like me.'

Brynhild's smile was confessional. 'You are much more beautiful. And much nicer!'

She got up, remained bending over, stubbing out her cigarette; she did it with a clumsy movement. She was trembling.

Zulema got up too.

'No, don't go, I'll tell Leonard to turn off his highbrow concert, and come down. You wait here.'

She had come up close; Zulema suddenly felt an arm round her, a mouth on her cheek. It was a warm kiss. In a totally unpremeditated response her heart leaped towards the other woman.

'I know he's going to ask you tonight; I think it's always nicer if the girl knows beforehand!'

Zulema looked at her, unable to think of anything to say.

'You're just the girl for him; I'd have chosen you myself. I hope with all my heart you'll both be very happy.'

Zulema felt her thank you almost clumsy, but Brynhild didn't seem to notice, she was looking through the tall windows into the drawing room, pondering.

'You see . . . in spite of everything . . . Richard has been the only man in my life.'

Zulema waited.

'One can't stop loving a person just because of something they do to you. . . .'

A sentence fallen out of the night, connected more with the ocean invisible before them, the cosmic forces themselves; at first Zulema did not even connect it with Brynhild, who still wasn't looking at her, anyway.

'Can one?' Brynhild had turned.

Zulema realized that she, the younger woman, was being asked, as if Brynhild herself knew nothing of these things. She said: 'No,' and there was silence.

Brynhild looked into the drawing room again.

'I've never bothered to put plants in my house,' she said reflectively, and looked round in a sullen way, which Zulema recognized as the Brynhild everyone knew. 'I don't know . . . I suppose I must have a rather prosaic mind.'

Alone, Zulema realized she had sat down again in obedience to something other than herself. It was a moment to be reborn a generation later. She saw what awaited her should she remain married to Leonardo for more than eight or nine years. It would become too late; she would, like Ricardo, be expropriated, become his female counterpart: a travesty of an English lady. She would never feel completely at home there; that was probably to be expected. What was unendurable was the thought of it being made impossible for her ever to feel quite at home again among her own people—the ultimate ravage of the takeover.

From upstairs a pause in the music.

She strained her ears for noises of him. Suddenly the sounds raced out of the window as the Presto began; he would listen to the end of course. It infuriated him that she would put on a record, then perhaps forget about it. The symphony, to her, had become invested with the personality of Leonardo listening up there, so that somehow it was not Mozart she heard but Leonardo. It was not the first time this had happened.

She was in the next moment unable to think or do anything. A slow and stealthy uneasiness began to conquer her whole body. Her nerve centres trembled, and she could not control them. In this disquieting lassitude her legs weakened, her palms became moist, she swallowed less. She felt that when he came down she would scarcely be able to stand. And all the time the rumours of the outside world were receding: the shrilling grillos, cars rushing back to the capital, the heavy muffle of the waves, they were going, fading, becoming part of unreality; for reality was only this feeling of waiting for him. It enveloped her like a cocoon, insulating her from everything else she knew, so that finally, when the music cut off in the middle of a phrase, a light went out, a door slammed, something inside her loosened, broke; it was the only time she could wholeheartedly agree with Brynhild.

V. S. NAIPAUL

A Christmas Story

THOUGH it is Christmas Eve my mind is not on Christmas. I look forward instead to the day after Boxing Day, for on that day the inspectors from the Audit Department in Port-of-Spain will be coming down to the village where the new school has been built. I await their coming with calm. There is still time, of course, to do all that is necessary. But I shall not do it, though my family, from whom the spirit of Christmas has, alas, also fled, have been begging me to lay aside my scruples, my new-found faith, and to rescue us all from disgrace and ruin. It is in my power to do so, but there comes a time in every man's life when he has to take a stand. This time, I must confess, has come very late for me.

It seems that everything has come late to me. I continued a Hindu, though of that religion I saw and knew little save meaningless and shameful rites, until I was nearly eighteen. Why I so continued I cannot explain. Perhaps it was the inertia with which that religion deadens its devotees. It did not, after all, require much intelligence to see that Hinduism, with its animistic rites, its idolatry, its emphasis on mango leaf, banana leaf and—the truth is the truth—cowdung, was a religion little fitted for the modern world. I had only to contrast the position of the Hindus with that of the Christians. I had only to consider the differing standards of dress, houses, food. Such differences have today more or less disappeared, and the younger generation will scarcely understand what I mean. I might even be reproached with laying too great a stress on the superficial. What can I say? Will I be believed if I say that to me the superficial has always symbolized the profound? But it is enough, I feel, to state that at eighteen my eyes were opened. I did not have to be 'converted' by the Presbyterians of the Canadian Mission. I had only to look at the work they were doing among the backward Hindus and

Moslems of my district. I had only to look at their schools, to look at the houses of the converted.

My Presbyterianism, then, though late in coming, affected me deeply. I was interested in teaching—there was no other thing a man of my limited means and limited education could do—and my Presbyterianism was a distinct advantage. It gave me a grace in the eyes of my superiors. It also enabled me to be a good teacher, for between what I taught and what I felt there was no discordance. How different the position of those who, still unconverted, attempted to teach in Presbyterian schools!

And now that the time for frankness has come I must also remark on the pleasure my new religion gave me. It was a pleasure to hear myself called Randolph, a name of rich historical associations, a name, I feel, thoroughly attuned to the times in which we live and to the society in which I found myself, and to forget that once—I still remember it with shame—I answered, with simple instinct, to the name of—Choonilal. That, however, is so much in the past. I have buried it. Yet I remember it now, not only because the time for frankness has come, but because only two weeks ago my son Winston, going through some family papers—clearly the boy had no right to be going through my private papers, but he shares his mother's curiosity—came upon the name. He teased, indeed reproached me, with it, and in a fit of anger, for which I am now grievously sorry and for which I must make time, while time there still is, to apologize to him, in a fit of anger I gave him a sound thrashing, such as I often gave in my schoolteaching days, to those pupils whose persistent shortcomings were matched by the stupidity and backwardness of their parents. Backwardness has always roused me to anger.

As much as by the name Randolph, pleasure was given me by the stately and *clean*—there is no other word for it—rituals sanctioned by my new religion. How agreeable, for instance, to rise early on a Sunday morning, to bathe and breakfast and then, in the most spotless of garments, to walk along the still quiet and cool roads to our place of worship, and there to see the most respectable and respected, all dressed with a similar purity, addressing themselves to the devotions in which I myself could participate, after for long being an outsider, someone to whom the words *Christ* and *Father* meant no more than *winter* or *autumn* or *daffodil*. Such of the unconverted village folk who were energetic enough to be awake and alert at that hour gaped at us as we walked in white procession to our church. And though their admiration was sweet, I must confess that at the same time it filled me with shame to reflect that not long before I too formed part of the gaping crowd. To walk past their gaze was peculiarly painful to me, for I, more perhaps than anyone in that slow and stately procession, *knew*—and by my silence had for nearly eighteen years condoned—the practices those people indulged in in the name of religion. My attitude towards them was therefore somewhat stern, and it gave me some little consolation to know that though we were in some ways alike, we were distinguished from them not only by our names, which after all no man carries pinned to his lapel, but also by our dress. On these Sundays of which I speak the men wore trousers and jackets of white drill, quite unlike the leg-revealing dhoti which it still pleased those others to wear, a garment which I have always felt makes the wearer ridiculous. I even sported a white solar topee. The girls and ladies wore the short frocks which the others held in abhorrence; they wore hats; in every respect, I am pleased to say, they resembled their sisters who had come all the way from Canada and other countries to work among our people. I might be accused of laying too much stress on superficial things. But I ought to say in my own defence that it is my deeply held conviction that progress is not a matter of outward show, but an attitude of mind; and it was this that my religion gave me.

It might seem from what I have so far said that the embracing of Presbyterianism conferred only benefits and pleasure. I wish to make no great fuss of the trials I had to endure, but it is sufficient to state that, while at school and in other associations my fervent adherence to my new faith was viewed with favour, I had elsewhere to put up with the constant ridicule of those of my relations who continued, in spite of my example, in the ways of darkness. They spoke my name, Randolph, with accents of the purest mockery. I bore this with fortitude. It was what I expected, and I was greatly strengthened by my faith, as a miser is by the thought of his gold. In time, when they saw that their ridiculing of my name had not the slightest effect on me—on the contrary, whereas before I had in my signature suppressed my first name behind the blank initial C, now I spelt out Randolph in full—in time they desisted.

But that was not the end of my trials. I had up to that time eaten with my fingers, a manner of eating which is now so repulsive to me, so ugly, so unhygienic, that I wonder how I managed to do it until my eighteenth year. Yet I must now confess that at that time food never tasted as sweet as when eaten with the fingers, and that my first attempts to eat with the proper implements of knife and fork and spoon were almost in the nature of shameful experiments, furtively carried out; and even when I was by myself I could not get rid of the feeling of self-consciousness. It was easier to get used to the name of Randolph than to knife and fork.

Eating, then, in my determined manner one Sunday lunch-time, I heard that I had a visitor. It was a man; he didn't knock, but came straight into my room, and I knew at once that he was a relation. These people have never learned to knock or to close doors behind them.

I must confess I felt somewhat foolish to be caught with those implements in my hand.

'Hello, Randolph,' the boy Hori said, pronouncing the name in a most offensive manner.

'Good afternoon, *Hori*.'

He remained impervious to my irony. This boy, Hori, was the greatest of my tormentors. He was also the grossest. He strained charity. He was a great lump of a man and he gloried in his brutishness. He fancied himself a debater as well, and many were the discussions and arguments we had had, this lout—he strained charity, as I have said—insisting that to squat on the ground and eat off banana leaves was hygienic and proper, that knives and forks were dirty because used again and again by various persons, whereas the fingers were personal and could always be made thoroughly clean by washing. But he never had *his* fingers clean, that I knew.

'Eating, Randolph?'

'I am having my lunch, *Hori*.'

'Beef, Randolph. You are progressing, Randolph.'

'I am glad you note it, *Hori*.'

I cannot understand why these people should persist in this admiration for the cow, which has always seemed to me a filthy animal, far filthier than the pig, which they abhor. Yet it must be stated that this eating of beef was the most strenuous of my tests. If I persevered it was only because I was strengthened by my faith. But to be found at this juncture—I was in my Sunday suit of white drill, my prayer book was on the table, my white solar topee on the wall, and I was eating beef with knife and fork—to be found thus by Hori was a trifle embarrassing. I must have looked the picture of the over-zealous convert.

My instinct was to ask him to leave. But it occurred to me that that would have been too easy, too cowardly a way out. Instead, I plied my knife and fork with as much skill as I could command at that time. He sat, not on a chair, but on the table, just next to my plate, the lout, and gazed at me while I ate. Ignoring his smile, I ate, as one might eat of sacrificial food. He crossed his fat legs, leaned back on his palms and examined me. I paid no attention. Then he took one of the forks that were about and began picking his teeth with it. I was angry and revolted. Tears sprang to my eyes. I rose, pushed away my plate, pushed back my chair, and asked him to leave. The violence of my reaction surprised him, and he did as I asked. As soon as he had gone I took the fork he had handled and bent it and stamped on it and then threw it out of the window.

Progress, as I have said, is an attitude of mind. And if I relate this trifling incident with such feeling, it is because it demonstrates how difficult that attitude of mind is to acquire, for there are hundreds who are ready to despise and ridicule those who they think are getting above themselves. And let people say what they will, the contempt even of the foolish is hard to bear. Let no one think, therefore, that my new religion did not bring its share of trials and tribulations. But I was sufficiently strengthened by my faith to bear them all with fortitude.

My life thereafter was a lonely one. I had cut myself off from my family, and from those large family gatherings which had hitherto given me so much pleasure and comfort, for always, I must own, at the back of my mind there had been the thought that in the event of real trouble there would be people to whom I could turn. Now I was deprived of this solace. I stuck to my vocation with a dedication which surprised even myself. To be a teacher it is necessary to be taught; and after much difficulty I managed to have myself sent to the Training College in Port-of-Spain. The competition for these places was fierce, and for many years I was passed over, because there were many others who were more fitting. Some indeed had been born of Presbyterian parents. But my zeal, which ever mounted as the failures multiplied, eventually was rewarded. I was twenty-eight when I was sent to the Training College, considerably older than most of the trainees.

It was no pleasure to me to note that during those ten years the boy Hori had been prospering. He had gone into the trucking business and he had done remarkably well. He had bought a second truck, then a third, and it seemed that to his success there could be no limit, while my own was always restricted to the predictable contents of the brown-paper pay-packet at the end of the month. The clothes in which I had taken such pride at first became less resplendent, until I felt it as a disgrace to go to church in them. But it became clear to me that this was yet another of the trials I was called upon to undergo, and I endured it, until I almost took pleasure in the darns on my sleeves and elbows.

At this time I was invited to the wedding of Hori's son, Kedar. They marry young, these people! It was an occasion which surmounted religious differences, and it was a distinct pleasure to me to be again with the family, for their attitude had changed. They had become reconciled to my Presbyterianism and indeed treated me with respect for my profession, a respect which, I fear, was sometimes missing in the attitude of my superiors and even my pupils. The marriage rites distressed me. The makeshift though beautiful tent, the coconut-palm arches hung with clusters of fruit, the use of things like mango leaves and grass and saffron, the sacrificial fire, all these things filled me with shame rather than delight. But the rites were only a small part of the celebrations. There was much good food, strictly vegetarian but somehow extremely tempting; and after a period of distaste for Indian food, I had come back to it again. The food, I say, was rich. The music and the dancers were thrilling. The tent and the illuminations had a charm which not even our school hall had on concert nights, though the marriage ceremony did not of course have the grace and dignity of those conducted, as proper marriages should be, in a church.

Kedar received a fabulous dowry, and his bride, of whose face I had just a glimpse when her silk veil was parted, was indeed beautiful. But such beauty has always appeared to me skin deep. Beauty in women is a disturbing thing. But beyond the beauty it is always necessary to look for the greater qualities of manners and—a thing I always remind Winston of—no one is too young or too old to learn—manners and *ways*. She was beautiful. It was sad to think of her joined to Kedar for life, but she was perhaps fitted for nothing else. No need to speak of the resplendent regalia of Kedar himself: his turban, the crown with tassels and pendant glass, his richly embroidered silk jacket, and all those other adornments which for that night concealed so well the truck-driver that he was.

I left the wedding profoundly saddened. I could not help reflecting on my own position and contrasting it with Hori's or even Kedar's. I was now over forty, and marriage, which in the normal way would have come to me at the age of twenty or thereabouts, was still far from me. This was my own fault. Arranged marriages like Kedar's had no part in my scheme of things. I wished to marry, as the person says in *The Vicar of Wakefield*, someone who had qualities that would wear well.

My choice was severely restricted. I wished to marry a Presbyterian lady who was intelligent, well brought up and educated, and wished to marry me. This last condition, alas, I could find few willing to fulfil. And indeed I had little to offer. Among Hindus it would have been otherwise. There might have been men of substance who would have been willing to marry their daughters to a teacher, to acquire respectability and the glamour of a learned profession. Such a position has its strains, of course, for it means that the daughter remains, as it were, subject to her family; but the position is not without its charms.

You might imagine—and you would be correct—that at this time my faith was undergoing its severest strain. How often I was on the point of reneging I shudder to tell. I felt myself about to yield; I stiffened in my devotions and prayers. I reflected on the worthlessness of worldly things, but this was a reflection I found few to share. I might add here, in parenthesis and without vanity, that I had had several offers from the fathers of unconverted daughters, whose only condition was the one, about my religion, which I could not accept; for my previous caste had made me acceptable to many.

In this situation of doubt, of nightly wrestling with God, an expression whose meaning I came only then fully to understand, my fortune changed. I was appointed a headmaster. Now I can speak! How many people know of the tribulations, the pettiness, the intrigue which schoolteachers have to undergo to obtain such promotion? Such jockeying, such jealousy, such ill-will comes into play. What can I say of the advances one has to make, the rebuffs one has to suffer in silence, the waiting, the undoing of the unworthy who seek to push themselves forward for positions which they are ill-qualified to fill but which, by glibness and all the outward shows of respectability and efficiency and piety, they manage to persuade our superiors that they alone can fill? I too had my adversaries. My chief rival—but let him rest in peace! I am, I trust, a Christian, and will do no man the injustice of imagining him to persist in error even after we have left this vale of tears.

In my fortune, so opportune, I saw the hand of God. I speak in all earnestness. For without this I would surely have lapsed into the ways of darkness, for who among us can so steel himself as to resist temptation for all time? In my gratitude I applied myself with renewed dedication to my task. And it was this that doubtless evoked the gratification of my superiors which was to lead to my later elevation. For at a time when most men, worn out by the struggle, are content to relax, I showed myself more eager than before. I instituted prayers four times a day. I insisted on attendance at Sunday School. I taught Sunday School myself, and with the weight of my influence persuaded the other teachers to do likewise, so that Sunday became another day for us, a day of rest which we consumed with work for the Lord.

And I did not neglect the educational side. The blackboards all now sparkled with diagrams in chalks of various colours, projects which we had in hand. Oh, the school was such a pretty sight then! I instituted a rigid system of discipline, and forbade indiscriminate flogging by pupil teachers. All flogging I did myself on Friday afternoons, sitting in impartial judgement, as it were, on the school, on pupils as well as teachers. It is surely a better system, and I am glad to say that it has now been adopted throughout the island. The most apt pupils I kept after school, and for some trifling extra fee gave them private lessons. And the school became so involved with work as an ideal that had to be joyously pursued and not as something that had to be endured, that the usefulness of these private lessons was widely appreciated, and soon larger numbers than I could cope with were staying after school for what they affectionately termed their 'private'.

And I married. It was now in my power to marry virtually anyone I pleased and there were among the Sunday School staff not a few who made their attachment to me plain. I am not such a bad-looking fellow! But I wished to marry someone who had qualities that would wear well. I was nearly fifty. I did not wish to marry someone who was much younger than myself. And it was my good fortune at this juncture to receive an offer—I hesitate to use this word, which sounds so much like the Hindu custom and reminds one of the real estate business, but here I must be frank—from no less a person than a schools inspector, who had an unmarried daughter of thirty-five, a woman neglected by the men of the island because of her attainments—yes, you read right—which were considerable, but not of the sort that proclaims itself to the world. In our attitude to women much remains to be changed! I have often, during these past days, reflected on marriage. Such a turning, a point in time whence so many consequences flow. I wonder what Winston, poor boy, will do when his time comes.

My establishment could not rival Hori's or Kedar's for splendour, but within it there was peace and culture such as I had long dreamed of. It was a plain wooden house, but well built, built to last, unlike so many of these modern monstrosities which I see arising these days: and it was well ordered. We had simple bentwood chairs with cane bottoms. No marble-topped tables with ball-fringed lace! No glass cabinets! I hung my treasured framed teaching diploma on the wall, with my religious pictures and some scenes of the English countryside. It was also my good fortune at this time to get an old autographed photograph of one of our first missionaries. In the decoration of our humble home my wife appeared to release all the energy and experience of her thirty-five years which had so far been denied expression.

To her, as to myself, everything came late. It was our fear, confirmed by the views of many friends who behind their expressions of goodwill concealed as we presently saw much uncharitableness, that we would be unable to have children, considering our advanced years. But they, and we, underestimated the power of prayer, for within a year of our marriage Winston was born.

The birth of Winston came to us as a grace and a blessing. Yet it also filled me with anxiety, for I could not refrain from assessing the difference between our ages. It occurred to me, for instance, that he would be thirty when I was eighty. It was a disturbing thought, for the companionship of children is something which, perhaps because of my profession, I hold especially dear. My anxiety had another reason. It was that

Winston, in his most formative years, would be without not only my guidance—for what guidance can a man of seventy give to a lusty youngster of twenty?—but also without my financial support.

The problem of money, strange as it might appear, considering my unexpected elevation and all its accruing benefits, was occupying the minds of both my wife and myself. For my retirement was drawing near, and my pension would scarcely be more than what I subsisted on as a simple pupil teacher. It seemed then that like those pilgrims, whose enthusiasm I admire but cannot share, I was advancing towards my goal by taking two steps forward and one step back, though in my case a likelier simile might be that I was taking one step forward and one step back. So success always turns to ashes in the mouth of those who seek it as ardently as I had! And if I had the vision and the depth of faith which I now have, I might have seen even then how completely false are the things of this world, how much they flatter only to deceive.

We were both, as I say, made restless. And now the contemplation of baby Winston was a source of much pain to both of us, for the poor innocent creature could scarcely know what anguish awaited him when we would both be withdrawn from this vale of tears. His helplessness, his dependence tortured me. I was past the age when the taking out of an insurance policy was a practicable proposition; and during my days as a simple teacher I never had the resources to do so. It seemed, then, that I was being destroyed by my own good fortune, by the fruits of all my endeavour. Yet I did not heed this sign.

I continued while I could giving private lessons. I instituted a morning session as well, in addition to the afternoon one. But I did so with a heavy heart, tormented by the thought that in a few years this privilege and its small reward would be denied me, for private lessons, it must be understood, are considered the prerogative of a headmaster: in this way he stamps his character on the school. My results in the exhibition examinations for boys under twelve continued to be heartening; they far surpassed those of many other country schools.

My religious zeal continued unabated; and it was this zeal which, burning in those years when most men in my position would have relaxed—they, fortunate souls, having their children fully grown—it was this surprising zeal, I say, which also contributed, I feel, to my later elevation which, as you will see from the plain narration of these events, I did not seek.

My retirement drew nearer. I became fiercer at school. I wished all the boys under me could grow up at once. I was merciless towards the backward. My wife, poor creature, could not control her anxiety with as much success as myself. She had no occupation, no distracting vocation, in which her anxiety might have been consumed. She had only Winston, and this dear infant continually roused her to fears about his future. For his sake she would, I believe, have sacrificed her own life! It was not easy for her. And it required but the exercise of the mildest Christian charity to see that the reproaches she flung with increased acerbity and frequency at my head were but expressions of her anxiety. Sometimes, I must confess, I failed! And then my own unworthiness would torment me, as it torments me now.

We confided our problems to my wife's father, the schools inspector. Though we felt it unfair to let another partake of our troubles, it is none the less a recognized means of lightening any load which the individual finds too heavy to bear. But he, poor man, though as worried on his daughter's behalf as she was on Winston's, could offer only sympathy and little practical help. He reported that the authorities were unwilling to give me an extension of my tenure as headmaster. My despondency found expression in a display of temper, which he charitably forgave; for though he left the house, promising not to do another thing for us, he presently returned, and counselled patience.

So patient we were. I retired. I could hardly bear to remain at home, so used had I been to the daily round, the daily trials. I went out visiting, for no other reason than that I was afraid to be alone at home. My zeal, I believe, was remarked upon, though I took care to avoid the school, the scene of my late labours. I sought to take in for private lessons two or three pupils whose progress had deeply interested me. But my methods were no longer the methods that found favour! The parents of these children reported that the new headmaster had expressed himself strongly, and to my great disfavour, on the subject, to such a degree, in fact, that the progress of their children at school was being hampered. So I desisted; or rather, since the time has come for frankness, they left me.

The schools inspector, a regular visitor now at our humble, sad home, continued to counsel patience. I have so far refrained in this narrative from permitting my wife to speak directly; for I wish to do nothing that might increase the load she will surely have to bear, for my wife, though of considerable attainments, has not had the advantages of a formal education on which so much stress is nowadays laid. So I will refrain from chronicling the remark with which she greeted this advice of her father's. Suffice it to say that she spoke a children's rhyme without any great care for its metre or rhyme, the last of which indeed she destroyed by accidentally, in her haste, pulling down a vase from the centre-table on to the floor, where the water ran like one of the puddles which our baby Winston so lately made. After this incident relations between my wife and her father underwent a perceptible strain; and I took care to be out of the house as often as possible, and indeed it was pleasant to forget one's domestic troubles and walk abroad and be greeted as 'Headmaster' by the simple village folk.

Then, as it appears has happened so regularly throughout my life, the clouds rolled away and the sky brightened. I was appointed a School Manager. The announcement was made in the most heart-warming way possible, by the schools inspector himself, anticipating the official notification by a week or so. And the occasion became a family reunion. It was truly good to see the harassed schools inspector relaxing at last, and to see father and daughter reasonably happy with one another. My delight in this was almost as great as the delight in my new dignity.

For a school managership is a good thing to come to a man

in the evening of his days. It permits an exercise of the most benign power imaginable. It permits a man at a speech day function to ask for a holiday for the pupils; and nothing is as warming as the lusty and sincere cheering that follows such a request. It gives power even over headmasters, for one can make surprise visits and it is in one's power to make reports to the authorities. It is a position of considerable responsibility as well, for a school manager manages a school as much as a managing director manages a company. It is in his power to decide whether the drains, say, need to be remade entirely or need simply be plastered over to look as new; whether one coat of paint or two are needed; whether a ceiling can be partially renovated and painted over or taken out altogether and replaced. He orders the number of desks and blackboards which he considers necessary, and the chalks and the stationery. It is, in short, a dignity ideally suited to one who has led an active life and is dismayed by the prospect of retirement. It brings honour as well as reward. It has the other advantage that school managers are like civil servants; they are seldom dismissed; and their honours tend to increase rather than diminish.

I entered on my new tasks with zeal, and once again all was well at our home. My wife's father visited us regularly, as though, poor man, anxious to share the good fortune for which he was to a large measure responsible. I looked after the school, the staff, the pupils. I visited all the parents of the pupils under my charge and spoke to them of the benefits of education, the dangers of absenteeism, and so on. I know I will be forgiven if I add that from time to time, whenever the ground appeared ripe, I sowed the seed of Presbyterianism or at any rate doubt among those who continued in the ways of darkness. Such zeal was unknown among school managers. I cannot account for it myself. It might be that my early austerity and ambition had given me something of the crusading zeal. But it was inevitable that such zeal should have been too much for some people to stomach.

For all his honour, for all the sweet cheers that greet his

request for a holiday for the pupils, the school manager's position is one that sometimes attracts adverse and malicious comment. It is the fate of anyone who finds himself in a position of power and financial responsibility. The rumours persisted; and though they did not diminish the esteem in which I was so clearly held by the community—at the elections, for example, I was approached by all five candidates and asked to lend my voice to their cause, a situation of peculiar difficulty, which I resolved by promising all five to remain neutral, for which they were effusively grateful—it is no good thing for a man to walk among people who every day listen eagerly—for flesh is frail, and nothing attracts our simple villagers as much as scurrilous gossip—to slanders against himself. It was beneath my dignity, or rather, the dignity of my position, to reply to such attacks; and in this situation I turned, as I was turning with growing frequency, to my wife's father for advice. He suggested that I should relinquish one of my managerships, to indicate my disapproval of the gossip and the little esteem in which I held worldly honour. For I had so far succeeded in my new functions that I was now the manager of three schools, which was the maximum number permitted.

I followed his advice. I relinquished the managership of a school which was in a condition so derelict that not even repeated renovations could efface the original gimcrackery of its construction. This school had been the cause of most of the rumours, and my relinquishing of it attracted widespread comment and was even mentioned in the newspapers. It remained dear to me, but I was willing for it to go into other hands. This action of mine had the effect of stilling rumours and gossip. And the action proved to have its own reward, for some months later my wife's father, ever the bearer of good tidings, intimated that there was a possibility of a new school being put up in the area. I was thoroughly suited for its management; and he, the honest broker between the authorities and myself, said that my name was being mentioned in this connection. I was at that time manager of only two schools; I was entitled to a third. He warmly urged me to accept. I hesitated, and my hesitations were later proved to be justified. But the thought of a new school fashioned entirely according to my ideas and principles was too heady. I succumbed to temptation. If now I could only go back and withdraw that acceptance! The good man hurried back with the news; and within a fortnight I received the official notification.

I must confess that during the next few months I lost sight of my doubts in my zeal and enthusiasm for the new project. My two other schools suffered somewhat. For if there is a thing to delight the heart of the school manager, it is the management of a school not yet built. But, alas! We are at every step reminded of the vanity of worldly things. How often does it happen that a person, placed in the position he craves, a position which he is in every way suited to fill, suddenly loses his grip! Given the opportunity for which he longs, he is unable to make use of it. The effort goes all into the striving.

So now it happened with me. Nearly everything I touched failed to go as it should. I, so careful and correct in assessments and estimates, was now found repeatedly in error. None of my calculations were right. There were repeated shortages and stoppages. The school progressed far more slowly than I would have liked. And it was no consolation to me to find that in this moment I was alone, in this long moment of agony! Neither to my wife nor to her father could I turn for comfort. They savoured the joy of my managership of a new school without reference to me. I had my great opportunity; they had no doubt I would make use of it; and I could not bear disillusioning them or breaking into their happiness with my worries.

My errors attracted other errors. My errors multiplied, I tell you! To cover up one error I had to commit twenty acts of concealment, and these twenty had to be concealed. I felt myself caught in a curious inefficiency that seemed entirely beyond my control, something malignant, powered by forces hostile to myself. Until at length it seemed that failure was staring me in the face, and that my entire career would be forgotten in this crowning failure. The building went up, it is true. It had a respectable appearance. It looked a building. But it was far from what I had visualized. I had miscalculated badly, and it was too late to remedy the errors. Its faults, its weaknesses would be at once apparent even to the scantily trained eye. And now night after night I was tormented by this failure of mine. With the exercise of only a little judgement it could so easily have been made right. Yet now the time for that was past! Day after day I was drawn to the building, and every day I hoped that by some miracle it would have been effaced during the night. But there it always stood, a bitter reproach.

Matters were not made easier for me by the reproaches of my wife and her father. They both rounded on me and said with justice that my failure would involve them all. And the days went by! I could not—I have never liked bickering, the answering of insult with insult—I could not reproach them with having burdened me with such an enterprise at the end of my days. I did it for their glory, for I had acquired sufficient to last me until the end of my days. I did it for my wife and her father, and for my son Winston. But who will believe me? Who will believe that a man works for the glory of others, except he work for the glory of God? They reproached me. They stood aside from me. In this moment of need they deserted me.

They were bitter days. I went for long walks through our villages in the cool of the evening. The children ran out to greet me. Mothers looked up from their cooking, fathers from their perches on the roadside culverts, and greeted me, 'Headmaster!' And soon my failure would be apparent even to the humblest among them. I had to act quickly. Failures should be destroyed. The burning down of a school is an unforgiveable thing, but there are surely occasions when it can be condoned, when it is the only way out. Surely this was such an occasion! It is a drastic step. But it is one that has been taken more than once in this island. So I argued with myself. And always the answer was there; my failure had to be destroyed, not only for my own sake, but for the sake of all those, villagers included, whose fates were involved with mine.

Once I had made up my mind, I acted with decision. It was that time of year, mid-November, when people are beginning to think of Christmas to the exclusion of nearly everything else. This served my purpose well. I required—with what shame I now confess it—certain assistants, for it was necessary for me to be seen elsewhere on the day of the accident. Much money, much of what we had set aside for the future of our son Winston, had to go on this. And already it had been necessary to seal the lips of certain officials who had rejoiced in my failure and were willing to proclaim it to the world. But at last it was ready. On Boxing Day we would go to Port-of-Spain, to the races. When we returned the following day, the school would be no more. I say 'we', though my wife had not been apprised of my intentions.

With what fear, self-reproach, and self-disgust I waited for the days to pass! When I heard the Christmas carols, ever associated for me with the indefinable sweetness of Christmas Eve—which I now once more feel, thanks to my decision, though underneath there is a sense of doom and destruction, deserved, but with their own inevitable reward—when I heard carols and Christmas commercials on the radio, my heart sank; for it seemed that I had cut myself off from all about me, that once more I had become a stranger to the faith which I profess. So these days passed in sorrow, in nightly frenzies of prayer and self-castigation. Regret assailed me. Regret for what might have been, regret for what was to come. I was sinking, I felt, into a pit of defilement whence I could never emerge.

Of all this my wife knew nothing. But then she asked one day, 'What have you decided to do?' and, without waiting for my reply, at once drew up such a detailed plan, which corresponded so closely to what I had myself devised, that my heart quailed. For if, in this moment of my need, when the deepest resource was needed, I could devise a plan which might have been devised by anyone else, then discovery was certain. And to my shame, Winston, who only two or three days before had been teasing me with my previous unbaptized name, Winston took part in this discussion, with no appearance of shame on his face, only thrill and—sad am I to say it—a pride in me greater than I had ever seen the boy display.

How can one tell of the workings of the human heart? How

can one speak of the urge to evil—an urge of which Christians more than anyone else are so aware—and of the countervailing urge to good? You must remember that this is the season of goodwill. And goodwill it was. For goodwill was what I was feeling towards all. At every carol my heart melted. Whenever a child rushed towards me and cried, 'Headmaster!' I was tormented by grief. For the sight of the unwashed creatures, deprived, so many of them, of schooling, which matters so much in those early years, and the absence of which ever afterwards makes itself felt, condemning a human being to an animal-like existence, the sight of these creatures, grateful towards me who had on so many evenings gone among them propagating the creed with what energy I could, unmanned me. They were proud of their new school. They were even prouder of their association with the man who had built it.

Everywhere I felt rejected. I went to church as often as I could, but even there I found rejection. And as the time drew nearer the enormity of what I proposed grew clearer to me. It was useless to tell myself that what I was proposing had been often done. The carols, the religious services, the talk of birth and life, they all unmanned me.

I walked among the children as one who had it in his power to provide or withhold blessing, and I thought of that other Walker, who said of those among whom I walked that they were blessed, and that theirs was the kingdom of heaven. And as I walked it seemed that at last I had seized the true essence of the religion I had adopted, and whose worldly success I had with such energy promoted. So that it seemed that these trials I was undergoing had been reserved to the end of my days, so that only then I could have a taste of the ecstasy about which I had so far only read. With this ecstasy I walked. It was Christmas Eve. It was Christmas Eve. My head felt drawn out of my body. I had difficulty in assessing the size and distance of objects. I felt myself tall. I felt myself part of the earth and yet removed.

And: 'No!' I said to my wife at teatime. 'No, I will not disgrace myself by this action of cowardice. Rather, I will proclaim my failure to the world and ask for my due punishment.'

She behaved as I expected. She had been busy putting up all sorts of Christmas decorations, expensive ones from the United States, which are all the rage now, so unlike the simple decorations I used to see in the homes of our early missionaries before the war. But how changed is the house to which we moved! How far has simplicity vanished and been replaced by show! And I gloried in it!

She begged me to change my mind. She summoned Winston to her help. They both wept and implored me to go through with our plan. But I was firm. I do believe that if the schools inspector were alive, he would also have been summoned to plead with me. But he, fortunate man, passed away some three weeks ago, entrusting his daughter and grandson to my care; and this alone is my fear, that by gaining glory for myself I might be injuring them. But I was firm. And then there started another of those scenes with which I had become only too familiar, and the house which that morning was filled with the enthusiasm of Winston was changed into one of mourning. Winston sobbed, tears running down his plump cheeks and down his well-shaped nose to his firm top lip, pleading with me to burn the school down, and generally behaving as though I had deprived him of a bonfire. And then a number of things were destroyed by his mother, and she left the house with Winston, vowing never to see me again, never to be involved in the disgrace which was sure to come.

And so here I sit, waiting not for Christmas, but in this house where the autographed photograph of one of our earliest missionaries gazes down at me through his rich beard and luxuriant eyebrows, and where the walls carry so many reminders of my past life of endeavour and hardship and struggle and triumph and also, alas, final failure, I wait for the day after Boxing Day, after the races to which we were to have gone, for the visit of the inspectors of the Audit Department. The house is lonely and dark. The radios play the Christmas songs. I am very lonely. But I am strong. And here I lay down my pen. My hand tires; the beautiful letters we were taught to fashion at the mission school have begun to weaken and to straggle untidily over the ruled paper; and someone is knocking.

December 27. How can one speak of the ways of the world, how can one speak of the tribulations that come one's way? Even expiation is denied me. For even as I wrote the last sentence of the above account, there came a knocking at my door, and I went to open unto him who knocked. And lo, there was a boy, bearing tidings. And behold, towards the west the sky had reddened, the boy informed me that the school was ablaze. What could I do? My world fell about my ears. Even final expiation, final triumph, it seemed, was denied me. Certain things are not for me. In this moment of anguish and despair my first thought was for my wife. Where had she gone? I went out to seek her. When I returned, after a fruitless errand, I discovered that she and Winston had come back to seek me. Smiling through our tears, we embraced. So it was Christmas after all for us. And, with lightened heart, made heavy only by my wrestling with the Lord, we went to the races on Boxing Day, yesterday. We did not gamble. It is against our principles. The inspectors from the Audit Department sent word today that they would not, after all, come.

R. K. NARAYAN

A Horse and Two Goats

OF THE seven hundred thousand villages dotting the map of India, in which the majority of India's five hundred million live, flourish, and die, Kritam was probably the tiniest, indicated on the district survey map by a microscopic dot, the map being meant more for the revenue official out to collect tax than for the guidance of the motorist, who in any case could not hope to reach it since it sprawled far from the highway at the end of a rough track furrowed up by the iron-hooped wheels of bullock carts. But its size did not prevent its giving itself the grandiose name Kritam, which meant in Tamil 'coronet' or 'crown' on the brow of this subcontinent. The village consisted of less than thirty houses, only one of them built with brick and cement. Painted a brilliant yellow and blue all over with gorgeous carvings of gods and gargoyles on its balustrade, it was known as the Big House. The other houses, distributed in four streets, were generally of bamboo thatch, straw, mud, and other unspecified material. Muni's was the last house in the fourth street, beyond which stretched the fields. In his prosperous days Muni had owned a flock of forty sheep and goats and sallied forth every morning driving the flock to the highway a couple of miles away. There he would sit on the pedestal of a clay statue of a horse while his cattle grazed around. He carried a crook at the end of a bamboo pole and snapped foliage from the avenue trees to feed his flock; he also gathered faggots and dry sticks, bundled them, and carried them home for fuel at sunset.

His wife lit the domestic fire at dawn, boiled water in a mud pot, threw into it a handful of millet flour, added salt, and gave him his first nourishment for the day. When he started out, she would put in his hand a packed lunch, once again the same millet cooked into a little ball, which he could swallow with a raw onion at midday. She was old, but he was older and needed all the attention she could give him in order to be kept alive.

His fortunes had declined gradually, unnoticed. From a flock of forty which he drove into a pen at night, his stock had now come down to two goats which were not worth the rent of a half rupee a month the Big House charged for the use of the pen in their back yard. And so the two goats were tethered to the trunk of a drumstick tree which grew in front of his hut and from which occasionally Muni could shake down drumsticks. This morning he got six. He carried them in with a sense of triumph. Although no one could say precisely who owned the tree, it was his because he lived in its shadow.

She said, 'If you were content with the drumstick leaves alone, I could boil and salt some for you.'

'Oh, I am tired of eating those leaves. I have a craving to chew the drumstick out of sauce, I tell you.'

'You have only four teeth in your jaw, but your craving is for big things. All right, get the stuff for the sauce, and I will prepare it for you. After all, next year you may not be alive to ask for anything. But first get me all the stuff, including a measure of rice or millet, and I will satisfy your unholy craving. Our store is empty today. Dhal, chili, curry leaves, mustard, coriander, gingelley oil, and one large potato. Go out and get all this.' He repeated the list after her in order not to miss any item and walked off to the shop in the third street.

He sat on an upturned packing case below the platform of the shop. The shopman paid no attention to him. Muni kept clearing his throat, coughing, and sneezing until the shopman could not stand it any more and demanded, 'What ails you? You will fly off that seat into the gutter if you sneeze so hard, young man.' Muni laughed inordinately, in order to please the shopman, at being called 'young man'. The shopman softened and said, 'You have enough of the imp inside to keep a second wife busy, but for the fact the old lady is still alive.' Muni laughed appropriately again at this joke. It completely won the shopman over; he liked his sense of humour to be appreciated. Muni engaged his attention in local gossip for a few minutes, which always ended with a reference to the postman's wife who had eloped to the city some months before.

The shopman felt most pleased to hear the worst of the postman, who had cheated him. Being an itinerant postman, he returned home to Kritam only once in ten days and every time managed to slip away again without passing the shop in the third street. By thus humouring the shopman, Muni could always ask for one or two items of food, promising repayment later. Some days the shopman was in a good mood and gave in, and sometimes he would lose his temper suddenly and bark at Muni for daring to ask for credit. This was such a day, and Muni could not progress beyond two items listed as essential components. The shopman was also displaying a remarkable memory for old facts and figures and took out an oblong ledger to support his observations. Muni felt impelled to rise and flee. But his self-respect kept him in his seat and made him listen to the worst things about himself. The shopman concluded, 'If you could find five rupees and a quarter, you would pay off an ancient debt and then could apply for admission to swarga. How much have you got now?'

'I will pay you everything on the first of the next month.'

'As always, and whom do you expect to rob by then?'

Muni felt caught and mumbled, 'My daughter has sent word that she will be sending me money.'

'Have you a daughter?' sneered the shopman. 'And she is sending you money! For what purpose, may I know?'

'Birthday, fiftieth birthday,' said Muni quietly.

'Birthday! How old are you?'

Muni repeated weakly, not being sure of it himself, 'Fifty'. He always calculated his age from the time of the great famine when he stood as high as the parapet around the village well, but who could calculate such things accurately nowadays with so many famines occurring? The shopman felt encouraged when other customers stood around to watch and comment. Muni thought helplessly, My poverty is exposed to everybody. But what can I do?

'More likely you are seventy,' said the shopman. 'You also forget that you mentioned a birthday five weeks ago when you wanted castor oil for your holy bath.'

'Bath! Who can dream of a bath when you have to scratch

the tank-bed for a bowl of water? We would all be parched and dead but for the Big House, where they let us take a pot of water from their well.' After saying this Muni unobtrusively rose and moved off.

He told his wife, 'That scoundrel would not give me anything. So go out and sell the drumsticks for what they are worth.'

He flung himself down in a corner to recoup from the fatigue of his visit to the shop. His wife said, 'You are getting no sauce today, nor anything else. I can't find anything to give you to eat. Fast till the evening, it'll do you good. Take the goats and be gone now,' she cried and added, 'Don't come back before the sun is down.' He knew that if he obeyed her she would somehow conjure up some food for him in the evening. Only he must be careful not to argue and irritate her. Her temper was undependable in the morning but improved by evening time. She was sure to go out and work—grind corn in the Big House, sweep or scrub somewhere, and earn enough to buy foodstuff and keep a dinner ready for him in the evening.

Unleashing the goats from the drumstick tree, Muni started out, driving them ahead and uttering weird cries from time to time in order to urge them on. He passed through the village with his head bowed in thought. He did not want to look at anyone or be accosted. A couple of cronies lounging in the temple corridor hailed him, but he ignored their call. They had known him in the days of affluence when he lorded over a flock of fleecy sheep, not the miserable gawky goats that he had today. Of course he also used to have a few goats for those who fancied them, but real wealth lay in sheep; they bred fast and people came and bought the fleece in the shearing season; and then that famous butcher from the town came over on the weekly market days bringing him betel leaves, tobacco, and often enough some bhang, which they smoked in a hut in the coconut grove, undisturbed by wives and well-wishers. After a smoke one felt light and elated and inclined to forgive everyone including that brother-in-law of his who had once tried to set fire to his home. But all this seemed like the memoirs of a previous birth. Some pestilence afflicted his cattle (he could of course guess who had laid his animals under a curse) and even the friendly butcher would not touch one at half the price . . . and now here he was left with the two scraggy creatures. He wished someone would rid him of their company too. The shopman had said that he was seventy. At seventy, one only waited to be summoned by God. When he was dead what would his wife do? They had lived in each other's company since they were children. He was told on their day of wedding that he was ten years old and she was eight. During the wedding ceremony they had had to recite their respective ages and names. He had thrashed her only a few times in their career, and later she had the upper hand. Progeny, none. Perhaps a large progeny would have brought him the blessing of the gods. Fertility brought merit. People with fourteen sons were always so prosperous and at peace with the world and themselves. He recollected the thrill he had felt when he mentioned a daughter to that shopman; although it was not believed, what if he did not have a daughter?—his cousin in the next village had many daughters, and any one of them was as good as his; he was fond of them all and would buy them sweets if he could afford it. Still, everyone in the village whispered behind their backs that Muni and his wife were a barren couple. He avoided looking at anyone; they all professed to be so high up, and everyone else in the village had more money than he. 'I am the poorest fellow in our caste and no wonder that they spurn me, but I won't look at them either', and so he passed on with his eyes downcast along the edge of the street, and people left him also very much alone, commenting only to the extent, 'Ah, there he goes with his two great goats; if he slits their throats, he may have more peace of mind.' 'What has he to worry about anyway? They live on nothing and have nobody to worry about.' Thus people commented when he passed through the village. Only on the outskirts did he lift his head and look up. He urged and bullied the goats until they meandered along to the foot of the horse statue on the edge of the village. He sat on its pedestal for the rest of the day. The advantage of this was that he could watch the highway and see the lorries and buses pass through to the hills, and it gave him a sense of belonging to a larger world. The pedestal of the statue was broad enough for him to move around as the sun travelled up and westward; or he could also crouch under the belly of the horse, for shade.

The horse was nearly life-size, moulded out of clay, baked, burnt, and brightly coloured, and reared its head proudly, prancing its forelegs in the air and flourishing its tail in a loop; beside the horse stood a warrior with scythe-like mustachios, bulging eyes, and aquiline nose. The old image-makers believed in indicating a man of strength by bulging out his eyes and sharpening his moustache tips, and also had decorated the man's chest with beads which looked today like blobs of mud through the ravages of sun and wind and rain (when it came), but Muni would insist that he had known the beads to sparkle like the nine gems at one time in his life. The horse itself was said to have been as white as a dhobi-washed sheet, and had had on its back a cover of pure brocade of red and black lace, matching the multicoloured sash around the waist of the warrior. But none in the village remembered the splendour as no one noticed its existence. Even Muni, who spent all his waking hours at its foot, never bothered to look up. It was untouched by the young vandals of the village who gashed tree trunks with knives and tried to topple off milestones and inscribed lewd designs on all the walls. This statue had been closer to the population of the village at one time, when this spot bordered the village; but when the highway was laid through (or perhaps when the tank and wells dried up completely here) the village moved a couple of miles inland.

Muni sat at the foot of the statue, watching his two goats graze in the arid soil among the cactus and lantana bushes. He looked at the sun; it had tilted westward no doubt, but it was not the time yet to go back home; if he went too early his wife would have no food for him. Also he must give her time to cool off her temper and feel sympathetic, and then she would scrounge and manage to get some food. He watched the mountain road for a time signal. When the green bus appeared around the bend he could leave, and his wife would feel pleased that he had let the goats feed long enough.

He noticed now a new sort of vehicle coming down at full speed. It looked both like a motor car and a bus. He used to be intrigued by the novelty of such spectacles, but of late work was going on at the source of the river on the mountain and an assortment of people and traffic went past him, and he took it all casually and described to his wife, later in the day, not everything as he once did, but only some things, only if he noticed anything special. Today, while he observed the yellow vehicle coming down, he was wondering how to describe it later when it sputtered and stopped in front of him. A red-faced foreigner who had been driving it got down and went round it, stooping, looking, and poking under the vehicle; then he straightened himself up, looked at the dashboard, stared in Muni's direction, and approached him. 'Excuse me, is there a gas station nearby, or do I have to wait until another car comes——' He suddenly looked up at the clay horse and cried, 'Marvellous!' without completing his sentence. Muni felt he should get up and run away, and cursed his age. He could not readily put his limbs into action; some years ago he could out-run a cheetah, as happened once when he went to the forest to cut fuel and it was then that two of his sheep were mauled—a sign that bad times were coming. Though he tried, he could not easily extricate himself from his seat, and then there was also the problem of the goats. He could not leave them behind.

The red-faced man wore khaki clothes—evidently a police-man or a soldier. Muni said to himself, 'He will chase or shoot if I start running. Sometimes dogs chase only those who run—O Shiva protect me. I don't know why this man should be after me.' Meanwhile the foreigner cried, 'Marvellous!' again, nodding his head. He paced around the statue with his eyes fixed on it. Muni sat frozen for a while, and then fidgeted and tried to edge away. Now the other man suddenly pressed his palms together in a salute, smiled, and said, 'Namaste! How do you do?'

At which Muni spoke the only English expressions he had learnt, 'Yes, no.' Having exhausted his English vocabulary, he started in Tamil: 'My name is Muni. These two goats are mine, and no one can gainsay it—though our village is full of slanderers these days who will not hesitate to say that what belongs to a man doesn't belong to him.' He rolled his eyes and shuddered at the thought of evil-minded men and women peopling his village.

The foreigner faithfully looked in the direction indicated by Muni's fingers, gazed for a while at the two goats and the rocks, and with a puzzled expression took out his silver cigarette-case and lit a cigarette. Suddenly remembering the courtesies of the season, he asked, 'Do you smoke?' Muni answered, 'Yes, no.' Whereupon the red-faced man took a cigarette and gave it to Muni, who received it with surprise, having had no offer of a smoke from anyone for years now. Those days when he smoked bhang were gone with his sheep and the large-hearted butcher. Nowadays he was not able to find even matches, let alone bhang. (His wife went across and borrowed a fire at dawn from a neighbour.) He had always wanted to smoke a cigarette; only once had the shopman given him one on credit, and he remembered how good it had tasted. The other flicked the lighter open and offered a light to Muni. Muni felt so confused about how to act that he blew on it and put it out. The other, puzzled but undaunted, flourished his lighter, presented it again, and lit Muni's cigarette. Muni drew a deep puff and started coughing; it was racking, no doubt, but extremely pleasant. When his cough subsided he wiped his eyes and took stock of the situation, understanding that the other man was not an inquisitor of any kind. Yet, in order to make sure, he remained wary. No need to run away from a man who gave him such a potent smoke. His head was reeling from the effect of one of those strong American cigarettes made with roasted tobacco. The man said, 'I come from New York,' took out a wallet from his hip pocket, and presented his card.

Muni shrank away from the card. Perhaps he was trying to present a warrant and arrest him. Beware of khaki, one part of his mind warned. Take all the cigarettes or bhang or whatever is offered, but don't get caught. Beware of khaki. He wished he weren't seventy as the shopman had said. At seventy one didn't run, but surrendered to whatever came. He could only

ward off trouble by talk. So he went on, all in the chaste Tamil
for which Kritam was famous. (Even the worst detractors
could not deny that the famous poetess Avvaiyar was born in
this area, although no one could say whether it was in Kritam
or Kuppam, the adjoining village.) Out of this heritage the
Tamil language gushed through Muni in an unimpeded flow.
He said, 'Before God, sir, Bhagwan, who sees everything, I tell
you, sir, that we know nothing of the case. If the murder was
committed, whoever did it will not escape. Bhagwan is all-
seeing. Don't ask me about it. I know nothing.' A body had
been found mutilated and thrown under a tamarind tree at the
border between Kritam and Kuppam a few weeks before,
giving rise to much gossip and speculation. Muni added an
explanation, 'Anything is possible there. People over there will
stop at nothing.' The foreigner nodded his head and listened
courteously though he understood nothing.

'I am sure you know when this horse was made,' said the red
man and smiled ingratiatingly.

Muni reacted to the relaxed atmosphere by smiling himself,
and pleaded, 'Please go away, sir, I know nothing. I promise
we will hold him for you if we see any bad character around,
and we will bury him up to his neck in a coconut pit if he tries
to escape; but our village has always had a clean record. Must
definitely be the other village.'

Now the red man implored, 'Please, please, I will speak
slowly, please try to understand me. Can't you understand
even a simple word of English? Everyone in this country seems
to know English. I have got along with English everywhere in
this country, but you don't speak it. Have you any religious or
spiritual scruples for avoiding the English speech?'

Muni made some indistinct sounds in his throat and shook
his head. Encouraged, the other went on to explain at length,
uttering each syllable with care and deliberation. Presently he
sidled over and took a seat beside the old man, explaining,
'You see, last August, we probably had the hottest summer in
history, and I was working in shirt-sleeves in my office on the
fortieth floor of the Empire State Building. You must have
heard of the power failure, and there I was stuck for four hours,

no elevator, no air conditioning. All the way in the train I kept thinking, and the minute I reached home in Connecticut, I told my wife Ruth, "We will visit India this winter, it's time to look at other civilizations." Next day she called the travel agent first thing and told him to fix it, and so here I am. Ruth came with me but is staying back at Srinagar, and I am the one doing the rounds and joining her later.'

Muni looked reflective at the end of this long peroration and said, rather feebly, 'Yes, no,' as a concession to the other's language, and went on in Tamil, 'When I was this high,' he indicated a foot high, 'I heard my uncle say . . .'

No one can tell what he was planning to say as the other interrupted him at this stage to ask, 'Boy, what is the secret of your teeth? How old are you?'

The old man forgot what he had started to say and remarked, 'Sometimes we too lose our cattle. Jackals or cheetahs may carry them off, but sometimes it is just theft from over in the next village, and then we will know who has done it. Our priest at the temple can see in the camphor flame the face of the thief, and when he is caught . . .' He gestured with his hands a perfect mincing of meat.

The American watched his hands intently and said, 'I know what you mean. Chop something? Maybe I am holding you up and you want to chop wood? Where is your axe? Hand it to me and show me what to chop. I do enjoy it, you know, just a hobby. We get a lot of driftwood along the backwater near my house, and on Sundays I do nothing but chop wood for the fireplace. I really feel different when I watch the fire in the fireplace, although it may take all the sections of the Sunday *New York Times* to get a fire started,' and he smiled at this reference.

Muni felt totally confused but decided the best thing would be to make an attempt to get away from this place. He tried to edge out, saying, 'Must go home,' and turned to go. The other seized his shoulder and said desperately, 'Is there no one, absolutely no one here, to translate for me?' He looked up and down the road, which was deserted in this hot afternoon; a sudden gust of wind churned up the dust and dead leaves on

the roadside into a ghostly column and propelled it towards the
mountain road. The stranger almost pinioned Muni's back to
the statue and asked, 'Isn't this statue yours? Why don't you
sell it to me?'

The old man now understood the reference to the horse,
thought for a second, and said in his own language, 'I was an
urchin this high when I heard my grandfather explain this
horse and warrior, and my grandfather himself was this high
when he heard his grandfather, whose grandfather . . .'

The other man interrupted him with, 'I don't want to seem
to have stopped here for nothing. I will offer you a good price
for this,' he said, indicating the horse. He had concluded without the least doubt that Muni owned this mud horse. Perhaps
he guessed by the way he sat at its pedestal, like other souvenir-
sellers in this country presiding over their wares.

Muni followed the man's eyes and pointing fingers and
dimly understood the subject matter and, feeling relieved that
the theme of the mutilated body had been abandoned at least
for the time being, said again, enthusiastically, 'I was this high
when my grandfather told me about this horse and the warrior,
and my grandfather was this high when he himself . . .' and he
was getting into a deeper bog of reminiscence each time he
tried to indicate the antiquity of the statue.

The Tamil that Muni spoke was stimulating even as pure
sound, and the foreigner listened with fascination. 'I wish I had
my tape-recorder here,' he said, assuming the pleasantest
expression. 'Your language sounds wonderful. I get a kick out
of every word you utter, here'—he indicated his ears—'but you
don't have to waste your breath in sales talk. I appreciate the
article. You don't have to explain its points.'

'I never went to a school, in those days only Brahmin went
to schools, but we had to go out and work in the fields morning
till night, from sowing to harvest time . . . and when Pongal
came and we had cut the harvest, my father allowed me to go
out and play with others at the tank, and so I don't know the
Parangi language you speak, even little fellows in your country
probably speak the Parangi language, but here only learned
men and officers know it. We had a postman in our village who

could speak to you boldly in your language, but his wife ran
away with someone and he does not speak to anyone at all
nowadays. Who would if a wife did what she did? Women
must be watched; otherwise they will sell themselves and the
home,' and he laughed at his own quip.

The foreigner laughed heartily, took out another cigarette,
and offered it to Muni, who now smoked with ease, deciding to
stay on if the fellow was going to be so good as to keep up his
cigarette supply. The American now stood up on the pedestal
in the attitude of a demonstrative lecturer and said, running
his finger along some of the carved decorations around the
horse's neck, speaking slowly and uttering his words syllable by
syllable, 'I could give a sales talk for this better than anyone
else . . . This is a marvellous combination of yellow and indigo,
though faded now . . . How do you people of this country
achieve these flaming colours?'

Muni, now assured that the subject was still the horse and
not the dead body, said, 'This is our guardian, it means death
to our adversaries. At the end of Kali Yuga, this world and all
other worlds will be destroyed, and the Redeemer will come in
the shape of a horse called Kalki; this horse will come to life
and gallop and trample down all bad men.' As he spoke of bad
men the figures of his shopman and his brother-in-law assumed
concrete forms in his mind, and he revelled for a moment in
the predicament of the fellow under the horse's hoof: served
him right for trying to set fire to his home . . .

While he was brooding on this pleasant vision, the foreigner
utilized the pause to say, 'I assure you that this will have the
best home in the U.S.A. I'll push away the bookcase, you know
I love books and am a member of five book clubs, and the
choice and bonus volumes really mount up to a pile in our
living-room, as high as this horse itself. But they'll have to go.
Ruth may disapprove, but I will convince her. The T.V. may
have to be shifted too. We can't have everything in the living-
room. Ruth will probably say what about when we have a
party? I'm going to keep him right in the middle of the room.
I don't see how that can interfere with the party—we'll stand
around him and have our drinks.'

Muni continued his description of the end of the world. 'Our pundit discoursed at the temple once how the oceans are going to close over the earth in a huge wave and swallow us—this horse will grow bigger than the biggest wave and carry on its back only the good people and kick into the floods the evil ones—plenty of them about,' he said reflectively. 'Do you know when it is going to happen?' he asked.

The foreigner now understood by the tone of the other that a question was being asked and said, 'How am I transporting it? I can push the seat back and make room in the rear. That van can take in an elephant —waving precisely at the back of the seat.

Muni was still hovering on visions of avatars and said again, 'I never missed our pundit's discourses at the temple in those days during every bright half of the month, although he'd go on all night, and he told us that Vishnu is the highest god. Whenever evil men trouble us, he comes down to save us. He has come many times. The first time he incarnated as a great fish, and lifted the scriptures on his back when the floods and sea-waves . . .'

'I am not a millionaire, but a modest businessman. My trade is coffee.'

Amidst all this wilderness of obscure sound Muni caught the word 'coffee' and said, 'If you want to drink "kapi", drive further up, in the next town, they have Friday market, and there they open "kapi-otels"—so I learn from passers-by. Don't think I wander about. I go nowhere and look for nothing.' His thoughts went back to the avatars. 'The first avatar was in the shape of a little fish in a bowl of water, but every hour it grew bigger and bigger and became in the end a huge whale which the seas could not contain, and on the back of the whale the holy books were supported, saved, and carried.' Having launched on the first avatar it was inevitable that he should go on to the next, a wild boar on whose tusk the earth was lifted when a vicious conqueror of the earth carried it off and hid it at the bottom of the sea. After describing this avatar Muni concluded, 'God will always save us whenever we are troubled by evil beings. When we were young we staged at full moon the story of the avatars. That's how I know the stories; we played them all night until the sun rose, and sometimes the European collector would come to watch, bringing his own chair. I had a good voice and so they always taught me songs and gave me the women's roles. I was always Goddess Laxmi, and they dressed me in a brocade sari, loaned from the Big House . . .'

The foreigner said, 'I repeat I am not a millionaire. Ours is a modest business; after all, we can't afford to buy more than sixty minutes' T.V. time in a month, which works out to two minutes a day, that's all, although in the course of time we'll maybe sponsor a one-hour show regularly if our sales graph continues to go up . . .'

Muni was intoxicated by the memory of his theatrical days and was about to explain how he had painted his face and worn a wig and diamond earrings when the visitor, feeling that he had spent too much time already, said, 'Tell me, will you accept a hundred rupees or not for the horse? I'd love to take the whiskered soldier also but I've no space for him this year. I'll have to cancel my air ticket and take a boat home, I suppose. Ruth can go by air if she likes, but I will go with the horse and keep him in my cabin all the way if necessary,' and he smiled at the picture of himself voyaging across the seas hugging this horse. He added, 'I will have to pad it with straw so that it doesn't break . . .'

'When we played *Ramayana*, they dressed me as Sita,' added Muni. 'A teacher came and taught us the songs for the drama and we gave him fifty rupees. He incarnated himself as Rama, and he alone could destroy Ravana, the demon with ten heads who shook all the worlds; do you know the story of Ramayana?'

'I have my station wagon as you see. I can push the seat back and take the horse in if you will just lend me a hand with it.'

'Do you know *Mahabharata*? Krishna was the eighth avatar of Vishnu, incarnated to help the Five Brothers regain their kingdom. When Krishna was a baby he danced on the thousand-hooded giant serpent and trampled it to death; and then he suckled the breasts of the demoness and left them flat as a disc though when she came to him her bosoms were large, like mounds of earth on the banks of a dug-up canal.' He indicated two mounds with his hands. The stranger was completely mystified by the gesture. For the first time he said, 'I really wonder what you are saying because your answer is crucial. We have come to the point when we should be ready to talk business.'

'When the tenth avatar comes, do you know where you and I will be?' asked the old man.

'Lend me a hand and I can lift off the horse from its pedestal after picking out the cement at the joints. We can do anything if we have a basis of understanding.'

At this stage the mutual mystification was complete, and there was no need even to carry on a guessing game at the meaning of words. The old man chattered away in a spirit of balancing off the credits and debits of conversational exchange, and said in order to be on the credit side, 'O honourable one, I hope God has blessed you with numerous progeny. I say this because you seem to be a good man, willing to stay beside an old man and talk to him, while all day I have none to talk to except when somebody stops by to ask for a piece of tobacco. But I seldom have it, tobacco is not what it used to be at one time, and I have given up chewing. I cannot afford it nowadays.' Noting the other's interest in his speech, Muni felt encouraged to ask, 'How many children have you?' with appropriate gestures with his hands. Realizing that a question was being asked, the red man replied, 'I said a hundred,' which encouraged Muni to go into details, 'How many of your children are boys and how many girls? Where are they? Is your daughter married? Is it difficult to find a son-in-law in your country also?'

In answer to these questions the red man dashed his hand into his pocket and brought forth his wallet in order to take immediate advantage of the bearish trend in the market. He flourished a hundred-rupee currency note and asked, 'Well, this is what I meant.'

The old man now realized that some financial element was entering their talk. He peered closely at the currency note, the like of which he had never seen in his life; he knew the five and ten by their colours although always in other people's hands, while his own earning at any time was in coppers and nickels. What was this man flourishing the note for? Perhaps asking for change. He laughed to himself at the notion of anyone coming to him for changing a thousand- or ten-thousand-rupee note. He said with a grin, 'Ask our village headman, who is also a moneylender; he can change even a lakh of rupees in gold sovereigns if you prefer it that way; he thinks nobody knows, but dig the floor of his puja room and your head will reel at the sight of the hoard. The man disguises himself in rags just to mislead the public. Talk to the headman yourself because he goes mad at the sight of me. Someone took away his pumpkins with the creeper and he, for some reason, thinks it was me and my goats . . . that's why I never let my goats be seen anywhere near the farms.' His eyes travelled to his goats nosing about, attempting to wrest nutrition from minute greenery peeping out of rock and dry earth.

The foreigner followed his look and decided that it would be a sound policy to show an interest in the old man's pets. He went up casually to them and stroked their backs with every show of courteous attention. Now the truth dawned on the old man. His dream of a lifetime was about to be realized. He understood that the red man was actually making an offer for the goats. He had reared them up in the hope of selling them some day and, with the capital, opening a small shop on this very spot. Sitting here, watching the hills, he had often dreamt how he would put up a thatched roof here, spread a gunny sack out on the ground, and display on it fried nuts, coloured sweets, and green coconut for the thirsty and famished wayfarers on the highway, which was sometimes very busy. The animals were not prize ones for a cattle show, but he had spent his occasional savings to provide them some fancy diet now and then, and they did not look too bad. While he was reflecting thus, the red man shook his hand and left on his palm one hundred rupees in tens now. 'It is all for you or you may share it if you have the partner.'

The old man pointed at the station wagon and asked. 'Are you carrying them off in that?'

'Yes, of course,' said the other, understanding the transportation part of it.

The old man said, 'This will be their first ride in a motor car. Carry them off after I get out of sight, otherwise they will never follow you, but only me even if I am travelling on the path to Yama Loka.' He laughed at his own joke, brought his palms together in a salute, turned round and went off, and was soon out of sight beyond a clump of thicket.

The red man looked at the goats grazing peacefully. Perched on the pedestal of the horse, as the westerly sun touched the ancient faded colours of the statue with a fresh splendour, he ruminated, 'He must be gone to fetch some help, I suppose!' and settled down to wait. When a truck came downhill, he stopped it and got the help of a couple of men to detach the horse from its pedestal and place it in his station wagon. He gave them five rupees each, and for a further payment they siphoned off gas from the truck and helped him to start his engine.

Muni hurried homeward with the cash securely tucked away at his waist in his dhoti. He shut the street door and stole up softly to his wife as she squatted before the lit oven wondering if by a miracle food would drop from the sky. Muni displayed his fortune for the day. She snatched the notes from him, counted them by the glow of the fire, and cried, 'One hundred rupees! How did you come by it? Have you been stealing?'

'I have sold our goats to a red-faced man. He was absolutely crazy to have them, gave me all this money and carried them off in his motor car!'

Hardly had these words left his lips when they heard bleating outside. She opened the door and saw the two goats at her door. 'Here they are!' she said. 'What's the meaning of all this?'

He muttered a great curse and seized one of the goats by its ears and shouted, 'Where is that man? Don't you know you are his? Why did you come back?' The goat only wriggled in his grip. He asked the same question of the other too. The goat shook itself off. His wife glared at him and declared, 'If you have thieved, the police will come tonight and break your bones. Don't involve me. I will go away to my parents. . . .'

JEAN RHYS

Tigers are Better-Looking

'MEIN LIEB, Mon Cher, My Dear, Amigo,' the letter began.

I'm off. I've been wanting to go for some time, as I'm sure you know, but was waiting for the moment when I had the courage to step out into the cold world again. Didn't feel like a farewell scene.

Apart from much that it is *better* not to go into, you haven't any idea how sick I am of all the phoney talk about Communism—and the phoney talk of the other lot too, if it comes to that. You people are exactly alike, whatever you call yourselves—Untouchable. Indispensable is the motto, and you'd pine to death if you hadn't someone to look down on and insult. I got the feeling that I was surrounded by a pack of timid tigers waiting to spring the moment anybody is in trouble or hasn't any money. *But tigers are better-looking, aren't they?*

I'm taking the coach to Plymouth. I have my plans.

I came to London with high hopes, but all I got out of it was a broken leg and enough sneers to last me for the next thirty years if I live so long, which may God forbid.

Don't think I'll forget how kind you were after my accident—having me to stay with you and all that. But assez means enough.

I've drunk the milk in the refrigerator. I was thirsty after that party last night, though if you call that a party I call it a wake. Besides, I know how you dislike the stuff (Freud! Bow-wow-wow!!) So you'll have to have your tea straight, my dear.

Good-bye. I'll write you again when times are better.

HANS

There was a postscript:

Mind you write a swell article today, you tame grey mare.

Mr. Severn sighed. He had always known Hans would hop it sooner or later, so why this taste in his mouth, as if he had eaten dust?

A swell article.

The band in the Embankment Gardens played. It's the same old song once again. It's the same old tender refrain. *As the carriages came into sight some of the crowd cheered and a fat man said he couldn't see and he was going to climb a lamp-post. The figures in the carriages bowed from right to left—victims bowed to victimized. The bloodless sacrifice was being exhibited, the reminder that somewhere the sun is shining, even if it doesn't shine on everybody.*

"E looked just like a waxwork, didn't 'e?" a woman said with satisfaction. . . .

No, that would never do.

He looked out of the window at the Lunch Edition placards outside the newspaper shop opposite. 'JUBILEE PICTURES—PICTURES—PICTURES' and 'HEAT WAVE COMING'.

The flat over the shop was occupied by a raffish middle-aged woman. But today her lace-curtained windows, usually not unfriendly, added to his feeling of desolation. So did the words 'PICTURES—PICTURES—PICTURES'.

By six o'clock the floor was covered with newspapers and crumpled, discarded starts of the article which he wrote every week for an Australian paper.

He couldn't get the swing of it. The swing's the thing, as everybody knows—otherwise the cadence of the sentence. Once into it, and he could go ahead like an old horse trotting, saying anything that anybody liked.

'The tame grey mare,' he thought. Then he took up one of the newspapers and, because he had the statistical mania, began to count the advertisements. Two remedies for constipation, three for wind and stomach pains, three face creams, one skin food, one cruise to Morocco. At the end of the personal column, in small print, 'I will slay in the day of My wrath and spare not, saith the Lord God.' Who pays to put these things in anyway, who pays?

'This perpetual covert threat,' he thought. 'Everything's based on it. Disgusting. What Will They Say? And down at the bottom of the page you see what will happen to you if you don't toe the line. You will be slain and not spared. Threats and mockery, mockery and threats. . . .' And desolation, desertion, and crumpled newspapers in the room.

The only comfort allowed was the money which would buy the warm glow of drink before eating, the Jubilee laughter afterwards. Jubilant—Jubilee—Joy. . . . Words whirled round in his head, but he could not make them take shape.

'If you won't, you bloody well won't,' he said to his typewriter before he rushed down the stairs, counting the steps as he went.

After two double whiskies at his usual pub, time, which had dragged so drearily all day, began to move faster, began to gallop.

At half-past eleven Mr. Severn was walking up and down Wardour Street between two young women. The things one does on the rebound.

He knew one of them fairly well—the fatter one. She was often at the pub and he liked talking to her, and sometimes stood her drinks because she was good-natured and never made him feel nervous. That was her secret. If fair was fair, it would be her epitaph: 'I have never made anybody feel nervous—on purpose.' Doomed, of course, for that very reason. But pleasant to talk to and, usually, to look at. Her name was Maidie— Maidie Richards.

He had never seen the other girl before. She was very young and fresh, with a really glittering smile and an accent he didn't quite recognize. She was called Heather Something-or-other. In the noisy pub he thought she said Hedda. 'What an unusual name!' he had remarked. 'I said Heather, not Hedda. Hedda! I wouldn't be seen dead with a name like that.' She was sharp, bright, self-confident—nothing flabby there. It was she who had suggested this final drink.

The girls argued. They each had an arm in one of Mr. Severn's, and they argued across him. They got to Shaftesbury Avenue, turned and walked back.

'I tell you the place is in this street,' Heather said. 'The "Jim-Jam"—haven't you ever heard of it?'

'Are you sure?' Mr. Severn asked.

'Of course I'm sure. It's on the left-hand side. We've missed it somehow.'

'Well, I'm sick of walking up and down looking for it,' Maidie said. 'It's a lousy hole anyway. I don't particularly want to go, do you?'

'Not particularly,' said Mr. Severn.

'There it is,' Heather said. 'We've passed it twice. It's changed its name, that's what.'

They went up a narrow stone staircase and on the first landing a man with a yellow face appeared from behind drawn curtains and glared at them. Heather smiled. 'Good evening, Mr. Johnson. I've brought two friends along.'

'Three of you? That'll be fifteen shillings.'

'I thought it was half a crown entrance,' Maidie said so aggressively that Mr. Johnson looked at her with surprise and explained, 'This is a special night.'

'The orchestra's playing rotten, anyway,' Maidie remarked when they got into the room.

An elderly woman wearing steel-rimmed glasses was serving behind the bar. The mulatto who was playing the saxophone leaned forward and whooped.

'They play so rotten,' Maidie said, when the party was seated at a table against the wall, 'that you'd think they were doing it on purpose.'

'Oh stop grumbling,' Heather said. 'Other people don't agree with you. The place is packed every night. Besides, why should they play well. What's the difference?'

'Ah-ha,' Mr. Severn said.

'There isn't any difference if you ask me. It's all a lot of talk.'

'Quite right. All an illusion,' Mr. Severn agreed. 'A bottle of ginger ale,' he said to the waiter.

Heather said, 'We'll have to have a bottle of whisky. You don't mind, do you, dear?'

'Don't worry, child, don't worry,' Mr. Severn said. 'It was only my little joke . . . a bottle of whisky,' he told the waiter.

'Will you pay now, if you please?' the waiter asked when he brought the bottle.

'What a price!' Maidie said, frowning boldly at the waiter. 'Never mind, by the time I've had a few goes at this I ought to have forgotten my troubles.'

Heather pinched up her lips. 'Very little for me.'

'Well, it's going to be drunk,' Mr. Severn said. 'Play *Dinah*,' he shouted at the orchestra.

The saxophonist glanced at him and tittered. Nobody else took any notice.

'Sit down and have a drink, won't you?' Heather clutched at Mr. Johnson's sleeve as he passed the table, but he answered loftily, 'Sorry, I'm afraid I can't just now,' and passed on.

'People are funny about drinking,' Maidie remarked. 'They get you to buy as much as they can and then afterwards they laugh at you behind your back for buying it. But on the other hand, if you try to get out of buying it, they're damned rude. Damned rude, they can be. I went into a place the other night where they have music—the International Café, they call it. I had a whisky and I drank it a bit quick because I was thirsty and feeling down and so on. Then I thought I'd like to listen to the music—they don't play so badly there because they say they're Hungarians—and a waiter came along, yelling "Last drinks". "Can I have some water?" I said. "I'm not here to serve you with water," he said. "This isn't a place to drink water in," he said, just like that. So loud! Everybody was staring at me.'

'Well, what do you expect?' Heather said. 'Asking for water! You haven't got any sense. No more for me, thank you.' She put her hand over her glass.

'Don't you trust me?' Mr. Severn asked, leering.

'I don't trust anybody. For why? Because I don't want to be let down, that's why.'

'Sophisticated, she is,' said Maidie.

'I'd rather be sophisticated than a damned pushover like you,' Heather retorted. 'You don't mind if I go and talk to some friends over there, do you, dear?'

'Admirable.' Mr. Severn watched her cross the room. 'Admirable. Disdainful debonair and with a touch of the tarbrush too, or I'm much mistaken. Just my type. One of my types. Why is it that she isn't quite—Now, why?' He took a yellow pencil out of his pocket and began to draw on the tablecloth.

Pictures, pictures, pictures. . . . Face, faces, faces. . . . Like hyaenas, like swine, like goats, like apes, like parrots. But not tigers, because tigers are better-looking, aren't they? as Hans says.

Maidie was saying, 'They've got an awfully nice "Ladies" here. I've been having a chat with the woman; she's a friend of mine. The window was open and the street looked so cool and peaceful. That's why I've been so long.'

'London is getting very odd, isn't it?' Mr. Severn said in a thick voice. 'Do you see that tall female over there, the one in the backless evening gown? Of course, I've got my own theory about backless evening gowns, but this isn't the moment to tell you of it. Well, that sweetiepie's got to be at Brixton tomorrow morning at a quarter-past nine to give a music lesson. And her greatest ambition is to get a job as stewardess on a line running to South Africa.'

'Well, what's wrong with that?' Maidie said.

'Nothing—I just thought it was a bit mixed. Never mind. And do you see that couple over there at the bar? The lovely dark brown couple. Well, I went over to have a change of drinks and got into conversation with them. I rather palled up with the man, so I asked them to come and see me one day. When I gave them my address the girl said at once "Is that in Mayfair?" "Good Lord, no; it's in the darkest, dingiest Bloomsbury." "I didn't come to London to go to the slums," she said with the most perfect British accent, high, sharp, clear and shattering. Then she turned her back on me and hauled the man off to the other end of the bar.'

'Girls always cotton on to things quicker,' Maidie asserted.

'The social climate of a place?' said Mr. Severn. 'Yes, I suppose they do. But some men aren't so slow either. Well, well, tigers are better-looking, aren't they?'

'You haven't been doing too badly with the whisky, dear, have you?' Maidie said rather uneasily. 'What's all this about tigers?'

Mr. Severn again addressed the orchestra in a loud voice. 'Play *Dinah*. I hate that bloody tune you keep playing. It's always the same one too. You can't fool me. Play *Dinah, is there anyone finer?* That's a good old tune.'

'I shouldn't shout so loud,' Maidie said. 'They don't like it here if you shout. Don't you see the way Johnson's looking at you?'

'Let him look.'

'Oh, do shut up. He's sending the waiter to us now.'

'Obscene drawings on the tablecloths are not allowed here,' the waiter said as he approached.

'Go to hell,' Mr. Severn said. 'What obscene drawings?'

Maidie nudged him and shook her head violently.

The waiter removed the tablecloth and brought a clean one. He pursed his lips up as he spread it and looked severely at Mr. Severn. 'No drawings of any description on tablecloths are allowed here,' he said.

'I'll draw as much as I like,' Mr. Severn said defiantly. And the next thing he knew two men had him by the collar and were pushing him towards the door.

'You let him alone,' said Maidie. 'He hasn't done anything. You are a lot of sugars.'

'Gently, gently,' said Mr. Johnson, perspiring. 'What do you want to be so rough for? I'm always telling you to do it quietly.'

As he was being hauled past the bar, Mr. Severn saw Heather, her eyes beady with disapproval, her plump face lengthened into something twice the size of life. He made a hideous grimace at her.

'My Lawd,' she said, and averted her eyes. 'My Lawd!'

Only four men pushed them down the stairs, but when they were out in the street it looked more like fourteen, and all howling and booing. 'Now, who are all these people?' Mr. Severn thought. Then someone hit him. The man who had hit him was exactly like the waiter who had changed the tablecloth. Mr. Severn hit back as hard as he could and the waiter, if he was the waiter, staggered against the wall and toppled slowly to the ground. 'I've knocked him down,' Mr. Severn thought. 'Knocked him down!'

'Tally-ho!' he yelled in a high voice. 'What price the tame grey mare?'

The waiter got up, hesitated, thought better of it, turned round and hit Maidie instead.

'Shut up, you bloody basket,' somebody said when she began to swear, and kicked her. Three men seized Mr. Severn, ran him off the pavement and sprawled him in the middle of Wardour Street. He lay there, feeling sick, listening to Maidie. The lid was properly off there.

'Yah!' the crowd round her jeered. 'Boo!' Then it opened up, servile and respectful, to let two policemen pass.

'You big blanks,' Maidie yelled defiantly. 'You something somethings. I wasn't doing anything. That man knocked me down. How much does Johnson pay you every week for this?'

Mr. Severn got up, still feeling very sick. He heard a voice: 'That's 'em. That's the chap. That 'im what started every-thing.' Two policemen took him by the arms and marched him along. Maidie, also between two policemen, walked in front, weeping. As they passed through Piccadilly Circus, empty and desolate, she wailed, 'I've lost my shoe. I must stop and pick it up. I can't walk without it.'

The older policeman seemed to want to force her on, but the younger one stopped, picked the shoe up and gave it to her with a grin.

'What's she want to cry for?' Mr. Severn thought. He shouted 'Hoi, Maidie, cheer up. Cheer up, Maidie.'

'None of that,' one of his policemen said.

But when they arrived at the police station she had stopped crying, he was glad to see. She powdered her face and began to argue with the sergeant behind the desk.

'You want to see a doctor, do you?' the sergeant said.

'I certainly do. It's a disgrace, a perfect disgrace.'

'And do you also want to see a doctor?' the sergeant asked, coldly polite, glancing at Mr. Severn.

'Why not?' Mr. Severn answered.

Maidie powdered her face again and shouted, 'God save Ireland. To hell with all dirty sneaks and Comic Cuts and what-have-yous.'

'That was my father speaking,' she said over her shoulder as she was led off.

As soon as Mr. Severn was locked into a cell he lay down on the bunk and went to sleep. When they woke him to see the doctor he was cold sober.

'What time is it?' the doctor asked. With a clock over his head, the old fool!

Mr. Severn answered coldly 'A quarter-past four.'

'Walk straight ahead. Shut your eyes and stand on one leg,' the doctor demanded, and the policeman watching this performance sneered vaguely, like schoolboys when the master baits an unpopular one.

When he got back to his cell Mr. Severn could not sleep. He lay down, stared at the lavatory seat and thought of the black eye he would have in the morning. Words and meaningless phrases still whirled tormentingly round in his head.

He read the inscriptions on the grim walls. 'Be sure your sins will find you out. B. Lewis.' 'Anne is a fine girl, one of the best, and I don't care who knows it. (Signed) Charlie S.' Somebody else had written up, 'Lord, save me; I perish.' and underneath, 'SOS, SOS, SOS (Signed) G.R.'

'Appropriate,' Mr. Severn thought, took his pencil from his pocket, wrote, 'SOS, SOS, SOS (Signed) N.S.', and dated it.

Then he lay down with his face to the wall and saw, on a level with his eyes, the words, 'I died waiting'.

Sitting in the prison van before it started, he heard somebody whistling *The Londonderry Air* and a girl talking and joking with the policemen. She had a deep, soft voice. The appropriate adjective came at once into his mind—a sexy voice.

'Sex, sexy,' he thought. 'Ridiculous word! What a give-away!'

'What is wanted,' he decided, 'is a brand-new lot of words, words that will mean something. The only word that means anything now is death—and then it has to be my death. Your death doesn't mean much.'

The girl said, 'Ah, if I was a bird and had wings, I could fly away, couldn't I?'

'Might get shot as you went,' one of the policemen answered.

'This must be a dream,' Mr. Severn thought. He listened for Maidie's voice, but there was not a sound of her. Then the van started.

It seemed a long way to Bow Street. As soon as they got out of the van he saw Maidie, looking as if she had spent the whole night in tears. She put her hand up to her hair apologetically.

'They took my handbag away. It's awful.'

'I wish it had been Heather,' Mr. Severn thought. He tried to smile kindly.

'It'll soon be over now, we've only got to plead guilty.'

And it was over very quickly. The magistrate hardly looked at them, but for reasons of his own he fined them each thirty shillings, which entailed telephoning to a friend, getting the money sent by special messenger and an interminable wait.

It was half-past twelve when they were outside in Bow Street. Maidie stood hesitating, looking worse than ever in the yellowish, livid light. Mr. Severn hailed a taxi and offered to take her home. It was the least he could do, he told himself. Also the most.

'Oh, your poor eye!' Maidie said. 'Does it hurt?'

'Not at all now. I feel astonishingly well. It must have been good whisky.'

She stared into the cracked mirror of her handbag.

'And don't I look terrible too? But it's no use; I can't do anything with my face when it's as bad as this.'

'I'm sorry.'

'Oh, well,' she said, 'I was feeling pretty bad on account of the way that chap knocked me down and kicked me, and afterwards on account of the way the doctor asked me my age. "This woman's very drunk," he said. But I wasn't, was I? . . . Well, and when I got back into the cell, the first thing I saw was my own name written up. My Christ, it did give me a turn! Gladys Reilly—that's my real name. Maidie Richards is only what I call myself. There it was staring me in the face.

"Gladys Reilly, October 15th, 1934. . . ." Besides, I hate being locked up. Whenever I think of all these people they lock up for years I shiver all over.'

'Yes,' Mr. Severn said, 'so do I.' *I died waiting.*

'I'd rather die quick, wouldn't you?'

'Yes.'

'I couldn't sleep and I kept on remembering the way the doctor said, "How old are you?" And all the policemen round were laughing, as if it was a joke. Why should it be such a joke. But they're hard up for jokes, aren't they? So when I got back I couldn't stop crying. And when I woke up I hadn't got my bag. The wardress lent me a comb. She wasn't so bad. But I do feel fed up. . . .'

'You know the room I was waiting in while you were telephoning for money?' she said. 'There was such a pretty girl there.'

'Was there?'

'Yes, a very dark girl. Rather like Dolores del Rio, only younger. But it isn't the pretty ones who get on—oh no, on the contrary. For instance, this girl. She couldn't have been prettier—lovely, she was. And she was dressed awfully nicely in a black coat and skirt and a lovely clean white blouse and a little white hat and lovely stockings and shoes. But she was frightened. She was so frightened that she was shaking all over. You saw somehow that she wasn't going to last it out. No, it isn't being pretty that does it. . . . And there was another one, with great hairy legs and no stockings, only sandals. I do think that when people have hairy legs they ought to wear stockings, don't you? Or do something about it. But no, she was just laughing and joking and saw whatever happened to her she'd come out all right. A great big, red, square face she had, and those hairy legs. But she didn't care a damn.'

'Perhaps it's being sophisticated,' Mr. Severn suggested, 'like your friend Heather.'

'Oh, her—no, she won't get on either. She's too ambitious, she wants too much. She's so sharp she cuts herself, as you might say. . . . No, it isn't being pretty and it isn't being sophisticated. It's being—adapted, that's what it is. And it isn't any good *wanting* to be adapted, you've got to be born adapted.'

'Very clear,' Mr. Severn said. Adapted to the livid sky, the ugly houses, the grinning policemen, the placards in shop windows.

'You've got to be young, too. You've got to be young to enjoy a thing like this—younger than we are,' Maidie said as the taxi drew up.

Mr. Severn stared at her, too shocked to be angry.

'Well, good-bye.'

'*Good*-bye,' said Mr. Severn, giving her a black look and ignoring her outstretched hand. 'We' indeed!

Two-hundred and ninety-six steps along Coptic Street. One-hundred and twenty round the corner. Forty stairs up to his flat. A dozen inside it. He stopped counting.

His sitting-room looked well, he thought, in spite of the crumpled papers. It was one of its good times, when the light was just right, when all the incongruous colours and shapes became a whole—the yellow-white brick wall with several of the Museum pigeons perched on it, the silvered drainpipe, the chimneys of every fantastical shape, round, square, pointed, and the odd one with the mysterious hole in the middle through which the grey, steely sky looked at you, the solitary trees—all framed in the silver oilcloth curtains (Hans's idea), and then with a turn of his head he saw the woodcuts from Amsterdam, the chintz-covered arm-chairs, the fading bowl of flowers in the long mirror.

An old gentleman wearing a felt hat and carrying a walking-stick passed the window. He stopped, took off his hat and coat and, balancing the stick on the end of his nose, walked backwards and forwards, looking up expectantly. Nothing happened. Nobody thought him worth a penny. He put his hat and coat on again and, carrying the stick in a respectable manner, vanished round the corner. And, as he did so, the tormenting phrases vanished too—'Who pays? Will you pay now, please? You don't mind if I leave you, dear? I died waiting, I died waiting. (Or was it I died hating?) That was my father speaking. Pictures, pictures, pictures. You've got to be young. But tigers are better-looking, aren't they? SOS, SOS,

SOS. If I was a bird and had wings I could fly away, couldn't I? Might get shot as you went. But tigers are better-looking aren't they? You've got to be younger than we are. . . .' Other phrases, suave and slick, took their place.

The swing's the thing, the cadence of the sentence. He had got it.

He looked at his eye in the mirror, then sat down at the typewriter and with great assurance rapped out 'JUBILEE. . . .'

FRANK SARGESON

A Hen and Some Eggs

I THINK that one time when my mother set a hen on some eggs was about the most anxious time I've ever experienced in my life.

The hen was a big black Orpington, and mother set her inside a coop in the warmest corner of our yard. My brother and I went out one night and held a candle, and mother put the hen in the coop and gave her thirteen eggs to hatch out. And the next morning we ran out and looked inside the coop, and it was wonderful to see the hen looking bigger than ever as she sat on the thirteen eggs.

But besides being wonderful to see the hen sitting on the eggs, it was a worry to see that she had one egg showing. And it was the same way each time we looked. It wouldn't have been so bad if we could have been sure that it was the same egg each time, because mother had put the thirteenth egg in just to see if thirteen was an unlucky number, and if it hadn't hatched out it wouldn't have mattered much. But we couldn't be sure, and we'd go to school thinking that if our hen was silly enough to let each one of the thirteen eggs get cold in turn, then we wouldn't have any of the eggs hatch out at all.

Then an even worse worry was trying to get the hen to eat. We'd put her food just by the hole in the coop but she'd take no notice. And after we'd got tired of waiting to see her come out and eat and had gone away and left her, sometimes the food would disappear, but as often as not it wouldn't. And when it did disappear we could never be sure that it wasn't the sparrows that had taken it. So each time we looked inside the coop we thought our hen was getting thinner and thinner, and if there happened to be two eggs showing instead of one we were sure that it was so, and we said that after all our trouble there probably wouldn't be one egg that'd hatch out after all.

And we thought that our hen might be even silly enough to let herself starve to death.

Then one Saturday morning when it was nearly time for the eggs to hatch out, something terrible happened. My brother and I were chopping kindling wood in the yard and suddenly my brother said, Look! And there was the hen walking up and down inside the wire-netting part of the coop, something which we had never seen her doing before.

We thought she must be hungry, so as fast as we could we took her some wheat. But the hen didn't seem to be hungry, and instead of eating the wheat she started cackling, and if we stayed near her she'd run up and down inside the wire-netting instead of just walking. Well, we went and told mother, and mother told us to leave the hen alone and she'd go back to the eggs. So we stood in the yard and watched, and the hen went on walking up and down, so we went and told mother again. And mother looked at the clock and said, Give her five minutes from now and see what happens.

Well, the hen went on walking up and down, and we could hardly bear it. It was awful to think of the thirteen eggs getting colder and colder. Anyhow mother made us wait another five minutes, then she came out and we tried to shoo the hen back into the coop. But it was no good, the hen went on like a mad thing, and mother said we'd just have to leave her alone and trust to luck. We all went inside to look at the clock and we reckoned that the hen must have been off the nest for at least twenty minutes, and we said that the eggs couldn't help being stone cold by that time.

Then when we came outside again we saw the most astonishing thing happen. The hen suddenly left off cackling and walking up and down. She stood there without moving just as if she was trying to remember something, then she ran for the hole in the coop and disappeared inside.

Well, it was ourselves who went on like mad things then. But after a few minutes we started talking in whispers, and we chopped our kindling wood round the front of the house so as not to disturb the hen, and we'd keep coming back into the yard to creep towards the coop and look in from a distance, and it was more wonderful than ever to see the hen sitting there, even though she had the one egg showing as usual.

And a few days later twelve of the eggs hatched out, but the thirteenth egg was no good. To this day I've wondered whether it was the same one that was always showing, and whether that was the one that was no good. My brother said that the hen knew it was no good and didn't bother to keep it warm. He may have been right. Children are rather like hens. They know things that men and women don't know, but when they grow up they forget them.

ELIZABETH TAYLOR

A Dedicated Man

In the dark, raftered dining-room, Silcox counted the coned napkins and, walking among the tables, lifted the lids of the mustard pots and shook salt level in the cellars.

At the beginning of their partnership as waiter and waitress, Edith had liked to make mitres or fleurs-de-lis or water-lilies of the napkins, and Silcox, who thought this great vulgarity, waited until after he had made his proposal and been accepted before he put a stop to it. She had listened meekly. 'Edwardian vulgarity,' he had told her. Taking a roll of bread from the centre of the petalled linen, he whipped the napkin straight, then turned it deftly into a dunce's cap.

Edith always came down a little after Silcox. He left the bedroom in plenty of time for her to change into her black dress and white apron. His proposal had not included marriage or any other intimacy and, although they lay every night side by side in twin beds, they were always decorous in their behaviour, fanatically prim, and he had never so much as seen her take a brush to her hair, as he himself might have said. However, there was no one to say it to, and to the world they were Mr. and Mrs. Silcox, a plain, respectable couple. Both were ambitious, both had been bent on leaving the hotel where they first met—a glorified boarding-house, Silcox called it. Both, being snobbish, were galled at having to wait on noisy, sunburnt people who wore freakish and indecent holiday clothes and could not pronounce *crêpes de volaille*, let alone understand what it meant.

By the time Silcox heard of the vacancy at the Royal George, he had become desperate beyond measure, irritated at every turn by the vulgarities of seaside life. The Royal George was mercifully as inland as anywhere in England can be. The thought of the Home Counties soothed him. He visualized the landscape embowered in flowering trees.

In his interview with the manageress he had been favourably impressed by the tone of the hotel. The Thames flowed by beyond the geranium-bordered lawns; there would be star occasions all summer—the Fourth of June, Henley, Ascot. The dining-room, though it was small, had velvet-cushioned banquettes and wine-lists in padded leather covers. The ashtrays advertised nothing and the flowers had not come out of the garden.

'My wife,' he said repeatedly during the interview. He had been unable to bring her, from consideration to their employer. The manageress respected him for this and for very much else. She could imagine him in tails, and he seemed to wear the grey suit as if it were a regrettable informality he had been unable to escape. He was stately, eyes like a statue's, mouth like a carp's. His deference would have that touch of condescension which would make customers angle for his good will. Those to whom he finally unbent, with a remark about the weather or the compliments of the season, would return again and again, bringing friends to whom they could display their status. 'Maurice always looks after me,' they would say.

Returning to the pandemonium—the tripperish hotel, the glaring sky—he made his proposal to Edith. 'Married couple', the advertisement had stipulated and was a necessary condition, he now understood, for only one bedroom was available. 'It has twin bedsteads, I ascertained,' he said.

Marriage, he explained, could not be considered, as he was married already. Where the person in question (as he spoke of his wife) was at present, he said he did not know. She had been put behind him.

Until that day, he had never spoken to Edith of his personal affairs, although they had worked together for a year. She was reserved herself and embarrassed by this unexpected lapse, though by the proposal itself she felt deeply honoured. It set the seal on his approval of her work.

'I think I am right in saying that it is what matters most to both of us,' he observed, and she nodded. She spoke very little and never smiled.

The manageress of the Royal George, when Edith went for

her separate interview, wondered if she were not too grim. At forty-five, her hair was a streaked grey and clipped short like a man's at the back. She had no make-up and there were deep lines about her mouth which had come from the expression of disapproval she so often wore. On the other hand, she was obviously dependable and efficient, would never slop soup or wear dirty cuffs or take crafty nips of gin in the still room whenever there was a lull. Her predecessor had done these things and been flighty, too.

So Edith and Silcox were engaged. Sternly and without embarrassment they planned arrangements for bedroom privacy. These were simply a matter of one staying in the bathroom while the other dressed or undressed in the bedroom. Edith was first to get into bed and would then turn out the light. Silcox was meanwhile sitting on a laundry basket in his dressing-gown, glancing at his watch until it was time to return. He would get into bed in the dark. He never wished her goodnight and hardly admitted to himself that she was there.

Now a week had gone by and the arrangements had worked so smoothly that he was a little surprised this evening that on the stroke of seven o'clock she did not appear. Having checked his tables, he studied the list of bookings and was pleased to note the name of one of his *bêtes-noires*. This would put a spur to his pride and lift the evening out of the ordinary ruck. Pleasant people were not the same challenge.

Upstairs, Edith was having to hurry, something she rarely deigned to do. She was even a little excited as she darted about the room, looking for clean cuffs and apron, fresh dress preservers, and some pewter-coloured stockings, and she kept pausing to glance at a photograph on the chest of drawers. It was postcard size and in a worn leather frame and was of an adolescent boy wearing a school blazer.

When she had gone back to the bedroom after breakfast she saw the photograph for the first time. Silcox had placed it there without a word. She ignored it for a while and then became nervous that one of the maids might question her about it, and it was this reason she gave Silcox for having asked him who it was.

'Our son,' he said.

He deemed it expedient, he added, that he should be a family man. The fact would increase their air of dependability and give them background and reality and solid worth. The boy was at a public school, he went on, and did not divulge to his friends the nature of his parents' profession. Silcox, Edith realized with respect, was so snobbish that he looked down upon himself.

'How old is he?' she asked in an abrupt tone.

'He is seventeen and working for the Advanced Level.'

Edith did not know what this was and wondered how she could manage to support the fantasy.

'We shall say nothing ourselves,' said Silcox, 'as we are not in the habit of discussing our private affairs. But he is there if wanted.'

'What shall we . . . what is his name?'

'Julian,' Silcox said and his voice sounded rich and musical.

Edith looked with some wonder at the face in the photograph. It was a very ordinary face and she could imagine the maids conjecturing at length as to whom he took after.

'Who is he really?' she asked.

'A young relative,' said Silcox.

In Edith's new life there were one or two difficulties—one was trying to remember not to fidget with the wedding ring as if she were not used to wearing it, and another was being obliged to call Silcox 'Maurice'. This she thought unseemly, like all familiarities, and to be constant in it required continual vigilance. He, being her superior, had called her Edith from the start.

Sleeping beside him at night worried her less. The routine of privacy was established and sleep itself was negative and came immediately to both of them after long hours of being on their feet. They might have felt more sense of intimacy sitting beside one another in deckchairs in broad daylight, for then there would be the pitfalls of conversation. (How far to encroach? How much interest to show that could be shown without appearing inquisitive?)

Edith was one of those women who seem to know from childhood that the attraction of men is no part of their equipment, and from then on to have supported nature in what it had done for them, by exaggerating the gruffness and the gracelessness and becoming after a time sexless. She strode heavily in shoes a size too large, her off-duty coat and skirt were as sensible as some old Nannie's walking-out attire. She was not much interested in people, although she did her duty towards them and wrote each week to her married sister in Australia: and was generous to her at Christmas. Her letters, clearly written as they were, were still practically unreadable —so full of facts and times: where she took the bus to on her day off and the whole route described, where this road forked and that branched off and what p.m. she entered this or that café to progress from the grapefruit to the trifle of the table d'hôte (five and sixpence). Very poor service usually, she wrote—odd knives and forks left on the table while she drank her coffee, for no one took any pride nowadays.

Edith had no relations other than her sister; her world was peopled with hotel staff and customers. With the staff she was distant and sometimes grim if they were careless in their work, and with her customers she was distant and respectful. She hardly responded to them, although there were a very few— usually gay young men or courtly and jovial elderly ones—to whom she behaved protectively, as Nannie-ish as she looked when she wore her outdoor clothes.

The other person in her life—Silcox—was simply to her the Establishment. She had never worked with anyone she respected more—in her mind, he was always a waiter and she always thought of him dressed as a waiter. On his day off, he seemed lowered by wearing the clothes of an ordinary man. Having to turn her eyes away from him when she glimpsed him in a dressing-gown was really no worse. They were not man and woman in one another's eyes, and hardly even human beings.

No difficulties they were beset with in their early days at the Royal George could spoil the pleasures of their work. The serenity of the dining-room, the elaborate food which made demands upon them (to turn something over in flaming brandy in a chafing-dish crowned Silcox's evening), the superiority of the clientele and the glacial table linen. They had suffered horrors from common people and this escape to elegance was precious to them both. The hazards that threatened were not connected with their work, over which both had mastery from the beginning, but with their private lives. It was agonizing to Edith to realize that now they were expected to spend their free time together. On the first day off they took a bus to another hotel along the river and there had luncheon. Silcox modelled his behaviour on that of his own most difficult customers, and seemed to be retaliating by doing so. He was very lordly and full of knowledge and criticism. Edith, who was used to shopping ladies' luncheons in cafés, became nervous and alarmed. When she next wrote to her sister, she left this expedition altogether out of the letter and described instead some of the menus she had served at the Royal George, with prices. Nowadays, there was, for the first time in her life, an enormous amount that had to be left out of the letters.

She was dreading their next free day and was relieved when Silcox suggested that they should make a habit of taking the train to London together and there separating. If they came back on the same train in the evening, no suspicions would be roused.

In London, she enjoyed wandering round the department stores, looking without surprise or envy at all the frivolous extravagancies. She made notes of prices, thinking that her sister would be interested to compare them with those in Melbourne, and she could spend a whole day over choosing a pair of gloves, going from shop to shop, studying the quality. One day, she intended to visit the Zoo.

Silcox said that he liked to look in the jewellers' windows. In the afternoons, he went to a News Cinema. Going home in the train, he read a newspaper and she looked at the backs of houses and little gardens, and later, fields or woods, staring as if hypnotized.

One morning, when she had returned to their bedroom after breakfast, he surprised her by following her there. This was the time of day when he took a turn about the garden or strolled along by the river.

When he had shut the door, he said quietly, 'I'm afraid I must ask you something. I think it would be better if you were less tidy in here. It struck me this morning that by putting everything away out of sight, you will give rise to suspicion.'

Once, he had been a floor waiter in an hotel and knew, from taking breakfast in to so many married people, what their bedrooms usually looked like. His experience with his own wife he did not refer to.

'I overheard Carrie saying what a tidy pair we were and she had never met anyone like it, not a pin in sight when she came into this room, she said.'

'I respect your intentions,' he said grandly, 'but the last thing to serve our purpose is to appear in any way out of the ordinary. If you could have one or two things lying about—your hairbrush, perhaps—well, I leave it to you—just a pot of something or other on the dressing-table. A wife would never hide everything away in the drawers. Carrie's right, as it is there isn't even a pin to be seen. Nothing to show it's anyone's room at all, except for the photograph.'

Edith blushed and pressed her lips tightly together. She turned away and made no reply. Although she knew that it had been difficult for him to make the suggestion, and sensible and necessary as she saw it to be, she was angry with him. She wondered why his words had so humiliated her, and could find no reason. He had reproved her before about her work—the water-lily napkins, for instance—but he had never angered her.

She waited for him to leave her and then she removed from the drawer a large, harsh-bristled brush, a boxful of studs and safety pins and a pot of Vaseline which she used in cold weather when her lips were chapped. In the early evening, when she came up to change, she found Silcox's brushes beside hers, a shoe-horn dangled from the side of the mirror and his dressing-gown had been taken from his clothes' cupboard and was hanging at the back of the door.

She felt very strange about it all and when she went downstairs she tried to direct all her thoughts towards her work.

'He couldn't be anyone else's,' said Carrie Hurt, the maid, looking at the photograph. She had the impertinence to take it up and go over to the window with it, to see it better.

'He is thought to take more after his father's side.' Edith said, tempted to allow the conversation to continue, then wondering why this should be.

'I expect it's his father's side that says it,' Carrie replied. 'Oh, I can see you. The way his hair grows on his forehead. His father's got quite a widow's peak.'

Edith found herself looking over Carrie's shoulder, as if she had never seen the photograph before.

'As a matter of fact, he is a little like my sister's eldest boy,' she conceded. 'His cousin,' she added, feeling wonder at the words.

'Well, you must be proud of him. Such an open face.' Carrie said, replacing the photograph in its right position and passing a duster over the glass.

'Yes,' said Edith. 'He's a good boy.'

She left Carrie and went downstairs and walked in the garden until it was time to go on duty. She went up and down the gravel paths and along by the river, but she could not overcome the excitement which lately disturbed her so, the sensation of shameful pleasure.

By the river's edge, she came upon Silcox, who had taken up fishing in his spare time—a useful excuse for avoiding Edith's company. He stood on the bank, watching the line where it entered the water, and hardly turned his head as Edith approached him.

'Where does he—where does Julian go to in the holidays?' she asked.

'He goes to relatives.' Silcox answered.

She knew that she was interrupting him and that she must move on. As she did, he heard her murmuring anxiously, 'I do so hope they're kind.'

He turned his head quickly and looked after her, but she

had gone mooning back across the lawn. The expression of astonishment stayed on his face for a long time after that, and when she took up her position in the dining-room before lunch, he looked at her with concern, but she was her usual forbidding and efficient self again.

'Don't we ever go to see him?' she asked a few days later. 'Won't they think us strange not going?'

'What we do in our free time is no concern of theirs,' he said.

'I only thought they'd think it strange.'

He isn't real, none of it's true, she now constantly reminded herself, for sometimes her feelings of guilt about that abandoned boy grew too acute.

Sometimes, on Sunday outings from school, boys were brought by their parents to have lunch at the hotel, and Edith found herself fussing over them, giving them huge helpings, discussing their appetites with their parents.

'They're all the same at that age,' she would say. 'I know.'

It was so unlike her to chat with the customers and quite against Silcox's code. When he commented disdainfully upon her unusual behaviour, she seemed scarcely to listen to his words. The next Sunday, serving a double portion of ice cream to a boy, she looked across at his mother and smiled. 'I've got a son myself, madam,' she said. 'I know.'

Silcox, having overheard this, was too enraged to settle down to his fishing that afternoon. He looked for Edith and found her in the bedroom writing a letter to her sister.

'It was a mistake—this about the boy,' he said, taking up the photograph and glaring at it. 'You have not the right touch in such matters. You carry the deception to excess. You go too far.'

'Too far?' she said brightly, but busy writing.

'Our position is established. I think the little flourishes I thought up had their result.'

'But they were all *your* little flourishes,' she said, looking up at him. 'You didn't let *me* think of any, did you?'

He stared back at her and soon her eyes flickered, and she returned to her writing.

'There won't be any more,' he said. 'From me, or from you. Or any more discussion of our affairs, do you understand? Carrie in here every morning gossiping, you chatting to customers, telling them such a pack of lies—as if it were all true, and as if they could possibly be interested. You know as well as I do how unprofessional it is. I should never have credited it of you. Even when we were at that dreadful place at Paignton, you conducted yourself with more dignity.'

'I don't see the harm,' she said mildly.

'And I don't see the necessity. It's courting danger for one thing—to get so involved. We'll keep our affairs to ourselves or else we'll find trouble ahead.'

'What time does the post go?'

Without reading her letter through, she pushed it into an envelope. Goodness knows what she has written, he thought. A mercy her sister was far away in Australia.

The photograph—the subject of their contention—he pushed aside, as if he would have liked to be rid of it.

'You don't seem to be paying much attention,' he said. 'I only warn you that you'd better. Unless you hope to make laughing stocks of both of us.'

Before she addressed the envelope, she looked gravely at him for a moment, thinking that perhaps the worst thing that could happen to him, the thing he had always dreaded most, was to be laughed at, to lose his dignity. I used to be the same, she thought, taking up her pen.

'Yes, I made a mistake,' he said. 'I admit it freely. But we shall stand by it, since it's made. We can hardly kill the boy off, now we've got him.'

She jerked round and looked at him, her face even paler than usual, then seemed to gather her wits again and bent her head. Writing rather slowly and unsteadily, she finished addressing the envelope.

'I hope I shan't have further cause for complaint,' he said— rather as if he were her employer, as in fact he always felt himself to be. The last word duly spoken, he left her, but was frowning as he went downstairs. She was behaving oddly, something was not quite right about her and he was apprehensive.

Edith was smiling while she tidied herself before slipping out to the pillar box. 'That's the first tiff we've ever had,' she thought. 'In all our married life.'

'I find *her* all right,' Carrie Hurt said to the still-room maid. 'Not stand-offish, really, when you get to know her.'

'It's him I can't abide.'

'I'm sorry for her. The way he treats her.'

'And can't you tell he's got a temper? You get that feeling, don't you, that for two pins he'd boil over?'

'Yes, I'm sorry for her. When he's not there, she likes to talk. And dotes on that boy of theirs.'

'Funny life it must be, not hardly ever seeing him.'

'She's going to soon, so she was telling me, when it's his birthday. She was showing me the sweater she was knitting for him. She's a lovely knitter.'

Silcox found Edith sitting in a secluded place at the back of the hotel where the staff were allowed to take the air. It was a cobbled courtyard, full of empty beer-crates and strings of tea-towels hung to dry. Pigeons walked up and down the out-house roofs and the kitchen cat sat at Edith's feet watching them. Edith was knitting a white, cable-stitch sweater and she had a towel across her lap to keep the wool clean.

'I have just overheard that Carrie Hurt and the still-room girl discussing you,' Silcox said, when he had looked round to make sure that there was no one to overhear him. 'What is this nonsense about going to see the boy, or did my ears deceive me?'

'They think we're unnatural. I felt so ashamed about it that I said I'd be going on his birthday.'

'And when is *that*, pray?'

'Next month, the eighteenth. I'll have the sweater done by then.'

She picked up the knitting pattern, studied it frowning.

'Oh, it is, is it? You've got it all cut and dried. But his birthday happens to be in March.'

'You can't choose everything,' she said. She was going on with her knitting and smiling.

'I forbid you to say any more about the boy.'

'You can't, you see. People ask me how he's getting on.'

'I wish I hadn't started the damn fool business.'

'I don't. I'm so glad you did.'

'You'll land us in gaol, do you realize that? And what is this you're knitting?' He knew, from the conversation he had overheard.

'A sweater for him, for Julian.'

'Do you know what?' he said, leaning towards her and almost spitting the words at her, one after the other, 'I think you're going out of your mind. You'll have to go away from here. Maybe we'd both better go, and it will be the parting of the ways.'

'I don't see any cause for that,' said Edith. 'I've never been so happy.'

But her happiness was nearly at an end: even before she could finish knitting the sweater, the spell had been broken.

A letter came from her sister, Hilda, in Melbourne. She wrote much less frequently than Edith and usually only when she had something to boast about—this time it was one of the boys having won a tennis tournament.

'She has always patronized me,' Edith thought. 'I have never harped on in that way about Julian. I don't see why I should have hidden his light under a bushel all these years.'

She sat down at once and wrote a long letter about his different successes. Whatever Hilda's sons may have done, Julian seemed to find it easy to do better. 'We are sending him for a holiday on the Continent as a reward for passing his exams,' she finished up. She was tired of silence and modesty. Those qualities had never brought her any joy, none of the wonderful exhilaration and sense of richness she had now. Her attitude towards life had been too drab and undemanding; she could plainly see this.

She took her letter to the village and posted it. She imagined her sister looking piqued—not puzzled—when she read it.

Silcox was in the bedroom when she returned. A drawer slid
quickly shut and he was suddenly busy winding his watch.
'Well, I suppose it's time to put my hand to the wheel,' he said
in a voice less cold than it had been of late, as he went
out.

Edith was suspicious of this voice, which was too genial, she
thought, and she looked round to see if anything of hers had
been tampered with. She was especially anxious about her
knitting, which was so precious to her; but it was still neatly
rolled up and hanging in a clean laundry-bag in her cupboard.

She opened the drawer which Silcox had so smartly closed
and found a letter lying on top of a pile of black woollen socks.
A photograph was half out of the envelope. Though he had
thrust it out of sight when she came into the room, she realized
that he had been perfectly easy in his mind about leaving it
where it was, for it would be contrary to his opinion of her that
she would pry or probe. 'He knows nothing about me,' she
thought, taking the photograph to the window so that she
could see it better.

She was alarmed at the way her heart began to leap and
hammer, and she pressed her hand to her breast and whispered, 'Hush' to its loud beating. 'Hush, hush,' she implored
it, and sat down on her bed to wait for the giddiness to
pass.

When she was steadier, she looked again at the two faces in
the photograph. There was no doubt that one of them was
Julian's, though older than she had imagined and more defined
than in the other photograph—the one that stood always on
the chest of drawers.

It was so much like the face of the middle-aged woman
whom his arm encircled affectionately, who wore the smug,
pleased smile of a mother whose son has been teasing her. She
glowed with delight, her lips ready to shape fond remon-
strances. She looked a pretty, silly woman and wore a flowered,
full-skirted dress, too girlish for her, too tight across the bust.
They were standing by the wooden fence of a little garden.
Behind them, hollyhocks grew untidily and a line of washing,
having flapped in the wind as the camera clicked, hung there,

blurred, above their heads. Julian had stared at the photographer, grinning foolishly, almost pulling a face. 'It's all put on,' thought Edith. 'All for effect.'

When her legs stopped trembling, she went again to the drawer and fetched the letter. She could only read a little of it at a time, because the feeling of faintness and nausea came upon her in waves and she would wait, with closed eyes, till each receded. After seeing 'Dear Father' she was as still as a stone, until she could brace herself for more, for the rest of the immaturely-written, facetious letter. It contained abrupt and ungracious thanks for a watch he had received for what he referred to as his twenty-first. He seemed, Edith thought, to have expected more. A good time had been had by all, with Mum pushing the boat out to the best of her ability. They were still living in Streatham and he was working in a car showroom, where, he implied, he spent his time envying his customers. Things weren't too easy, although Mum was wonderful, of course. When he could afford to take her out, which he only wished he were able to do more often, she enjoyed herself as if she were a young girl. It was nice of his father to have thought of him, he ended reproachfully.

Carrie Hurt pushed the bedroom door open at the same time as she rapped on it with her knuckles. 'I was to say would you come down at once, Edith. There's some people in the dining-room already.'

'I shan't be coming down,' Edith said.

'Don't you feel well?'

'Tell him I shan't be coming down.'

Edith turned her head away and remained like that until Carrie had gone. Quietly, she sat and waited for Silcox to arrive. He would do so, she knew, as soon as he could find the manageress or a maid to take his place for a moment. It would offend his pride to allow such a crisis, but he would be too seriously alarmed to prevent it.

Her hatred was now so heavy that it numbed her and she was able to sit, quite calm and patient, waiting for him, rehearsing no speeches, made quite incapable by the suddenness of the calamity and the impossibility of accepting the truth of it.

It was not so very long before she heard his hurrying foot-steps. He entered the room as she had thought he would, brimming with pompous indignation. She watched this fade and another sort of anger take its place when he saw the letter in her hand, the photograph on the bed.

'No, your eyes don't deceive you,' she said.

At first, he could think of nothing better to say than 'How dare you!' He said this twice, but as it was clearly inadequate, he stepped forward and grasped her wrists, gripping them tightly, shook her back and forth until her teeth were chatter-ing. Not for years, not since the days of his brief marriage, had he so treated a woman and he had forgotten the overwhelming sensations to be derived from doing so. He released her, but only to hit her across her face with the back of one hand then the other.

Shaken, but unfrightened, she stared at him. 'It was true all the time,' she said. 'He was really yours and you disowned him. Yet you made up that story just to have a reason for put-ting out the photograph and looking at it every day.'

'Why should I want to do that? He means nothing to me.' He hoped to disconcert her by a quick transition to indiffer-ence.

'And his mother—*I* was supposed to be his mother.'

He laughed theatrically at the absurdity of this idea. It was a bad performance. When he had finished being doubled-up, he wiped his eyes and said: 'Excuse me.' The words were breathed on a sigh of exquisite enjoyment.

Coming to the door for the second time, Carrie Hurt waited after knocking. She had been surprised to hear Silcox laughing so loudly as she came along the passage. She had never heard him laugh in any way before and wondered if he had gone suddenly mad. He opened the door to her, looking grave and dignified.

'Yes, I am coming now,' he said.

'They're very busy. I was told to say if you could please . . .'

'I repeat, I am coming now. Edith is unwell and we must manage for today as best we may without her. She will stay here and rest,' he added, turning and saying this directly to

Edith and stressing his even tone by a steady look. He would have locked the door upon her if Carrie had not been standing by.

Edith was then alone and began to cry. She chafed her wrists that were still reddened from his grasp, and moved her head from side to side, as if trying to evade the thoughts that crowded on her.

Carrie Hurt returned presently with a glass of brandy. 'It can't do any harm,' she said. 'He told me to leave you alone, but there might be something she wants, I thought.'

She put the glass on the table beside the bed and then went over to draw the curtains. Edith sat still, with her hands clasped in her lap, and waited for her to go.

'My mother has these funny spells,' Carrie told her. Then, noticing the letter lying on the bed, she asked, 'Oh you haven't had any bad news, have you?'

'Yes,' Edith said.

She leaned forward to take the glass, sipped from it and shuddered.

'Not your *boy*?' Carrie whispered.

Edith sighed. It seemed more than a sigh—a frightening sound, seeming to gather all the breath from her body, shuddering expelling it.

'He isn't ill, is he?' Carrie asked, expecting worse—though Silcox, to be sure, had seemed controlled enough. And what had his dreadful laughter meant?

Edith was silent for a moment and took a little more brandy. Then she said, in a forced and rather high-pitched voice: 'He is much worse than ill. He is disgraced.'

'Oh, my God!' said Carrie eagerly.

Edith's eyes rested for a second on the photograph lying beside her on the bed and then she covered it with her hand. 'For theft,' she said, her voice strengthening, 'thieving,' she added.

'Oh dear, I'm ever so sorry,' Carrie said softly. 'I can't believe it. I always said what an open face he'd got. Don't you remember—I always said that? Who could credit it? No one could. Not that I should breathe a word about it to a single soul.'

'Mention it to whoever you like,' Edith said. 'The whole world will know, and may decide where they can lay the blame.'

She drained the glass, her eyes closed. Then, 'There's bad blood there,' she said.

When Silcox had finished his duties, he returned, but the door was locked from inside, and there was no answer when he spoke, saying her name several times in a low voice, his head bent close to the keyhole.

He went away and walked by the river in his waiter's clothes, stared at by all who passed him. When he returned to the hotel, he was stared at there, too. The kitchen porter seemed to be re-assessing him, looked at him curiously and spoke insolently. The still-room maid pressed back against the passage wall as he went by. Others seemed to avoid him.

The bedroom door was still shut, but no longer locked. He stood looking at the empty room, the hairbrush had gone from the dressing-table and only a few coat-hangers swung from the rail in the clothes' cupboard. He picked up the brandy glass and was standing there sniffing it when Carrie Hurt, who had enjoyed her afternoon, appeared in the doorway.

'I don't know if you know, she's packed and gone,' she said, 'and had the taxi take her to the train. I thought the brandy would pull her together,' she went on, looking at the glass in Silcox's hand. 'I expect the shock unhinged her and she felt she had to go. Of course, she'd want to see him, whatever happened. It must have been her first thought. I should like to say how sorry I am. You wouldn't wish such a thing on your worst enemy.'

He looked at her in bewilderment and then, seeing her glance, as it swerved from his in embarrassment, suddenly checked by something out of his sight, he walked slowly round the bed and saw there what she was staring at—the waste-paper basket heaped high with her white knitting, all cut into little shreds; even the needles had been broken in two.

Before the new couple arrived, Silcox prepared to leave.

Since Edith's departure, he had spoken to no one but his customers, to whom he was as stately as ever—almost devotional he seemed in his duties, bowed over chafing-dish or bottle— almost as if his calling were sacred and he felt himself worthy of it.

On the last morning, he emptied his bedroom cupboard and then the drawers, packing with his usual care. In the bottom drawer, beneath layers of shirts, and rolled up in a damask napkin, he was horrified to discover a dozen silver-plated soup-spoons from the dining-room.

WILLIAM TREVOR

In at the Birth

O NCE upon a time there lived in a remote London suburb
an elderly lady called Miss Efoss. Miss Efoss was a spry
person, and for as long as she could control the issue she was
determined to remain so. She attended the cinema and the
theatre with regularity; she read at length; and she preferred
the company of men and women forty years her junior. Once
a year Miss Efoss still visited Athens and always on such visits
she wondered why she had never settled in Greece: now, she
felt, it was rather too late to make a change; in any case, she
enjoyed London.

In her lifetime, nothing had passed Miss Efoss by. She had
loved and been loved. She had once, even, given birth to a
child. For a year or two she had known the ups and downs of
early family life, although the actual legality of marriage had
somehow been overlooked. Miss Efoss's baby died during a
sharp attack of pneumonia; and shortly afterwards the child's
father packed a suitcase one night. He said goodbye quite
kindly to Miss Efoss, but she never saw him again.

In retrospect, Miss Efoss considered that she had run the
gamut of human emotions. She settled down to the lively
superficiality of the everyday existence she had mapped for
herself. She was quite content with it. And she hardly noticed
it when the Dutts entered her life.

It was Mr. Dutt who telephoned. He said: 'Ah, Miss Efoss,
I wonder if you can help us. We have heard that occasionally
you baby-sit. We have scoured the neighbourhood for a reliable
baby-sitter. Would you be interested, Miss Efoss, in giving us
a try?'

'But who are you?' said Miss Efoss. 'I don't even know you.
What is your name to begin with?'

'Dutt,' said Mr. Dutt. 'We live only a couple of hundred
yards from you. I think you would find it convenient.'

'Well——'

'Miss Efoss, come and see us. Come and have a drink. If you like the look of us perhaps we can arrange something. If not, we shan't be in the least offended.'

'That is very kind of you, Mr. Dutt. If you give me your address and a time I'll certainly call. In fact, I shall be delighted to do so.'

'Good, good.' And Mr. Dutt gave Miss Efoss the details, which she noted in her diary.

Mr. and Mrs. Dutt looked alike. They were small and thin with faces like greyhounds. 'We have had such difficulty in finding someone suitable to sit for us,' Mrs. Dutt said. 'All these young girls, Miss Efoss, scarcely inspire confidence.'

'We are a nervous pair, Miss Efoss,' Mr. Dutt said, laughing gently as he handed her a glass of sherry. 'We are a nervous pair and that's the truth of it.'

'There is only Mickey, you see,' explained his wife. 'I suppose we worry a bit. Though we try not to spoil him.'

Miss Efoss nodded. 'An only child is sometimes a problem.'

The Dutts agreed, staring intently at Miss Efoss, as though recognizing in her some profound quality.

'We have, as you see, the television,' Mr. Dutt remarked. 'You would not be lonely here of an evening. The radio as well. Both are simple to operate and are excellent performers.'

'And Mickey has never woken up,' said Mrs. Dutt. 'Our system is to leave our telephone behind. Thus you may easily contact us.'

'Ha, ha, ha.' Mr. Dutt was laughing. His tiny face was screwed into an unusual shape, the skin drawn tightly over his gleaming cheek-bones.

'What an amusing thing to say, Beryl! My wife is fond of a joke, Miss Efoss.'

Unaware that a joke had been made, Miss Efoss smiled.

'It would be odd if we did *not* leave our telephone behind,' Mr. Dutt went on. 'We leave the telephone *number* behind, Beryl. The telephone number of the house where we are dining. You would be surprised, Miss Efoss, to receive guests who carried with them their telephone receiver. Eh?'

'It would certainly be unusual.'

' "We have brought our own telephone, since we do not care to use another." Or: "We have brought our telephone in case anyone telephones us while we are here." Miss Efoss, will you tell me something?'

'If I can, Mr. Dutt.'

'Miss Efoss, have you ever looked up the word *joke* in the *Encyclopaedia Britannica*?'

'I don't think I have.'

'You would find it rewarding. We have the full *Encyclopaedia* here, you know. It is always at your service.'

'How kind of you.'

'I will not tell you now what the *Encyclopaedia* says on the subject. I will leave you to while away a minute or two with it. I do not think you'll find it a wasted effort.'

'I'm sure I won't.'

'My husband is a great devotee of the *Encyclopaedia*,' Mrs. Dutt said. 'He spends much of his time with it.'

'It is not always pleasure,' Mr. Dutt said. 'The accumulation of information on many subjects is part of my work.'

'Your work, Mr. Dutt?'

'Like many, nowadays, Miss Efoss, my husband works for his living.'

'You have some interesting job, Mr. Dutt?'

'Interesting, eh? Yes, I suppose it is interesting. More than that I cannot reveal. That is so, eh, Beryl?'

'My husband is on the secret list. He is forbidden to speak casually about his work. Alas, even to someone to whom we trust our child. It's a paradox, isn't it?'

'I quite understand. Naturally, Mr. Dutt's work is no affair of mine.'

'To speak lightly about it would mean marching orders for me,' Mr. Dutt said. 'No offence, I hope?'

'Of course not.'

'Sometimes people take offence. We have had some unhappy occasions, eh, Beryl?'

'People do not always understand what it means to be on the secret list, Miss Efoss. So little is taken seriously nowadays.'

Mr. Dutt hovered over Miss Efoss with his sherry decanter. He filled her glass and his wife's. He said:

'Well, Miss Efoss, what do you think of us? Can you accept the occasional evening in this room, watching our television and listening for the cry of our child?'

'Naturally, Miss Efoss, there would always be supper,' Mrs. Dutt said.

'With sherry before and brandy to finish with,' Mr. Dutt added.

'You are very generous. I can quite easily have something before I arrive.'

'No, no, no. It is out of the question. My wife is a good cook. And I can be relied upon to keep the decanters brimming.'

'You have made it all so pleasant I am left with no option. I should be delighted to help you out when I can manage it.'

Miss Efoss finished her sherry and rose. The Dutts rose also, smiling benignly at their satisfactory visitor.

'Well then,' Mr. Dutt said in the hall, 'would Tuesday evening be a time you could arrange, Miss Efoss? We are bidden to dine with friends near by.'

'Tuesday? Yes, I think Tuesday is all right. About seven?'

Mrs. Dutt held out her hand. 'Seven would be admirable. Till then, Miss Efoss.'

On Tuesday Mr. Dutt opened the door to Miss Efoss and led her to the sitting-room. His wife, he explained, was still dressing. Making conversation as he poured Miss Efoss a drink, he said:

'I married my wife when she was on the point of entering a convent, Miss Efoss. What d'you think of that?'

'Well,' Miss Efoss said, settling herself comfortably before the cosy-stove, 'it is hard to know what to say, Mr. Dutt. I am surprised, I suppose.'

'Most people are surprised. I often wonder if I did the right thing. Beryl would have made a fine nun. What d'you think?'

'I'm sure you both knew what you were doing at the time. It is equally certain that Mrs. Dutt would have been a fine nun.'

'She had chosen a particularly severe order. That's just like Beryl, isn't it?'

'I hardly know Mrs. Dutt. But if it is like her to have made that choice, I can well believe it.'

'You see my wife as a serious person, Miss Efoss? Is that what you mean?'

'In the short time I have known her, yes I think I do. Yet you also say she relishes a joke.'

'A joke, Miss Efoss?'

'So you remarked the other evening. In relation to a slip in her speech.'

'Ah yes. How right you are. You must forgive me if my memory is often faulty. My work is wearing.'

Mrs. Dutt, gaily attired, entered the room. 'Here, Miss Efoss,' she said, proffering a piece of paper, 'is the telephone number of the house we are going to. If Mickey makes a sound please ring us up. I will immediately return.'

'Oh but I'm sure that's not necessary. It would be a pity to spoil your evening so. I could at least attempt to comfort him.'

'I would prefer the other arrangement. Mickey does not take easily to strangers. His room is at the top of the house, but please do not enter it. Were he to wake suddenly and catch sight of you he might be extremely frightened. He is quite a nervous child. At the slightest untoward sound do not hesitate to telephone.'

'As you wish it, Mrs. Dutt. I only suggested——'

'Experience has taught me, Miss Efoss, what is best. I have laid you a tray in the kitchen. Everything is cold, but quite nice, I think.'

'Thank you.'

'Then we will be away. We should be back by eleven-fifteen.'

'Do have a good evening.'

The Dutts said they intended to have a good evening, whispered for a moment together in the hall, and were on their way. Miss Efoss looked critically about her.

The room was of an ordinary kind. Utrillo prints on plain grey walls. Yellowish curtains, yellowish chair-covers, a few pieces of simple furniture on a thick grey carpet. It was warm, the sherry was good and Miss Efoss was comfortable. It was pleasant, she reflected, to have a change of scene without the obligation of conversation. In a few moments, she carried her supper tray from the kitchen to the fire. As good as his word, Mr. Dutt had left some brandy. Miss Efoss began to think the Dutts were quite a find.

She had dropped off to sleep when they returned. Fortunately, she heard them in the hall and had time to compose herself.

'All well?' Mrs. Dutt asked.

'Not a sound.'

'Well, I'd better change him right away. Thank you so much, Miss Efoss.'

'Thank you. I have spent a very pleasant evening.'

'I'll drive you back,' Mr. Dutt offered. 'The car is still warm.'

In the car Mr. Dutt said: 'A child is a great comfort. Mickey is a real joy for us. And company for Beryl. The days hang heavy when one is alone all day.'

'Yes, a child is a comfort.'

'Perhaps you think we are too careful and fussing about Mickey?'

'Oh no, it's better than erring in the other direction.'

'It is only because we are so grateful.'

'Of course.'

'We have much to be thankful for.'

'I'm sure you deserve it all.'

Mr. Dutt had become quite maudlin by the time he delivered Miss Efoss at her flat. She wondered if he was drunk. He pressed her hand warmly and announced that he looked forward to their next meeting. 'Any time,' Miss Efoss said as she stepped from the car. 'Just ring me up. I am often free.'

After that, Miss Efoss baby-sat for the Dutts many times. They became more and more friendly towards her. They left her little bowls of chocolates and drew her attention to articles in magazines that they believed might be of interest to her. Mr. Dutt suggested further words she might care to look up in the *Encyclopaedia* and Mrs. Dutt wrote out several of her recipes.

One night, just as she was leaving, Miss Efoss said: 'You know, I think it might be a good idea for me to meet Mickey some time. Perhaps I could come in the daytime once. Then I would no longer be a stranger and could comfort him if he woke.'

'But he *doesn't* wake, Miss Efoss. He has never woken, has he? You have never had to telephone us.'

'No. That is true. But now that I have got to know you, I would like to know him as well.'

The Dutts took the compliment, smiling at one another and at Miss Efoss. Mr. Dutt said: 'It is kind of you to speak like this, Miss Efoss. But Mickey is rather scared of strangers. Just at present at any rate, if you do not mind.'

'Of course not, Mr. Dutt.'

'I fear he is a nervous child,' Mrs. Dutt said. 'Our present arrangement is carefully devised.'

'I'm sorry,' Miss Efoss said.

'No need. No need. Let us all have a final brandy,' Mr. Dutt said cheerfully.

But Miss Efoss was sorry, for she feared she had said something out of place. And then for a week or so she was worried whenever she thought of the Dutts. She felt they were mistaken in their attitude about their child; and she felt equally unable to advise them. It was not her place to speak any further on the subject, yet she was sure that to keep the child away from people just because he was nervous of them was wrong. It sounded as though there was a root to the trouble somewhere, and it sounded as though the Dutts had not attempted to discover it. She continued to baby-sit for them about once every ten days and she held her peace. Then, quite unexpectedly, something happened that puzzled Miss Efoss very much indeed.

It happened at a party given by some friends of hers. She was talking about nothing in particular to an elderly man called Summerfield. She had known him for some years but whenever they met, as on this occasion, they found themselves with little to say beyond the initial courteous greetings. Thinking that a more direct approach might yield something of interest, Miss Efoss, after the familiar lengthy silence, said: 'How are you coping with the advancing years, Mr. Summerfield? I feel I can ask you, since it is a coping I have to take in my own stride.'

'Well, well, I think I am doing well enough. My life is simple since my wife died, but there is little I complain of.'

'Loneliness is a thing that sometimes strikes at us. I find one must regard it as the toothache or similar ailment, and seek a cure.'

'Ah yes. I'm often a trifle alone.'

'I baby-sit, you know. Have you ever thought of it? Do not shy off because you are a man. A responsible person is all that is required.'

'I haven't thought of baby-sitting. Not ever I think. Though I like babies and always have done.'

'I used to do quite a lot. Now I have only the Dutts, but I go there very often. I enjoy my evenings. I like to see the TV now and again and other people's houses are interesting.'

'I know the Dutts,' said Mr. Summerfield. 'You mean the Dutts in Raeburn Road? A small weedy couple?'

'They live in Raeburn Road, certainly. They are small too, but you are unkind to call them weedy.'

'I don't particularly mean it unkindly. I have known Dutt a long time. One takes liberties, I suppose, in describing people.'

'Mr Dutt is an interesting person. He holds some responsible position of intriguing secrecy.'

'Dutt? 25 Raeburn Road? The man is a chartered accountant.'

'I feel sure you are mistaken——'

'I cannot be mistaken. The man was once my colleague. In a very junior capacity.'

'Oh, well . . . then I must be mistaken.'

'What surprises me is that you say you baby-sit for the Dutts. I think you must be mistaken about that too.'

'Oh no, I am completely certain about that. It is for that reason that I know them at all.'

'I cannot help being surprised. Because, Miss Efoss—and of this I am certain—the Dutts have no children.'

Miss Efoss had heard of the fantasy world with which people, as they grow old, surround themselves. Yet she could not have entirely invented the Dutts in this way because Mr. Summerfield had readily agreed about their existence. Was it then for some other reason that she visited them? Did she, as soon as she entered their house, become so confused in her mind that she afterwards forgot the real purpose of her presence? Had they hired her in some other capacity altogether? A capacity she was so ashamed of that she had invented, even for herself, the euphemism of baby-sitting? Had she, she wondered, become some kind of servant to these people—imagining the warm comfortable room, the sherry, the chocolates, the brandy?

'We should be back by eleven, Miss Efoss. Here is the telephone number.' Mrs. Dutt smiled at her and a moment later the front door banged gently behind her.

It is all quite real, Miss Efoss thought. There is the sherry. There is the television set. In the kitchen on a tray I shall find my supper. It is all quite real: it is old Mr. Summerfield who is wandering in his mind. It was only when she had finished her supper that she had the idea of establishing her role beyond question. All she had to do was to go upstairs and peep at the child. She knew how to be quiet: there was no danger of waking him.

The first room she entered was full of suitcases and cardboard boxes. In the second she heard breathing and knew she was right. She snapped on the light and looked around her. It was brightly painted, with a wallpaper with elves on it. There was a rocking horse and a great pile of coloured bricks. In one of the far corners there was a large cot. It was very large and very high and it contained the sleeping figure of a very old man.

When the Dutts returned Miss Efoss said nothing. She was frightened and she didn't quite know why she was frightened. She was glad when she was back in her flat. The next day she telephoned her niece in Devon and asked if she might come down and stay for a bit.

Miss Efoss spoke to nobody about the Dutts. She gathered her strength in the country and returned to London at the end of a fortnight feeling refreshed and rational. She wrote a note to the Dutts saying she had decided to baby-sit no more. She gave no reason, but she said she hoped they would understand. Then, as best she could, she tried to forget all about them.

A year passed and then, one grey cold Sunday afternoon, Miss Efoss saw the Dutts in one of the local parks. They were sitting on a bench, huddled close together and seeming miserable. For a reason that she was afterwards unable to fathom Miss Efoss approached them.

'Good afternoon.'

The Dutts looked up at her, their thin, pale faces unsmiling and unhappy.

'Hello, Miss Efoss,' Mr. Dutt said. 'We haven't seen you for a long time, have we? How are you this nasty weather?'

'Quite well, thank you. And you? And Mrs. Dutt?'

Mr. Dutt rose and drew Miss Efoss a few yards away from his wife. 'Beryl has taken it badly,' he said. 'Mickey died. Beryl has not been herself since. You understand how it is?'

'Oh, I am sorry.'

'I try to cheer her up, but I'm afraid my efforts are all in vain. I have taken it hard myself too. Which doesn't make anything any easier.'

'I don't know what to say, Mr. Dutt. It's a great sadness for both of you.'

Mr. Dutt took Miss Efoss's arm and led her back to the seat. 'I have told Miss Efoss,' he said to his wife. Mrs. Dutt nodded.

'I'm very sorry,' Miss Efoss said again.

The Dutts looked at her, their sad, intent eyes filled with a pathetic desire for comfort. There was something almost hypnotic about them.

'I must go,' Miss Efoss said. 'Goodbye.'

'They have all died, Miss Efoss,' Mr. Dutt said. 'One by one they have all died.'

Miss Efoss paused in her retreat. She could think of nothing to say except that she was sorry.

'We are childless again,' Mr. Dutt went on. 'It is almost unbearable to be childless again. We are so fond of them and here we are, not knowing what to do on a Sunday afternoon because we are a childless couple. The human frame, Miss Efoss, is not built to carry such misfortunes.'

'It is callous of me to say so, Mr. Dutt, but the human frame is pretty resilient. It does not seem so at times like this I know, but you will find it is so in retrospect.'

'You are a wise woman, Miss Efoss, but, as you say, it is hard to accept wisdom at a moment like this. We have lost so many over the years. They are given to us and then abruptly they are taken away. It is difficult to understand God's infinite cruelty.'

'Goodbye, Mr. Dutt. Goodbye, Mrs. Dutt.'

They did not reply, and Miss Efoss walked quickly away.

Miss Efoss began to feel older. She walked with a stick; she found the cinema tired her eyes; she read less and discovered that she was bored by the effort of sustaining long conversations. She accepted each change quite philosophically, pleased that she could do so. She found too that there were compensations; she enjoyed, more and more, thinking about the past. Quite vividly, she re-lived the parts she wished to re-live. Unlike life itself, it was pleasant to be able to pick and choose.

Again by accident, she met Mr. Dutt. She was having tea one afternoon in a quiet, old-fashioned teashop, not at all the kind of place she would have associated with Mr. Dutt. Yet there he was, standing in front of her. 'Hello, Miss Efoss,' he said.

'Why, Mr. Dutt. How are you? How is your wife? It is some time since we met.'

Mr. Dutt sat down. He ordered some tea and then he leaned forward and stared at Miss Efoss. She wondered what he was thinking about: he had the air of someone who through politeness, makes the most of a moment but whose mind is busily occupied elsewhere. As he looked at her, his face suddenly cleared. He smiled, and when he spoke he seemed to be entirely present.

'I have great news, Miss Efoss. We are both so happy about it. Miss Efoss, Beryl is expecting a child.'

Miss Efoss blinked a little. She spread some jam on her toast and said:

'Oh, I'm so glad. How delightful for you both! Mrs. Dutt will be pleased. When is it—when is it due?'

'Quite soon. Quite soon.' Mr. Dutt beamed. 'Naturally Beryl is beside herself with joy. She is busy preparing all day.'

'There is a lot to see to on these occasions.'

'Indeed there is. Beryl is knitting like a mad thing. It seems as though she can't do enough.'

'It is the biggest event in a woman's life, Mr. Dutt.'

'And often in a man's, Miss Efoss.'

'Yes, indeed.'

'We have quite recovered our good spirits.'

'I'm glad of that. You were so sadly low when last I saw you.'

'You gave us some wise words. You were more comfort than you think, you know.'

'Oh, I was inadequate. I always am with sorrow.'

'No, no. Beryl said so afterwards. It was a happy chance to have met you so.'

'Thank you, Mr. Dutt.'

'It's not easy always to accept adversity. You helped us on our way. We shall always be grateful.'

'It is kind of you to say so.'

'The longing for a child is a strange force. To attend to its needs, to give it comfort and love—I suppose there is that in all of us. There is a streak of simple generosity that we do not easily understand.'

'The older I become, Mr. Dutt, the more I realize that one understands very little. I believe one is meant not to understand. The best things are complex and mysterious. And must remain so.'

'How right you are! It is often what I say to Beryl. I shall be glad to report that you confirm my thinking.'

'On my part it is instinct rather than thinking.'

'The line between the two is less acute than many would have us believe.'

'Yes, I suppose it is.'

'Miss Efoss, may I do one thing for you?'

'What is that?'

'It is a small thing but would give me pleasure. May I pay for your tea? Beryl will be pleased if you allow me to.'

Miss Efoss laughed. 'Yes, Mr. Dutt, you may pay for my tea.' And it was as she spoke this simple sentence that it dawned upon Miss Efoss just what it was she had to do.

Miss Efoss began to sell her belongings. She sold them in many directions, keeping back only a few which she wished to give away. It took her a long time, for there was much to see to. She wrote down long lists of details, finding this method the best for arranging things in her mind. She was sorry to see the familiar objects go, yet she knew that to be sentimental about them was absurd. It was for other people now to develop a sentiment for them; and she knew that the fresh associations they would in time take on would be, in the long run, as false as hers.

Her flat became bare and cheerless. In the end there was nothing left except the property of the landlord. She wrote to him, terminating her tenancy.

The Dutts were watching the television when Miss Efoss arrived. Mr. Dutt turned down the sound and went to open the door. He smiled without speaking and brought her into the sitting-room.

'Welcome, Miss Efoss,' Mrs. Dutt said. 'We've been expecting you.'

Miss Efoss carried a small suitcase. She said: 'Your baby, Mrs. Dutt. When is your baby due? I do hope I am in time.'

'Perfect, Miss Efoss, perfect,' said Mr. Dutt. 'Beryl's child is due this very night.'

The pictures flashed silently, eerily, on the television screen. A man dressed as a pirate was stroking the head of a parrot.

Miss Efoss did not sit down. 'I am rather tired,' she said. 'Do you mind if I go straight upstairs?'

'Dear Miss Efoss, please do.' Mrs. Dutt smiled at her. 'You know your way, don't you?'

'Yes,' Miss Efoss said. 'I know my way.'

FRANK TUOHY

The Licence

Aunt Cynthia rarely made personal use of the chairs in her London drawing-room. She was kneeling now on the hearth rug, and poking at the grate from time to time with a pair of tongs. When she turned round, her face would be full of endeavour at sympathy and understanding. It is a great effort to talk to boys of Peter's age.

Awkwardly waiting for her to speak again, he looked as if he might break the chair he was sitting in.

'Does your father write to you?'

'Yes, of course.'

'Often?'

'Yes.' Adolescence still made Peter's voice thrum like a slack guitar string. 'At school we're meant to write home every week, so, as I usually do, he pretty well has to; I mean he writes something, not much though.'

His aunt struck a heated coal and it split satisfactorily, emitting branches of flame. 'What does he write about?'

Peter laughed oafishly. 'About my future mostly.'

'Surely that can wait. What about himself? Has he told you any plans?'

'We're going to Austria this summer. He wants me to learn to drive.'

'You're too young.'

'I won't be then.' He laughed again, to help things on.

She was agitated and fussed. The boy had a train to catch in half an hour's time. Though partly impelled by curiosity, her sympathy was genuine; but he deflected it at every opportunity.

'Please don't always try to shut me out, Peter.'

He looked at her with hatred and desperation.

'I suppose it isn't any use. You're just a child.'

Her husband, a barrister, came in with the evening papers.

'Hullo, Pete, old boy.'

'Hullo, Uncle Raymond.'

Raymond Pelham issued a big grin: everybody felt they had to start off cheerfully with Peter.

'Darling, Carla's been pressing your dinner jacket. Do go and see if it's all right.'

'What did she want to do that for?'

'Because we're dining at the Messiters. Darling, please.'

'I expect it's all right. Is Pete old enough to have a glass of sherry?'

'Darling, please,' Aunt Cynthia went on signalling until her husband left the room, first winking at Peter on the way.

She put a hand on Peter's knee.

'This housekeeper, Mrs. What's-her-name.'

'Mrs. Macdonnell.'

'Yes. What does your father write about her?'

'Nothing much. Why?'

His aunt turned back to the fire, armed this time with the poker.

'He got her from an agency,' Peter said, trying to help.

'Oh, God. How difficult it is!' Aunt Cynthia hit a smoking coal with some violence, but it failed to crumble. 'He's my favourite brother. I was fond of your mother too. She could be a very very sweet person.'

At this, Peter was locked in silence.

'You'd better go to your train. I'll ring the taxi rank.'

'I can go by tube.'

'With your squash racket and record-player and everything?'

'Oh, all right.'

In the hall, they listened for the taxi. When they heard it stop outside, Aunt Cynthia kissed him. He still reeked of boarding school, as men do of prison; in her arms he held himself quite still, like an animal tense and ready to leap away at the first relaxation. She let him go, with a hurt little laugh.

Afterwards she said to her husband: 'I sometimes think he hates me.'

'He probably still feels like hell, poor Pete.'

'That's no answer. It's five months now—I was counting this morning.'

She moved into his arms. Raymond knew that for her the problem was, not Peter, but her own childlessness.

Because his father had evening surgery, Peter could not be met at Shereham station. He took another taxi to the house, which lay a mile away, among bird-haunted shrubberies. The drive spat and crackled with new gravel.

'There he is at last! I expect you know who I am, don't you?'

The woman in the doorway spoke in a soft Edinburgh voice. She was about forty, and wore a knitted suit and her dark hair done up in a bun. On her bright, bird-like face, the lips were thin and scarlet.

Peter dropped his squash racket to shake hands.

'I'm Mrs. Macdonnell. When you've got over your first shyness, I expect you'll want to call me Helen. Come along up, then.'

Peter picked up his bags again and made off up the stairs, with Mrs. Macdonnell following him.

'There's a big strong laddy.'

The room was small, on the sunless side of the house, a museum of Peter's past. He put his record-player and a case of records on the bed.

'Those'll be all the latest smash-hits.'

'No,' Peter said.

'What are they then? Dixieland?' She was showing him she knew all the modern words.

'Bach mostly.'

'Gloomy stuff, eh? Well, I never.'

She seemed put out, and left him, shaking her head as though she knew he'd be growing out of this phase. 'You'll be coming down when you're ready.'

Peter's trunk would arrive later. He unpacked his suitcase quickly and put the clothes in the drawer; if he left it, she might do it for him. He hid under his handkerchiefs the photograph of his mother, and the letter she had written to him before she died.

Dr. Hesketh was standing in front of the drawing-room fire with a whisky and soda. He had reddish hair, which was growing colourless, and a bristly moustache. He always looked ruffled and embarrassed; everyone over the past few months had conspired to expect too much of him.

Peter and his father shook hands. It was, nowadays, their only way of touching, and they hardly glanced at each other.

Mrs. Macdonnell said: 'You know I think he's got quite a look of you, Jack. Quite a look.'

At the sound of his father's Christian name, Peter flinched visibly. His father stared at the logs in the grate.

'He's taller, though. The wee bairn's taller than his daddy.' She drained her sherry. 'Well, then, I'll be going through to get you your supper. I expect you two have lots to talk about.'

Relieved of her presence, they could talk to each other quite easily.

'Aunt Cynthia's got seats for Covent Garden next week. She wants me to go up.'

'You go then. It's no fun for you now, moping around down here.'

'Have you thought any more about my driving lessons?'

'Yes, I don't see why you shouldn't begin as soon as you can.'

'Mr. Beaman—he's the history master—let me practise stopping and starting in his mini. In the school grounds, so I didn't need a licence.'

'Well then, you know the rudiments.'

'Yes.'

Both Peter and his father knew they would over-discuss this subject: they exploited to the utmost the few topics for conversation that now remained to them.

Mrs. Macdonnell called them.

'Not much for supper, I'm afraid. Today's the day I have my hair done.'

His father ate in silence, pouring tomato ketchup onto the thawed-out fishcakes. When they had finished, he whispered to Peter: 'Give her a hand with the dishes, there's a good lad.'

He went through to the kitchen.

'That's nice of you, Peter. I see they look after your manners at that school, not like some of these places.'

Peter seized a cloth and began drying plates strenuously.

'How do you think Dad is looking?'

He did not answer.

'Lost your tongue, have you? Never mind. As I say, you'll soon get over your shyness with Helen.'

'Actually, I call him Pa.'

She laughed, 'Do you now? Old-fashioned, aren't we?'

'He's all right, I suppose.'

Mrs. Macdonnell put down the dish-mop. 'Your father's a fine good man, Peter. He wears himself out for those patients of his, but they're not grateful, not a bit of it.'

She poured bleach into the basin.

'They don't know they're lucky. I was an ill woman when I came here, Peter. You're not old enough to know about these things. Your father's been a trump to me, a real trump.'

She unbuttoned her apron. Her sentimentality was full of menace.

'There's not many like him, these days. People down here don't know they're well off. And all these foreigners that work at the big houses!—They're not healthy, you know. I wouldn't have one of them in my house. And they don't do the work, either.'

Peter ducked away as soon as he could. Upstairs he lay flat on his bed, and put a Haydn quartet on the record-player. A few minutes later she was at his door.

'D'ye like the sound o' the pipes, Peter? D'ye no like the sound of the good Scots pipes?'

'I don't know much about them,' he said politely.

'There's nothing to beat them.'

She gave no signs of going away. Soon she tried whistling and humming a bit, to help Haydn along; it was the allegretto, however, and he was too quick for her.

'What do you have, Peter?'

'What?'

'What! Did ye never learn to say "pardon"? What'll you be

having for your nightcap? Will it be Horlick's or Ovaltine or cocoa or hot milk?'

'Nothing, thank you.'

'Ah, come now. Not even a nice cup of tea? Won't you join Helen in a nice cup of tea? She always has one, this time o' nights.'

'No, thank you.'

Huffed, she finally went away. Peter raised the arm of the pickup and put it back to where it had been when she first came in.

Later Peter stayed awake, listening. But the silence in the house was absolute. There was only a faint ringing sound out of the spring darkness, which might have been the blood encircling the walls of his own brain.

And then across the corridor, a small regular noise: Mrs. Macdonnell snoring. A guileless innocent murmur, it seemed to fill the whole house until Peter went to sleep.

Coming out of his bedroom, where he had been rearranging his long-playing records, Peter bumped into a small grey figure armed with a feather mop.

'They never tell me you was back! How are you then, dear?'

'I'm fine, Mrs. Parkes. How are things?'

'Oh, it's not the same.' The old woman's eyes sparkled with grief and mischief. 'It's not the same by a long chalk.'

Mrs. Macdonnell called upstairs: 'Mrs. Parkes, I've left the vacuum cleaner out, so's you can give downstairs a proper doing today.'

Mrs. Parkes made a face at Peter. 'See what I mean? Only I'm loyal, see? I won't let Doctor down. I said that to your poor mother, I won't let Doctor down.'

Relishing this, she was going to repeat it, but Mrs. Macdonnell had come half-way up the stairs, her head raised, scenting trouble.

'Your father's just off, Peter, once I've made his list out. You're going with him, aren't you?'

'Oh, all right.'

Dr. Hesketh was downstairs drinking a cup of tea. Mrs.

Macdonnell stood dutifully beside him with his list. She gave Peter a little smile, which indicated the regularity and reliability of this event.

Peter's father pointed to one name. 'Who's that?'

'I can't spell the foreign names, Jack. It's that cook at Shereham Hall.'

'Right ho. Nothing going to hold us up for long there.' He pocketed his stethoscope.

'Now, boys, don't you go being late for lunch. One o'clock sharp, mind.'

Peter followed his father out to the garage.

'It's probably only corned beef, anyway,' his father said, starting the car. Peter giggled.

The houses round Shereham were bright with new paint and daffodils and pink cherry-trees were in flower in the easily run gardens. On the few remaining bits of pasture, horses and ponies which belonged to the daughters of London businessmen were frisking in the sunshine. Dr. Hesketh visited two or three council houses and a thatched cottage, in which a family waited for a grandmother to die: they had already an offer from London people. Sometimes he stopped for a moment behind the car, out of sight of the windows. He came out of the last cottage whistling, and drove to Shereham Hall.

'Got something to read, old man? I may be a bit of time here.'

'Is the cook very ill?'

'No, not really. Be a bit of time, though.'

Shereham Hall was a square Palladian mansion built of pale sandstone. In the Portico there were croquet mallets, and some hooded basket-chairs. The garden was very large and would soon be opened to the public, in aid of the District Nurses.

After half an hour, there were voices, especially his father's, which sounded louder than before. Mr. and Mrs. Tyrell Bailey, both with pale hair and long whey-coloured faces, came out with him.

Mrs. Tyrell Bailey leaned towards the car. 'So this is the boy.'

'Oh yes, the boy,' Mr. Tyrell Bailey said.

Peter was trapped, like a fish under observation in an aquarium, but before he could get out of the car, they had lost interest in him. With the slow saunter of garden-viewers, they had crossed the drive and were approaching a large magnolia-tree, which stood in full blossom near the lake. Mrs. Tyrell Bailey was telling his father about the tree, and his father was nodding a great many times.

After a few minutes Peter's father returned across the lawn, smiling to himself and mopping his hands with a handkerchief. He got into the car in silence. As a child Peter had once said to his mother: 'Pa smells like the cocktail cabinet.' This joke had not been funny a second time.

'Well, off we go.'

Gravel roared under the tyres, Shereham Hall, the basket chairs and the magnolia-tree spun round, and the car raced towards a wall of rhododendrons. Beside the lake, the faces of the Tyrell Baileys flashed by, identically aghast. The car reached the bottom of the drive, swooped into the main road, and came to a halt.

'Get out, get out, you little fool,' Dr. Hesketh shouted. 'See what it is.'

Peter scrambled out and ran to the front of the car.

A schoolboy, several years younger than himself, was kneeling on his hands and knees in the road. The wheels of his bicycle were still spinning furiously.

'Are you all right?'

The boy got up. He wore shorts and a county school cap, and his overfed face was white with fear. His smooth knees were grazed and the palms of his hands pitted with the marks of stones.

'I think . . .' Tame, neuter-looking, he was ready to apologize. 'P'raps I should've rung my bell.'

'Are you sure you're all right? My father's a doctor, he could probably help.'

'No, I'm all right.' Nearly crying, the boy wanted to be left to himself.

Peter rummaged in his pocket and produced five shillings. 'Here, take this.'

Startled, the boy said, 'Thank you, sir,' and they both blushed. He picked up his bicycle, spun the pedals once or twice, then mounted and wobbled slowly away up the hill. Peter watched him until he had disappeared round a corner.

In the car Peter's father was leaning forward with forehead resting on the top of the steering wheel.

Peter sat beside him in silence.

'Sorry, Pete. Sometimes, I can't see things—I can't——'

'Let's stay here a bit.'

His father leaned back, showing that his cheeks were wet. 'No, better get back. Helen'll be waiting lunch.' He took out a cigarette with violently trembling hands. Peter pulled out the dashboard lighter to help him.

'Now, you see, Pete, why you'd better learn to drive.'

'I want to, anyway.'

'Peter, you'd better know about this. I've been under a lot of strain lately. Very private strain.'

The expression sounded peculiar. After a moment he inquired cautiously: 'Is it about Ma?'

'No, it isn't.'

'Oh,' Peter said.

Late that night Peter heard somebody moving about the house. Without thinking, he put on his dressing-gown and crept to the end of the corridor. Mrs. Macdonnell was standing at the top of the stairs. Wearing no make-up, with her hair hanging in two long dark braids down her frilly white night-dress, she looked both archaic and sexy, like somebody out of the Brontës.

'Who is it?'

'Hesketh. I mean, Peter.'

'Must I be always after you two laddies? Somebody left the light on in the hallway.'

He shivered, clutching his shrunken fawn dressing-gown— someone at school had pinched the cord years ago. His large greyish feet were cold on the floorboards. She came closer to him.

'Off to bed with you now.'

Her eyes were an entire shock: they were hard with hatred,

like little darts of steel. He turned and without dignity made his way back to his room. She was watching him the whole time, and his hair prickled and his skin crawled.

'So you're off today, are you, dear?' Mrs. Parkes said. Peter was wearing his London suit. 'Well, I can't say I blame you. That auntie of yours, Mrs. Pelham, she's a kind soul. She spoke quite nicely to me after the funeral. I told her I'd stick with Doctor, and I done it up to now. But this isn't a happy house. You're well out of it.'

Peter's provisional driving licence had arrived by the morning's post. He showed it to his father at breakfast.

'Good man. I'll fix up those driving lessons before you come back. You may as well have something to do in the last week of the holidays.'

'Do you think I'll be able to drive in Austria?'

'I don't see why not.' His father was silent, buttering a piece of toast. 'It probably won't be Austria, in fact. Helen thinks she'd prefer Switzerland.'

Their eyes failed to meet across the tablecloth.

'Oh, I see.'

When they had both finished, Peter stacked the breakfast things and carried them through to the kitchen. Mrs. Macdonnell was standing at the sink, doing the flowers.

'Well, you're off now, are you, Peter? No doubt that aunt of yours will be spoiling you again. Funny, I thought you were a nice polite boy, first of all. Well, we live and learn and that's our misfortune.'

She cut through the stalks of a bunch of jonquils; they fell stickily, one by one.

'No, don't go yet. Listen to me a moment, Peter.' Her voice dropped. 'Now, young feller me lad, don't you be talking out of turn. No telling tales out of school, got it? Because if you do, laddie, you'll live to regret it. You'll live to regret it very much. Helen can be real nasty, when she's the mind to it. And one thing she doesn't take to is dirty little sneaking eavesdroppers. There's your daddy calling. Now remember what I said.'

Peter got into the car beside his father.

'I'll ring up about the lessons today. And you can start driving me around for practice.'

Peter did not answer. His father accepted this, and looked straight ahead, his face twitching with guilt.

Cynthia Pelham had been taking Peter out to lunch.

She had made an immense effort to stop making remarks like 'I suppose it's no use suggesting you do something about your hair?' She had refrained from straightening him up altogether, apart from insisting he got his shoes cleaned by the man on the corner of Piccadilly Circus. He bought the clothes he wanted, including two frightful ties. In the restaurant she had let him order what he liked, and allowed him, with certain afterthoughts, to drink a glass of wine. Now she pushed money under the table at him, whispering: 'The man pays.'

'It's obvious you're paying,' Peter said. 'The waiters all know.'

They returned home exhausted.

Tea was waiting and with it, by prearrangement, was Juliet, Cynthia's oldest friend.

'Washing his hands.'

'How are things?' Juliet asked.

'Worse, if anything. Of course, I scrupulously refrain from mentioning, and all that. But really, it's been half a year now. And it isn't as if everything between Jack and Elizabeth had been so absolutely marvellous, because I happen to know——'

'What on earth difference should that make to Peter?'

'No, none, I suppose.' Cynthia sighed. 'I'm sorry, darling, I'm tired. He'll be down in a minute. Try a spot of charm, will you?'

'I'm sure he's a perfectly normal boy,' Juliet said. 'It's just that——'

'It's just that he's going through a phase. I know. Jolly long phase. I wonder if a psychiatrist——'

'I'd leave him alone if I were you.'

Kneeling on the rug, Cynthia bit into a piece of bread and butter. 'Nobody helps.'

'Honestly, I'd skip it. What good bread you always have—though of course I shouldn't be eating it.'

'He's impossible.'

'I can remember when everyone said "Cynthia's impossible".'

Peter's aunt blushed a little. 'You know perfectly well that was about something quite different.'

The stairs shook overhead and the pictures began rattling.

'Peter, darling, come and have some tea.' His aunt had not called him 'darling' before, and this embarrassed both herself and him.

He shook hands with Juliet and sat down. Fair and gleaming and beautifully dressed, the two women filled the immediate view. They tried to talk about Covent Garden, but since Peter was the only one of them with any knowledge of opera, conversation did not progress. Juliet had been to Glyndebourne three or four times, but couldn't remember any of the names.

'When do you go back?' she asked him. 'I'm sorry, I don't mean school—I know everybody always asks that. I meant to Shereham.'

'The day after tomorrow.'

'So soon!'

'Peter's having driving lessons,' Aunt Cynthia said.

'Yes?'

'My father wants me to drive when we go on holiday. We're going to Austria.' He stopped, then continued: 'At least, I mean, Switzerland. Also he wants me to drive him when he visits patients.'

To Juliet, Cynthia made a tiny elbow-lifting gesture, which Peter observed.

'I think that's marvellous,' Juliet said. 'Your father will be pleased. How's he getting on with his new housekeeper?'

Peter stared at the floor between his feet. 'She does her job.'

Cynthia, collecting the teacups, muttered: 'Yes, but what job, that's what we'd all like to know.'

Peter got up and walked out of the room.

'Darling!' Juliet said.

'Have I said something awful?'

'Yes, you have.'

Cynthia went scarlet. 'Well, everything one says is awful. It's absolute hell, you don't know what I've been through.'

This evening Peter's father was waiting for him at Shereham Station.

'Hullo, old boy. Got your luggage?'

'Yes.'

'How's Aunt Cynthia?'

'She's all right,' Peter said. 'She sent you her love.'

He handed in his ticket and followed his father into the car park.

'Not too tired after all your junketings?'

'No, of course not. Why?'

'I thought of going over for a bite at the Ram at Chillington. They do quite a decent meal there. It's outside my parish, so there's no risk of meeting patients. We used to go there a lot in the old days.'

'That'd be lovely.'

'Mrs. Parkes has been leaving me something in the oven, but I told her not to bother tonight, as you were coming down.'

His father spoke excitedly and rather fast, and Peter had to wait until they got into the car before asking: 'Where's Mrs. Macdonnell?'

His father was silent a moment. 'I—I gave her the sack. We had a bit of a bust up, so I said she could leave at once. Come, now, her cooking wasn't so fancy, was it?'

Peter giggled. 'It certainly wasn't.'

His father drove very slowly through Shereham and swerved out onto the dark Chillington road.

'Pa, can I have wine at dinner?'

'Well, that's not really the object of the exercise, but I should think so. In moderation.'

A minute or two later his father drew up at the roadside.

'Got your licence on you?'

'Yes, I have.'

'Like to drive?'

'Yes, I would.'

'Good man. Hop out then, and I'll move over.'

Peter let in the clutch perfectly and the car slid off towards Chillington.

JOHN UPDIKE

Should Wizard Hit Mommy?

I N T H E evenings and for Saturday naps like today's, Jack
told his daughter Jo a story out of his head. This custom,
begun when she was two, was itself now nearly two years old,
and his head felt empty. Each new story was a slight variation
of a basic tale: a small creature, usually named Roger (Roger
Fish, Roger Squirrel, Roger Chipmunk), had some problem
and went with it to the wise old owl. The owl told him to go to
the wizard, and the wizard performed a magic spell that
solved the problem, demanding in payment a number of pennies greater than the number Roger Creature had but in the
same breath directing the animal to a place where the extra
pennies could be found. Then Roger was so happy he played
many games with other creatures, and went home to his mother
just in time to hear the train whistle that brought his daddy
home from Boston. Jack described their supper, and the story
was over. Working his way through this scheme was especially
fatiguing on Saturday, because Jo never fell asleep in naps any
more, and knowing this made the rite seem futile.

The little girl (not so little any more; the bumps her feet
made under the covers were halfway down the bed, their big
double bed that they let her be in for naps and when she was
sick) had at last arranged herself, and from the way her fat face
deep in the pillow shone in the sunlight sifting through the
drawn shades, it did not seem fantastic that something magic
would occur, and she would take her nap like an infant of two.
Her brother, Bobby, was two, and already asleep with his
bottle. Jack asked, 'Who shall the story be about today?'

'Roger . . .' Jo squeezed her eyes shut and smiled to be thinking she was thinking. Her eyes opened, her mother's blue.
'Skunk,' she said firmly.

A new animal; they must talk about skunks at nursery
school. Having a fresh hero momentarily stirred Jack to creative

enthusiasm. 'All right,' he said. 'Once upon a time, in the deep dark woods, there was a tiny little creature name of Roger Skunk. And he smelled very bad——'

'Yes,' Jo said.

'He smelled so bad none of the other little woodland creatures would play with him.' Jo looked at him solemnly; she hadn't foreseen this. 'Whenever he would go out to play,' Jack continued with zest, remembering certain humiliations of his own childhood, 'all of the other tiny animals would cry, "Uh-oh, here comes Roger Stinky Skunk," and they would run away, and Roger Skunk would stand there all alone, and two little round tears would fall from his eyes.' The corners of Jo's mouth drooped down and her lower lip bent forward as he traced with a forefinger along the side of her nose the course of one of Roger Skunk's tears.

'Won't he see the owl?' she asked in a high and faintly roughened voice.

Sitting on the bed beside her, Jack felt the covers tug as her legs switched tensely. He was pleased with this moment—he was telling her something true, something she must know—and had no wish to hurry on. But downstairs a chair scraped, and he realized he must get down to help Clare paint the living-room woodwork.

'Well, he walked along very sadly and came to a very big tree, and in the tiptop of the tree was an enormous wise old owl.'

'Good.'

' "Mr. Owl," Roger Skunk said, "all the other little animals run away from me because I smell so bad." "So you do," the owl said. "Very, very bad." "What can I do?" Roger Skunk said, and he cried very hard.'

'The wizard, the wizard,' Jo shouted, and sat right up, and a Little Golden Book spilled from the bed.

'Now, Jo. Daddy's telling the story. Do you want to tell Daddy the story?'

'No. You me.'

'Then lie down and be sleepy.'

Her head relapsed onto the pillow and she said, 'Out of your head.'

'Well. The owl thought and thought. At last he said, "Why
don't you go see the wizard?" '

'Daddy?'

'What?'

'Are magic spells *real*?' This was a new phase, just this last
month, a reality phase. When he told her spiders eat bugs, she
turned to her mother and asked, 'Do they *really*?' and when
Clare told her God was in the sky and all around them, she
turned to her father and insisted, with a sly yet eager smile,
'Is He *really*?'

'They're real in stories,' Jack answered curtly. She had made
him miss a beat in the narrative. 'The owl said, "Go through
the dark woods, under the apple trees, into the swamp, over
the crick——" '

'What's a crick?'

'A little river. "Over the crick, and there will be the wizard's
house." And that's the way Roger Skunk went, and pretty soon
he came to a little white house, and he rapped on the door.'
Jack rapped on the window sill, and under the covers Jo's tall
figure clenched in an infantile thrill. 'And then a tiny little old
man came out, with a long white beard and a pointed blue hat,
and said, "Eh? Whatzis? Whatcher want? You smell awful." '
The wizard's voice was one of Jack's own favorite effects; he
did it by scrunching up his face and somehow whining through
his eyes, which felt for the interval rheumy. He felt being an
old man suited him.

' "I know it," Roger Skunk said, "and all the little animals
run away from me. The enormous wise owl said you could
help me." '

' "Eh? Well, maybe. Come on in. Don't git too close." ' Now,
inside, Jo, there were all these magic things, all jumbled together in a big dusty heap, because the wizard did not have
any cleaning lady.'

'Why?'

'Why? Because he was a wizard, and a very old man.'

'Will he die?'

'No. Wizards don't die. Well, he rummaged around and
found an old stick called a magic wand and asked Roger Skunk

what he wanted to smell like. Roger thought and thought and said, "Roses." ' '

'Yes. Good,' Jo said smugly.

Jack fixed her with a trancelike gaze and chanted in the wizard's elderly irritable voice:

> ' "Abracadabry, hocus-poo,
>   Roger Skunk, how do you do,
>   Roses, boses, pull an ear,
>   Roger Skunk, you never fear:
>   *Bingo!*" '

He paused as a rapt expression widened out from his daughter's nostrils, forcing her eyebrows up and her lower lip down in a wide noiseless grin, an expression in which Jack was startled to recognize his wife feigning pleasure at cocktail parties. 'And all of a sudden,' he whispered, 'the whole inside of the wizard's house was full of the smell of—*roses!* "Roses!" Roger Fish cried. And the wizard said, very cranky, "That'll be seven pennies." '

'Daddy.'

'What?'

'Roger *Skunk*. You said Roger Fish.'

'Yes. Skunk.'

'You said Roger *Fish*. Wasn't that silly?'

'Very silly of your stupid old daddy. Where was I? Well, you know about the pennies.'

'Say it.'

'O.K. Roger Skunk said, "But all I have is four pennies," and he began to cry.' Jo made the crying face again, but this time without a trace of sincerity. This annoyed Jack. Downstairs some more furniture rumbled. Clare shouldn't move heavy things; she was six months pregnant. It would be their third.

'So the wizard said, "Oh, very well. Go to the end of the lane and turn around three times and look down the magic well and there you will find three pennies. Hurry up." So Roger Skunk went to the end of the lane and turned around three times and

there in the magic well were *three pennies!* So he took them back
to the wizard and was very happy and ran out into the woods
and all the other little animals gathered around him because he
smelled so good. And they played tag, baseball, football,
basketball, lacrosse, hockey, soccer, and pick-up-sticks.'

'What's pick-up-sticks?'

'It's a game you play with sticks.'

'Like the wizard's magic wand?'

'Kind of. And they played games and laughed all afternoon
and then it began to get dark and they all ran home to their
mommies.'

Jo was starting to fuss with her hands and look out of the
window, at the crack of day that showed under the shade. She
thought the story was all over. Jack didn't like women when
they took anything for granted; he liked them apprehensive,
hanging on his words. 'Now, Jo, are you listening?'

'Yes.'

'Because this is very interesting. Roger Skunk's mommy
said, "What's that awful smell?" '

'Wha-at?'

'And Roger Skunk said, "It's me, Mommy. I smell like
roses." And she said, "Who made you smell like that?" And he
said, "The wizard," and she said, "Well, of all the nerve. You
come with me and we're going right back to that very awful
wizard." '

Jo sat up, her hands dabbling in the air with genuine fright.
'But Daddy, then he said about the other little aminals run
away!' Her hands skittered off, into the underbrush.

'All right. He said, "But Mommy, all the other little animals
run away," and she said, "I don't care. You smelled the way a
little skunk should have and I'm going to take you right back
to that wizard," and she took an umbrella and went back with
Roger Skunk and hit that wizard right over the head.'

'No,' Jo said, and put her hand out to touch his lips, yet even
in her agitation did not quite dare to stop the source of truth.
Inspiration came to her. 'Then the wizard hit *her* on the head
and did not change that little skunk back.'

'No,' he said. 'The wizard said "O.K." and Roger Skunk

did not smell of roses any more. He smelled very bad again.'

'But the other little amum—*oh!*—amum——'

'Joanne. It's Daddy's story. Shall Daddy not tell you any more stories?' Her broad face looked at him through sifted light, astounded. 'This is what happened, then. Roger Skunk and his mommy went home and they heard *Woo-oo, woooo-oo* and it was the choo-choo train bringing Daddy Skunk home from Boston. And they had lima beans, pork chops, celery, liver, mashed potatoes, and Pie-Oh-My for dessert. And when Roger Skunk was in bed Mommy Skunk came up and hugged him and said he smelled like her little baby skunk again and she loved him very much. And that's the end of the story.'

'But Daddy.'

'What?'

'Then did the other little ani-mals run away?'

'No, because eventually they got used to the way he was and did not mind it at all.'

'What's evenshiladee?'

'In a little while.'

'That was a stupid mommy.'

'It was *not*,' he said with rare emphasis, and believed, from her expression, that she realized he was defending his own mother to her, or something as odd. 'Now I want you to put your big heavy head in the pillow and have a good long nap.' He adjusted the shade so not even a crack of day showed, and tiptoed to the door, in the pretense that she was already asleep. But when he turned, she was crouching on top of the covers and staring at him. 'Hey. Get under the covers and fall faaast asleep. Bobby's asleep.'

She stood up and bounced gingerly on the springs. 'Daddy.'

'What?'

'Tomorrow, I want you to tell me the story that that wizard took that magic wand and hit that mommy'—her plump arms chopped fiercely—'right over the head.'

'No. That's not the story. The point is that the little skunk loved his mommy more than he loved aaalll the other little animals and she knew what was right.'

'No. Tomorrow you say he hit that mommy. Do it.' She kicked her legs up and sat down on the bed with a great heave and complaint of springs, as she had done hundreds of times before, except that this time she did not laugh. 'Say it, Daddy.'

'Well, we'll see. Now at least have a rest. Stay on the bed. You're a good girl.'

He closed the door and went downstairs. Clare had spread the newspapers and opened the paint can and, wearing an old shirt of his on top of her maternity smock, was stroking the chair rail with a dipped brush. Above him footsteps vibrated and he called, '*Joanne*. Shall I come up there and spank you?' The footsteps hesitated.

'That was a long story,' Clare said.

'The poor kid,' he answered, and with utter weariness watched his wife labor. The woodwork, a cage of moldings and rails and baseboards all around them, was half old tan and half new ivory and he felt caught in an ugly middle position, and though he as well felt his wife's presence in the cage with him, he did not want to speak with her, work with her, touch her, anything.

PATRICK WHITE

Five-Twenty

MOST evenings, weather permitting, the Natwicks sat on the front veranda to watch the traffic. During the day the stream flowed, but towards five it began to thicken, it sometimes jammed solid like: the semi-trailers and refrigeration units, the decent old-style sedans, the mini-cars, the bombs, the Holdens and the Holdens. She didn't know most of the names. Royal did, he was a man, though never ever mechanical himself. She liked him to tell her about the vehicles, or listen to him take part in conversation with anyone who stopped at the fence. He could hold his own, on account of he was more educated, and an invalid has time to think.

They used to sit side by side on the tiled veranda, him in his wheelchair she had got him after the artheritis took over, her in the old cane. The old cane chair wasn't hardly presentable any more; she had torn her winter cardy on a nail and laddered several pair of stockings. You hadn't the heart to get rid of it, though. They brought it with them from Sarsaparilla after they sold the business. And now they could sit in comfort to watch the traffic, the big steel insects of nowadays, which put the wind up her at times.

Royal said, 'I reckon we're a shingle short to'uv ended up on the Parramatta Road.'

'You said we'd still see life,' she reminded, 'even if we lost the use of our legs.'

'But look at the traffic! Worse every year. And air. Rot a man's lungs quicker than the cigarettes. You should'uv headed me off. You who's supposed to be practical!'

'I thought it was what you wanted,' she said, keeping it soft; she had never been one to crow.

'Anyway, I already lost the use of me legs.'

As if she was to blame for that too. She was so shocked the chair sort of jumped. It made her blood run cold to hear the metal feet screak against the little draught-board tiles.

'Well, I 'aven't!' she protested. 'I got me legs, and will be able to get from 'ere to anywhere and bring 'ome the shopping. While I got me strength.'

She tried never to upset him by any show of emotion, but now she was so upset herself.

They watched the traffic in the evenings, as the orange light was stacked up in thick slabs, and the neon signs were coming on.

'See that bloke down there in the parti-coloured Holden?'

'Which?' she asked.

'The one level with our own gate.'

'The pink and brown?' She couldn't take all that interest tonight, only you must never stop humouring a sick man.

'Yairs. Pink. Fancy a man in a pink car!'

'Dusty pink is fashionable.' She knew that for sure.

'But a man!'

'Perhaps his wife chose it. Perhaps he's got a domineering wife.'

Royal laughed low. 'Looks the sort of coot who might like to be domineered, and if that's what he wants, it's none of our business, is it?'

She laughed to keep him company. They were such mates, everybody said. And it was true. She didn't know what she would do if Royal passed on first.

That evening the traffic had jammed. Some of the drivers began tooting. Some of them stuck their heads out, and yarned to one another. But the man in the pink-and-brown Holden just sat. He didn't look to either side.

Come to think of it, she had noticed him pass before. Yes. Though he wasn't in no way a noticeable man. Yes. She looked at her watch.

'Five-twenty,' she said. 'I seen that man in the pink-and-brown before. He's pretty regular. Looks like a business executive.'

Royal cleared his throat and spat. It didn't make the edge of the veranda. Better not to notice it, because he'd only create if she did. She'd get out the watering-can after she had pushed him inside.

'Business executives!' she heard. 'They're afraid people are gunner think they're poor class without they *execute*. In our day nobody was ashamed to *do*. Isn't that about right, eh?' She didn't answer because she knew she wasn't meant to. 'Funny sort of head that cove's got. Like it was half squashed. Silly-lookun bloody head!'

'Could have been born with it,' she suggested. 'Can't help what you're born with. Like your religion.'

There was the evening the Chev got crushed, only a young fellow too. Ahhh, it had stuck in her throat, thinking of the wife and kiddies. She ran in, and out again as quick as she could, with a couple of blankets, and the rug that was a present from Hazel. She had grabbed a pillow off their own bed.

She only faintly heard Royal shouting from the wheel-chair.

She arranged the blankets and the pillow on the pavement, under the orange sky. The young fellow was looking pretty sick, kept on turning his head as though he recognized and wanted to tell her something. Then the photographer from the *Mirror* took his picture, said she ought to be in it to add a touch of human interest, but she wouldn't. A priest came, the *Mirror* took his picture, administering what Mrs. Dolan said they call Extreme Unkshun. Well, you couldn't poke fun at a person's religion any more than the shape of their head, and Mrs. Dolan was a decent neighbour, the whole family, and clean.

When she got back to the veranda, Royal, a big man, had slipped down in his wheel-chair.

He said, or gasped, 'Wotcher wanter do that for, Ella? How are we gunner get the blood off?'

She hadn't thought about the blood, when of course she was all smeared with it, and the blankets, and Hazel's good Onka-parinka. Anyway, it was her who would get the blood off.

'You soak it in milk or something,' she said. 'I'll ask. Don't you worry.'

Then she did something. She bent down and kissed Royal on the forehead in front of the whole Parramatta Road. She regretted it at once, because he looked that powerless in his invalid chair, and his forehead felt cold and sweaty.

But you can't undo things that are done.

It was a blessing they could sit on the front veranda. Royal suffered a lot by now. He had his long-standing hernia, which they couldn't have operated on, on account of he was afraid of his heart. And then the artheritis.

'Arthritis.'

'All right,' she accepted the correction. 'Arth-er-itis.'

It was all very well for men, they could manage more of the hard words.

'What have we got for tea?' he asked.

'Well,' she said, fanning out her hands on the points of her elbows, and smiling, 'it's a surprise.'

She looked at her watch. It was five-twenty.

'It's a coupler nice little bits of fillet Mr. Ballard let me have.'

'Wotcher mean let you have? Didn't you pay for them?'

She had to laugh. 'Anything I have I pay for!'

'Well? Think we're in the fillet-eating class?'

'It's only a treat, Royal,' she said. 'I got a chump chop for myself. I like a nice chop.'

He stopped complaining, and she was relieved.

'There's that gentleman,' she said, 'in the Holden.'

They watched him pass, as sober as their own habits.

Royal—he had been his mother's little king. Most of his mates called him 'Roy'. Perhaps only her and Mrs. Natwick had stuck to the christened name, they felt it suited.

She often wondered how Royal had ever fancied her: such a big man, with glossy hair, black, and a nose like on someone historical. She would never have said it, but she was proud of Royal's nose. She was proud of the photo he had of the old family home in Kent, the thatch so lovely, and Grannie Natwick sitting in her apron on a rush-bottom chair in front, looking certainly not all that different from Mum, with the aunts gathered round in leggermutton sleeves, all big nosey women like Royal.

She had heard Mum telling Royal's mother, 'Ella's a plain

little thing, but what's better than cheerful and willing?' She had always been on the mousey side, she supposed, which didn't mean she couldn't chatter with the right person. She heard Mum telling Mrs. Natwick, 'My Ella can wash and bake against any comers. Clever with her needle too.' She had never entered any of the competitions, like they told her she ought to, it would have made her nervous.

It was all the stranger that Royal had ever fancied her.

Once as they sat on the veranda watching the evening traffic, she said, 'Remember how you used to ride out in the old days from "Bugilbar" to Cootramundra?'

'Cootamundra.'

'Yes,' she said. 'Cootramundra.' (That's why they'd called the house 'Coota' when they moved to the Parramatta Road.)

She had been so dazzled on one occasion by his parti-coloured forehead and his black hair, after he had got down from the saddle, after he had taken off his hat, she had run and fetched a duster, and dusted Royal Natwick's boots. The pair of new elastic-sides was white with dust from the long ride. It only occurred to her as she polished she might be doing something shameful, but when she looked up, it seemed as though Royal Natwick saw nothing peculiar in Ella McWhirter dusting his boots. He might even have expected it. She was so glad she could have cried.

Old Mr. Natwick had come out from Kent when a youth, and after working at several uncongenial jobs, and studying at night, had been taken on as book-keeper at 'Bugilbar'. He was much valued in the end by the owners, and always made use of. The father would have liked his son to follow in his footsteps, and taught him how to keep the books, but Royal wasn't going to hang around any family of purse-proud squatters, telling them the things they wanted to hear. He had ideas of his own for becoming rich and important.

So when he married Ella McWhirter, which nobody could ever understand, not even Ella herself, perhaps only Royal, who never bothered to explain (why should he?) they moved to Juggerawa, and took over the general store. It was in a bad way, and soon was in a worse, because Royal's ideas were above those of his customers.

Fulbrook was the next stage. He found employment as book-keeper on a grazing property outside. She felt so humiliated on account of his humiliation. It didn't matter about herself because she always expected less. She took a job in Fulbrook from the start, at the 'Dixie Cafe' in High Street. She worked there several years as waitress, helping out with the scrubbing for the sake of the extra money. She had never hated anything, but got to hate the flies trampling in the sugar and on the necks of the tomato sauce bottles.

At weekends her husband usually came in, and when she wasn't needed in the shop, they lay on the bed in her upstairs room, listening to the corrugated iron and the warping white-washed weatherboard. She would have loved to do something for him, but in his distress he complained about 'wet kisses'. It surprised her. She had always been afraid he might find her a bit too dry in her show of affection.

Those years at the 'Dixie Cafe' certainly dried her up. She got those freckly patches and seams in her skin in spite of the lotions used as directed. Not that it matters so much in anyone born plain. Perhaps her plainness helped her save. There was never a day when she didn't study her savings-book, it became her favourite recreation.

Royal, on the other hand, wasn't the type that dried up, being fleshier, and dark. He even put on weight out at the grazing property, where they soon thought the world of him. When the young ladies were short of a man for tennis the book-keeper was often invited, and to a ball once at the home-stead. He was earning good money, and he too saved a bit, though his instincts weren't as mean as hers. For instance, he fancied a choice cigar. In his youth Royal was a natty dresser.

Sometimes the young ladies, if they decided to inspect the latest at Ryan's Emporium, or Mr. Philup, if he felt like grog-ging up with the locals, would drive him in, and as he got out they would look funny at the book-keeper's wife they had heard about, they must have, serving out the plates of frizzled steak and limp chips. Royal always waited to see his employers drive off before coming in.

In spite of the savings, this might have gone on much longer than it did if old Mr. Natwick hadn't died. It appeared he had been a very prudent man. He left them a nice little legacy. The evening of the news, Royal was driven in by Mr. Philup and they had a few at the Imperial. Afterwards the book-keeper was dropped off, because he proposed to spend the night with his wife and catch the early train to attend his father's funeral.

They lay in the hot little room and discussed the future. She had never felt so hectic. Royal got the idea he would like to develop a grocery business in one of the posh outer suburbs of Sydney. 'Interest the monied residents in some of the luxury lines. Appeal to the imagination as well as the stomach.'

She was impressed, of course, but not as much as she should have been. She wasn't sure, but perhaps she was short on imagination. Certainly their prospects had made her down-right feverish, but for no distinct, sufficient reason.

'And have a baby.' She heard her own unnatural voice.

'Eh?'

'We could start a baby.' Her voice grew word by word drier.

'There's no reason why we couldn't have a baby. Or two.' He laughed. 'But starting a new life isn't the time to start a baby.' He dug her in the ribs. 'And you the practical one!'

She agreed it would be foolish, and presently Royal fell asleep.

What could she do for him? As he lay there breathing she would have loved to stroke his nose she could see faintly in the light from the window. Again unpractical, she would have liked to kiss it. Or bite it suddenly off.

She was so disgusted with herself she got creaking off the bed and walked flat across the boards to the washstand and swallowed a couple of Aspros to put her solidly to sleep.

All their life together she had to try in some way to make amends to Royal, not only for her foolishness, but for some of the thoughts that got into her head. Because she hadn't the imagination, the thoughts couldn't have been her own. They must have been put into her.

It was easier of course in later life, after he had cracked up, what with his hernia, and heart, and the artheritis taking over. Fortunately she was given the strength to help him into the wheel-chair, and later still, to lift, or drag him up on the pillows and over, to rub the bed-sores, and stick the pan under him. But even during the years at Sarsaparilla she could make amends in many little ways, though with him still in his prime, naturally he mustn't know of them. So all her acts were mostly for her own self-gratification.

The store at Sarsaparilla, if it didn't exactly flourish, gave them a decent living. She had her problems, though. Some of the locals just couldn't accept that Royal was a superior man. Perhaps she had been partly to blame, she hardly dared admit it, for showing one or two 'friends' the photo of the family home in Kent. She couldn't resist telling the story of one of the aunts, Miss Ethel Natwick, who followed her brother to New South Wales. Ethel was persuaded to accept a situation at Government House, but didn't like it and went back, in spite of the Governor's lady insisting she valued Ethel as a close personal friend. When people began to laugh at Royal on account of his auntie and the family home, as you couldn't help finding out in a place like Sarsaparilla, it was her, she knew, it was her to blame. It hurt her deeply.

Of course Royal could be difficult. Said stockbrokers had no palate and less imagination. Royal said no Australian grocer could make a go of it if it wasn't for flour, granulated sugar, and tomato sauce. Some of the customers turned nasty in retaliation. This was where she could help, and did, because Royal was out on delivery more often than not. It embarrassed her only when some of them took it for granted she was on their side. As if he wasn't her husband. Once or twice she had gone out crying afterwards, amongst the wormy wattles and hens' droppings. Anyone across the gully could have heard her blowing her nose behind the store, but she didn't care. Poor Royal.

There was that Mr. Ogburn said, 'A selfish, swollen-headed

slob who'll chew you up and swallow you down.' She wouldn't let herself hear any more of what he had to say. Mr. Ogburn had a hare-lip, badly sewn, opening and closing. There was nothing frightened her so much as even a well-disguised hare-lip. She got the palpitations after the scene with Mr. Ogburn.

Not that there was anything wrong with her.

She only hadn't had the baby. It was her secret grief on black evenings as she walked slowly looking for the eggs a flighty hen might have hid in the bracken.

Dr. Bamforth said, looking at the nib of his fountain pen, 'You know, don't you, it's sometimes the man?'

She didn't even want to hear, let alone think about it. In any case she wouldn't tell Royal, because a man's pride could be so easily hurt.

After they had sold out at Sarsaparilla and come to live at what they called 'Coota' on the Parramatta Road, it was both easier and more difficult, because if they were not exactly elderly they were getting on. Royal used to potter about in the beginning, while taking care, on account of the hernia and his heart. There was the business of the lawn-mowing, not that you could call it lawn, but it was what she had. She loved her garden. In front certainly there was only the two square of rather sooty grass which she would keep in order with the push-mower. The lawn seemed to get on Royal's nerves until the artheritis took hold of him. He had never liked mowing. He would lean against the veranda post, and shout, 'Don't know why we don't do what they've done down the street. Root the stuff out. Put down a green concrete lawn.'

'That would be copying,' she answered back.

She hoped it didn't sound stubborn. As she pushed the mower she bent her head, and smiled, waiting for him to cool off. The scent of grass and a few clippings flew up through the traffic fumes reminding you of summer.

While Royal shuffled along the veranda and leaned against another post. 'Or pebbles. You can buy clean, river pebbles. A few plastic shrubs, and there's the answer.'

He only gave up when his trouble forced him into the chair.

You couldn't drive yourself up and down a veranda shouting at someone from a wheel-chair without the passers-by thinking you was a nut. So he quietened.

He watched her, though. From under the peak of his cap. Because she felt he might still resent her mowing the lawn, she would try to reassure him as she pushed. 'What's wrong, *eh*? While I still have me health, me *strength*—I was always what they call *wiry*—why shouldn't I cut the *grass*?'

She would come and sit beside him, to keep him company in watching the traffic, and invent games to amuse her invalid husband.

'Isn't that the feller we expect?' she might ask. 'The one that passes at five-twenty,' looking at her watch, 'in the old pink-and-brown Holden?'

They enjoyed their snort of amusement all the better because no one else knew the reason for it.

Once when the traffic was particularly dense, and that sort of chemical smell from one of the factories was thickening in the evening air, Royal drew her attention. 'Looks like he's got something on his mind.'

Could have too. Or it might have been the traffic block. The way he held his hands curved listlessly around the inactive wheel reminded her of possums and monkeys she had seen in cages. She shifted a bit. Her squeaky old chair. She felt uneasy for ever having found the man, not a joke, but half of one.

Royal's chair moved so smoothly on its rubber-tyred wheels it was easy to push him, specially after her practice with the mower. There were ramps where necessary now, to cover steps, and she would sometimes wheel him out to the back, where she grew hollyhock and sunflower against the palings, and a vegetable or two on raised beds.

Royal would sit not looking at the garden from under the peak of his cap.

She never attempted to take him down the shady side, between them and Dolans, because the path was narrow from plants spilling over, and the shade might have lowered his spirits.

She loved her garden.

The shady side was where she kept her staghorn ferns, and fishbones, and the pots of maidenhair. The water lay sparkling on the maidenhair even in the middle of the day. In the blaze of summer the light at either end of the tunnel was like you were looking through a sheet of yellow cellophane, but as the days shortened, the light deepened to a cold, tingling green, which might have made a person nervous who didn't know the tunnel by heart.

Take Mrs. Dolan the evening she came in to ask for the loan of a cupful of sugar. 'You gave me a shock, Mrs. Natwick. What ever are you up to?'

'Looking at the plants,' Mrs. Natwick answered, whether Mrs. Dolan would think it peculiar or not.

It was the season of cinerarias, which she always planted on that side, it was sheltered and cold-green. The wind couldn't bash the big spires and umbrellas of blue and purple. Visiting cats were the only danger, messing and pouncing. She disliked cats for the smell they left, but didn't have the heart to disturb their elastic forms curled at the cineraria roots, exposing their colourless pads, and sometimes pink, swollen teats. Blushing only slightly for it, she would stand and examine the details of the sleeping cats.

If Royal called she could hear his voice through the window. 'Where'uv you got to, Ella?'

After he was forced to take to his bed, his voice began to sort of dry up like his body. There were times when it sounded less like a voice than a breath of drowsiness or pain.

'Ella?' he was calling. 'I dropped the paper. Where are yer all this time? You know I can't pick up the paper.'

She knew. Guilt sent her scuttling to him, deliberately composing her eyes and mouth so as to arrive looking cheerful.

'I was in the garden,' she confessed, 'looking at the cinerarias.'

'The what?' It was a name Royal could never learn.

The room was smelling of sickness and the bottles standing on odd plates.

'It fell,' he complained.

She picked up the paper as quick as she could.

'Want to go la-la first?' she asked, because by now he depended on her to raise him and stick the pan under.

But she couldn't distract him from her shortcomings; he was shaking the paper at her. 'Haven't you lived with me long enough to know how to treat a newspaper?'

He hit it with his set hand, and certainly the paper looked a mess, like an old white battered brolly.

'Mucked up! You gotter keep the pages *aligned*. A paper's not readable otherwise. Of course you wouldn't understand because you don't read it, without it's to see who's died.' He began to cough.

'Like me to bring you some Bovril?' she asked him as tenderly as she knew.

'Bovril's the morning,' he coughed.

She knew that, but wanted to do something for him.

After she had rearranged the paper she walked out so carefully it made her go lopsided, out to the front veranda. Nothing would halt the traffic, not sickness, not death even.

She sat with her arms folded, realizing at last how they were aching.

'He hasn't been,' she had to call after looking at her watch.

'Who?' she heard the voice rustling back.

'The gentleman in the pink Holden.'

She listened to the silence, wondering whether she had done right.

When Royal called back, 'Could'uv had a blow-out.' Then he laughed. 'Could'uv stopped to get grogged up.' She heard the frail rustling of the paper. 'Or taken an axe to somebody like they do nowadays.'

She closed her eyes, whether for Royal, or what she remembered of the man sitting in the Holden.

Although it was cold she continued watching after dark. Might have caught a chill, when she couldn't afford to. She only went inside to make the bread-and-milk Royal fancied of an evening.

She watched most attentively, always at the time, but he didn't pass, and didn't pass.

'Who?'

'The gentleman in the Holden.'

'Gone on holiday.' Royal sighed, and she knew it was the point where a normal person would have turned over, so she went to turn him.

One morning she said on going in, 'Fancy, I had a dream, it was about that man! He was standing on the side path alongside the cinerarias. I know it was him because of his funny-shaped head.'

'What happened in the dream?' Royal hadn't opened his eyes yet; she hadn't helped him in with his teeth.

'I dunno,' she said, 'it was just a dream.'

That wasn't strictly truthful, because the Holden gentleman had looked at her, she had seen his eyes. Nothing was spoken, though.

'It was a sort of red and purple dream. That was the cinerarias,' she said.

'I don't dream. You don't when you don't sleep. Pills aren't sleep.'

She was horrified at her reverberating dream. 'Would you like a nice soft-boiled egg?'

'Eggs all have a taste.'

'But you gotter eat *something*!'

On another morning she told him—she could have bitten off her tongue—she *was* stupid, *stupid*, 'I had a dream.'

'What sort of dream?'

'Oh,' she said, 'a silly one. Not worth telling. I dreamed I dropped an egg on the side path, and it turned into two. Not two. A double-yolker.'

She never realized Royal was so much like Mrs. Natwick. It was as she raised him on his pillows. Or he had got like that in his sickness. Old men and old women were not unlike.

'Wasn't that a silly one?' she coaxed.

Every evening she sat on the front veranda and watched the traffic as though Royal had been beside her. Looked at her watch. And turned her face away from the steady-flowing stream. The way she bunched her small chest she could have had a sour breath mounting in her throat. Sometimes she had, it was nervousness.

When she went inside she announced, 'He didn't pass.'

Royal said—he had taken to speaking from behind his eyelids. 'Something muster happened to 'im. He didn't go on holiday. He went and died.'

'Oh, no! He wasn't of an age!'

At once she saw how stupid she was, and went out to get the bread-and-milk.

She would sit at the bedside, almost crouching against the edge of the mattress, because she wanted Royal to feel she was close, and he seemed to realize, though he mostly kept his eyelids down.

Then one evening she came running, she felt silly, her calves felt silly, her voice, 'He's come! At five-twenty! In a new cream Holden!'

Royal said without opening his eyes, 'See? I said 'e'd gone on holiday.'

More than ever she saw the look of Mrs. Natwick.

Now every evening Royal asked, 'Has he been, Ella?'

Trying not to make it sound irritable or superior, she would answer, 'Not yet. It's only five.'

Every evening she sat watching, and sometimes would turn proud, arching her back, as she looked down from the veranda. The man was so small and ordinary.

She went in on one occasion, into the more than electric light, lowering her eyelids against the dazzle. 'You know, Royal, you could feel prouder of men when they rode horses. As they looked down at yer from under the brim of their hats. Remember that hat you used to wear? Riding in to Cootramundra?'

Royal died quietly that same year before the cinerarias had folded, while the cold westerlies were still blowing; the back page of the *Herald* was full of those who had been carried off. She was left with his hand, already set, in her own. They hadn't spoken, except about whether she had put out the garbage.

Everybody was very kind. She wouldn't have liked to admit it was enjoyable being a widow. She sat around for longer than she had ever sat, and let the dust gather. In the beginning acquaintances and neighbours brought her little presents of food: a billy-can of giblet soup, moulded veal with hard-boiled egg making a pattern in the jelly, cakes so dainty you couldn't taste them. But when she was no longer a novelty they left off coming. She didn't care any more than she cared about the dust. Sometimes she would catch sight of her face in the glass, and was surprised to see herself looking so calm and white.

Of course she was calm. The feeling part of her had been removed. What remained was a slack, discardable eiderdown. Must have been the pills Doctor gave.

Well-meaning people would call to her over the front fence, 'Don't you feel lonely, Mrs. Natwick?' They spoke with a restrained horror, as though she had been suffering from an incurable disease.

But she called back proud and slow, 'I'm under sedation.'

'Arrr!' They nodded thoughtfully. 'What's 'e given yer?'

She shook her head. 'Pills,' she called back. 'They say they're the ones the actress died of.'

The people walked on, impressed.

As the evenings grew longer and heavier she sat later on the front veranda watching the traffic of the Parramatta Road, its flow becoming syrupy and almost benign: big bulbous sedate buses, chrysalis cars still without a life of their own, clinging in line to the back of their host-articulator, trucks loaded for distances, empty loose-sounding jolly lorries. Sometimes women, looking out from the cabins of trucks from beside their men, shared her lack of curiosity. The light was so fluid nobody lasted long enough. You would never have thought boys could kick a person to death, seeing their long soft hair floating behind their sports models.

Every evening she watched the cream Holden pass. And looked at her watch. It was like Royal was sitting beside her. Once she heard herself, 'Thought he was gunner look round tonight, in our direction.' How could a person feel lonely?

She was, though. She came face to face with it walking through the wreckage of her garden in the long slow steamy late summer. The Holden didn't pass of course of a Saturday or Sunday. Something, something had tricked her, not the pills, before the pills. She couldn't blame anybody, probably only herself. Everything depended on yourself. Take the garden. It was a shambles. She would have liked to protest, but began to cough from running her head against some powdery mildew. She could only blunder at first, like a cow, or runty starved heifer, on breaking into a garden. She had lost her old wiriness. She shambled, snapping dead stems, uprooting. Along the bleached palings there was a fretwork of hollyhock, the brown fur of rotting sunflower. She rushed at a praying mantis, a big pale one, and deliberately broke its back, and was sorry afterwards for what was done so easy and thoughtless.

As she stood panting in her black, finally yawning, she saw all she had to repair. The thought of the seasons piling up ahead made her feel tired but necessary, and she went in to bathe her face. Royal's denture in a tumbler on top of the medicine cabinet, she ought to move, or give to the Sallies. In the meantime she changed the water. She never forgot it. The teeth looked amazingly alive.

All that autumn, winter, she was continually amazed, at the dust she had let gather in the house, at old photographs, books, clothes. There was a feather she couldn't remember wearing, a scarlet feather, she *can't* have worn, and gloves with little fussy ruffles at the wrists, silver piping, like a snail had laid its trail round the edges. There was, she knew, funny things she had bought at times, and never worn, but she couldn't remember the gloves or the feather. And books. She had collected a few, though never a reader herself. Old people liked to give old books, and you took them so as not to hurt anybody's feelings. *Hubert's Crusade*, for instance. Lovely golden curls. Could have been Royal's father's book. Everybody was a child once. And almost everybody had one. At least if she had had a child she would have known it wasn't a white turnip, more of a praying mantis, which snaps too easy.

In the same box she had put away a coloured picture, *Cities of the Plain*, she couldn't remember seeing it before. The people escaping from the burning cities had committed some sin or other nobody ever thought, let alone talked, about. As they hurried between rocks, through what must have been the 'desert places', their faces looked long and wooden. All they had recently experienced could have shocked the expression out of them. She was fascinated by what made her shiver. And the couples with their arms still around one another. Well, if you were damned, better hang on to your sin. She didn't blame them.

She put the box away. Its inlay as well as its contents made it something secret and precious.

The autumn was still and golden, the winter vicious only in fits. It was what you could call a good winter. The cold floods of air and more concentrated streams of dark-green light poured along the shady side of the house where her cinerarias had massed. She had never seen such cinerarias: some of the spired ones reached almost as high as her chin, the solid heads of others waited in the tunnel of dark light to club you with their colours, of purple and drenching blue, and what they called 'wine'. She couldn't believe wine would have made her drunker.

Just as she would sit every evening watching the traffic, evening was the time she liked best to visit the cinerarias, when the icy cold seemed to make the flowers burn their deepest, purest. So it was again evening when her two objects converged: for some blissfully confident reason she hadn't bothered to ask herself whether she had seen the car pass, till here was this figure coming towards her along the tunnel. She knew at once who it was, although she had never seen him on his feet; she had never seen him full-face, but knew from the funny shape of his head as Royal had been the first to notice. He was not at all an impressive man, not much taller than herself, but broad. His footsteps on the brickwork sounded purposeful.

'Will you let me use your phone, please, madam?' he asked in a prepared voice. 'I'm having trouble with the Holden.'

This was the situation she had always been expecting: somebody asking to use the phone as a way to afterwards murdering you. Now that it might be about to happen she couldn't care.

She said yes. She thought her voice sounded muzzy. Perhaps he would think she was drunk.

She went on looking at him, at his eyes. His nose, like the

shape of his head, wasn't up to much, but his eyes, his eyes, she dared to think, were filled with kindness.

'Cold, eh? but clean cold!' He laughed friendly, shuffling on the brick paving because she was keeping him waiting.

Only then she noticed his mouth. He had a hare-lip, there was no mistaking, although it was well sewn. She felt so calm in the circumstances. She would have even liked to touch it.

But said, 'Why, yes—the telephone,' she said, 'it's this way,' she said, 'it's just off the kitchen—because that's where you spend most of your life. Or in bed,' she ended.

She wished she hadn't added that. For the first time since they had been together she felt upset, thinking he might suspect her of wrong intentions.

But he laughed and said, 'That's correct! You got something there!' It sounded manly rather than educated.

She realized he was still waiting, and took him to the telephone.

While he was phoning she didn't listen. She never listened when other people were talking on the phone. The sight of her own kitchen surprised her. While his familiar voice went on. It was the voice she had held conversations with.

But he was ugly, real ugly, *deformed*. If it wasn't for the voice, the eyes. She couldn't remember the eyes, but seemed to know about them.

Then she heard him laying the coins beside the phone, extra loud, to show.

He came back into the kitchen smiling and looking. She could smell him now, and he had the smell of a clean man.

She became embarrassed at herself, and took him quickly out.

'Fair bit of garden you got.' He stood with his calves curved through his trousers. A cocky little chap, but nice.

'Oh,' she said, 'this', she said, angrily almost, 'is nothing. You oughter see it. There's sunflower and hollyhock all along the palings. I'm famous for me hollyhocks!' She had never boasted in her life. 'But not now—it isn't the season. And I let it go. Mr. Natwick passed on. You should'uv seen the cassia this autumn. Now it's only sticks, of course. And hibiscus. There's cream, gold, cerise, scarlet—double and single.'

She was dressing in them for him, revolving on high heels and changing frilly skirts.

He said, 'Gardening's not in my line,' turning his head to hide something, perhaps he was ashamed of his hare-lip.

'No,' she agreed. 'Not everybody's a gardener.'

'But like a garden.'

'My husband didn't even like it. He didn't have to tell me,' she added.

As they moved across the wintry grass, past the empty clothes-line, the man looked at his watch, and said, 'I was reckoning on visiting somebody in hospital tonight. Looks like I shan't make it if the N.R.M.A. takes as long as usual.'

'Do they?' she said, clearing her throat. 'It isn't somebody close, I hope? The sick person?'

Yes he said they was close.

'Nothing serious?' she almost bellowed.

He said it was serious.

Oh she nearly burst out laughing at the bandaged figure they were sitting beside particularly at the bandaged face. She would have laughed at a brain tumour.

'I'm sorry,' she said. 'I understand. Mr. Natwick was for many years an invalid.'

Those teeth in the tumbler on top of the medicine cabinet. Looking at her. Teeth can look, worse than eyes. But she couldn't help it, she meant everything she said, and thought.

At this moment they were pressing inside the dark-green tunnel, her sleeve rubbing his, as the crimson-to-purple light was dying.

'These are the cinerarias,' she said.

'The what?' He didn't know, any more than Royal.

As she was about to explain she got switched to another language. Her throat became a long palpitating funnel through which the words she expected to use were poured out in a stream of almost formless agonized sound.

'What is it?' he asked, touching her.

If it had happened to herself she would have felt frightened, it occurred to her, but he didn't seem to be.

'What is it?' he kept repeating in his familiar voice, touching, even holding her.

And for answer, in the new language, she was holding him. They were holding each other, his hard body against her eider-downy one. As the silence closed round them again, inside the tunnel of light, his face, to which she was very close, seemed to be unlocking, the wound of his mouth, which should have been more horrible, struggling to open. She could see he had recognized her.

She kissed above his mouth. She kissed as though she might never succeed in healing all the wounds they had ever suffered.

How long they stood together she wasn't interested in know-ing. Outside them the river of traffic continued to flow be-tween its brick and concrete banks. Even if it overflowed it couldn't have drowned them.

When the man said in his gentlest voice, 'Better go out in front. The N.R.M.A. might have come.'

'Yes,' she agreed. 'The N.R.M.A.'

So they shuffled, still holding each other, along the narrow path. She imagined how long and wooden their faces must look. She wouldn't look at him now, though, just as she wouldn't look back at the still faintly smouldering joys they had experienced together in the past.

When they came out, apart, and into the night, there was the N.R.M.A., his pointed ruby of a light burning on top of the cabin.

'When will you come?' she asked.

'Tomorrow.'

'Tomorrow. You'll stay to tea.'

He couldn't stay.

'I'll make you a *pot* of tea?'

But he didn't drink it.

'Coffee, then?'

He said, 'I like a nice cup of coffee.'

Going down the path he didn't look back, or opening the gate. She would not let herself think of reasons or possibilities, she would not think, but stood planted in the path, swayed slightly by the motion of the night.

Mrs. Dolan said, 'You bring the saucepan to the boil. You got that?'

'Yeeehs.' Mrs. Natwick had never been a dab at coffee.

'Then you throw in some cold water. That's what sends the gravel to the bottom.' This morning Mrs. Dolan had to laugh at her own jokes.

'That's the part that frightens me,' Mrs. Natwick admitted.

'Well, you just do it, and see,' said Mrs. Dolan; she was too busy.

After she had bought the coffee Mrs. Natwick stayed in the city to muck around. If she had stayed at home her nerves might have wound themselves tighter, waiting for evening to come. Though mucking around only irritated in the end. She had never been an idle woman. So she stopped at the cosmetics as though she didn't have to decide, this was her purpose, and said to the young lady lounging behind one of the counters, 'I'm thinking of investing in a lipstick, dear. Can you please advise me?'

As a concession to the girl she tried to make it a laughing matter, but the young person was bored, she didn't bat a silver eyelid. 'Elderly ladies,' she said, 'go for the brighter stuff.'

Mrs. Natwick ('my little Ella') had never felt so meek. Mum must be turning in her grave.

'This is a favourite.' With a flick of her long fingers the girl exposed the weapon. It looked too slippery-pointed, crimson-purple, out of its golden sheath.

Mrs. Natwick's knees were shaking. 'Isn't it a bit noticeable?' she asked, again trying to make it a joke.

But the white-haired girl gave a serious laugh. 'What's wrong with noticeable?'

As Mrs. Natwick tried it out on the back of her hand the way she had seen others do, the girl was jogging from foot to foot behind the counter. She was humming between her teeth, behind her white-smeared lips, probably thinking about a lover. Mrs. Natwick blushed. What if she couldn't learn to get the tip of her lipstick back inside its sheath?

She might have gone quickly away without another word if the young lady hadn't been so professional and bored. Still humming, she brought out a little pack of rouge.

'Never saw myself with mauve cheeks!' It was at least dry, and easy to handle.

'It's what they wear.'

Mrs. Natwick didn't dare refuse. She watched the long fingers with their silver nails doing up the parcel. The fingers looked as though they might resent touching anything but cosmetics; a lover was probably beneath contempt.

The girl gave her the change, and she went away without counting it.

She wasn't quiet, though, not a bit, booming and clanging in front of the toilet mirror. She tried to make a thin line, but her mouth exploded into a purple flower. She dabbed the dry-feeling pad on either cheek, and thick, mauve-scented shadows fell. She could hear and feel her heart behaving like a squeezed, rubber ball as she stood looking. Then she got at the lipstick again, still unsheathed. Her mouth was becoming enormous, so thick with grease she could hardly close her own lips underneath. A visible dew was gathering round the purple shadows on her cheeks.

She began to retch like, but dry, and rub, over the basin, scrubbing with the nailbrush. More than likely some would stay behind in the pores and be seen. Though you didn't have to see, to see.

There were Royal's teeth in the tumbler on top of the medicine cabinet. Ought to hide the teeth. What if somebody wanted to use the toilet? She must move the teeth. But didn't. In the present circumstances she couldn't have raised her arms that high.

Around five she made the coffee, throwing in the cold water at the end with a gesture copied from Mrs. Dolan. If the gravel hadn't sunk to the bottom he wouldn't notice the first time, provided the coffee was hot. She could warm up the made coffee in a jiffy.

As she sat on the veranda waiting, the cane chair shifted and squealed under her. If it hadn't been for her weight it might have run away across the tiles, like one of those old planchette boards, writing the answers to questions.

There was an accident this evening down at the intersection. A head-on collision. Bodies were carried out of the crumpled cars, and she remembered a past occasion when she had run with blankets, and Hazel's Onkaparinka, and a pillow from their own bed. She had been so grateful to the victim. She could not give him enough, or receive enough of the warm blood. She had come back, she remembered, sprinkled.

This evening she had to save herself up. Kept on looking at her watch. The old cane chair squealing, ready to write the answers if she let it. Was he hurt? Was he killed, then? Was he —what?

Mrs. Dolan it was, sticking her head over the palings. 'Don't like the accidents, Mrs. Natwick. It's the blood. The blood turns me up.'

Mrs. Natwick averted her face. Though unmoved by present blood. If only the squealing chair would stop trying to buck her off.

'Did your friend enjoy the coffee?' Mrs. Dolan shouted; nothing nasty in her: Mrs. Dolan was sincere.

'Hasn't been yet,' Mrs. Natwick mumbled from glancing at her watch. 'Got held up.'

'It's the traffic. The traffic at this time of evenun.'

'Always on the dot before.'

'Working back. Or made a mistake over the day.'

Could you make a mistake? Mrs. Natwick contemplated. Tomorrow had always meant tomorrow.

'Or he could'uv,' Mrs. Dolan shouted, but didn't say it. 'I better go inside,' she said instead. 'They'll be wonderun where I am.'

Down at the intersection the bodies were lying wrapped in someone else's blankets, looking like the grey parcels of mice cats sometimes vomit up.

It was long past five-twenty, not all that long really, but drawing in. The sky was heaped with cold fire. Her city was burning.

She got up finally, and the chair escaped with a last squeal, writing its answer on the tiles.

No, it wasn't lust, not if the Royal God Almighty with bared teeth should strike her down. Or yes, though, it was. She was lusting after the expression of eyes she could hardly remember for seeing so briefly.

In the effort to see, she drove her memory wildly, while her body stumbled around and around the paths of the burning city there was now no point in escaping. You would shrivel up in time along with the polyanthers and out-of-season hibiscus. All the randy mouths would be stopped sooner or later with black.

The cinerarias seemed to have grown so luxuriant she had to force her way past them, down the narrow brick path. When she heard the latch click, and saw him coming towards her.

'Why,' she screamed laughing though it sounded angry, she *was*, 'I'd given you up, you know! It's long after five-twenty!'

As she pushed fiercely towards him, past the cinerarias, snapping one or two of those which were most heavily loaded, she realized he couldn't have known that she set her watch, her life, by his constant behaviour. He wouldn't have dawdled so.

'What is it?' she called at last, in exasperation at the distance which continued separating them.

He was far too slow, treading the slippery moss of her too shaded path. While she floundered on. She couldn't reach the expression of his eyes.

He said, and she could hardly recognize the faded voice, 'There's something—I been feeling off colour most of the day.' His mis-shapen head was certainly lolling as he advanced.

'Tell me!' She heard her voice commanding, like that of a man, or a mother, when she had practised to be a lover; she could still smell the smell of rouge. 'Won't you tell me— *dearest*?' It was thin and unconvincing now. (As a girl she had once got a letter from her cousin Kath Salter, who she hardly knew: *Dearest Ella* . . .)

Oh dear. She had reached him. And was given all strength— that of the lover she had aimed at being.

Straddling the path, unequally matched—he couldn't

compete against her strength—she spoke with an acquired, a deafening softness, as the inclining cinerarias snapped.

'You will tell me what is wrong—dear, dear.' She breathed with trumpets.

He hung his head. 'It's all right. It's the pain—here—in my arm—no, the shoulder.'

'Ohhhhh!' She ground her face into his shoulder forgetting it wasn't *her* pain.

Then she remembered, and looked into his eyes and said, 'We'll save you. You'll see.'

It was she who needed saving. She knew she was trying to enter by his eyes. To drown in them rather than be left.

Because, in spite of her will to hold him, he was slipping from her, down amongst the cinerarias, which were snapping off one by one around them.

A cat shot out. At one time she had been so poor in spirit she had wished she was a cat.

'It's all right,' either voice was saying.

Lying amongst the smashed plants, he was smiling at her dreadfully, not his mouth, she no longer bothered about that lip, but with his eyes.

'More air!' she cried. 'What you need is air!' hacking at one or two cinerarias which remained erect.

Their sap was stifling, their bristling columns callous.

'Oh! Oh!' she panted. 'Oh God! Dear love!' comforting with hands and hair and words.

Words.

While all he could say was, 'It's all right.'

Or not that at last. He folded his lips into a white seam. His eyes were swimming out of reach.

'Eh? Dear—dearest—darl—darlig—darling love—*love*—LOVE?' All the new words still stiff in her mouth, that she had heard so far only from the mouths of actors.

The words were too strong she could see. She was losing him. The traffic was hanging together only by charred silences.

She flung herself and covered his body, trying to force kisses—no, breath, into his mouth, she had heard about it.

She had seen turkeys, feathers sawing against each other's feathers, rising afterwards like new noisy silk.

She knelt up, and the wing-tips of her hair still dabbled limply in his cheeks. 'Eh? Ohh luff!' She could hardly breathe it.

She hadn't had time to ask his name, before she must have killed him by loving too deep, and too adulterously.

BIOGRAPHICAL NOTES

CHINUA ACHEBE was born in 1930. He was educated at the University of Ibadan and worked for the Nigerian Broadcasting Corporation after a period as Senior Research Fellow at the Institute of African Studies, Nsukka. After teaching in the United States he returned to his country as Professor of English, University of Nigeria, Nsukka. His books include the novels *Things Fall Apart* (1958) and *The Anthills of the Savannah* (1987) and the collection of short stories *Girls at War* (1972).

KINGSLEY AMIS was born in Norbury in 1922 and educated at the City of London School and St. John's College, Oxford. From *Lucky Jim* (1954) onwards he has been the author of numerous novels. He has edited selected stories by G. K. Chesterton (1972) and written a book on Kipling and his background. His earlier short stories are collected as *My Enemy's Enemy* (1962). His novel *The Old Devils* won the Booker Prize in 1986.

GEORGE MACKAY BROWN was born in 1921 and educated at the University of Edinburgh. He lives in his native Orkney and writes about the life of its people. As well as poems and a play he has published the novels *Greenvoe* and *Magnus*, and several volumes of short stories, including *Hawkfall* (1974).

MORLEY CALLAGHAN, Canadian novelist, was born in Toronto in 1903. He attended the University of Toronto, followed by law school, and lives in the city. His books include *Native Argosy* (1929), *They Shall Inherit the Earth* (1935), *The Loved and the Lost* (1951), *The Man with the Coat* (1955, McLean's Prize), *A Passion in Rome* (1961), and a collection of short stories, *Stories* (1964). Later volumes are *A Fine and Private Place* (1976), *Close to the Sun Again* (1977), and *No Man's Meat* (1978).

ELSPETH DAVIE is an Edinburgh writer and former art-school student married to a philosopher. She is represented in the anthology of experimental writing edited by Giles Gordon, *Beyond the Words* (1975) and has published two collections of her stories, *The High Tide Talkers* (1976) and *The Night of the Funny Hats* (1980) as well as a novel *Climate on a Stair* (1978). She was awarded the Katherine Mansfield Prize in 1978.

SUSAN HILL was born in 1942 and after grammar schools in Scarborough and Coventry read English at King's College, London. Married to the Shakespearian scholar Stanley Wells, she lives with her family in a village near Oxford. Her books include *Do Me a Favour* (1963), *A Change for the Better* (1969), *The Albatross* (1971, stories), *Strange Meeting* (1971), *In the Springtime of the Year* (1974), and many other stories and radio plays.

DAN JACOBSON was born in Johannesberg in 1929 and educated at the University of Witwatersrand. After working in South Africa as a journalist and in commerce he came to London to write in 1954. His books include *The Trap* (1955) and *A Dance in the Sun* (1956), these two novellas reissued together by OUP in 1988, *A Long Way from London* (1958), *The Evidence of Love* (1960), *Inklings* (1972, stories), *Through the Wilderness: Selected Stories* (1973; Penguin, 1977), and *Her Story* (1987).

BENEDICT KIELY was born at Dromore in County Tyrone in 1919 and is a graduate of the National University of Ireland. He has been a journalist, a visiting professor at American universities, and now lectures in Dublin. His books include *Land Without Stars* (1946), *Modern Irish Fiction* (1948), *Honey Seems Bitter* (1954), *The Captain with the Whiskers* (1960), *Dogs Enjoy the Morning* (1968), and *A Ball of Malt* (1970, stories).

BERNARD MALAMUD was born in 1914 and teaches at Bennington College, Vermont. He was born in New York City and educated at City College and Columbia University. In 1979 he became President of the American PEN Center. Among his books are *The Natural* (1952), *The Assistant* (1957), *The Magic Barrel* (1958, stories; National Book Award), *The Fixer* (1966, Pulitzer Prize), *Rembrandt's Hat* (1973, stories), *Dubin's Lives* (1979).

OLIVIA MANNING was born in Portsmouth and married to Professor R.D. Smith. She died in 1980. During the 1939–45 war she was with her husband in Romania and Greece and her best-known series of novels, *Balkan Trilogy*, is based on this period (*The Great Fortune* (1960); *The Spoilt City* (1962); *Friends and Heroes* (1965)). *A Romantic Hero* (1967) is a volume of short stories.

GORDON MEYER was educated at Oxford and worked for an import-export firm in Buenos Aires before his early death in 1968. He wrote travel books on his experiences in Bolivia and Paraguay. Many of his stories about South America were collected in the volume *Exiles* (1967).

V. S. NAIPAUL was born in 1932 and brought up in Trinidad. He was educated at Queen's Royal College there and at University College, Oxford. His books include *A House for Mr. Biswas* (1961), *Mr. Stone and the Knights Companion* (1963), *The Mimic Men* (1967), *A Flag on the Island* (1967, short stories), *In a Free State* (1971, a novel which won the Booker Prize), *A Bend in the River* (1979), and *The Enigma of Arrival* (1987).

R. K. NARAYAN was born in Madras in 1907 and educated at Maharaja's College, Mysore. His books published in England include *The Man-Eaters of Malgudi* (1961), *Gods, Demons and Others* (1964), *The Sweet Vendor* (1967), *A Horse and Two Goats* (1970, short stories), and *The Painter of Signs* (1977). Autobiography: *Reminiscences* (1973). He has translated the *Ramayana* (1973) and the *Maha bharata* (1978).

JEAN RHYS was born in Dominica in 1894. After a period at the RADA she lived and wrote in Paris between the wars. Her earlier novels *After Leaving Mr.*

Mackenzie (1930), *Voyage in the Dark* (1934), and *Good Morning Midnight* (1939), which had enjoyed a coterie reputation, were reissued in the Sixties as a result of a revival of interest in her work. Collections of short stories are *The Left Bank* (1927) and *Tigers Are Better-Looking* (1967).

FRANK SARGESON, born in 1903, is the most distinguished New Zealand short-story writer and has been described as the founding father of the literature of his country. He was born in Hamilton and educated at Auckland University. His books include *That Summer* (1946, a long story which first made him known to British readers), *I Saw in My Dream* (1949), *Collected Stories 1935–63* (1965), *The Stories of Frank Sargeson* (Auckland, 1973; New York, 1974).

ELIZABETH TAYLOR was born in Reading in 1912 and died in 1975. Her first novel, *At Mrs. Lippincote's*, was published in 1945. As well as other novels she published several collections of short stories. These books include *Hester Lilly and Other Stories* (1958), *A Dedicated Man* (1965) and *Mrs. Palfrey at the Claremont* (1972).

WILLIAM TREVOR was born in 1928 in Mitchellstown, County Cork. He lives and works in London. His novel *The Old Boys* was published in 1964 and he has published many short stories. Other books include *The Children of Dynmouth* (1976), *Lovers of their Time* (1978), *Other People's Worlds* (1980), and *Fools of Fortune* (1983), which won the Whitbread Award.

FRANK TUOHY was born in 1925 and educated at Stowe and King's College, Cambridge. He lectured abroad for the British Council in Finland, Sweden, Poland, and Brazil. Among his books are a collection of short stories, *The Admiral and the Nuns* (1962), and *The Ice Saints* (1964), one of several novels. His *Live Bait* (1978) won the Heinemann Award.

JOHN UPDIKE was born in 1932 in Shillington, Pennsylvania, and educated at Harvard and the Ruskin School of Art, Oxford. For two years he was a staff contributor to the *New Yorker* magazine. Among his numerous books are the following collections of short stories: *Pigeon Feathers*, *The Same Door*, *Too Far to Go: The Maples Stories*, *Problems and Other Stories*. His novels include *The Poorhouse Fair*, *Rabbit Run*, *Couples*, *Rabbit Redux*, *Bech: A Book*, *Bech is Back*, and *Roger's Version*.

PATRICK WHITE is the son of an Australian sheep-grazing family but was born in England in 1912 and educated at Cheltenham and King's College, Cambridge. During the war he served in the RAF. His novels include *The Tree of Man* (1955), *Voss* (1957), *The Solid Mandala* (1966), *The Vivisector* (1970), *A Fringe of Leaves* (1976), *The Twyborn Affair* (1979). His two collections of short stories are *The Burnt Ones* (1964) and *The Cockatoos* (1974). He published his autobiography in 1981. In 1972 he was awarded the Nobel Prize for Literature.

ACKNOWLEDGEMENTS

We are grateful for permission to include the following copyright stories.

Chinua Achebe: 'Uncle Ben's Choice' from *Girls at War and Other Stories*. Copyright © 1972, 1973 by Chinua Achebe. Reprinted by permission of David Bolt Associates, and of Doubleday, A Division of Bantam, Doubleday, Dell Publishing, Inc.

Kingsley Amis: 'The Green Man Revisited'. © 1973 Kingsley Amis. Reprinted by permission of Jonathan Clowes on behalf of Kingsley Amis.

George Mackay Brown: 'Tithonus' from *Hawkfall*. Reprinted by permission of the Hogarth Press on behalf of the author.

Morley Callaghan: 'The Runaway' from *Stories*. Reprinted by permission of the author.

Elspeth Davie: 'Concerto' from *Beyond the Words*. ed. Giles Gordon (Hutchinson). Reprinted by permission of Anthony Sheil Associates Ltd.

Susan Hill: 'Cockles and Mussels' from *The Albatross and Other Stories* (Hamish Hamilton). Reprinted by permission of Richard Scott Simon Ltd.

Dan Jacobson: 'The Zulu and the Zeide' from *Inklings*. Reprinted by permission of A. M. Heath & Co. Ltd., for the author.

Benedict Kiely: 'God's Own Country' reprinted from *A Ball of Malt and Madame Butterfly* by permission of A. P. Watt Ltd., and from *The State of Ireland*, copyright © 1963, 1973, 1978, 1979, 1980 by Benedict Kiely, by permission of David R. Godine, Publisher.

Bernard Malamud: 'The Silver Crown' from *Rembrandt's Hat*. Copyright © 1972, 1973 by Bernard Malamud. Reprinted by permission of Chatto & Windus on behalf of the Estate of Bernard Malamud, and Farrar, Straus & Giroux, Inc.

Olivia Manning: 'A Spot of Leave' from *A Romantic Hero*. Reprinted by permission of William Heinemann Ltd.

Gordon Meyer: 'The Circle' from *Exiles*. Reprinted by permission of Alan Ross, London Magazine Editions.

V. S. Naipaul: ' A Christmas Story' from *A Flag on the Island*. Reprinted by permission of Aitken & Stone Ltd.

R. K. Narayan: 'A Horse and Two Goats' from *A Horse and Two Goats*. Reprinted by permission of David Higham Associates Ltd.

Jean Rhys: 'Tigers are Better-Looking', Copyright © 1974, 1987 by the Estate of Jean Rhys. Reprinted from *Tigers are Better-Looking* by permission of André Deutsch, and from *Jean Rhys: The Collected Short Stories*, published by W. W. Norton & Company, Inc., by permission of Wallace & Sheil Agency, Inc.

Frank Sargeson: 'A Hen and Some Eggs' from *Collected Stories* (Longman Paul Ltd).

Elizabeth Taylor: 'A Dedicated Man' from *A Dedicated Man*. Reprinted by permission of A. M. Heath on behalf of the Estate of the Late Elizabeth Taylor.

William Trevor: 'In at the Birth' from *The Day We Got Drunk on Cake*. Reprinted by permission of John Johnson (Authors' Agent) Ltd.

Frank Tuohy: 'The Licence' from *The Collected Stories of Frank Tuohy*. Reprinted by permission of A. D. Peters & Co. Ltd.

John Updike: 'Should Wizard Hit Mommy?' from *Pigeon Feathers and Other Stories*. Copyright © 1960 by John Updike. Reprinted by permission of André Deutsch, and Alfred A. Knopf, Inc.

Patrick White: 'Five-Twenty' from *The Cockatoos*. Reprinted by permission of Barbara Mobbs, Literary Agent.

Every effort has been made to contact copyright holders before publication. However in some cases this has not been possible. If contacted the publisher will ensure that full credit is given at the earliest opportunity.

OXFORD

MORE OXFORD PAPERBACKS

Details of a selection of other books follow. A complete list of Oxford Paperbacks, including The World's Classics, Twentieth-Century Classics, OPUS, Past Masters, Oxford Authors, Oxford Shakespeare, and Oxford Paperback Reference, is available in the UK from the General Publicity Department, Oxford University Press (JN), Walton Street, Oxford OX2 6DP.

In the USA, complete lists are available from the Paperbacks Marketing Manager, Oxford University Press, 200 Madison Avenue, New York, NY 10016.

Oxford Paperbacks are available from all good bookshops. In case of difficulty, customers in the UK can order direct from Oxford University Press Bookshop, 116 High Street, Oxford, Freepost, OX1 4BR, enclosing full payment. Please add 10 per cent of published price for postage and packing.

THE KILLING BOTTLE

Chosen by Dan Davin

This collection brings together 12 very different authors whose short stories, written in the 1940s and 1950s, helped establish or extend their reputations as writers of stories, novels or poetry. Preface and biographical notes by Dan Davin.

The authors are Elizabeth Bowen, Joyce Cary, Walter de la Mare, Graham Greene, L. P. Hartley, Somerset Maugham, Frank O'Connor, V. S. Pritchett, William Sansom, Dylan Thomas, Evelyn Waugh, and Angus Wilson.

CLASSIC ENGLISH SHORT STORIES

THE DRAGON'S HEAD

This collection contains short stories written in the years between the turn of the century and the outbreak of the Second World War—'a restless and impatient age'.

The authors are Stella Benson, John Gallsworthy, Richard Hughes, M. R. James, Somerset Maugham, Leonard Merrick, Naomi Mitchison, Geoffrey Moss, 'Saki', Frank O'Connor, Dorothy L. Sayers, Sir Hugh Walpole, and H. G. Wells.

CLASSIC ENGLISH SHORT STORIES

CHARMED LIVES

Chosen by T. S. Dorsch

This collection contains stories written in the 1950s and 1960s, many of which demonstrate the impressive and accomplished skills of Commonwealth writers who began to achieve world-wide reputations during that period. The writers, chosen by T. S. Dorsch (who has also written a preface and biographical notes), come from countries as diverse as Australia, Canada, India, New Zealand, South Africa, Nigeria, and the West Indies.

The writers are Mary Lavin, William Sansome, Dal Sivens, Viola Meynell, Maurice Shadbolt, H. E. Bates, Bill Naughton, L. P. Hartley, Ruth Prawer Jhabvala, John Wain, L. E. Jones, Nadine Gordimer, Peter Ustinov, May C. Jenkins, Morely Callaghan, Norah Lofts, David Owoyele, Angus Wilson, Rhys Davies, and George Lamming.

CLASSIC ENGLISH SHORT STORIES

DR STRANGELOVE

Peter George

The novel that made the Stanley Kubrick film possible: a hilarious, serious, savage farce.

Major Kong is the commander of the air bomber nicknamed Leper Colony. He has orders to proceed to their primary target. General Jack D. Ripper, in command of Burpelson Air Force Base, sips his glass of grain alcohol and rainwater and calmly puts the base on condition Red. President Merkin Muffley is reminded by General Buck Turgidson about Operation Ultech, the emergency war plan which allows a junior commander to order a nuclear 'retaliation'. Kissof, the Russian Premier, reminds President Muffley about the Russian counter-weapon, the Doomsday Machine. Full-scale nuclear war is inevitable.

Only one man can save the situation, and he has the reputation of a dangerous, if brilliant, madman—Dr Strangelove.

TWENTIETH-CENTURY CLASSICS

THE TRAP DANCE *and* A DANCE IN THE SUN

Dan Jacobson

Dan Jacobson's first novels—stories of drama and confrontation on the sun-baked South African veld.

In both stories the real subject is, as Dan Jacobson says in his introduction, the dramatic and inimical relationships between 'uneasily triumphant whites and truculently dispossessed blacks locked together in a kind of throttled domesticity, in a pattern of betrayal and self-betrayal from which not even their own acts of violence could release them'.

'it is hard to believe that *The Trap* and *A Dance in the Sun* are already a quarter of a century old . . . Jacobson's story is as disturbing today as ever' *New Statesman*

TWENTIETH-CENTURY CLASSICS

WHY ARE WE IN VIETNAM

Norman Mailer

It is 1967 and DJ, 18 year-old self-proclaimed genius, existentialist disciple of William Burroughs, is very much a product of his time. The novel is recounted by him at a frenetic pace in a mixture of Texas slang, hippy jargon, and disc-jockey jingles. But despite his fizz and humour, DJ is determined to embrace and exorcise the darker side of the American Dream— the corruption of wealth and the horrors of machismo.

A safari in Alaska in search of the grizzly, ultimate in hunting trophies, turns into an initiation rite. Against the spectacular backdrop of glaciers and forests, the confrontation of man and animal, and of man and man, takes place.

'he writes with the speed and rawness of insight of a Dostoevsky' *Observer*

TWENTIETH-CENTURY CLASSICS

KING, QUEEN, KNAVE

Vladimir Nabokov

'KING is Dreyer, wealthy and biosterous proprietor of a male clothing emporium. He has a taste for tennis and automata. Ruddy with health, tawny body hair, and self-satisfaction, he is perfectly repugnant to his cold QUEEN who is Martha, his exquisite middle-class wife. She is warmed by his fortune but repelled by his oblivious passion. Martha hungers for their nephew, the thin and furry KNAVE of hearts, myopic Franz. Newly arrived in Berlin, the awkward Franz repays his uncle's condescension in his aunt's bed.'

'(Nabokov) writes prose the only way it should be written—that is ecstatically' John Updike

TWENTIETH-CENTURY CLASSICS

DIARY OF A MAD OLD MAN

Junichiro Tanizaki

'I know very well that I am an ugly, wrinkled old man. When I look in the mirror at bedtime after taking out my false teeth, the face I see is really weird. I don't have a tooth of my own in either jaw. I can hardly even have gums. If I clamp my mouth shut, my lips flatten together and my nose hangs down my chin.'

A dying man's diary records, alongside the details of his final illness, an obsessive desire for his beautiful, gaudy, westernized daughter-in-law.

'it is important that the British public should become acquainted with this great twentieth-century Japanese fiction writer' Anthony Burgess

TWENTIETH-CENTURY CLASSICS

THE OXFORD BOOK OF SHORT STORIES

Chosen by V. S. Pritchett

'by a writer with a distinctive and distinguished taste . . . could hardly have been done better' *Sunday Times*

V. S. Pritchett, one of our greatest living short-story writers, has chosen some forty stories, written in the English language, to produce a collection that successfully displays the wealth and variety of an art that spans some 200 years.

'(a) treasure trove of an anthology . . . marvellous . . . . The enormous variety of tone and intention allows each story to make its own impact without detracting from that of those that precede and follow it.' *Times Educational Supplement*

TWENTIETH-CENTURY CLASSICS

THE DESIRE AND PURSUIT OF THE WHOLE

Frederick Rolfe
(Baron Corvo)

'The desire and pursuit of the whole is called love' Plato

The Desire and Pursuit of the Whole, one of Frederick Rolfe's most autobiographical novels, was written in Venice during 1909, a year of hardship and near-starvation for the author. Feeling himself abandoned by his friends, he produced a masterpiece of invective, a bitter attack against all those around him. And yet the book celebrates life, and more importantly love. It is, in fact, one of the first English novels to celebrate homosexual love. Though for a quarter of a century after his death his book was considered too libellous and subversive to publish, Rolfe's love for Venice demonstrates his enduring optimism and faith in human nature.

'extraordinary and magnificent' W. H. Auden

TWENTIETH CENTURY CLASSIC

IN YOUTH IS PLEASURE

Denton Welch

Introduced by John Lehmann

In Youth is Pleasure tells of fifteen-year-old Orvil Pym, during a summer holiday with his father and two older brothers in a grand hotel in Surrey. Suffering acutely the agonies of adolescence, Orvil spends his days alone and isolated. His senses, particularly his visual sense, are heightened and taut, so that every incident becomes an adventure, every adventure an intense and often terrifying experience.

Denton Welch's writing displays a remarkable mixture of naivety and sophistication. His purity of style and command of words combines to give an exactness of observation, providing an utterly convincing and profoundly disturbing vision of the world.

TWENTIETH CENTURY CLASSIC

THE UNBEARABLE BASSINGTON

Saki

At the centre of the book is Cormus Bassington, 'the beautiful wayward laughing boy, with his naughtiness, his exasperating selfishness, his insurmountable folly and perverseness, his cruelty that spared not even himself', in whom Saki invested his own ambiguous feelings for youth in his fierce indignation at the ravages of time.

KIPPS

H. G. Wells

Introduced by Benny Green

The story of Arthur Kipps, a poor, uneducated draper's assistant who inherits not only a fortune, but all the problems that a sudden elevation in social status can bring, recalls Wells's early life in the drapery trade.

'*Kipps* is the finest of H. G. Wells's deeply personal novels using his early experience in the draper's shop, an autobiographical theme explored by Benny Green in a fine introduction.' *Sunday Times*

ROMAN TALES

Alberto Moravia

Twenty-seven short stories, by Italy's foremost writer of short fiction, describe the low-life of Rome—the secret lives of washerwomen, barmen, caretakers, and the like, with their broken dreams, thwarted ambitions, unrequited loves, and unsatisfied desires.

'Alberto Moravia needs no introduction and no praise. He is an artist.' *Literary Guide*

'a major novelist' *Spectator*

TWENTIETH-CENTURY CLASSICS

THE WOMAN IN THE DUNES
Kobo Abe

Introduced by Anthony Thwaite

'One day in August a man disappeared . . .' Seven years later he is declared a missing person, presumed dead. What happens in the interim is the substance of this novel.

Niki Jumpei is a rare person, a loner. When, on one of his solitary insect-hunting expeditions to a nearby beach, he finds himself stranded in the dunes, the prisoner of a mysterious woman, it is not clear whether he is properly to be considered lost or found. As he struggles to escape, 'escape' itself becomes oddly ambiguous. At the same time his captor, a mixture of enigmatic reserve and earthly sensuality, arouses both his fear and his desire.

The Woman in the Dunes won the Yomiuri Prize in 1960 and Hiroshi Teshigahare's film won the jury prize at the 1963 Cannes Film Festival.

THE CHERRY TREE
Adrian Bell

Introduced by Humphrey Phelps

This is the final novel of Adrian Bell's Suffolk trilogy, completing the story begun in *Corduroy* and continued in *Silver Ley*. It is a deeply personal account of two loves, for his wife and for the land she helped him farm, and it vividly evokes a rural life that was changing even as he wrote.

HIS MONKEY WIFE

John Collier

Introduced by Paul Theroux

The work of this British poet and novelist who lived for many years in Hollywood has always attracted a devoted following. This, his first novel, concerns a chimpanzee called Emily who falls in love with her owner—an English schoolmaster—and embarks on a process of self-education which includes the reading of Darwin's *Origin of Species*.

'John Collier welds the strongest force with the strangest subtlety . . . It is a tremendous and terrifying satire, only made possible by the suavity of its wit.' Osbert Sitwell

'Read as either a parody of thirties' fiction or just crazy comedy, it deserves its place as a 20th-century classic.' David Holloway, *Sunday Telegraph*

RICEYMAN STEPS

Arnold Bennett

Introduced by Frank Kermode

Bennett's reputation as a novelist waned after the publication of his great pre-war novels, *Anna of the Five Towns, The Old Wives' Tale,* and *Clayhanger,* but it was emphatically restored by the appearance in 1923 of *Riceyman Steps,* the story of a miserly bookseller who not only starves himself to death, but infects his wife with a passion for economy that brings her also to an untimely end.